A

WEB

OF

CONSPIRACIES

BY

ALLAN TURNER

Trilogy

Steven Pinder, Ian Turner Series

Book 1. A Web of Conspiracies
Book 2. A Time on the Hill
Book 3. A Seeker

FOREWORD

An office in Queen Anne's Gate, London, is the current home of a small organisation known as the 'British Intelligence Special Service'. This organisation is believed to have been in existence, in one form or another for many years, albeit having several name changes along the way. It is also believed, was initially set up by Elizabeth I for her personal protection. The existence of BISS known only by a few was formally recognised in 1837 when, after the death of William IV, Lord Melbourne informed the young Victoria of its existence. In 1841 according to some notes made by Robert Peel, Queen Victoria advised him and the then Home secretary Graham, that they should be aware of the Royal Secret Service, which at that time was headed by Lord Palmerstone. Today this organisation is government funded, although its first allegiance is still to the Monarch.

The current Director of BISS is Sir Peter Thompson-Smythe, a former officer in the 'Household Cavalry.' Sir Peter's involvement with the other National Security Services is limited to a consultancy basis only. However, all matters deemed secret and of national interest are formally passed over Sir Peter's desk.

It is thought by the higher echelons of MI5, MI6, Special Branch and SAS, that BISS, over the years, had put together its own very secret and elite force of agents. Although never remarked upon by Sir Peter, it has been noticed on many occasions, just how often BISS manages to come up with facts that could have only been obtained by someone on the inside of a terrorist or some other anti-British group.

One such agent was Steven Pinder, code name, Spider.

CHAPTER 1

GADFLY

The motorcade of five vehicles sped across London Bridge and turned left into the, now closed to all other traffic, St Thomas Street. The cars eased towards Guys Hospital, amid large crowds lining both sides of the Street. Many in the crowd were waving flowers or placards on which was proclaimed 'We (heart) Princess Alice' and most of them also had small paper Union flags on little sticks, which they waved with gusto.

In the middle of the motorcade was a Rolls Royce Silver Shadow which had Royal standards in the form of two small flags secured to the vehicles front wings. Seated in rear, were Prince Edward and his wife Princess Alice.

Edward, the elder son of King Henry's now deceased younger brother William, is claiming succession to the throne by birthright, due to the failure of the King to produce an heir. In acknowledgement of this right, the crown, under some pressure from Westminster, has bestowed upon him the honorary title of the Prince of Wight and in so doing have given the small Isle off England's south coast, Principality status.

'For god sake smile woman, you're supposed to be enjoying the occasion.' The Prince managed to say through clenched teeth, while still maintaining a broad grin on his face.

The Princess turned to him. 'You are pathetic Edward; you think the people can't see through your silly fixed grin.'

At that they both turned to look out of their respective window, smiled, albeit falsely and waved to the crowd.

Prince Edward pressed the intercom button that was just below the glass dividing screen.

'Stop here Harold, we will go walkabout for the last fifty yards to the hospital.'

'Will do Sir, just give me a moment to organise your protection.'

'You know Edward, we should stop this charade, you stopped loving me a long time ago... That's if you ever did. Why don't you give me a divorce and then you can have your Mrs Grey at your leisure.'

'You're quite right dear, I've never loved you, - you were my father's choice not mine, - unfortunately with the state of the monarchy as it is, my uncle will never allow us to divorce.'

'Have you asked?'

'Not quite, but I know he's aware of the situation.'

'What situation would that be....The Mrs Grey, married woman situation, or the how you sneak off to her bed at the drop of a hat, situation?'

The Prince inhaled loudly through his nose, pursed his lips and stared blankly at Alice. 'Thought so.' She said, tapping her fingers lightly on her knee as spoke. 'You haven't told him you're screwing a married woman...Why am I not surprised; you're just as spineless as you are deceitful.'

Prince Edwards face began to redden, this was not the time or place to loose ones temper, but he was finding it damn difficult to restrain himself. 'Hold your tongue women! How dare you talk to me in that manner,' he said trying hard to restrain the volume of his effervescing anger, 'I demand some respect from a common ----.'

'You pompous pr—.'

Before any further retort could be exchanged between them, the doors on each side of the car opened simultaneously.

'We're ready for you now, sir.'

Princess Alice walked the nearside to admiring cheers, handing of flowers and shouts of. 'We love you Princess Alice.' The Prince decided to walk on the other side of the street and although he grasped many a hand, he could hardly help noticing the vast majority of the crowd on that side, were attempting to break through the barriers and police cordons, just to be in the proximity of his wife. Those who hadn't or couldn't get across the street were shouting their love for her, over his head.

The Prince turned to one his aides. 'It's like I'm none existent.'

'She is a very popular young lady sir.' The aide responded.

'So it seems. I think it is about time I had a word with my uncle.' The Prince mumbled to himself.

Sir Peter Thompson-Smythe, Head of the British Intelligence Special Service was at his desk in his office in Queen Anne's Gate, London when the red secure telephone rang. The noise startled him and he shot bolt upright knowing that the old fashioned contraption was a dedicated line and a direct link to the palace. Pressing the receiver firmly against his ear, he listened before replying. 'Yes Sir, as you wish, I'll give the matter my utmost attention. Goodbye Sir.' He replaced the receiver and sank back into his chair. Deep in thought he stared blankly at the desk top, the fingers of one hand gently massaged his chin. 'Now there lies a problem, - problem indeed.' He mused.

Why not. He thought with revelation as the germ of an idea entered his mind. Leaning forward he pressed the button on the intercom, 'Marj bring me the Gadfly file would you please.' A few moments later Marjorie entered the office with a sealed file in her hand. She knew Sir Peter well enough to know by his posture when he wanted to share his thoughts, and in this instance, she picked up the vibes that said he was playing this one close to his chest. Dropping the file on his desk she turned and headed back to the door.'

'Thank you Marj.'

Sir Peter broke the seal and perused the file. A few moments later, he typed in a text message on his mobile phone. 'Gadfly, need to meet, today at four.'

That afternoon at four pm, Sir Peter was sat on a cushioned bench seat set in the middle of the floor in one of the many rooms on the second floor of the Tate Gallery. He was contemplating the beauty and the artist's skill in the painting of 'The Lady of Shallot' by John Waterhouse. A man walked slowly into the room his head turned toward the same painting as he moved. He stopped, his eyes still fixed upon the artistry and slowly lowered himself onto the cushioned seat next to Sir Peter.

He spoke quietly, almost a whisper. 'Wonderful painting is it not?'

'It is indeed,' Sir Peter replied without turning his attention away from the painting.

'Just look at the detail in the blanket, the bird and even the insects, could that be a Gadfly, do you think?'

'Perhaps, but I think may be a Dragonfly.' Sir Peter said as he discreetly slid his hand so that it brushed against the stranger's and with a delicate movement passed over a miniature tape recording.

Without another word or even a glance in either's direction, Sir Peter and the stranger got up and left the Gallery room.

CHAPTER 2

DESERT ROSE

The Toyota Land Cruiser lumbered laboriously at a crawl over the desert wastelands on the outskirts of Baghdad. The vehicle was heading Northward, at night without the aid of the headlights. It bumped jarringly as it pitched over boulders almost to the point of rolling over and slued uncontrollably as a wheel periodically caught the drifts of soft sand. The five occupants were being thrown and bounced about and signs of irritation began to show with their discomfort.

'Mossoud, do you not know the way?'

'Yes I know it, but I cannot see the track at all well.'

Ahmed was in the front with the driver, throwing up his hands in the direction he hoped to be heading. 'Then why not put on the lights?'

'Do you not think the Americans would see us?'

The vehicle lurched again, accompanied by the groans of the passengers. 'This must be a track suitable only for the goat.' A voice muttered from the back seat.

'From where will anyone see us?' Ahmed said out of frustration, throwing his hands up again, as he spoke.

'From there!' Mossoud pointed to a hardly discernable halo of light far off into the distance. The others strained their eyes scanning the dark line of the horizon.

'I see it.' A voice from the back declared.

'Good, now you understand we must proceed with caution.'

At that, silence prevailed for the remainder of the journey. Despite their discomfort all that was heard from the passengers was the occasional grunt.

The Land Cruiser travelled along a Wadi, eventually coming to a stop within about three hundred yards of a USAAF Base and the twelve foot high concrete perimeter wall that surrounded it. The banks of the dry river bed were of sufficient depth to prevent the vehicle being seen from the base's observation posts. Three of occupants alighted from the vehicle and began to unload the weapon. Mossoud and Ahmed remained in the vehicle engrossed in conversation.

'Mossoud you must take the highway on our return, we cannot hope to getaway over that terrain.'

'As I have planned Ahmed, we will have no need then for the surprise.'

Spider together with the other two occupants carried the mortar launching tube and twelve rounds of shells up to and set on a small sandy plateau part way up the Wadi side.

'Abdullah, do you know this weapon?' Akhmed asked in a very low voice, seemingly not wanting to be overheard by either the Americans or indeed, his companions.

'There are mortars, I think, but you should know, are you not a soldier in our jihad against the infidel?'

'Yes, but I am also a citizen and a father. I, and the others,' he said making a sideward movement of his head in the direction of the vehicle, 'have had little time to prepare for this. We have used only the land mine, planting them at night on the road.'

Despite the low volume of Akhmed voice, Amir picked up on the conversation as he climbed the bank carrying four mortar rounds.

'Perhaps Mossoud will know how it will work.'

Mossoud and Ahmed made to join the other three dark shapes.

'Is the weapon set in the firing position?' Mossoud asked, in an exaggerated whisper.

All three shrugged their shoulders, at least that's what Mossoud thought they did, but in the darkness he could not be sure.

'We thought you knew what to do Mossoud.' Amir said.

'Do I have to do it all?' Mossoud said angrily and pushed his way forward making sure he barged Akhmed the smallest of the three out of the way.

Mossoud picked up the pieces, studied each one in the dim light emitting from the base and put them back down again. The other four were now gathered around him straining their eyes in the darkness to watch and learn, well for three of them it was a lesson. Mossoud, obviously unsure, decided to ask the newest member of the group, not knowing if he'd had any previous weapons training.

'Abdullah, do you not know how this thing works?'

Abdullah held out his hands palms up, gesturing his ignorance of all things ballistic. 'Alas I am but a car mechanic; I know nothing of these things.'

'I think the mortars have to be primed,' Amir chimed in. Mossoud ignored him and bungled on, doing it in his own way and trying to look as if he knew what he was doing. No one was more surprised than he as the first round shot out of the firing tube with a *"Whoop"* and exploded in a cloud of debris on their side of the concrete wall, considerably short of the intended target. Shock and blind panic took over as Mossoud, with the help of the other three, dropped five more rounds in quick succession into the tube. Abdullah stood back unnoticed, a smile on his face as he watched them all fall harmlessly short of their target.

By now sirens were blaring and search lights began to comb the desert, the American base was now on full alert, it would not be long before bullets would be flying.

'Let's get out of here!' Mossoud shouted the tremble in his voice gave away the fact that he was scared out of his skin.

In his haste to get up off his knees, Mossoud stuck out a foot and accidentally kicked the tripod as he rose, just at the very moment Amir dropped another shell into the tube. Not one of them turned to see where that particular bomb landed; they were too busy scrambling down the loose gravel of the side of the Wadi, part running and part sliding back to the car.

The tracer bullets were now lighting the sky above their heads and kicking up the sand and stones on the opposite bank. Mossoud was first into the Toyota and had the engine gunned and the vehicle in motion before Akhmed was able to get in. Irrespective of the terrain, the Toyota took off at speed. Akhmed was hanging desperately onto the open door, unable to keep pace with the vehicle, was being dragged, his feet making contact with the occasional boulder on the former river bed. Spider leaned out, took a firm hold on Akhmed's clothing and yanked him into the vehicle. Nothing was said about that incident and Akhmed's plaintive sighs were immediately out done by the audible gasps of the others, as the vehicle seemed periodically to take off, crash land and rear up again as it bounced its way over the rough terrain.

Eventually the vehicle found a road, unmade, but by comparison, it was like riding on a cloud. The atmosphere inside the vehicle was now more relaxed and even Akhmed seemed to have gotten over his trauma. 'Allah akbah' somebody shouted, but not in a very convincing fashion.

'Mossoud, we have left the mortar and the bombs behind,' Amir declared in a loud voice, suddenly realising the result of their panic.

'The Mullah is not going to be pleased with us Mossoud, we have failed in our mission and we have left the weapon.' Ahmed shook his head from side to side as he spoke.

'Do not worry my friend,' Mossoud replied casually, 'it was our first time I'm sure there will be other opportunities to prove ourselves....Imshallah.'

Spider, seated in the back with the other two, made a hardly discernible shake of his head and rolled his eyes in disbelief.

It was at that point that he realised, despite the rigorous vetting he'd received at their hands, these were not hardened terrorists. *Well not yet, they aren't.*

John Godfrey was quite a handsome guy; he had a fair complexion with neatly groomed blond hair which kinked over his forehead in a superman type style. He was five-ten, medium build and in good physical condition for a thirty-six year old. John held the position as the Foreign Affairs Advisor to the Ambassador in Iraq. Unofficially, however, it was a cover for the real purpose of his posting, which was as an Intelligence Operations Executive controlling an undercover operation, code name, 'Desert Rose', a conduit for a soon to be network of undercover agents, in Iraq.

He stood, hands clasped behind his back, deep in thought, gazing out of an office window in the British Embassy, Baghdad. 'At last, must be all of ten months,' John mumbled. He took a deep breath, raising himself on his toes in an attempt to peer between the bladed leaves of the date palms in the garden and over the perimeter wall out into the Baghdad streets.

He rocked back on heels, looked at his wrist watch and did a quick calculation in his head. *About 8am UK time.* Turning away from the window he walked over to his desk and tapped enter on the computer keyboard, at the same time edging into his seat as the screen lit up.

'Good morning Sir Peter.' He said as Sir Peter's face appeared.

'Ah Good morning to you John, though I suppose it's well past noon where you are.'

John smiled and nodded. 'Yes Sir; I have some news, Spider has made contact.'

'About time, don't you think?'

'It has been a while.'

'Well, what's he got to say for himself?'

John shifted in his seat as he opened a file. 'I picked this note from the DLB this morning.' He extracted a creased up scrap of paper from the file and held it up to the screen.

'Yes yes I see it, what does it say man, or do you expect me to read the bloody thing, it's far too small. 'Sir Peter said with an edge of impatience in his voice.

'Sorry Sir.' John immediately replaced the paper to the file, pattered it and rolled his palm over it in an attempt to make it lie flat. 'Decoded sir, it reads; *'Have joined terrorist faction. Involved in mortar attack.'* He's drawn a map, no street names, but from buildings noted, looks like it could be somewhere in southwest Baghdad, there's a cross on the map and written under it, *'Arms cache, Russian, under floor.'*

There was a pause; John just stared blankly into a thoughtful face on the screen for what seemed an age, before Sir Peter made to reply. 'This place John, get me the coordinates, I'll arrange satellite surveillance twenty-four-seven.'

'Thought you'd say that sir, so I've posted a team for that very purpose, should have them for you within the hour. And I've also taken the liberty of asking Cheltenham if it would be possible to pick up audio traffic in that region, when I get the exact data....Hope you don't mind sir.'

'Of course not, initiative lad, - now then, what about this mortar attack?'

'Well sir, there was some terrorist action last night at the American air base. A Helicopter on the maintenance pad took a direct hit.' John gave out a little sigh before continuing. 'My feeling sir is that's the attack Spider is referring to.'

'Was there, be damned, should have report. Give me a moment to check this lot.' Sir Peter disappeared momentarily out of camera; John could hear the rustling of paper and then he reappeared. 'Ah yes, got it.' There a pause and some muttering as Sir Peter read through the report. 'Ah y-e-s, tend to agree John. It would appear that Spider is now an Iraqi terrorist.'

'Just the break we've been waiting for sir, isn't it?'

Sir Peter nodded and without further comment there was a click and the screen went blank. John leaned forward, tapped at the keyboard and shut down his computer. He closed the file and sank back into his plastic covered swivel chair, hands clasped behind his head. *What now Spider...What now.*

CHAPTER 3

SPIDER

BISS Headquarters London, two months later.

Sir Peter pressed the remote and the screen went blank, he pondered a moment as he lowered the device onto his desk. He pressed the intercom button and lent forward as he spoke.

'Marjorie, did you get all that?'

'Sure did.'

Sir Peter eased back, elbows on the desk, brought his fingers together, as if he was about to pray. 'Send a coded message, will you, to John Godfrey, he's still in the Baghdad embassy. Tell him to get his backside to Medina post haste. Then contact the Saudi Ambassador, have him set up a meeting for John with King Faud....See if we can get that loud mouthed son of his over here for a long holiday.' He paused a moment. 'Have a word with the Manager at the Ritz.... Try to arrange for

us to take over the whole top floor, to accommodate a Royal visit by the Crown Prince of Arabia...Probably need a month.'
'Okay Peter I'm on it.'
'If necessary, point out that its in the Countries interest...I'm sure he will oblige....And Marjorie.'
'Y-e-s.'

'When you've done that, bring in the Desert Rose file.'
'Didn't we shelve that operation?'
'Yes...but I'd like to check something, do you mind.'
'Okay give me ten, I'll have to dig it out.'

'He swivelled around in his chair got up and headed to the safe in the wall behind him, opened it and slid out a file marked SPIDER. Placing the file neatly on the desk he squared it up so that its edge was parallel with the desks before running a paperknife under the seal and extracting the contents.

Marjorie knew she could be flippant with Sir Peter, after all, she had been with him for twenty years and was his lover and confident as well as his Personal Assistant and Private Secretary.

Since the death of Sir Peter's wife some ten years ago, they have been in a relationship, living together in Sir Peter's Guildford home.

She is an elegant lady, tall and slim and still very attractive. When younger she would have been considered a good catch for any man, but had never married, always putting her career first. Now in her late fifties such thoughts of wedlock were far from her mind, content with the arrangement she had with Sir Peter.

Marjorie gave a brief knock on the door walked in headed for the desk and handed the file to Sir Peter. Taking it for granted that he wanted her to remain, she backed up and dropped into the Chesterfield armchair opposite, promptly producing a note pad which she rested on the thigh of her now crossed legs, pencil poised in anticipation of Sir Peter's instruction.

'No problem with the Ritz, but they will need two weeks notice, John's on his way and the Ambassador making arrangements.'

'Good, good.' Sir Peter said thoughtfully, as he reached for the Dessert Rose file, flicked it open and extracted a sheet of paper which he lightly tapped with his fore finger. 'This guy,' he said, 'I want you to put a call in to MI6, expedite their

Romanovski file, apparently the CIA already have a team on hand in Riyadh.'

'R-o-m-a-n-o-v-s-k-i … Got that.' She said looking up from her note pad.

Sir Peter slid the sheet of paper back into the file and turned his attention back to the neatly stacked paperwork in front of him at the same time making a beckoning movement in Marjorie's direction with his head. She got out of the chair and walked around the desk and gently laid her arm on his shoulder and browsed the paperwork.

'I think it's about time we sorted this Ivor Romanovski, can't do with him running loose, any longer.' Sir Peter muttered. Marjorie didn't know who Romanovski was, but she knew there must be a connection with this Saudi thing.

'I want you to familiarise yourself with this file Marj, it's time to use my number one asset.' He said sliding a photograph out of the file.

'W-h-o is that?' She said in an exaggerated tone.

Sir Peter held up the photograph to give her a better viewing angle. 'That's Steven Pinder...Code name Spider and by far my best agent.'

'So this is Spider...Bit of alright isn't he.'

'Umm, I suppose he is, not that I'd notice.' Marjorie gave him a playful nudge.

'Now that you mention it, his mother was and probably still is a very beautiful lady.' Sir Peter pondered thoughtfully. 'Y-e-s indeed, very beautiful, Spanish, dark hair, brown eyes.' Sir Peter rolled his eyes when spoke, inviting another nudge from Marjorie. He smiled. 'Built like his father, Richard, only more muscular, six foot six inches and two-hundred and thirty pounds, or he was then, lost a bit of weight last time out.'

'In Iraq?'

Sir Peter nodded. 'Dessert Rose.'

He extracted another sheet of paper from the file, laying it so that Marjorie could read it. 'I came across Steven fifteen years ago at Winchester Boys School, the son of the then British Ambassador in Saudi Arabia. He was born and raised in the Riyadh Embassy and was sent to school in England when he was eight. An old friend, a teacher at the school drew my attention to him. At that time Steven could speak fluent Arabic and Spanish as well as English of course. Within one term at Winchester he was also pretty adept at French, that's when I created this file. Steven has a natural gift for languages; by the time he had got to Oxford he was fluent in Russian, German and Hindi.'

'Hindi?'

'At one time he had an Indian room mate. It was while he was at Oxford, I formally enlisted him; he had just taken part in the boat race, good oarsman, mad about boats.'

'All very impressive I must say.'

Sir Peter gave out a little cough accompanied by a hardly perceptible nod as an affirmative to Marjorie's comment, before continuing the synopsis. 'As soon as he left the university I put him through three years of intensive training with Two Para, and the SAS at the special facility in the Scottish Highlands.'

Sir Peter turned to look at Marjorie who was still standing behind him. 'Steven turned out to be an outstanding agent.' Sir Peter turned his attention back to the file. 'Enough of this chit chat let's get down to business. This is his mobile number please send him a text.'

'Isn't he still in Iraq?' Marjorie interrupted.

'No, he's been back now. Anyway this text, say Papa will be at the usual place, noon tomorrow with Mama.'

'Am I to take it that I'm Mama?'

'You may indeed.'

'Good.' Marjorie made towards the door.

Sir Peter added as she opened it. 'Better tell Dennis we won't require his services tomorrow, we'll drive ourselves, ask him to leave the keys to the Jaguar at reception. You and I my darling, are going for a day out to Dorset, we shall leave from home first thing in the morning.'

Sir Peter was driving, Marjorie was seated in the front passenger seat nursing the recently acquired CIA file, marked 'Ivor Romanovski' from an MI6 courier.

The mobile phone on the dash peeped and Marjorie retrieved it.

'It's a text from John. He's outside of the Palace in Medina awaiting audience with King Faud.'

'Good, let's hope he can pull it off.' Sir Peter nodded at the file. 'Anything of interest?'

'I've only given it a quick once over, but there doesn't seem to be anything that we don't already know.'

'Won't hurt to let Steven read both of them.'

'Where are we going to meet him?' Marjorie asked as she replaced the telephone into the holder.

'A place called Hamworthy, part of Poole; it's where the SBS are based. But first, we shall take a little detour around some of Poole's back streets and ferry port perhaps, just to ensure we are not being followed. Then we'll head to a pier at

Hamworthy Common and hopefully take a boat ride. That's why I suggested you wore casual clothes.

Sir Peter parked the car at Hamworthy Common. They sat there, taking the time to look around the car park at the other three vehicles and their occupants, nothing was out of place. Leaving the car they walked along the short pier. At that moment a dark green army Zodiac came from out of the nearby Marines Base. Sitting at the central controls was a soldier wearing camouflage fatigues and a green crash helmet with a dark visor. The boat pulled along side of the pier ladder, the soldier dismounted and took hold of the ladder stringer, to steady the craft.

'Major Pinder I presume.' Sir Peter said looking down and smiling.

'Hello Sir.' Steven's voice emitted from the within the helmet.

'Down you go Marj.' Sir Peter said, relieving Marjorie of the briefcase so that she could descend the ladder and step out onto the boat with relative ease. Steven gently guided Marjorie with his free hand to the central seat. He then reached up for the briefcase, allowing Sir Peter to descend into the craft. All aboard, Steven took the Zodiac across Poole harbour to a stretch of water just off Brownsea Island, where his Sunseeker Predator 72 motor cruiser, Morning Star was moored.

Once on board, Steven removed his helmet and camouflage jacket. Now more relaxed, he made Sir Peter and Marjorie welcome on board his luxury boat.

'Good to meet you, you must be Mamma.'

'You also,' she said holding out her hand. 'You can call me Marjorie,' then turning her head toward Sir Peter she mouthed. *Not bad.*

'Good to see you again Sir.'

'Beautiful boat Steven must have cost a small fortune.'

'I bought her after Ireland, I had a lot of years back pay due, plus I had a bit put by. She was built for some millionaire, who suddenly woke up one morning and realised he no longer was, so he cancelled the order. Got me a discount I couldn't resist. Besides this is my home, so in one way I'm saving the cost of buying a house here in Poole.'

'Do you leave her on here all the time?'

'Oh no, Marjorie, I have berth all paid for in Dolphin Quay. I just brought her out here today to warm the engines and to avoid prying eyes.

Sir Peter had wandered to the helm position. 'It would appear to have a lot of equipment, Steven.'

'Yes Sir, she's full of the latest technology and I've even had a company computer installed.'

'Do you live on her all the time?'

'Only when I'm not on the Base.'

'The Marines?' Marjorie queried.

Sir Peter put in. 'Steven isn't really in Marines, it's his cover between assignments. The Base Commander Colonel Paul Bradley believes Steven is on transfer from another Marine Commando Company, specially selected for SBS training, which I suppose isn't too far from the truth. The rank of Major allows him certain privileges, like access to the latest technology. All that SBS training keeps him in shape.'

'Oh I can see that.' Marjorie said looking Steven up and down.

Steven felt his face redden and quickly changed the subject.

'I, - I take it this isn't just a social visit sir?' Sir Peter just nodded. 'You have some action for me?'

Sir Peter pursed his lips. 'A hum, y-e-s all your own doing I'm afraid,' Steven looked bewildered, 'a development from the arms you spotted in Baghdad.'

'Ah the Russian stuff in the Mullah's cellar.'

'Yes, the Mullah is a Shia Cleric by the name of Abu Al Dinahjahd, a known Al Qeader activist; we've got him on round the clock surveillance. However it was a contact he made that caught our interest and the reason we are here.'

Marjorie, pre-empting Sir Peter, withdrew the copied CIA file and handed it to Sir Peter who in turn placed the folder on the table between him and Steven, so that it was in front of and the correct way for Steven to read. He then reached over opened the folder and tapped with a forefinger at a photograph of a male face. 'He's the reason for concern, a nasty piece of work by the name of Ivor Romanovski, ex KGB hit man.'

'Haven't had the pleasure sir,'

'Well that's about to change, he's your target, I want you to eliminate him.'

Steven nodded. 'Can I ask what he's done?'

Sir Peter eased back in his seat. 'Watch much TV Steven?'

'Yeah, a little.' Steven said bemused by the question.

'Did you by any chance catch the speech made by that Saudi Prince?'

'Who didn't,' Steven responded, 'it was on all the channels, even on U tube.'

'Well I believe it was this fellow,' Sir Peter tapped the photograph again, 'who somehow put him up to it.'

Sir Peter tapped the file again. 'In short, Ivor here has been travelling the Middle East and Asia cavorting with terrorist factions selling them weapons, like those you saw in Dinahjahd's cellar.'

'Surely he's the delivery boy....Who's the supplyer?'

'Ahh, that would be a company registered in Belgium in the name of Randall Holdings, who just happen to be a wholly owned subsidiary of VOSOGE, Vostok Oil and Gas Exploration a Russian company, part of Vostok Industries.'

'Vladimir Vostok.' Steven put in.

'You know him?'

'Know of him, he's probably one of the richest men in Russia if not the world, owner of a third of Russia's oil reserve, the extent of which does not seem to be known outside of Russia, together with almost all of the vast Siberian gas fields, grabbed the lion share when Yeltsin divided up Russia's state ran industries.'

Sir Peter nodded in agreement. 'And he has his fingers in pharmaceuticals and steel production as well. '

'You think Vostok is behind this?'

'Without doubt, I believe Vostok is stirring up conflict between Arab Islamic fundamentalists and the Western alliance, with the intention, I can only assume, of resting control of the vast gulf oil fields.'

'What do you suggest we do?'

'About Vostok, not much at the moment, can't get near him, but we can get Romanovski. Even he isn't mixed up with this speech thing, which I very much doubt by the way; he is proving to be a bit of nuisance.' Sir Peter turned to Marjorie. 'Pass me the Prince Mohammed speech please Marj.'

She slid the paper copy across the table; Sir Peter trapped it with his hand and positioned it so that Steven could read it. Sir Peter nodded. 'No need to tell you how inflammatory that is.'

'Y-e-s, knew of him as a kid, never had him down as a radical. Out of character.' Steven said thoughtfully.

'I agree Steven that's why I'm convinced our Russian friend somehow set the whole thing up.' Sir Peter reached over and turned a few pages of the file and found another photograph. 'We caught up with Ivor last week in Riyadh seated in a very exclusive Riyadh restaurant. And the gentleman he just happens to be in deep conversation with is none other than Sheikh Ahmed Al Bosfar.'

'Who's he when he's at home?'

'A very wealthy and much respected businessman, he also has title to a large area of dessert, yet to be tapped, but surveys predict another large field. But more importantly the Sheikh just happens to be Prince Mohammed's friend and most trusted confidant.'

'So Romanovski gets to the Prince through the Sheikh....Possible.'

Sir Peter nodded and cocked an eyebrow. 'In my book very probable.'

'But in any event you still want Romanovski taken out and you want me to do it.'

Sir Peter nodded solemnly.

'Okay....When and where?'

Marjorie slid another file across the table; it was stamped "Top Secret". 'That's what we've got so far,' Sir Peter said, 'It's a CIA file on Romanovski goes back to his KGB days. Marj and I will have a cuppa while you sift through them.'

'I can do better than that; I've prepared lunch for you.'

'Thank you, very thoughtful, point me in the right direction I'll do the rest.' Marjorie said.

'In the fridge, down there in the galley, you will find two smoked salmon and prawn salads and there's French bread and a bottle of Merlot already corked, set out on a tray.'

Steven took the files down into the lower saloon, leaving his guests to enjoy their lunch in the deck saloon dining area.

Half an hour later he wandered back. 'Interesting,' Steven said as he lightly tapped the CIA folder. 'Romanovski is still in Riyadh with three heavies... Why, what are they hanging around for?'

'Whatever the reason Steven, I guess you're going to find out. I would suggest you liaise with George Carter the CIA agent running the surveillance op. I've taken the liberty of setting up a meeting with him through the British Embassy... Familiar territory, is it not...Steven.' Sir Peter added thoughtfully.

'I'll try not to let it show sir.'

Marjorie opened her note book and began to read. 'You are scheduled to leave the day after tomorrow at ten am, out of Brise Norton to Dhahran. John Godfrey will be waiting to meet you the moment you land.'

'I thought John was still in Baghdad.'

'Was, got him to Medina when this lot blew up. He's had a meeting with King Faud and made arrangements for Prince Mohammed to visit England.' Sir Peter answered. 'Sorry Marj, do continue.'

Marjorie gave out a little cough for no other reason than to let the men know that she did not want to be interrupted again. 'Both of you are then fly to Riyadh on a British Aerospace Dhahran military training flight. At Riyadh John will use his diplomatic status to get you through Saudi customs and immigration. Your journey will not appear on any flight manifest and the Saudis will not have any record of your presence in their country.'

'As you know the Embassy has a well-stocked arsenal, you can collect whatever you need when you get there.' Sir Peter put in and then turned to Marjorie. 'Have you got Steven's cover and paperwork Marj.'

'Right Steven.' she said as she fumbled in the pocket compartment of the briefcase, extracting an envelope which she opened, tipping out the contents onto the table. 'This is your passport and this is your MI6 security clearance, I have digitally lifted your finger prints and photograph from your file and transferred them. You are now Charles Evans MI6 special agent. Who does exist by the way and is now spending some time in the agency safe house.'

Sir Peter took a miniature recorder out of his pocket and handed it to Steven. 'The tape is an outline of all you will need to know about your new cover, listen and digest while on the airplane and then destroy it. Suffice to say Charles Evans can speak Russian, but only a little Arabic and has never been to Saudi Arabia.' Reaching into his pocket again he pulled out a brown MOD envelope. 'Nearly forgot this. It's a letter from the

MOD to Colonel Bradley, requesting your immediate release. Oh and one other thing Steven, John Godfrey has no idea that you are Spider, better we should leave it that way.'

Washington (USA)

Henry Forbes stepped from the limousine as his chauffer held open the rear door; he was greeted by a smart young marine with a crisp salute. 'This way sir, the President is expecting you.'

Henry followed the soldier to the oval office of the White House, a journey he had made many times before, although he was not any kind of government official or politician. He just happened to be without doubt, the richest man in America and as it happened, the main contributor to President Baxter's campaign fund.

The marine tapped the office door, opened it and announced, 'Mister Forbes sir' and then withdrew as Henry marched past him hand extended.

'Mister President.'

'Nice to see you Henry.'

'And you sir.'

A brief handshake, President James Baxter motioned Henry to sit, and resumed his position, seated behind a walnut desk.

'Okay Henry, I don't expect this is just a social call, so let's cut to the chase. What can I do for you?'

Henry dispensed with the small talk and got straight to the point. 'Day before yesterday Prince Mohammed of Saudi Arabia made a pretty damming speech,' the President pursed his lips and nodded, 'if he is allowed to carry out these treats, the affect on the US economy would be devastating, sir.'

'For sure, I know all about it, plans are in motion as we speak to get the situation resolved.'

'Can I ask you what, sir?'

'Uh –uh, no way, this is a government situation, not open for public discussion. - Hells bells Henry, that's how it works, - you know that.'

The President eased forward in his leather-upholstered chair and looked at Henry long and hard, he saw the determined look fixed on Henry's face. 'Augh come on now Henry.' He said as he slumped back into in his chair, leaving one arm extended over the desk. 'This ain't the kind of situation that's gonna involve you now, is it?'

'Very much so, Mister President; which ever way this cookie crumbles, some where along the line, I'm about to get shafted, sir.'

'For Christ sake lighten up, we've known each other too long, cut the sir and the Mister President crap, just plain Jim, alright!'

'Alright Jim, I really need to know what you are going to do about this situation.'

'It's not a big deal, we, that is, the joint chiefs, I and the Brits, have decided to resolve the situation with a little diplomatic gesturing. The Brits have been quick off the mark and have had an audience with King Faud, we want to show the world we still have his backing despite his son's ill contrived speech.'

'Is that all Jim?'

'Isn't that enough?'

'No.'

Then the President sat up straight in his seat, and stared hard again at Henry. – 'Explain yourself.'

'I want to know if you have any intention to zap the son of a bitch.'

'I'll just forget you said that Henry.'

'What would you say if I told you that everything Prince Mohammed said about us in that speech was true?'

The President a little taken aback by that comment took a moment to gather himself. 'I can't answer that Henry.'

'Can't or won't Jim.'

'You got a problem with that Henry, I suggest you leave right now, this issue is no longer open for discussion.'

Henry Forbes left the White House feeling that very little progress had been made. He'd achieved dick shit, status quo. What the hell was he thinking, why should he have expected a solution from the President. He half wished he'd kept his big mouth shut. Seated in the back of his limousine he reached for his mobile phone and punched in a number. A few seconds later, it was answered, with a very British sounding. 'Hello.'

'York, this is Washington, we have a situation.'

'What level do you require?'

'The whole family.'

'That would take the best part of three weeks to organise.'

'Three weeks! But this is urgent, couldn't you make it sooner?'

'Fraid not old chum, we must consider the availability and all that.'

'Okay understood, please make the necessary arrangements for three weeks from today.'

'As you wish, goodbye.'

Henry pressed the key to end the call, and return the telephone to his pocket he muttering to himself. 'Yeah and goodbye to you.'

CHAPTER 4
STAKE OUT
Riyadh Saudi Arabia

'This is your room Charles; I'm just down the hall. Get some rest; we've a busy day tomorrow. Oh and while I remember, breakfast is laid on for nine in the conference room. I'm expecting George Carter to join us, - good night Charles.'

'Err, thank you John, goodnight.'

Spider knew all about the Embassy, its conference rooms, offices and the very sparsely furnished guest rooms. Although as far as the Embassy staff and John Godfrey in particular were concerned, this was Charles Evans first visit to Arabia. To fit the part Spider acted a little vague about the locations of the rooms. So that John had found it necessary to escort him.

In the morning, right on cue, George Carter turned up at reception. A Corporal from the Military Police escorted him to the conference room just in time for coffee. Introductions were exchanged and John stated, for the benefit of Charles Evans. 'Here in the Middle East we have a shared information policy with our American cousins.' Which basically meant security at the Embassy was very relaxed, especially where the CIA are involved. 'Well George what's the situation?'

'Not good John, we have lost them.'

John's former assured demeanour change instantly to an expression of shock horror. 'What! You lost them! I don't believe it....Don't you realize how important it is to deactivate this Russian? We've spent months tracking him over half the world and you manage to lose him in a few days.' John shook his head in dismay.

'Look John these things happen, I guess the guys on surveillance let themselves get blinkered by their routine. You know, same thing day in day out, leave the hotel at nine each morning, visit to various locations in the city, then returning to the hotel late afternoon. Until yesterday, that is.'

George now shook his head in dismay. 'Our man should have realised something was different, when they emerged earlier than usual with suit cases. He took it that they were leaving and radioed ahead to alert the airport surveillance team, only the Ruskies never showed.'

'And this guy watching the hotel didn't bother to follow them?' John was now wild eyed and getting very irate.

'Apparently not, he decided to remain on station and check at the hotel that they had checked out.'

'You mean they left the hotel with suitcases and you wanted to know if they were coming back. The mind boggles.' John put his head in his hands and stared down into his coffee cup. George remained silent.

'This is your shout we are only helping you guys out.'

John slammed his fist down hard on the table sending the coffee cup momentarily into the air, as it bounced back, several globules of the liquid were ejected and splashed across the table top. The anger was now showing clearly on his face. 'If you'd bothered to read the files, you would know that these Russians are much more of a threat to US-Middle East stability than they are to us Brits.'

'So much for a shared information policy.' A thin smile cut across Charles's face as he spoke. John and George looked hard at Charles, who just shrugged his shoulders.

John continued to ball out George. 'Bloody hell George what a cock up.'

'Now just steady on John, we're not that incompetent; if it's of any help, we know they didn't go to the airport, so that means they're still in the city.'

John got to his feet and began to pace up and down, moving his head from side to side. 'What on earth are we going to do now?'

Charles, give a little cough to catch the attention of the other two and he spoke with a voice of authority. 'John would you like to sit down, please.' John obeyed, surprisingly without question. 'Well gentlemen a small hiccup, but at this moment not a big problem.'

He turned to John who was now sat head in hands rocking it from side to side. 'John!' John snapped to attention, sitting bolt upright. 'Would Romanovski and friends have any idea they were under surveillance before coming to Saudi?'

'Definitely not, we were most discreet. And much of our surveillance was by satellite.'

Spider nodded thoughtfully. 'And George, do you think the Russians spotted your surveillance?'

'No way Charlie, we used different vehicles never parked in the same spot, never got close to the targets and as we had a pretty good idea where they were heading, we didn't always tail them.'

'That's obvious,' John snidely put in. George shot him a stare; Charles chose to ignore him and continued his analysis.

'Good....So we can assume their departure from the hotel, if indeed they have departed, was pre-arranged and had nothing to do with our surveillance.'

'I'd go along with that Charlie boy.'

'Yes, I tend to agree.' John said.

'You mentioned the airport George; can we assume that your agents were covering the airport when the Russians arrived?'

'Not really, we caught the group on a random satellite sweep; our computers came up with an instant match on Romanovski coming off an inbound from Beirut. Didn't put any credence on it until we got the nod that you guys had an interest and wanted us to keep tabs on them.'

Until yesterday!' John said as he raised himself out of the chair, about to have another go at George, when he caught the hard look in Charles's eyes, and lowered himself back down, without further comment.

'So one would presume that they have complied with Saudi immigration.'

'Guess so.'

'In that case, as non-Arabs, they probably had a sponsor. If so, the car they were driving would more than likely traced back to him.'

'Why the hell didn't I think of that?' George put in.

'I take it you do have the number?'

'Yeah, sure we do.'

John was more sceptical. 'Well I think you're grasping at straws, if you knew anything about Saudi Arabia, you'd know that you can get in on a visit visa, you don't need a sponsor in all cases.'

'Quite,' Spider agreed. 'Indulge me if you will John, I've got a theory. George, would it be possible to find out who supplied their car?' And could you get a copy of the flight manifest, I want to know the names of all passengers arriving on that flight from Beirut.'

'No problem Charlie, I'm on it.' George got up and began to make for the door.

'I am not quite finished George. I'd also like to take a look at the surveillance reports, covering their movement.'

'Okay, can do.'

Charles smiled at George. 'And what's the chance you could have all this information back to me by four this afternoon?'

'Sure, not a problem.'

'Oh and one more thing.' Charles said, as George was about to open the door. 'If our Russian friends have been sponsored and I suspect they have, perhaps the connection with Sheikh Ahmed Al Bosfar amounts to more than a chance meeting in a restaurant. It may prove beneficial if you put a tail on the Sheikh.'

'Yeah good thinking Charlie, I'll get a team organised.' As George walked through the door, the MP Corporal came to attention ready to show him out. George turned and called back. 'Good to have you on board Charlie.'

Charles and John were still seated in the conference room, pondering the situation.

'John, could you get me an advance, say 10,000 Riyals? Should be enough, I would also like an automatic pistol with a silencer, PNG night vision glasses, a Leatherman multi function tool set, the one with pliers and a set of skeleton keys.' John listed the requirements on a scribble pad, looking up when Charles had finished.

'That all?'

'Yes.'

'No problem.'

'And I don't think it would be wise for me to spend another night here. It would be difficult to maintain any kind of cover if I'm clocked coming and going from the Embassy'

'That's your prerogative, but if you ask me, you'd stick out like a sore thumb out there.'

'The same goes for George Carter, a known CIA agent. After this afternoons meeting, it won't be necessary for George to visit the Embassy. At least, not until this operation has been put to bed.'

'As you wish. How do you envisage we will maintain contact?'

'Can you get hold of three fixed contact radio transmitters? .... Must be secure.'

'I can do better than that. - We've got the very latest technology in mobile telephones, linked through a secret service satellite, calls are un-detectable.' John was referring to the latest BISS communication system, but was not about to inform Charles Evans, of the existence of BISS. However Spider was way ahead of him. 'What do you think?'

'Sound's good to me John.'

'I'll get everything organized. If you are going to leave the Embassy, where will you go? You will need a valid passport and possibly a permit to allow you to stay in a hotel.'

'Don't worry John I can take care of myself.' John shook his head in disbelief, thinking to himself. *Silly bugger, just who does he think he is, James Bond, this is Saudi Arabia, for Christ sake.*

George Carter returned to the Embassy that afternoon bang on four, Charles met him at the conference room door, reaching out to shake his hand. Still standing in the doorway and still holding hands as a gesture of friendship, Charles explained his new arrangement for security and communications. George nodded in agreement with everything Charles had to say on the matter. He'd formed an instant liking for the MI6 agent and would willingly comply with his requests.

John came into the room with a tray and three cups of coffee.

'Hi George, that's yours, on the right.'

'Thanks John.' George said as he walked over to the table, placed his briefcase on it, hesitating before turning to face the others.

The expression on George's face notably turned very serious. 'I have to tell you that I have discovered something very disturbing, in fact so disturbing that I'm going to have to inform Langley.'

'And what would that be George?' John asked brusquely, failing to disguise his frustration. 'Are you going to let us in on this disturbing discovery of yours, or is that a secret for CIA ears only.'

Charles held up a hand to quieten John. 'What's the problem George, anything we need to know?'

George nodded, flipped the clasps on his briefcase and extracted a single sheet of paper. 'We got a hold of the passenger manifest for that flight.' George waved the paper.

'There were no Russians on it, - or for that matter, on any flight that week. However there were four non Arabs on it.'

'Americans?'

'Yeah Charlie, but how ---?'

'Sort of runs along the lines of a theory of mine, -- but I'm sorry to interrupt, please continue.'

George was somewhat taken aback, the serious look on his face being transformed into a look of confusion. And he took a moment before he continued. 'Ah em..' He cleared his throat. 'This changes things dramatically.'

'Not really, logical, in view of the circumstances,' Charles put in. George obviously needed to relate his thoughts on this discovery despite Charles's broadside.

'This is now a whole new ball game makes the situation solely a US issue.'

John reacted swiftly. 'What you fail to realize George, it always has been a US issue, but until now you were quite content to let us Brits sort it out for you. If it weren't for us you wouldn't even know a situation existed.' John glared at George as he tried to calm the rage building inside him. 'We have spent a lot of time and effort chasing these Russians around the Middle East, in and out of countries illegally and everything else involved with long term surveillance. And now you have the nerve to suggest Uncle Sam should get involved, perhaps take over the operation, now that there is more than a hint, the good old US of A, could be in deep shit.'

'A little unfair don't you think John; we have fully cooperated on this.'

'Well lets face it George you didn't really give it your best shot did you, the hotel surveillance for example.'

'Okay, okay back off John, I hear what your saying, point taken. It's still your operation until someone tells me different and I'll will do all I can to help. But I will still be advising Langley of the situation.' George turned back to his briefcase and took out a bunch of A4 size of reports clipped into a manila folder. 'Got the surveillance reports you wanted Charlie, wanna take look?' He slid the folder across the desk. 'Sure.' Charles picked it up and began to browse.

'I also found another piece of information you may find interesting.' George lifted a photo from the briefcase. 'I got it from the tapes.' He said as he placed the picture in front of Charles, lightly tapping it with his finger and a smile on his face. 'George you bloody beauty!' The three of them studied the photo in front of them.

'Sheikh Ahmed Al Bosfar is in the airport car park with the four Russians and it looks like he is meeting and greeting them.

George nodded with satisfaction. 'And,' he added, 'the Saudi Police verified that the car they are using is registered to the Sheikh.'

'Well we now know the sponsor, the car and the fact that they are posing as Americans. Charles picked up the surveillance folder and wandered over to a street map of Riyadh set on one wall. After a short while studying, jerking his head from the reports to the map and back from the map to the reports, he mumbled. 'Yes it all fits,' more to himself than a general comment. The other two who were sipping their coffee in silence, looked at him.

'What fits?' John queried.

'My theory is proving to be near the mark, very near the mark.' John and George looked at each other; problems seemingly forgot and shrugged their collective shoulders.

'What do we know here, umm?' The Spider was again talking to and answering himself as he perused the map in front of him. 'Four Russians posing as Americans, enter Saudi Arabia. Purpose, let's assume is to somehow influence a Prince's speech.' Spider turned to face the others. 'How do they achieve this?' He looked enquiringly at them, but didn't wait for a response.

'Well for a start they would need to find someone with connections to the Prince.'

'The Sheikh.' George put in.

'Exactly, but they would also need some kind of leverage, something that would influence the Prince.'

'Blackmail?'

'Possible George, but whatever, we have to consider that was only phase one.'

'Why only phase one?

'Because John, nobody comes to Saudi for a holiday, once the Prince had made the speech, why hang around, phase two has got to involve something bad enough to make the Saudi's angry at the Americans, hence the pretence when they arrived.'

'What do yah reckon that would be Charlie?

Spider turned back to the map and began to stick pins in various locations taken from the CIA surveillance reports.

'Well my theory would be assassination.' He said nonchantly over his shoulder.

'Assassination!' John and George exclaimed in unison.

'George, these places I've marked, would you say there are high rise? Although Spider knew very well that there were. John responded. 'Yeah from what I know most of them I'd consider high rise.

George was now standing next to Charles looking at the various locations, now identified on the map with a marker pin.

'What yah thinking Charlie?

Spider pondered a moment before wagging a finger at the map.

'This Ivor Romanovski is an ex KGB hit man who favours the long range deal.'

'Sniper?'

'Huh huh,' Spider nodded, 'no doubt looking for high spot from which to make the shot.'

'Shit, we thought they were just looking to set up a business office.'

'Feasible, but I'll wager they're not planning on writing letters.'

'Guess not.'

'This last place, they visited several times, I'll lay odds that's the set up point. Have you by any chance got this place under surveillance?'

'Hell no Charlie, don't have the man power, we concentrated on watching them.'

'Not hard enough.' John put in, George turned and was about to react, when Spider spoke.

'Might I suggest George, you get a team over there now, I'm betting that they have rented an office space on or above the fourth floor and will probably be there as we speak.'

'I'm on it.' George picked up the telephone. 'Okay to use this John?'

John nodded. 'Dial nine for an outside line.'

Spider continued to stare at the map. 'Now we ask ourselves, if this office is the set up, where is the target?'

John sidled up to stand at Spider's shoulder 'All this seems a bit extreme to me Charles, I mean, what evidence do you have? And just who are you expecting to be killed?'

'I don't know at this juncture John, but whoever it is, it'll be someone very important to the Saudis, and I've a feeling it will happen very soon.'

'How the hell did you deduce that? The very soon bit.'

'Well, I would guess that they need to make an impact after the speech, soon as, probably made to look like a retaliation gesture by the Americans, hence the pretence. And the number of visits to this particular office block,' Spider tapped the map with a finger, 'tells me that they're must be nearly ready.'

'You're right Charlie, we've got em, they're at that office.' George said with telephone pressed against his ear relaying the information from CIA headquarters. 'We're picking them up on satellite.'

'Good, so now we know for sure where they are.'

'Two of them carrying a crate Charlie.' Then he said into the phone. 'Zoom in on the goddamn box.'

A brief moment passed and then George covered the mouthpiece and looked toward Spider. 'The crate's marked, 'MACHINE PARTS BOSTON USA'.'

'Interesting...The gun, you think?' Spider said thoughtfully.

'It figures.' George agreed, then speaking into the phone he said. 'Get a team over there like now, and keep that satellite camera on them.' At that he replaced the receiver and returned to the table. John wandered back nodded and smiled thinly at George as if to say all's forgiven, before seating himself next to his CIA buddy.

Spider still perusing the map, now had a pencil and a rule in hand and began to project arcs from each of the marked locations. Standing back he studied the area encompassed within the bounds of the intersecting arcs. 'George, John, you know this city better than me, is there anything of note within this area?' Spider circled an area as he spoke.

'What's the significance, Charles?' John said as he and George headed towards him.

'I've projected the killing field up to a mile range from their present location, if I'm right Romanovski's target will be somewhere within the arc.'

John didn't hesitate. 'It's a large area, but the football stadium is only about half a mile away and bag in the centre. Soccer to you George.'

'Hell, I know that John, I've followed the game for years, in fact I've got a ticket for Thursday's game.'

Spider slowly turned his attention away from the wall map and looked quizzically towards George, noting that John seemed to be doing the same.

Oblivious to their reaction, George continued, 'Promises to be a great game, Saudi verses the Emirates, a world cup qualifier. In fact, this is the last engagement......Holy shit! Surely you don't think?'

'Before his trip to England.' Spider nodding finished the sentence.

George, for a moment he was gob smacked.

'Of course, it makes perfect sense Charlie; - it'll look like a get even attack by us Americans.'

'My thoughts exactly.... Thursday, day after tomorrow, this must be their only opportunity, probably been the plan from the outset, this way it wouldn't of been a problem if the Prince hadn't of made the speech.'

'Hang on Charles, don't you think you're jumping the gun, we can't be sure they are going to shoot the Prince, if indeed they are going to shoot anybody, just because we think they may have rented some office near the stadium.'

George interrupted to dismiss any further comment from John. 'It's a hit on the Arab Prince for sure.'

'Well I'm not convinced.' But John's objection fell on deaf ears; the others were now planning moves to counter the supposed assassination plot. So without further comment he decided to go along with them, after all, the objective was to eliminate this Russian and his pals before they could do further damage to the West.

Spider fingered his chin thoughtfully, thinking aloud. 'In order for their objective to be achieved, everything must point irrefutably at the Americans, notwithstanding retaliatory action for the speech. The Russians will leave a trail of incriminating evidence after the hit, to ensure the Americans take the blame.'

'The crate for one with Boston plastered all over it.' George added.

'For sure,' Spider agreed. He then turned to face the other two. 'Priority one, we must recover the false American passports before Thursdays game. When and if we do, we will need four diplomats to use them on the first plane out of here?'

'That shouldn't be a problem.' John said. 'I'll supply the bodies, you get the passports.'

'So we know where they are now, but I doubt they're sleeping there, we need to find out where. George, I need your guys to stay undercover at the office block, we'll need to tail the Russians when they leave.'

'You've got it Charlie, we'll track em with the sat-cam.' Spider walked back to the table and sat down. 'I'm fairly sure that they will also have changed their car, possibly an American job.'

'It's less than two days to go before the game; do you think they'll be still setting up the gun?'

'Probably already targeted.'

George nodded thoughtfully 'Yeah you're probably right.' Then a little hesitant he continued. 'I'm with you so far Charlie, just need to get a couple of things clear.'

'Fire away.'

'How do yah reckon these commies are getting out? I mean if their Russian passports haven't been stamped, - they sure as hell won't want to risk using the American ones.'

'Good point.' Spider pondered. My guess would be they'd head to the coast, probably the Gulf and rendezvous with one of the ships in the Vostok Fleet.'

'Yeah, I'll go along with that. What about the Sheikh guy?' He's got to be in on it, sponsors Russians and somehow gets to the Prince.'

'I'm not sure he is, my gut feeling is that he thinks he has sponsored four Americans, which would be further incrimination. I can't figure how they worked the speech thing, but I would have expected the Sheikh to report he's involvement with the Americans when the speech was broadcast. The worrying factor is that he hasn't. Why?'

'They may not have had anything to do with the speech thing.' John put in.

'You may be right John, but I doubt it.'

'This Al Bosfar guy probably knew all along they were Russian.' George added.

Spider nodded, pursed his lips and took a moment before responding. 'It's irrelevant George, it won't matter one iota either way. Sheikh Ahmed Al Bosfar is now expendable and will probably be eliminated as soon as, certainly before Thursday.'

'Yep for sure, they've got to do him before they take the Prince.'

'I think I'd better check out Bosfar while you locate where the Russians are staying.'

'What about the office?'

'Tell your guys to check it out just in case we need to get in there in a hurry. But don't attempt entry, these guys will know where every spec of dust is.'

After the meeting, Spider left the Embassy with a few personal bits and pieces together with the items John had gotten for him, all packed into a small duffle bag. He called in to what was once the local souk, but is now a very large shopping centre. He purchased a good quality white Saudi Dishdash, and to fit over it a black Abaya trimmed with gold embroidery. For his head he purchased a plain white Kofi which would be worn under a white silk Shoran held in place with a black Egal. From another shop he picked up a pair of black leather toe sandals and a good quality overnight leather bag. Spider then headed for the toilets at the far end of the centre.

About five minutes later he emerged from the hole in the floor smelly toilet cubicle looking every inch a wealthy Saudi businessman. He had no trouble hiring a car and after a very short drive in a familiar city, found a clean room in a small quiet hotel, an ideal place for keeping a low profile.

What a relief to be Spider again, he said to himself, *well almost.* He lay on the bed smiling as he contemplated his Arab passport and identification card in the name of Abdullah Ali Al Zamil.

The next morning, dressed as an affluent Arab, Spider set off to find Sheikh Ahmed Al Bosfar. He started at the restaurant where the Sheikh met Romanovski.

Spider entered the almost empty restaurant, and headed for the table in the corner, he believed was the one he'd seen in the BISS file photograph. An Indian waiter approached and was visibly taken aback when Spider not only greeted him, but ordered coffee and dates in Hindi. When the waiter returned, Spider drew him into conversation, in Hindi of course. 'I'm looking for a friend, Sheikh Ahmed Al Bosfar, he told me he comes here sometimes.'

'Indeed he does sir; he sits in this very same seat.

'When do you next expect him?'

'I am not sure sir; the Sheikh had a reservation for last night, but did not show, most unlike him.'

'You wouldn't happen to know were I could find him?'

The waiter paused for a moment before answering. Spider began to peel off Riyal notes from a roll. 'It may be possible sir, where I live there are many of us. My friend knows a man who is employed by the Sheikh, a moment please sahib.' The waiter returned ten minutes later, 'I have been fortunate enough to get for you the Sheikh's home address, I trust you will find him there, good fortune sahib.' Spider slid 600 Riyals across the table which promptly disappeared into the waiter's pocket. The Indian waiter then bowed, placed his hands together slightly touching his forehead, as he withdrew.

Half an hour later Spider was outside the gates of a walled area, the size of which he estimated to be in the region of ten acres. He could see a guard post just inside the gate, but it appeared to be empty. Getting out of the car he approached the gate and pressed the call button. He stood there for some time pressing the button persistently. Out of the corner of an eye he perceived the movement of the camera watching him. Now even more convinced someone was at home, he was not going to give up and continued to press the call button. It was a good twenty minutes before the buzz came and the gates began to swing open. Spider got back into the car and proceeded along the drive, the gardens on either side were planted with large palms, which screened the large house beyond.

He rang the bell on the double teak stained solid wood door and again waited an age for some response. Eventually the door eased open to reveal a small Arab boy. On seeing this tall well-dressed Arab, the boy swung the door fully open, at the same time, shouting as loud as he could, in a well-practised manner.

'Go away my father is not here.'

'But I have not asked to see your father.'

The boy repeated in a much quieter manner. 'Go away my father is not here.'

Spider was now sure that the boy's father, if he was the Sheikh, was indeed at home.

'Is your father the Sheikh Ahmed Al Bosfar?' The boy biting his bottom lip just nodded.

'Would you go and tell your father that Abdullah Ali Al Zamil of Saudi Arabian Internal Security wants to talk to him about a private matter.' The boy disappeared inside the house, returning a minute later and with a beckoning movement of the hand, ushered Spider in, and with a pointed finger directed him, to a door at the head of the stairs.

Giving the door a light tap he pushed it open and walked into a large but sparsely furnished room. A continuous multi coloured cushioned seat ran around the room against the walls, the floor was layered with brightly patterned carpets with a number of cushions scattered about. At the far end of the room sat Sheikh Ahmed looking rather agitated.

'May I see some identification?' He snapped, Spider stepped forward and presented a fake identification document, confirming him as the head of the Saudi Internal Security, a discreet organization that Sheikh Ahmed wasn't sure existed. Spider sensed the anxiety of his host and figured a little pressure might prove fruitful. As it turned out the Sheikh was anxious to get the whole matter off his chest.

'We are aware Sheikh Ahmed that you incited the Royal Prince Mohammed to make an anti western speech, which has caused our country and our King much embarrassment.

'I.....I was unaware of what the speech contained, believe me. I just delivered the message. I only knew Mohammed was to ask the West to pay more for our oil, but I did not expect the speech to be so demanding and phased so bitterly, I was shocked.'

'Frankly Sheikh, I believe you not only wrote the speech, but used your friendship with the Prince to influence him with your extreme radical views, to the extent that you are prepared to put his life in danger.'

'No, no I swear upon Allah, it was not like that.'

'Then how was it, Sheikh?'

The Sheikh hesitated and swallowed nervously. 'About a month ago, I received a telephone call from an Arab claiming to represent an American consortium. Apparently this consortium was interested in a joint venture with one of my companies, promising a very lucrative deal. I was asked to sponsor for visa purposes, a four-man American delegation coming to Saudi to broker the deal. It all seemed quite straightforward, they arrived, I loaned them a car and put them in a hotel. I later talked business with their leader a Mister Robinson and we struck up what I considered to be a very lucrative deal.'

The Sheikh paused while he reflected on the past events. 'To get to the point, I arranged a celebration dinner the night before they were due to leave Arabia; I waited at the restaurant for sometime. Eventually only this Mr Robinson turned up. He said that the deal was all set, I would be getting my share, ninety-five million dollars, but now this will depend on the Saudi Royal Family financing the scheme. Up until that point, the inclusion of the Royal family in this project had never been mentioned. Don't worry he assured me, some of the issues involved are of a delicate nature, you understand, some committees back in the US are raising objections. It would be a smart move if it appeared that Saudi Arabia had instigated and were financing the whole project and who better than the Saudi Royal family as the benefactors of the project. The funding will of course come from the American government indirectly by way of an increase of five cents per barrel of oil. Handing me a sealed envelope he said, we have set out these points and the agreement to the increased oil price in this document. It would be to all our benefit, if you could persuade your friend Prince Mohammed to announce the contents of this document at some public event. It is important, in order to ensure US funding you must convince the Prince, that the contents of the documents are genuine facts and must be read word for word. Mister Robinson said that the document did include some controversial statements that would in fact embarrass only those back home who have been dealing underhand with Saudi oil.'

The Sheikh inhaled with a tremble expelling the air with a deep sigh. 'I thought at the time, what a strange way to do business, but then I suppose the promise of money clouded my judgment. I just went along with whatever he said. I met the

Prince the next day and passed the envelope to him. I knew he was scheduled to visit Mecca the following day, so I suggested that he used it as a basis for his speech, emphasizing as I'd been requested, the validity of the facts it contained, without really knowing what it said. The rest, I am sad to say is history.'

'Why Sheikh, am I getting the feeling that you are not telling me the full story?' Spider stared long and hard into the Sheikhs eyes, he could see the fear, but the fear was not of him. 'How perceptive Al Zamil, yes, there is more.' The Sheikh buried his head in his hands and shook it from side to side, as if to emphasize the enormity of the tragic circumstances he had created. 'I was tricked, blinded by my own greed and was angry with myself. What could I do to put it all right, - nothing, it was too late, so I decided to say nothing, - soon Imsha Allah it will be all forgotten.

For a moment the look of fear in the Sheikh's eyes, changed to a wild stare. 'Yes I was angry with myself, but more so with these Americans, I wanted to face them, ask them why, - but at that point I believed they had already left the country.'

'You believed they'd left the country? - Are you now telling me that they haven't left?'

The Sheikh slowly nodded. 'I know now that they are still here, but I don't know where.'

'So how do you know this Ahmed?'

Sheikh Ahmed looked directly at Spider, now more composed, but Spider could sense the fear returning as the Sheikh began to think through the next set of events.

'Among my businesses I own Arabian Import Export Inc' here in Riyadh. Yesterday, I just happened to make an impromptu visit to the office. As I entered the building I came face to face with two of the Americans. I was flabbergasted. I attempted some form of confrontation in an attempt to get some answers, but I was totally ignored. In fact they rudely pushed by me and hurriedly headed toward the door. By the time I'd gathered myself together they had gone. Naturally I was curious as to what they where doing in my establishment. So I took the time to check the inventory only to find Ian Robinson had been in the day before. They had collected two boxes of machine parts shipped some months ago from Boston.' He paused momentarily in contemplation. 'I don't understand what is happening, I am extremely fearful. Why they are still here? What am I to tell Mohammed?'

'Well Sheikh Ahmed,' Spider drawled out slowly, 'I don't think your fears are unfounded, as a matter of fact I would be expecting them to visit you any time now, they no doubt have your execution well planned and the reason they waited is because they wanted you to report them, as Americans. The truth is, these infidels who have misled you and who have caused a problem for our country and the Royal family are not from the West, but from the North.' The Sheikh's head lifted and his eyes opened wide with surprise. Spider continued. 'The man you spoke with, is not Ian Robinson an American businessman, but Ivor Romanovski an ex KGB assassin. They have imported a weapon through your company made to look as if it was of American origin. A weapon that is intended for the assassination of..... Prince Mohammed.'

The Sheikh looked up to the ceiling and held out his arms. 'Oh Allah please be merciful forgive my stupidity.' And then brought his hands up to cradle his forehead, then he rocked back and forth.

Spider slowly shook his head from side to side, as if about to chastise a naughty child. 'It is clear that you are no longer of use to these Russians, in fact you could now be a hindrance. I suspect they will be heading this way with the intention of killing you.' Spider said the last bit with an air of nonchalance. The Sheiks eyes widen. 'It is as I feared.'

'You were foolish and greedy, but now you have got to pull yourself together and leave this place, there is little time left.' Sheikh Ahmed Al Bosfar lifted his head and stared at Spider with a mixture of surprise and relief. 'I have made preparations to go and I will not return until I am sure it is safe. All the servants have been sent away, they will find nothing when they come.'

Just as if on cue, Spider's telephone rang, the LCD told him it was George. Spider excused himself, and went outside the room before answering.

'Hello George.'

'Hi Charlie, just to let you know, I figured if we set up small fibre optic cables on each floor, linked to a camera, we would get the office location.'

'And did you?'

'Sure as hell we did. We filmed two of the cronies leaving, put a tail on them.'

'Well done, that man. What happened to the other two?'

'Romanovski and another are still in there, but there's only one car, so I guess the other two will be heading back to pick them up.'

'What kind of car?'

'You were on the ball with that too Charlie boy, it's an American Chevrolet Evanda, gold coloured, Arabic plates. You okay with Arabic numbers?'

'I'll manage.'

'Right, 376552.'

'Any idea where the two goons are heading?'

'Just had a call, the cars pulled up outside of Arabian Import Export Inc.'

There was a moment's pause, purely for George's benefit, before Spider continued.

'I think they are after the Sheikh, probably hoping to pick him up prior to zapping the poor sod.

'You sure?'

'Reasonably, Arabian Import Export Inc is one of the Sheikh's companies.

'Feasible, where are you now?'

'I'm with the Sheikh, at his home. They will never find this place without asking questions and I've an inkling that none of the goons speak much English, or for that matter, probably no Arabic.'

'They won't find it easy then?'

'I'm guessing the goons will head back for Romanovski when they draw a blank.'

'If that's the case, we've got the sat-cam on standby ready to follow them.'

'Yeah, sounds good, let me know how you get on.'

'Will do.'

Spider switched off the mobile, returned to the room to face the Sheikh and he relayed the relevant parts of the conversation he'd just had. As Spider spoke, the colour drained from the Sheikhs face, turning a ghostly shade of white, he was again visibly shaking.

'I would suggest Sheikh that you get your family together now, get into your car and drive to Mecca, you will be safe there.' The Sheikh hurried from the room and disappeared into vastness of the large house. Within a few minutes he was in the drive ushering the family of three wives and five children, into a Chrysler people carrier.

After checking that the Russians were not outside the gate, Spider pressed the car horn twice, a signal to the Sheikh that coast was clear. He waved to them as they passed and watched until their car was safely out of sight.

George rang again, just as Spider was getting back into the hire car after he'd closed and locked the large steel barred gates.

'Charlie.'

'Yes George.'

'The two goons returned, as expected and picked up the other two. We're following them now, looks like they could be heading to the restaurant.'

'That figures George, that's how I found this place. Now I'm positive they're after the Sheikh, it won't be too long before they turn up here.'

'Beats me Charlie, I thought they would let the Sheikh dangle until they were ready with the Prince hit.'

'That changed when he happened to bump into two of the goons at "Arabian Import and Export Inc".' They had to assume the Sheikh will realise they are building a weapon and that's something they don't want the police to know. Not just yet, anyway.'

'So Romanovski will have to eliminate the Sheikh before he concentrates on shooting the Prince, just in case he blabs.'

'That's the way I see it.'

'What's the next step?'

'Just keep them on satellite camera George, when they get here, I'll pick up the trail and let you know where it leads.'

'You aren't thinking of taking this lot by yourself....Are you Charlie boy?' Spider switched off the phone.

Spider drove the car a discreet distance down the road, parked up and settled back to keep watch on the gate to the Sheikh's house. Early evening some two hours after George's call, a gold Chevrolet slowly cruised by the house, five minutes later it returned. The road was devoid of any kind of activity. Spider had slumped way down in the seat and was watching the progress of the Russians through the re-angled rear view mirror. One of the Russians, with help from another scrambled over the eight-foot high wall and opened the gate. As their car disappeared up the drive, Spider drove the hire car to a carefully considered spot close to the surrounding wall; he got out and climbed binoculars in hand, onto the vehicle roof. Looking over the wall he had a clear view of the front of the house. Three of the Russians led by Romanovski made a surprisingly quick forced entry into the house. A few minutes later they emerged no doubt frustrated to find the place empty. Spider could tell by the silhouetted body language that the Ruskies were angry, just by the way they slammed back into the car.

Spider jumped down from the car roof and drove back to a discreet location before the Russians car appeared at the road junction just beyond the gates. As their Chevy passed, Spider eased his car out slowly, letting the Russians get to a good distance in front, before setting off to follow. He had no trouble tailing them.

About an hour later the car turned on to a long straight road which was the start of a new housing development. The newish properties were all of a good size, all individual and well spaced out. The development seemed to cover an extensive area which still had many vacant plots, the poor street lighting and lack of any activity gave the place a ghostly feel. Spider stopped the car a good distance away and watched the Russians put their car into the garage of a typical Arab suburban property. *So this is home.* He said to himself, *I think it would be prudent to wait a while, give them chance to settle.* He called George on the cell phone and gave him details of the address.

'Okay Charlie we've got them, I'm on my way.'

'Hang fire George there's no hurry wait until I get back to you.'

George wasn't happy as the phone went dead again cutting him off, but he'd had one outburst so this time he bit his lip. 'Son of bitch.' He mumbled to and about, no one in particular. He was after all, allowing Charlie to run the show. *At least we've found where the bastards are hiding.* He said to himself.

Spider had switched off the phone realising he'd pissed George off, but he wanted time to figure out some sort of plan and to get out of the Arab clothes he was wearing without having to explain why. So he began to undress putting aside the Arab clothes and pulling on dark blue jeans, black long sleeved cotton shirt with a high roll neck and a pair of black trainers, not the best choice, as the air was still very warm and humid even at that time of night. He contemplated putting on the air conditioner but decided against running the car engine. Then he checked his equipment, pistol with full magazine and silencer which he tucked in the waist of his jeans, PNG night vision head set, skeleton keys and a Leatherman multi-tool.

Reclining the seat, he laid back and closed his eyes. It was late when he roused himself and decided in was time to drive by and reconnoitre the property. The few very dim streetlights should be enough for him to see what he wants to see.

The perimeter wall was eight-foot high, there was an alarm box set in the peak under the gable overhang and there were bars on the visible upstairs window. He parked the car in a side street about a hundred yards past the house. Taking out his cell phone he called George again.

'Jesus H Christ Charlie, do yah know what time it is?'

'Ah, I make it three thirty George.'

'Don't get smart Charlie boy, I was asleep for the first time in weeks.'

'Sorry George, thought I'd let you know, I've decided to go in.'

'Okay, when?'

'No time like the present.'

'Now you just hold yah horse's there; give me a chance to get you some back up.'

'No problem George, they will only get in the way.'

'Just hang fire, you hear!'

The line was dead again.

'Son of a bitch!' George threw the phone down with such force that it bounced off the seat and crashed into the car window.

The wall was no problem, Spider took a run and jump at it, caught a hold on the top coping and effortlessly pulled himself up and over in one motion. The main entrance door would also be easy, the alarm, on the other hand is a concern. *Another guessing game.* He thought.

Spider selected a skeleton key and fiddled, a gentle click and the door was unlocked. 'No bolts, that's a relief,' easing the door slowly open, only just enough to peer in and establish that the door was not wired. It was very dark inside; Spider put on the PNG and squeezed himself into the house through the minimum gap he'd allowed the door to open. The glowing alarm sensor was positioned against the ceiling high in the corner, above his head and pointing along the entrance passageway. Spider figured as long as he stayed pressed against the door, he would not be picked up by the angle of the sensor. He could see the alarm remote panel; it had a cover which was open. 'Damn!' A row of red lights indicating active sensors appeared to be covering all the down stairs rooms. 'Calm you're self Spider old son,' he mumbled, 'there must be a way, -think.'

On the wall just a little way down the passage there was a small cupboard. Noting the cables going into the bottom of the cupboard, he adjudged it to be the mains electric box where the power comes into the property. 'If I can switch off the power I will have an advantage with the PNG, but the alarm system will probably have a battery back up.' Still standing with his back pressed against the door, he took the gun out of his belt, cocked the weapon and flicked off the safety. Holding the gun with the grip in his right hand and poised ready to turn off the power with his left hand. As he stood there, he tried to imagine the layout of the rooms.

The hall passage is about eight feet wide and thirty feet long, doors off each side, no interest.
The hall opens out into an atrium, possibly the stairwell to the bedrooms. Hopefully that's where the targets will be.
The moment I move, I will have about twenty seconds before the alarm to go off.....Just how far am I likely to get?

Spider stepped forward and almost instantly the sensor picked him up and began to beep. He threw open the mains cupboard door, hit the power out button and started his run, bringing the gun up to the aim position as he did so. He crashed through the door at the end of the passage into, as he'd figured, an atrium with a wide staircase curving around one side up to a curved gallery first floor landing. Spider took the stairs two at a time, pushing open the door to the first room on the landing. He checked inside. Damn! Empty. Moving quickly he turned his attention to the next door. Just as he reached for the handle, the alarm activated, a siren wailed loudly and although he couldn't see, he knew it would be accompanied with a flashing strobe light. As he pushed open the door, two Russians in single beds were rousing themselves, but were only semiconscious. Spit!- Spit! Two rounds left the silenced muzzle of his pistol, one bullet in each head. Spider spun around and almost collided with a third Russian who had stumbled onto the dark landing gun in hand, searching for the light switch with his free hand. Spit. Spider's shot hit the Russian somewhere about the midriff and he tumbled into Spider as he fell.

Bang! A shot from the other side of the landing rang out. The shot obviously aimed at the barrel flash from Spider's gun. The weapon was sent flying from Spider's hand. He felt the pain first, then just as quickly a tingling numbness and loss of all feeling in his right hand. Automatically he threw himself on the floor, in doing so landed on the Russian who he had just shot. The Russian gave out a loud groan as Spiders weight landed upon him. Bang! Bang! Two shots thudded into the back of the prostrate Russian and the body jumped in spasm with the impact. Spider could see the dim blurred shape of the man, undoubtedly Romanovski in a squatting position on the other side of the landing. He could just make out the barrel of Romanovski's gun protruding through the balustrade. The numbness left Spiders right hand only to be replaced with severe pain and the wet feeling from the oozing blood. The acrid smell of blood and cordite filled the air. The noise of the alarm siren persisted for what seemed like an age, in fact at that point, it was less than a minute. Spider shielded by the Russian's body managed to take the multi-tool out of pocket of his jeans with his left hand. Unable pull out the blade with one hand, he used the pointed pliers to rive and tear a strip off the Russians cotton vest. The tearing noise however invited two more rounds from Romanovski's pistol, which were also embedded into the Russians body.

The muzzle flash will spoil Romanovski's night vision for a few seconds.

Quickly wrapping the strip of material around the damaged right hand he picked up the Russians pistol and fought through the pain, aimed it as best as he could towards Romanovski and wildly fired off five rounds before the gun jammed, the rounds ricocheting around the stairwell. Although only a short distance between them he knew he hadn't hit the target, but the noise, flashes and ricochets, hopefully had created enough confusion for Romanovski's head to go down. Spider threw down the pistol, grasping the Leatherman in his left hand; he sprung to his feet and set off to run around the landing. After taking only a few paces, the lights came on. Without giving it a thought, he lifted his right forearm and in one quick movement, knocked the PNG gear off his head. 'Advantage gone.'

As the lights came on, Romanovski lifted his head allowing his vision to re-focus, but before the blur had left his eyes he saw the dark shape of the body hurtling towards him. He turned his face to the oncoming figure, at the same time he swung his pistol in the direction of the dark shape and fired. Bang! Missed, he levelled the pistol for another shot, a split second too late. The assailant's right foot caught the wrist of the gun hand square on, propelling the weapon across the landing. Romanovski rolled with it and tried to get up, but before he was able to straighten, he was met by a left hand uppercut. Something, metal, blunt, but pointed in the assailant's hand caught him under the chin with such force, that his head was pushed upward and the body was sent hurtling backwards across the landing. Whatever had hit him had penetrated through the lower jaw bone and into his mouth. The bitter taste of the metal and blood filled his mouth.

The pain was excruciating, blood oozed from the wound and ran down his bare chest. He staggered backwards almost falling with each step, in a painful kind of daze, but somehow managed to stay conscious. In a state of part fear, part panic he instinctively aimed a kick at the blood soaked cotton rag that was wrapped around his assailants hand with all the force he could muster. In doing so, he lost the little balance he had had and fell backward onto his bottom.

The kick connected all right, with some force, but if it had hurt Spider, it didn't stop him. In panic Romanovski tried to scurry away backwards on his bottom.. Spider not in any hurry ambled after the now whimpering Russian. Neither had realized that the alarm siren had stopped.

Quite by chance Romanovski found his gun, quickly grasping it, he rolled and brought the weapon up, aiming at the oncoming Spider.

Bang!

George was standing at the top of the stairs a smoking gun in his hand.

Romanovski stared wide eye at his assailant with a bewildered look as if now realising that his plan had failed. Blood now oozing from a hole in the heart side of his chest, but all he could feel was numbness, the gun in his hand wavered and he tried desperately to steady his aim and pull the trigger, but his finger would not move. He slowly fell backward and was dead before his head hit the floor.

'Good timing George.'

'You'd better believe it, one second more and we'd be digging you pit. I thought twice about coming, just as well for you I did.'

'Thanks anyway, glad you could make it.'

'Geez what a mess, better get the sanitary guys in here, get this place cleaned up.' George then notice the red blood stained rag wrapped around Spider's hand. 'You okay? He said nodding towards Spider's injured hand. 'Better let me take a look at that.'

'It's alright George, there's a medic at the embassy. I'll get him to check it out. To distract the conversation away from his injury he quickly changed the subject. 'How on earth did you manage to stop that dam alarm?'

'Easy, you didn't think I was going to let you have all the glory. I was parked at the end of the street when you rang. By the time I got here, I was just in time to see you disappearing over the wall. And then the porch light went out, I guessed you'd tripped the mains switch. I was taking my second jump at that dammed wall when the alarm started. Don't know how I managed to get over, nearly broke my bloody neck when I fell off. Anyway, I figured, new property, rented house, short stay tenants, the codes probably written on the inside of the box, I had to put the lights on, forgot my torch.'

'Good thinking, George.'

Two days later a tall well built man with his right hand heavily bandaged and supported in a sling, boarded an Emirates 747 jet to London Heathrow, with an American Passport in the name of Ian Robinson, duly exit stamped from Saudi Arabia. John Godfrey and two diplomats accompanied him each carrying American passports with the requisite exit stamp. Once airborne, John Godfrey turned to his travel companion.

'Bloody good job George and his CIA blokes did. Finding the Russians and eliminating them never would have these US passports without them.'

'Sure they did, but if I hadn't of smashed my hand trying to force my way through the Sheikh Bosfar's door, I would have sorted it.'

John smiled. 'Oh yeah.'

CHAPTER 5
THE RETURN
London Heath Row

At Heathrow terminal four arrivals, John Godfrey shook the hand of his travelling companions each in turn, collecting their US passports as he did so. The two diplomats left immediately heading to a waiting limousine pre arranged to convey them to the foreign office. John held onto Charles Evans left hand, as he watched the two depart.

'Thanks for everything Charles, suppose you'll be heading back to MI6 for debrief.'

'Something like that John.' Not wanting to elaborate on the subject of his intended direction, Spider cut the conversation short withdrawing his hand at the same time.

'You take care now, bye.' At that he turned and headed back towards to the underground and the Heathrow express train which would take him to Paddington and the Bakerloo line into Waterloo main line station.

'Yeah will do and the same to you.' John called after him. His mind no longer on Charles Evans, John turned and headed to the taxi rank jumping into the first available taxi. 'Queen Anne's Gate please' he told the driver.

A very tasty young lady in a mini skirt was on hand as the lift doors opened, to escort John to Sir Peter's office. Not that John didn't know the way, but rather because he had no security card, a necessity to gain access through several doors. John didn't at all mind, in fact this attractive young lady walking with him, gave him quite a buzz. As they entered into the outer office adjacent to Sir Peter's office, John automatically turned his head to watch the swing of her bottom as she walked away.

How long have I been away. As he turned his head back, Marjorie was stood holding out her hand.

'Hello John, nice to see you.'

John took it, 'Good to see you too, Marjorie.'

'Michelle.' Marjorie called over Johns shoulder. The girl stopped and began to walk back to Marjorie's desk; giving John the opportunity to ogle her again, this time from the front. 'Would you organize an office on the sixth floor for Mr. Godfrey?'

'Yes Miss Fawcett.'

'And get security to sort him out a pass.' Michelle nodded, turned and walked away. This time John resisted the temptation, only just, to watch the swing of Michelle's bottom as it floated into the corridor.

'Please take a seat John I'll see if Sir Peter is free.' Marjorie pressed the intercom. 'John Godfrey to see you, Sir Peter.'

'Wheel him in please Marjorie.'

She raised her eyebrows gave a slight nod to John, who having overheard the conversation, was up and heading towards the door.

Sir Peter was sitting behind his desk, seemingly in the process of making notes. As John walked in he looked up and straightened in his chair.

'Ah John, welcome back.' Sir Peter gestured to the chesterfield armchair. 'Make yourself comfortable. Good to see you, been a while.'

John lowered himself onto the leather cushions. 'Hum yes sir, quite a while.'

'By the way, good job, well done, well done.'

'Thank you sir.'

Sir Peter then pressed the intercom button. 'Marjorie will sort you out security clearance and an office, For John.'

'Already done.' Marjorie replied.

'Splendid, splendid.'

He then turned his attention back to John. 'I would like you to put together a full report on the Riyadh 'Stake Out' op as soon as possible.'

'No problem sir, I'll get on to it straight away.'

Sir Peter eased himself back into his chair. 'As I seem to have some free time at the moment, perhaps you can give me a brief rundown.'

'Fine sir, but before I start, can I ask, when you envisage sending me back to Iraq?'

'Let's not be concerned about Iraq for the time being John, we'll put 'Desert Rose' on the back burner. I may have something else in mind for you.' Sir Peter eased forward, elbows on the desk, fingers crossed beneath his chin. 'Now then, tell me about Riyadh?'

'Well sir, it turned out that the Russians were posing as Americans, entering Arabia with false passports.'

'Well I never.' Sir Peter chirped in.

'And they had, as you suspected sir, initiated the Prince's speech. Their plan was to assassinate the Prince making it look like American retaliation.'

'My word.' Sir Peter said in a more or less complacent manner, chin still resting on his hands as he spoke. 'So Mr Vostok is no doubt as devious as he is greedy.'

'George Carter and his CIA staff turned up trumps.' John continued.

'Did they indeed, CIA proved useful then?' Sir Peter responded, cocking an eyebrow as he spoke.

'They did indeed sir, they discovered the Russians hideout, eliminated them and recovered fake American passports.' At that John delved into his pocket, extracted and passed the passports across the desk.

'Ah – Thank you.' Sir Peter said as he sat back in his chair. 'What of the MI6 guy I sent you?'

'Charles, a good man, theoretically he was brilliant, it was Charles who worked it all out. What the Russians were up to and where they would probably be. I suppose Charles also gets the credit for pointing us in the right direction. By us I mean George and his CIA team, they did all the groundwork. However, my candid opinion is that Charles needs to brush up on his field skills.'

'Oh, what makes you say that?'

'Well sir, he never seemed to be where the action was. And he had this crazy idea that moving out of the Embassy would allow him to go undercover. It was obvious to me, a Westerner not speaking any Arabic would stick out like a sore thumb. Speaking of which, he was unfortunate enough to get his hand crushed trying to gain entry into the Sheikh's house, a door apparently, was slammed on him.'

'Was he badly hurt?'

'I would hazard a guess and say it must have been painful, but he seemed to be quite chirpy when I left him at Heathrow, so I think he'll recover.'

'What happened to the Sheikh?'

'Took off, I believe, him and his family just disappeared.'

'I see, was the Sheikh in league with the Russians?'

'Probably, but we don't know for sure.'

'Ah well I don't suppose it's that important now that the Russians have been eliminated.'

'No sir, but there is something else.'

'And what would that be?'

'Charles has lost some equipment.' Sir Peter's head and eyes rolled as if feigning disgust.

'Don't get me wrong sir, I don't mean to tell tales, Charles Evans is a first class bloke with a brilliant technical ability, just not good at the hands on stuff.'

'So you would recommend Charles to take a field retraining course.'

'Yes sir.'

'I'll see what I can do on the matter.' Sir Peter had already read and digested George Carter's full report, received from CIA Langley, so he knew John had been fed a cock and bull story to draw any credit for the successful operation away from Charles Evans. Spider had persuaded George to omit his part in operation from his report to John, so as to appear an insignificant player in the Riyadh affair.

'No doubt John, your report will prove to be interesting reading.'

Sir Peter shuffled some paperwork around the desktop as if looking for a lost letter, which was, as it happens, on the top of the pile. 'Now then, there's this little job I want you to do for me. Right up your street, couldn't think of anyone better.'

John had a bemused look on his face. *What on earth is he up to now.*

'As you know John, Prince Mohammed arrives here tomorrow. He will be staying at the Ritz and for security reasons, the whole top floor as been assigned to him and his entourage. At the governments expense, of course. That's why I have arranged for you to have an adjacent room.'

'Well, err, thank you sir,' John said, not really knowing why or if he should be, in anyway grateful.

'You are to organise his activities and accompany him everywhere.' John nodded thoughtfully.

'Stick to him like glue; he doesn't go anywhere or do anything without you.'

'A nursemaid sir?'

'I prefer "companion" John. In particular, avoid any contact with the press, I do not wish to read about the Prince's activities or whereabouts in the papers.'

'No problem sir, I'll do my best to keep a lid on the situation, as for Prince Mohammed, I'll do my best to take good care of him.'

'I'm quite sure you would make the perfect companion. Get to know the guy, how he thinks, what he likes, that sort of thing. All very tactfully of course.'

'Diplomacy is my forte, sir.'

Sir Peter looked at John, speaking almost in a whisper, to emphasize the discreet nature of his comment. 'Most important the Prince is shown our Western hospitality, you understand, show him a good time, maybe introduce him to someone of the fairer sex,' he gave John an exaggerated wink, 'and perhaps a taste of Scotland's finest.'

'Hearing you, loud and clear sir, what about the Saudi Ambassador and the Prince's entourage, wont they interfere?'

'No doubt there will be objections along the way John. I have it on good authority that the Ambassador is partial to a drop of the amber nectar. As for the rest of them, I've every confidence that a man with your diplomatic skills will tactfully handle any unwanted interference. Besides I've already let it be known, for security reasons, you understand. While the Prince is in this country, you will be solely responsible for him.'

'Okay sir, I think I can handle that.' John said thoughtfully. 'Am I to be his Bodyguard as well?'

'No no John, god forbid, it is hoped the Prince will have his own. One more thing, this is not the Prince's first visit to our shores, I do believe he was at Oxford and he speaks perfect English.... A quirk of mine perhaps, but I feel it would be prudent if you did not mention that you spoke Arabic.'

'Understood sir.'

John took that to be the end of the discussion and stood to leave.

'One more thing John,' Sir Peter rustled in the top draw of his desk while he spoke, 'I understand the Prince is a fine horseman. I thought you may be able to use these.' Sir Peter slid two invitations to the "Royal Windsor Horse Trials" across the desk.

As John left Sir Peters office, Marjorie discretely removed a small device from her ear. This was wired to a recorder in a locked draw of her desk and transmitted from a miniature microphone in Sir Peter's office. When he was sure John had left the outer office, Sir Peter pressed the button on the intercom.

'Get that Marj?' Knowing she had, but without waiting for a response, he continued. 'Oh and will you text Spider find out where he is?'

A few moments later Marjorie came back. 'He's having a coffee on Waterloo station, - he is expecting you.'

'Good, I think I'll go for a walk, hold the fort, would you dear heart.' Marjorie smiled and nodded.

Sir Peter put on his jacket and left the office.

A tall slim built man with thinning Grey hair wearing a charcoal Grey pinstripe suit with a guard's tie and carrying an overcoat over his left forearm perused the large destination board on Waterloo station. Two minutes later, another tall man, much broader with his right arm in a sling, approached.

'Missed your train sir?'

Without turning Sir Peter casually said. 'Good to hear your voice Steven lets walk.' The pair set off in the same direction, but avoided looking as if they were together. 'How's the hand?'

'Still a bit sore sir, but luckily there is no permanent damage.' Spider was lying; the index finger was so badly damaged, it was doubtful it could be saved. The pair mingled with the crowds perusing the destination screens on separate platforms, and then if by accident came together again. This manoeuvre was performed so well no one could have suspected they were together let alone holding a conversation. Steven held a rolled up newspaper in his left hand that he used to gently tap the side of his face as if musing a problem, but in actual fact was detracting attention from his mouth movement as he spoke. 'The trigger guard did some damage to the end of my index finger and the ricochet smashed the knuckle, just off to see our man in Harley Street.' Sir Peter covered his mouth with a handkerchief as if about blow his nose.

'To MI5 account, I'll sort it, how long do you think?'

'Two months at the outside.'

'Okay, what about the weapon?'

'Russians were using similar American jobs, did a swap, pocketed the silencer, and told John I'd lost it.' Sir Peter had great difficulty keeping the smile off his face as he thought of John back at the office writing his report.

'I'll be in touch,' he said as he turned and casually walked away.

Steven stared blankly at his own reflection in the dark window of the Southwest train as it eased out of Waterloo station bound for Weymouth via Poole. Thoughts of the past few days in Saudi-Arabia ran through his mind, in particular the probable extent of his wound and the possible affect it could have on his future. The Embassy doctor had been of little comfort; he had made the excuse that he did not have the facilities to do a proper job and had, in his words. 'Did a temporary patch up job.' Steven had not been convinced by the doctors' ineptitude and considered the guy to be short on training. However the doctor did attempt to cover his backside by insisting that he should get immediate attention in the UK. Steven didn't go to the MI5 Harley Street Doctor, knowing a detailed report, without doubt, would end up on Sir Peter's desk, and no way did he want that. He also had little doubt, although he tried to kid himself otherwise, the extent of the damage to his hand was serious, for one thing, it hurt like hell and he was taking a regular dose of paracetamol to nullify the throbbing. It was throbbing now as the trains wheels clicked over the track. *Bugger! Bugger!* He said to himself as he fumbled the foil tablet strip with his left hand. He popped two tablets and washed them down with a swig of water from the bottle he'd purchased on the station, then he sat back, biting on his bottom lip and waited for them to take effect.

I need time to become proficient with my left hand before Sir Peter learns the truth. And how am I going to play this down to Colonel Bradley. At least the thought of his predicament was a distraction from the pain. *I'll get rid of the sling and pass it off as insignificant; tell him I'm being treated at the hospital that ought to do it.*

Steven had already played down the extent of the injury; first to George Carter who was led to believe the blood soaked strip of Russians vest hid only a graze. Then John Godfrey was given to understand that the finger had been jammed in a door. And he never actually told Sir Peter that he probably would never be able to hold a gun in his right hand again, for fear of being taken off active duty.

In the immortal words of Sir Walter Scott... Oh what a tangled web we weave when first we practice to deceive....And that from a Spider.

'The next station is Poole - Poole' the guard announced. Steven collected his bag and headed for the carriage door.

Just outside the station he picked up a taxi to take him to the Marine Base in Hamworthy. Although it was getting late he somehow knew the base commander would still be in his office, so after passing through security, he headed straight to Colonel Bradley's office.

'Ah Steven, good to see you, I take it you're reporting back for duty.'

Steven not in uniform made no attempt to salute, handing over a bunch of papers with his left hand.

'Yes sir, thank you sir, it's good to be back.'

The Colonel, sitting at his desk began to thumb through the false MOD letters confirming Steven's posting. Steven stood to attention at the front of the desk. 'Relax Steven, take a seat.'

'Thank you sir.'

'I could hardly miss the fact that your hand is bandaged. No mention of it here. Care to enlighten me?' The Colonel sat back and looked across to Steven.

'It's nothing really sir, I had a little accident. I was about to ask for some time out to visit Poole Hospital.'

'You know better than that, we have our own very good Medical facility on camp.

'In fact-.' The Colonel picked up the telephone. 'Major Stanford MO, please. - Ah Christopher, would you have time to pop across to my office, there is something I would like you to take a look at? Oh and bring your tool bag.'

A minute later Major Christopher Stanford entered with white coat and medical bag, which he placed on the Colonel's desk. Following the Colonel's eyes, he turned to Steven and immediately noticed the bandaged hand.

'Hello Steven, nice to have you back. What have you been up to, eh?' Without waiting for an answer, he wandered over and picked up Steven's hand; a pair of scissors appeared as if by magic and deftly began to cut off the bandage securing tape.

'Suppose I'd better take a look.'

'Hello Chris, nice to be back.' Steven looked at his hand as the bandage was been removed.

'It's nothing really.'

'Your dammed right sunshine, there is nothing. Nothing left of the knuckle and the forefinger's had it. That will have to be removed, like now, before infection takes hold.'

The Colonel noticed the look of despair on Steven's face.

The MO continued, still examining the wound and talking mainly to himself. 'Mmm, quick patch up job, wonder if all bone fragments and damaged tissue, have been removed. The bullet seems to have struck the top of the forefinger, smashing its way through the flesh between the thumb. No damage to the thumb that I can see.'

'Bullet?' The Colonel looked at Steven, then back to the MO. 'Yes sir, in my opinion, a bullet wound.' Steven said nothing. 'Right sunshine let's have you over to the medical block, if I don't remove what's left of that finger soon, it could well be your hand.'

Colonel Paul Bradley had for a long time, suspected that Major Steven Pinder was involved in very secret government work. Seeing Steven's wounded hand and the MOD letters covering Steven's movements, which he felt were concocted, had only served to confirm his suspicions. But he was not going to make any mention of it. *This is something I must keep to myself.* He thought. He was inwardly very proud to have someone of Steven's calibre on his staff, albeit on a temporary posting. He was also wise enough to perceive Steven's anxiety, the thought of losing your trigger finger to a marksman of Steven's quality, must be devastating. Especially so if, as the Colonel believed, his job depended on the competent use of a gun. Sitting back in his chair, rubbing his chin, 'I wonder,' he mumbled, 'being in the Freemasons could have its uses.' Picking up the telephone he called a friend and a fellow mason, who happened to be a Plastic Surgeon with a private clinic in the town.

The Colonel took his cap from the stand placing it on his head as he made for the door, *I'd better let Christopher know what I'm doing.* As he entered the Medical Block surgery he saw Steven sitting in a chair with his damaged hand, now painted brown with iodine and resting on a table. Christopher knife in hand was poised over the limb. 'Ah Colonel, just waiting for the local anaesthetic to take effect,' occasionally jabbing Steven's hand with the scalpel. 'Feel that sunshine?' Steven shook his head. 'Then we shall begin.'

'Before you do Christopher, I think you should be aware. I've just been talking to a surgeon friend of mine. He with the help of an engineer feels it may be possible to rebuild the finger, and he wants to see Steven tomorrow.'

'Not this finger sir, believe me. I need to remove what's left of it now. I'll clean up what's left of the knuckle and perhaps this surgeon can do something with that.' At that the Major removed the digit.

The next day still feeling quite sore, Steven found himself sitting in the office Mr Marchants Westbourne clinic.

'Well Steven, Mr McPherson and I have studied your x-ray, and this is what we propose to do. Mr McPherson will manufacture a titanium finger and knuckle, ball and socket type joint.' Picking up a skeleton of a human hand, he pointed to the relevant area as he spoke. 'I will shape the bone here to fit tightly into the ball of the knuckle, where it will be pinned. I will then link artificial tendons to yours way back here and hopefully, after a little practice this will give the ability to move the false finger.'

'Hopefully!'

'You have to remember Major Pinder, what we are doing here is ground breaking; there are no guarantees of success. Also a lot will depend on your ability to adapt to having no sensation in that part of your hand, other than the discomfort you will have at the stub around the joint. It will not be easy.' The surgeon put down the hand and picked up a piece of material. 'Now to the cosmetic bit, this material will be moulded onto the titanium. It's a spongy plastic, skin coloured, which I will extend at the knuckle to fit over your skin. Speaking of which.' Mr Marchant walked around his desk and gently took hold of Steven's hand. 'You have suffered some tissue loss, what I intend to do is dress what you have here around the base of the new knuckle. The flap of skin you used to have between the thumb and forefinger will be built up from skin I intend to get from your posterior.' The surgeon returned to his seat behind his desk. 'Any questions, Major?'

'How much is this going to cost me, Doc?'

'I am assured that it will cost you nothing Major Pinder. The account, which will no doubt be expensive, is to be charged direct to Colonel Bradley. I am under specific instruction that no reference whatsoever is made to you, for this treatment.'

CHAPTER 6
THE COMPANION
London 10th November

The Prince and his entourage arrived at the Ritz in the company of the Saudi Arabian Ambassador. John was waiting with the hotel manager just inside the entrance. Introductions and greeting formalities complete, John accompanied the Prince to his suite, closely followed by two very large Egyptian bodyguards, a relatively diminutive Indian manservant, and four hotel porters carrying the baggage. The rest of the entourage, four advisors, of what, John didn't know and a holy man went to their allocated rooms. The Saudi Ambassador had excused himself with assurances that he would return in the morning.

'Leave the bags.' The Prince said, waving his hand at the porters. 'The rest of you may go and sort yourselves out. I would like some time to talk to Mr Godfrey.'

John and the Prince talked for sometime, the conversation was relaxed and cordial, never at any point was there reference made to the infamous speech. The conversation centred on Johns plans to keep the Prince occupied for the coming month and it was clear from the start that there was an affinity between them.

A day or so later, they were the best of friends and John was allowed to call the Prince, "Mohammed", but only in private. Mohammed's admiration of John was evident; a fact not lost on some of the entourage, in particular the bodyguards who were uneasy with familiarity of a non-Muslim. John had persuaded Mohammed to put aside all forms of Arab dress for security reasons and had taken him on shopping trips, filling the wardrobes of the suite with Western style clothes. From the security aspect the bodyguards and the Ambassador, approved of the Prince's new attire. The holy man on the other hand was quite outraged, and threatened to report the matter to the Saudi Palace. He however became strangely quiet after John had arranged for a pot of Arabic coffee accompanied with a bottle of Johnny Walker to be sent to his room. John soon came to realize, behind the Prince's noble facade, there was a naïve and gullible young man.

Initially John selected innocent fun things for them to do together, sight seeing, sporting events, theme parks and the like. But he knew that with some guile he had to corrupt this young man, a task that he did not relish.

Windsor Great Park 14th November

The first invitation on Sir Peter's insistence was to a Royal event in Windsor Great Park, which turned out to be a farcical race under the guise of a horse trial.

John and Mohammed on presentation of their invitations were directed towards a cluster of vehicles and horse boxes. Mohammed's two bodyguards were not permitted access without an invitation and were told to wait at the gate.

'Johnny Goddas! Well I'll be blowed, how the devil are you?' John spun around and saw a man with blond wavy hair, wearing a dark blue polo necked sweater and jodhpurs heading across the grass to meet them. John and Mohammed stopped and turned to face the stranger. 'Well I never.' John declared, 'Its Fishy.'

'W-w- what, who?' Mohammed stuttered.

'Fishy Salmons.' John noting the confused look on the Princes' face continued. 'It's James actually, James Salmons, an old Estonian chum.' John extended a hand and took a step forward. 'James! It's been an age, how's it going?'

'Absolutely fine old chum.' James said as their hands pumped. 'Last time I saw you, you were a lieutenant in the Household Cavalry.'

'Still am Johnny boy, in the Household Cavalry I mean, but I'm a Major now.'

'That's great, good for you.'

'And what pray tell, are you doing with yourself these days?'

'Oh – you know a bit of this bit of that.'

'No more navy then?'

'Gave that up, a long time ago.' At that point John suddenly seemed to realise what he was doing. – 'Oh, please excuse me James, awfully rude of me; I'd like you to meet my companion and friend.' John held out an arm to encourage Mohammed to step forward. 'This is his Royal Highness Prince Mohammed Bin Aziz Al Saud.' Mohammed made a slight nodding motion. 'Your Highness, please allow me to introduce you to an old school chum of mine, Major James Salmons.'

'Oh the sp--.' James stopped himself realising it could be awkward; instead he confidently took a step forward holding out his hand. 'Pleased to meet you, your Highness.' Surprisingly Mohammed took James's hand and shook it firmly. 'I am pleased to make your acquaintance -err Fishy.' He said looking to John for approval. All it seemed found the response amusing.

The three set off to walk together towards the array of horse boxes and the small wooden stand erected to seat the relatively few spectators. 'Are you here to watch the event, or whatever it is?' Mohammed enquired.

'I'm actually taking part sir; I'm the Captain of the visiting team.'

'Are you indeed and what does that entail, I mean, what's this Royal event about?'

'Hardly a Royal event, your Highness, it's more an excuse to exercise the horses from Royal stables.'

They approached the cluster of vehicles, where men were changing into their riding attire and the horses were being taken out of their boxes and saddled. 'It's Prince Edward's idea of course, this trial gives him the opportunity to winter exercise his polo ponies and to boost his overblown ego.' James suddenly realised that he may have overstepped the mark, being so flippant about royalty while addressing a Prince. 'I beg your pardon sir; I hope I have not caused offence.' Mohammed waved his hand dismissively and John said. 'Makes no difference to us James, don't know the guy.'

'Why should it boost his ego?'

'Because your Highness, he and his team always win and get to keep the cup that he kindly donated for this once a year event.'

'I'm not into horsy events, what happens?' John queried.

'The Prince of Wight leads a team of five riders to compete against a team of five visiting riders, usually made up of from the ranks of the Household Cavalry. I'm the Captain of the visitors. We ride two circuits around the park, over rough terrain and through the woods, over jumps and water hazards. First to finish gets 10 points down to 1 point for the last man, providing he finishes, that is.' 'Sounds like fun to me James.' 'It is your Highness. – Do you ride sir?'

John put in. 'Prince Mohammed is famous across Arabia as a skilled horseman.' James just nodded.

The group had reached James's horse box, John and Mohammed stood aside as James dropped the tail gate and backed out his black horse.

While James was busy saddling his mount, the accident happened. A young Lieutenant was in the process of backing his mount out of its box. As he reached the ramped tail gate, a car alarm shrieked, the horse reared with fright and the young Lieutenant was sent hurtling backwards off the ramp, landing heavily and awkwardly.

James looked concerned that the lad may be hurt, John couldn't help feeling the incident seemed somewhat contrived and Mohammed caught the horse and started to gently stroke its nose at the same time talking to it quietly; in a short time the animal was calm. The lieutenant held his arm and expressed great pain as he muttered through gritted teeth. 'I think I've broken it sir.'

'Don't worry David,' James said, 'there's an ambulance on its way, shouldn't be too long.'

Edward Prince of Wight rode up to the crowd now gathered around the injured man.

'Dammed hard luck eh what, if you chaps want to continue a man down, then you'd better hurry up and get mounted, I'm ready to start. - Well, what's it to be?'

James was somewhat incensed by the Prince's seemingly uncaring attitude, he declared. 'We shall fight on sir. My team will be with you in a moment'

'Five minutes Major Salmons, five minutes.' The Prince said over his shoulder as he galloped away.

James looked first at Mohammed and then at John. 'What do you think, John?'

'As I told you James, Mohammed's skill on horse back, is well known in Arabia.'

The officer turned to Mohammed. 'I've a spare kit and boots in the car; we are about the same size. Do you think it would be possible sir, for you to ride the Lieutenant's horse in the trial?'

'Oh yes - without a doubt.' Mohammed said eagerly and strode away with the Major, toward his car.

John couldn't help but wonder if Sir Peter had had a hand in this. 'No, no, couldn't have.' He said shaking his head from side to side.

By the time the injured man had been carried off the field to await the ambulance, Mohammed was ready and in the saddle for the start.

The ten horses and riders set off across an area of grass heading into the woods, not at a very fast pace. Mohammed considered the reason was to pace the horses over a long distance. He then noticed when a jump was coming the riders seemed to ease their mounts to allow horses in ones or two to go over so that the hazard wasn't crowded. It wasn't until he was into the second circuit that he realised the other riders were allowing Prince Edward to lead, and no doubt win.

Mohammed determined he was having none of this and dug his heels into the sides of his mount. The horse reacted, increasing its speed and its agility over the hazards. He began to pass the other riders with ease, coming up fast on Prince Edward's mount. James, seeing Mohammed zoom past him realised exactly what the Arab Prince was about to do.

Why not, he thought, *Edward could do with a dint in that ego.* With that James also heeled his horse. By this time Mohammed and Edward were neck and neck and both riders were pushing their mounts to the limit. As they came to the last jump, a bank of logs fronting a stream, Prince Edward reined to get his mount's head up for the jump. Mohammed just went for it, pushing his horse on without a change to its pace and it landed a good three lengths clear of Edward's mount.

Mohammed won the race and the Prince of Wight just scraped into second, ahead of a fast finishing James. When the points were totalled, the Prince of Wight team had twenty-four points, but the visitors had thirty-one.

Alice Princess of Wight presented the winners trophy to the Major, as captain of the visiting team.
'Very well rode James, I'm so pleased for you.'
'Thank you, your Highness.'
'Would you be so kind as to introduce me to the rest of your team?'
Mohammed heard the Princess and turned towards John who was carrying Mohammed's jacket over his arm.

'Quick John I must prepare.' Hastily he began to rummage through the jacket pockets, while John was still holding it.

'My word, she is so beautiful, isn't she John?'

'Yes she is, Mohammed.'

'Should I bow to her...Should I touch her hand. Look John, she is touching the others.'

'She is shaking their hand, Mohammed, perfectly acceptable.'

'But she's a woman.'

John just shuck his head. 'I feel it may be prudent to conform to protocol.' He said calmly.

Mohammed was last in the line, as the Princess approached all his resolve and Islamic ritual melted.

She's so beautiful.

'Finally Highness; this is our star man, our ace in the hole, His Royal Highness Prince Mohammed Bin Aziz Al Saud.'

'Yes I did notice, congratulations on a very fine ride your Highness.' Taking Mohammed's hand firmly, she held on to it. Mohammed made a weak attempt to bow, but their eye's locked and they stood like that for a long moment just staring at each other.

'Thank you your Highness.'

'Such skilled horsemanship I have rarely seen.'

'Thank you your Highness.'

'Please just call me Alice.'

'Then you must just call me Mohammed.'

They had now been together for some time and John could sense the anxiety of those around.

Clearly showing embarrassment tinged with a little impatience, the entourage with the Prince of Wight's party, started to disperse. Edward did not look at all happy, especially when he could see the look of admiration on both their faces. The very apparent angry look formed on the Prince's face and was becoming obvious to those around. One of the Prince Edwards party, Giles Fairchild, stepped forward and taking Edward by the arm began to engage him in conversation turning him away from a confrontation.

John somewhat naively hoped nobody else had noticed and in an attempt to avoid further embarrassment, moved forward toward the couple in an attempt to distract them. Eventually eye contact broke and Mohammed let go of Princess Alice's hand.

John turned to Mohammed as they walked back to the car. 'Thank goodness the press hasn't been invited.' The Prince had a huge beam on his face. 'Its not funny Mohammed you are getting into something that you shouldn't.' John said in a low voice to avoid being overheard.

'I passed her a card with my telephone number and she kept it.'

'You did what!' Do you not realise who she is?'

'But she's beautiful John, isn't she, isn't she?'

'Yes Mohammed, she is very beautiful, very beautiful indeed.' John agreed.

Prince Edward had moved away from his friends and bodyguards and was sitting on the tailgate of the Vogue, solemn faced and making a weak effort to remove his own riding boots. His manservant was about to go to his aid, when he saw Princes Alice arriving and stopped in his tracks, a discreet distance away, when he heard the Prince of Wight outburst.

'What the hell do you think you're playing at? – Trying to make a fool of me in front of my friends.'

'Come now Edward you don't need me to make a fool of you, you can manage that all by yourself. Besides they all know you don't give a dam about me, they know you're screwing that Mrs Grey. In fact it is rumoured that she's a better ride than that horse of yours, but not quite as handsome.' Prince Edward sprang to his feet, one boot on, the other shaking angrily in his hand and held under Princess Alice's nose. His voice lower now, but nevertheless the venom in his speech spat through his clenched teeth. 'You first class bitch, I want rid of you, out of my life once and for all.'

'Temper, temper Eddy, your pals are watching.' Alice smiled back at him, determined not to be bullied. 'Why don't you divorce me, please? Give me a chance to find someone else.'

'Like that Arab you mean...No way.'

'Huh,' she scoffed, throwing out her hip, 'I'm not stupid Edward, you won't give me a divorce, because uncle won't let you, not while I am more popular with the public than you are. And we've got to keep the Monarchy in touch with the love of the people, you know, - unfortunately for me.'

She tossed her hair back and stuck out her chin. 'But you had better be careful not to push me too far Edward, or you may find it is I who will be doing the divorcing, exposing your affair with that old nag Cecelia, for starters. I wonder what uncle would say to that.'

Edward glared at her. 'You tart.'

'We both know the life of the monarchy is hanging by a thread, the King knows it and your so called friends over there,' Alice nodded at the group of followers, as she spoke, 'know it. The last thing he or those sycophants would want is an unpopular successor to the throne.' Edwards head dropped, he knew, she was right.

'Enough! Enough!' Edward waved to one of his bodyguards and Special Branch officer Detective Mullen's made his way towards them. 'Mullen's, you and Detective Smithson get the Jag and take the Princess of Wight, along with the Forsythe woman, to Kensington Palace; see that they remain there until further notice.'

'Very well, sir.'

CHAPTER 7
THE ASSASSIN

London Heathrow 15thNovember

Lufthansa 737 from Berlin taxied off the east end of runway one onto its stand outside terminal three Heathrow Airport. Among the disembarking passengers milling their way along the corridors to passport control, was a thick set man of average height he had dark hair cut short in a crew cut fashion. A noticeable pink crescent shaped scar started from the top of his upper lip across the rounded cheek of his chubby face and ended below one socket of his brown eyes. The customs officer looked hard at the Russian passport then back to the man, a delaying tactic, as he had already depressed the button positioned under his desk, for assistance. Two officers approached, one collected the passport from the officer behind the desk, the other motioned to the man with the scarred face to follow. 'Would you like to come with us sir?' The scar faced mans body language gestured that he was not understanding the situation. 'No speak English.'

The officer spoke calmly as he took hold of scar faces arm. 'Just for a moment sir, shan't keep you too long.' The three of them then headed towards the customs office. 'Better get a Russian interrupter Reg.'

At that moment, scar face produced a letter, holding it out for the officer to read. 'Hang fire Reg, what's this about then?'

The customs officer took the note and read out loud.

'To whom it may concern. I speak no English.

My name is Demmitri Abramovich; I am a citizen of Russia. I am a salesman for Vostok Oil and Gas Industries.

I am in England to complete a deal with the British Energy Authority, for our supply of natural gas to your country. Depending upon the conclusion of my business I expect to be in your country for one week. My address while in your country will be the Savoy Hotel, London.'

'What do you reckon Bill?'

'All a bit too pat, if you ask me...And the Savoy, not on your nelly.'

'Yeah he did seem to produce this note right on cue, didn't he?' Then turning to scar face, hoping to catch him off guard, he shouted. 'Didn't you Demmitri!' The Russian just stared wide eyed back at the officer, feigning none comprehension. 'Inform Special Branch let them takeover.'

Reg dropped the telephone back into its cradle. 'They're on the way', he declared looking at the Russian for any tell tale sign of acknowledgement. Not a twitch. He then nodded to Bill and they both left the office leaving the Russian in the room by himself. 'I'd bet my arse that guy understands everything we say.'

'Yeah, but that's not a crime and we've haven't got a thing on him.'

'Hum I know... I'll check his bags.'

'I'll hold him in there for as long as I dare, hopefully special branch will be on the ball.'

Ten minutes later Reg came back into the room and discretely gestured with his head to the other Officer. They huddled in a corner out of earshot of the Russian. 'Instructions from Special Branch, we've to let him go.'

Demmitri Abramovich walked out through the nothing to declare green channel and out into the arrivals concourse. He stood and turned on the spot trying to take in the information and direction boards. Two Special Branch officers observed the Russian from a distance. A lady approached the Russian and handed him a note.

'What's going on?'

'She looks like a prostitute…Surely she isn't soliciting?'

'Grab her when she comes back.'

As she headed toward the exit, one of the officers moved to block her way. 'Just a minute Miss, mind if we have a quick word, I'm PC Martins.' He said flashing his warrant card.

'What for? I ain't done noffing wrong.'

'That note you have just given to that man.'

She shrugged her shoulders whilst masticating the gum in her mouth. 'What about it?' She said flippantly.

'Aiding and abetting a criminal activity, that's what.'

'Give over…You trying to stitch me up?'

'What was in the note?'

'Haven't an effin clue, mate. This geezer picks me up in Piccadilly, in a bloomin taxi, brings me here. Bungs me a hundred to give the note to scar face…That's it, end of.'

'Where's this guy now?'

The girl shrugged. 'Dunno.'

'Steve, the Russian's gone!'

'Shit, get Eddie on the radio.'

'Eddie this is Ron, come in.'

'Go ahead Ron.'

'Is the car still there?'

'That's an affirmative Ron.'

'Okay Ed, give us a call when it starts to move.'

'What you, still here, you can go now.' Steve said. The prostitute spun around and exaggeratedly pushed out her buttocks and swaggered towards the exit.

'Better start looking Ron.' At that the two officers started to work their way up the concourse checking all of the nooks and crannies as they went. They arrived at the far exit door just in time to see the Russian getting into a taxi. 'Damn! Damn! Damn!'

16ʰ November, Moscow

Vladimir Vostok picked up the telephone on the third ring; he placed the handset to his ear, but did not say anything.

'Hello it's me. Your envoy has arrived safely, I have made the necessary arrangements to accommodate him, but I may have another use for him.'

'I trust you have the scrambler on?'

'I do indeed.'

'So what are you proposing?'

'There's been a development, one which would cause the British much controversy, and if we play our cards right, the SAS will finish what Romanovski couldn't.'

'Interesting.....Pull it off, and all we would have to do, is point the finger.'

'My thoughts exactly.'

'And the asset?'

'I think he may be better employed as a photographer.'

'Then you must use him as you see fit, but please be reminded, whatever little game you are playing, I cannot afford another failure. Understand?'

'I will not fail.'

Queen Anne's Gate.16th November

Sir Peter swiped his security pass card through the detector to release the door lock. The click indicated acceptance and allowed him to pass into an anti chamber, where his palm and retina were scanned, before allowing him to proceed further. The door lock clicked and Sir Peter entered into the area known as the basement. This area was crammed full of the latest technology in surveillance and satellite communication. At one of the computer stations sat the head of the department, a Welshman, by the name of Terry Griffiths.

'Morning Terry.'

'Ah, good morning sir, thought you might want see this.'

'What is it?'

'Pointless you see to put it on speaker the buggers got a jammer running. Could break it down I suppose, but it'll take sometime.'

'Spit it out Tee.'

'It's a phone call sir, recorded earlier this morning at GCHQ.'

'Yes I gathered that, but from who to where?'

'Well sir, it's from somewhere in London to that office you see, the one we have under surveillance in Moscow.'

'Vladimir Vostok's office.'

'Aye that's the one.' Terry nodded towards whirling reels of recording tape feeding information into the computer terminal. 'Cheltenham did a triangulation check, but all they could get was somewhere in the centre of London.' Terry tapped the keyboard in response to a chiming sound and the screen lit up.

'PC Martins

Special Branch, sir.' Sir Peter faced the screen. 'Yes Martins, you were on duty at Heathrow I do believe.'

'That's correct sir.'

'And.'

'The suspect arrived as you envisaged, name of Demmitri Abramovich, we held him up, made him aware we considered him suspicious and then we let him escape as you instructed, but we made it look good, even if I say so myself.'

'Thank you PC Martins, good work.' Sir Peter nodded to Terry who in turn tapped a key to close the transmission and the screen went blank.

'This Demmitri Abramovich will be staying at this address,' Sir Peter passed a postit note to Terry, 'I would like a full twenty-four seven satellite surveillance on him.'

'No problem guv, leave it to me I'll have him in jiffy.'

'Thanks Tee.'

CHAPTER 8

THE BROTHERHOOD

North Yorkshire 17th November

A Range Rover Vogue driven by Henry Forbes, turned off the A64 onto a quiet narrow country road in North Yorkshire. As he drove, in his mind wrestled with the way he was going to approach the subject with the other nine members of the 'Brotherhood' and just how he was going to persuade them to arrive at the same conclusion that he already had. Henry knew that he could count on the support of his fellow Americans, if not out of friendship, certainly because of the secrete they shared.

The car turned to approach a large ornate wrought iron gate and gatehouse of a large country estate. Before the vehicle had come to a complete stop, a man had emerged from the house, gave the vehicle and driver a cursory glance and set about swinging open the gate. As the Vogue nosed through the opening the gateman held up a hand, signalling for the driver to stop. The Gateman approached, clipboard in hand. Henry pressed the button to lower the window.

'Name sir?'

'John Washington'

'Ah yes Mr Washington, you are expected. If you keep to the road on the right you will come to Ashmore house after five miles. Good day sir.'

'And a good day to you.' Henry raised the window and set off in the indicated direction. 'Dam these narrow English roads there's hardly enough road to be on the wrong side of.' Five miles down the road he eventually arrived at his destination, a large country house on a very large North Yorkshire estate. He swung the Range Rover around the circular, gravel covered drive and parked in front of the steps to the main entrance.

Henry was relieved to have finally completed his journey; it had been a long and harrowing drive from Heathrow. He sat for a moment, head back eyes closed, letting his mind go blank. Most of the journey had been spent, when road conditions allowed, deep in thought, going over and over the situation. He had done little else for the past three weeks since the meeting with the President. *The President, what a waste of time.* He mused.

Henry brought his head back, opened his eyes and switched off the ignition, threw back his head again and made a loud deflating noise blowing through his mouth. 'Thank fuck for that.' Before he'd had time to readjust, a tall slender silver haired man wearing a claw hammer coat and striped waistcoat opened the car door.

'Welcome to Ashmore sir, his grace is expecting you.' He then gestured to a young man standing by the main door. 'May we take yours bags sir?'

'Sure, there's only the one, in the trunk.' Henry lowered himself gingerly out of the vehicle and took a few stiff legged steps towards the house. The host came bounding down the sandstone steps meeting and greeting Henry at the bottom. The host looked around furtively ensuring he was at a discreet distance from the servants, before welcoming his guest. 'Ah Washington my old friend, so good to see you.'

'And you York.' They shook hands and York flung his left arm over Henry's shoulder, saying in a fairly loud voice so that the young man now carrying Henrys suitcase could hear. 'We have put you the blue room in the west wing.' Then in a much quieter tone, 'I've put you Americans together in the west wing, the other three arrived yesterday.' They walked side by side up the steps, through a large oak door and into the large hall. The host checked around again just to make sure that all the servants were now out of earshot. 'For the benefit of the staff, this weekend is scheduled for a shoot. By the way, you have shot before haven't you?'

'I've done a bit.'

'Good – good, we have all the equipment and attire ready for you. After the shoot tomorrow evening we can get down to the real reason we are gathered here.'

'Am I the last to arrive?'

'No not quite, London has yet to make an appearance.'

The host, York, clearly did not want to concern himself discussing the late arrival of any guest, turning instead his attention to his wrist watch. 'Err let me see, it's now six pm, dinner will be served at eight in the main dining hall. Err you've been here before? Henry attempted to nod, but he hardly made any movement before York continued. 'You'll know your way round then, eh.' He said gently patting Henry on the back as he spoke. 'Good show, good show, go and freshen up, see you at dinner.' Without waiting for any further comment or conversation, he gave Henry a final pat, turned on his heel and disappeared into the study closing the door behind him. Henry stood for a moment gathering his thoughts, then made his way up the staircase to his room.

His room, he knew, was at the end of the corridor which meant he would have to pass the rooms where the other three Americans would be staying. Pausing at the first door, he raised his hand about to knock, and then changed his mind, *plenty of time, 'I'll touch base later.'*

Although they knew each other, the ten members of this secretive and exclusive society, maintained the tradition of using a place name relative to that particular member as a form of address, when in connection with 'Brotherhood' business. This tradition was a carry over from the days of communications by mail or telegram and was a way of having some discretion and protection in respect of their identity. The 'Brotherhood' was formed some time ago, when a very rich Englishman got together with a few friends of similar fortune and decided between them it was time to make the world a better place, predominately for themselves. They used their combined financial muscle to influence governments, policies, industries and economies, anything in fact, to sustain their power. It has been rumoured in the corridors of power, that wars have been fought and won for the financial benefit of the 'Brotherhood.' Access to this society is by word of mouth recommendation alone and to qualify for recommendation, one must have a very substantial bank balance and preferably a tangible link with the people in power. Needless to say, these ten members are among the richest and influential men in the

Western world. Over time the emphasis of the membership changed to include Americans and Europeans, to the extent that the core of the society was no longer British. The current membership is made up of four Americans, two British, a Frenchman, a German, a Spaniard and a Swiss.

Henry pushed open the door to his designated large room and noted the luxury of the fittings, *very nice indeed, been awhile since I was here last.* His carryall had been placed on a chest at the foot of the bed and neatly laid out on the dresser were a set of clothes for tomorrows shoot, a green tweed jacket, matching tweed plus-fours, check shirt, with a green wool tie sporting a pheasant in flight and a pair of fawn coloured wool stocking with red garters. On the floor by the dresser was a pair of walking boots. Curiosity got the better of him, deciding that a partial inspection of the attire was necessary. This entailed a try on of the tweed jacket and the slipping of his right foot, being the slightly wider one, into one of the boots. *Godamit! How the hell did they know my size?* Henry exclaimed to himself. He was still pondering the matter when there was a knock on his door. 'Come in,' he shouted, 'I'm decent.' At that three guys walked in hands extended.

'Hey Washington, good to see yah man.'

'Yeah good to see you too Houston,' he acknowledged the other two with a nod and a warm hand shake, - 'Denver.... Portland.' A few pleasantries were exchanged, before Houston suggested that they all went out onto the balcony for a quiet word.

'Can't be too careful, the Limies may have the rooms bugged.'

'You could well be right Houston,' Washington agreed, 'better safe than sorry.' The four of them then edged out into the darkness.

'Okay, we're out here, in the cold and the dark, so what is it you want to know?'

'Well it's like this Washington, the three of us have had a conflab, and we were sorta won-dring,' Houston said acting as self appointed spokesperson.

'And?' Washington prompted.

'Is this meeting about the Arab speech thing?'

'Guess you'll find out sooner or later, - so the answers yes.'

'Well we were thinking—.'

'Get to the point Houston.' Denver said.

'Darn it, am about to ask the man.' Houston lowered his voice, just in case anyone was standing in the darkness, ear wigging.

'Are we going the full hog with the rest of them brothers?'

'You mean tell them the real reason for our concern with the Arab oil situation.'

'That's what we mean.' Portland chipped in.

'Don't know how he got that info, but the guy's signed his death warrant.' Denver added.

'Quiet both of you,' Huston said with some authority in his voice, 'let Washington tell us what he has in mind. – Well?'

'Not if I can help it, you've got to remember some of the companies where we offloaded our crude are represented here, disclosure at this point, would not be in our best interest.'

'How to win friends and influence people.' Portland muttered.

'Exactly.'

The day had gone well, a good bag of birds; the guests all felt that they had shot well. Keepers, beaters and picker ups with their dogs, had all gone away happy and under the impression that the shoot was the only reason for the visiting guns.

The ten members of the 'Brotherhood' had just finished a rather sumptuous five course dinner and had retired with their port and cigars to the privacy of the library. This was a large rectangular shaped room. The two long walls were adorned with large oil paintings in gilt frames. The entrance was at one end and an inglenook fireplace with a log fire burning, at the other.

'No windows and no books,' Henry noted, 'how very unusual for a library.'

In the centre of the room was a large oak table with ten chairs. As host, York took the head of the table, Henry as the instigator seated him self at the other end.

'Well gentlemen.' York said as he began to issue each member with a two page agenda. 'I'm quite sure you are all familiar with the matter in hand, but just to ensure that we are all singing off the same hymn sheet, perhaps we could all take time to digest this information.'

There was a pause for a minute or so to allow the agenda to be passed around and digested. After two minutes had elapsed, York assured himself that all was understood. 'I would now like to call upon our member from Washington to open the meeting.' Henry cleared his throat and was about to speak, when York got to his feet and set about collecting the agendas. 'Sorry old chap won't be a tick.' He took the now collected agendas and placed them into the fire, pausing until he was sure the paperwork was destroyed. 'Over to you Washington.' He said over his shoulder as the last black paper ash folded around a burning log. Henry didn't stand, just gave another cough to get attention and started.

'Mohammed Bin Aziz Al Saud, Crown Prince of Saudi Arabia, is destined to become the most influential person in the whole of the Middle East and possibly most of the Far East as well. Just over three weeks ago, Prince Mohammed made a very controversial speech to the multitudes in Mecca. I'm sure most of will have heard, or be aware of this speech, if not, the pertinent points were as briefly set out in the agenda you have just read. In short, Prince Mohammed wants to quadruple the cost of Saudi crude to the West and where the Saudi's go, there will follow the rest of the Middle East producers, sending oil prices across the globe sky high.' Washington took the time to look at the faces of each man sitting around the table; he then began the question and answer monologue that he rehearsed over and over in his head. 'Question, can he do it? Answer, yes he can, and probably will. Can we in the West afford such a hike? Probably yes in the short term, but as the knock on effect of the price rise filters through to the various industries we will not be able to sustain our output and compete in the world market place economically. Does the West need Arab oil? –We could probably manage without it, but would require supplementing our reserves from another

source if we are to maintain growth and stay world leaders.
Can we get the oil from another source? Markets in Russia and
the Far East are available, but potentially expensive, especially
when transportation costs are considered. This however may
prove to be our only viable option.' Again he paused, taking in
each of the faces that silently stared back at him. 'And what,
you might ask, are our governments prepared to do about the
situation? In essence, jack shit.'

'Are not you yanks looking at alternative sources?' London put
in curtly.

'True we are spending billions of dollars looking for a viable
renewable form of energy. Problem there is that no matter how
much cash we throw at it, the answer is way down line and to
put it frankly we don't have the luxury of time to wait.'
Washington paused to let the membership digest what he had
just said. 'Any suggestions gentlemen?'

Marseilles was the first to react. 'Almost everything Saudi
Arabia has, is imported from the West, if they force up the price
of these goods, surely it will be not beneficial for them?'

'Good point but not quite true I'm afraid. For one, the Saudi's,
in particular, have over the years become much less dependant
upon us and secondly, the huge Russian and Far Eastern
markets, will supply all their needs at a fraction of any price we

would be able to offer. Probably in return for the oil that we can no longer afford.'

'It may not come down to that, I'm sure this speech will soon be forgotten and I think our governments feel that too.'

'Not in my opinion Berlin, I doubt the many anti-west Middle East factions will allow him to forget his promise, irrespective of our governments' complacency.'

'If our governments aren't prepared to do anything, what do you expect from us?'

'Hell boy', Houston reacted to the Frenchman's apathetic comment. 'What the fuck do think we're doing here, or do yawl give a shit.'

'Steady on gentlemen.' York put in, before a situation could develop. An uncontrolled hubbub occurred with members muttering their comments to each other. Washington sat quiet, taking it all in. York was becoming red-faced trying to get order. A shout rang out above the level of the other voices.

'Eliminate the bastard!'

London's crude sounding comment brought instant silence for what seemed an age, Washington coolly responded.

'Yes, that would work, but only if it's done a certain way.' It was obvious to all that Washington had considered this option, so each remained silent, allowing him to expand on the theory.

'The most important thing is that his death is not connected in any way with the West and indeed us. An accident perhaps or even made to look like suicide. Preferably not in our backyards.' He paused a moment, to try to gauge an opinion, but no reaction was evident, so he continued. 'To have even a hint of Western involvement could provoke the anti-west element and we would be back to square one.' Washington paused again looking around the room at his colleagues, waiting for a response.

'We could be playing into the hands of our enemies.' Berlin spoke in almost perfect English with only the hint of an accent. 'There are many with opposing views who would not hesitate to point an accusing finger at the West, at any opportunity.'

Serville attempted to lighten the mood. 'I suppose the perfect solution would be, to have the Prince accidentally fall from a minaret in Mecca.'

'And just how would you arrange that!' Marseilles spat back. Serville shrugged his shoulders. 'If elimination of the Prince was the only option open to us, then I would consider that to be the perfect solution.'

'Please gentlemen let's try be serious about this.' York put in, attempting to get some semblance of order to the meeting. Zurich, not really wanting to contemplate the matter, reluctantly said. 'I am sorry, but I just can't think about killing another human being. I would not have any idea of how to go about such a thing.'

'Let's assume shall we that the deed has been done and this Prince is dead, what would happen then?' Berlin asked.

'His brother, Prince Abdul Bin Aziz Al Saud would automatically succeed to the Saudi throne. He is known to be pro-west and very much in his father's ilk.'

'Then we must find a way to dispose of this Prince with the runaway mouth.' Serville said.

'Way to go' Portland declared.

'Is that the consensus of us all?' York said as he looked around the table at the nodding heads. 'So be it.'

'About fucking time, I reached that conclusion an age ago.' Nobody approved of London's rudeness, but nothing was said as he continued. 'I have a contact that'll get the job done no questions asked.'

The majority of the membership seemed somewhat relieved that someone was prepared to sort the problem, remaining quiet and unquestioning. All that is, except Washington.

'You seem to have it all figured London, how do you suppose this contact of yours will go about it so that there will be no connection to the Brotherhood and indeed the West?'

'He's got that all figured, kidnap the geezer and dump his body, probably from a plane over Iraq.' Everyone silently contemplated the situation, until Washington responded. 'So let's get straight to the point London, how much is this going to cost us?'

'Twenty million, pounds of course.' There was an audible gasp from the rest of the membership. 'English pounds? Bit steep isn't it!' A statement rather than question from Denver. There were a lot of disgruntled murmurings from the members around the table. London stood to continue his point. 'Gentlemen, gentlemen, this is a mere pittance to achieve so much and there isn't anyone in this room who couldn't put his hands on two million pounds worth of untraceable assets, most of us have been salting it away for years.'

'Am feeling I'm about to git shafted' Houston said, clasping his hands behind his head as he leaned back in a nonchalant manner. Questions reined in from around the table.

'What if this contact of yours just fucks off with our dough?'

'Or what if he just fucks up?'

'How do we know he won't come back for more?'

'How do we stay anonymous?'

'Your contact, but you know us and I'm not sure I even trust you.'

'Yeah what's in it for you?'

The questions and comments reigned in from around the table, London still standing lifted his hands in a quieting gesture, 'I've never met, nor am I likely to meet the contact, so there would be no link to the 'Brotherhood.' Any future communication I have with this contact will be from a telephone box using a code name.' London could see the doubt on their faces.

'There's always going to be risk no matter how we play this, so this is what we'll do.'

Hmm not asking, but telling, this guy's giving me bad vibes, Washington thought.

'Firstly I'm sure Zurich can help us with the banking arrangements, I take it we all have a Swiss numbered account.' London looked around for the confirmatory nods from each member. 'Good then it shouldn't take long to transfer money into a separate account.'

'Whose account?' Marseilles asked.

'I would expect Zurich to set up another numbered account.' Washington jumped in before London could finish. 'For you to pass to your contact, or not, as the case maybe, I for one would not be happy with such an arrangement.'

'What would you suggest?' London snapped back.

Washington pondered the question for a moment, but that was a subterfuge, he had already analysed that problem in his own mind.

'I would not object to Zurich opening an interim account solely for holding of the two million from each of – 'us'.' Washington emphasized the word us looking directly at London. Pausing a while as if working things through in his mind, he turned to Zurich. 'Would it be possible to concoct our own account number and code?'

'Unusual, - may take some rearranging of the banks computer program, but I don't see why it cannot be done.'

Washington then turned to York. 'York would you please get us a writing pad, twenty small and two large envelopes please.'

'Er er yes, by all means, shant be a moment.' York left the library returning a little later, stationery in hand. 'You did say twenty small and two large envelopes?' Washington nodded as York passed him the stationery.

'Here's what I propose, we each take two pieces of paper and two envelopes. On both pieces write your Brotherhood initial on the top and two numbers underneath, place one piece of paper in each small envelope. The completed sealed envelopes will then be put into each larger envelope and sealed. One goes to the hit man via Mr. London, the other to Zurich, for safe keeping in the bank vault, in Switzerland. I suggest that we charge Zurich with the task of collecting and holding our two million pounds in a temporary account. When we are satisfied that the execution has been undertaken in accordance with our requirements, that is to say, no evidence of the Brotherhood or the West's involvement. I will organise for an advertisement to appear in the national press of the country where the hit occurs and in the Zurich press. The advert will simply relate your initials set out at random. As far as Zurich is concerned, and of course the hit man, this will dictate the sequence of the ten sets of numbers forming the special account for the twenty million.'

'Well thought out Washington that makes sure only Zurich and the executioner will know the number sequence.' Marseilles said.

'Or whoever it is who will have the other envelope.' Added Berlin.

'I can assure you, without guarantee of payment, no contract will be undertaken.' London retorted, staring hard at the German. 'So Berlin it would be in none of our interests to retain the envelope.

Zurich timorously interjected, tactfully defusing a probable altercation. 'I am expecting this transaction to be undertaken electronically through the World banking network, I and my banking network want as little as possible association with this affair.'

'That's understood Zurich.' Said Washington. 'Whoever it is who gets access to the account is of no interest to us, other than the completion of the task.' The rest of the members nodded and grunted their approval all that is, except London, a point that Washington mentally noted.

Houston piped in, 'I'm with you ole boy, but what if this guy wants something up front?'

'If London's assassin insists then I would expect we reconvene at another time to sort out another account, but I would like London to strongly resist any suggestion of an up front payment.'

'If London contacts me in this regard, it would be possible to fund the enterprise to one point five million Euros, if necessary? I would of course reduce the fee accordingly.' Zurich suggested.

'No problem with that Zurich, but it would be a lot tidier in one lump, if London can swing it.'

'What if the attempt fails?'

'I hadn't really contemplated failure, we cannot afford failure.' Washington turned to look London in the eye. 'You must impress upon your contact that failure to complete the task is not an option.'

London nodded. 'It will be done.'

'What if in the worse case scenario, the contact is discovered before the job's done, what then?'

'In that case Serville, we find another.'

'And if we are too late?'

Washington pursed his lips and considered his answer. 'In that case my friend we're fucked and all I can suggest is that we would expect to see a large donation into the funds of Africa's Famine Relief.' Washington looked at Zurich and nodded for approval, which Zurich returned with a similar affirmative gesture.

'I can live with that.' Portland said.

And comments of approval echoed around the table, again all except London, who appeared to be deep in thought, no doubt thinking about a relief of his own.

'Before I close this meeting, I do have a concern that I'd like London to clear up.'

'And what would that be, Yorky old chum, don't you trust me with the dough.'

'Err no; it's not that, only I'm aware, as I'm sure we all are that the Arab Prince is currently in England, how can you guarantee your contact won't kill him here?'

'I can't, other than the fact Washington would not release the cash and that the contact is of Middle East origin.' The room went quiet for a long moment, until York coughed and pushed back his chair as he stood up. 'Then gentleman there is nothing more to say.'

Moscow

Vladimir Vostok picked up the ringing telephone.

'Hello.'

'Hello, it's me. They have agreed that I will deal with the matter.'

'Good, then you should deal with it.'

'Not so fast, we may have a problem. There are conditions for which we have not allowed.'

'Such as?'

'The American is insisting on a code being used for the payment, one which would ensure the hit is made outside of the UK, and without the involvement of the Brotherhood.'

'You said you would not fail and the SAS would solve our problem; I warn you it would not be advisable to cross me.'

'I swear the Yank has come up with the scheme.'

There was a pause. 'How much?'

'Twenty million.'

The money is still to be handled by Zurich, as we planned?'

'Yes, but with one code to him and one code to the assassin.'

'Then you need to use the asset as intended and drop the Arab in the sea from your private jet, we can still point a finger can we not, so nothing has changed, goodbye.'

Without another word Vostok replaced the receiver.

England

At the crack of dawn, Henry Forbes started the journey back to Heathrow in the rented Vogue. 'Not a bad car this, driving on the wrong side of the road isn't that bad either, providing they are quiet,' which in fact there were at that time of day. It wasn't too long before his mind started to replay the weekend events, in particular the meeting. Something had really bothered him.

I called that meeting, with no reference at all to the Prince's speech. How come London was all prepared with an assassin in his pocket? Okay, so it wasn't that difficult to envisage the scenario and second-guess the outcome of the meeting. I myself had concluded, if the Prince were to die, under the right circumstances, it would be the best solution to the problem. Although, it did take me a couple of days to ponder the likely outcome. Hiring a hit man, even if you know a contact, is not a straightforward process, it can take months to put discreet negotiations together, I know, I've tried. Not an easy choice, but nevertheless, it's a long process. So this London guy is not only a smart arse and a sadistic bastard, he's way ahead of the game. – Something smells and I don't like it.

Peeeep! 'Fucking hell! Maniac.' Henry shouted at a car speeding past him in the middle lane, he was now on the M1 and he suddenly realised that he was ambling along at fifty mph in the fast lane, the traffic was now significantly heavier, and a lapse of concentration had sub-consciously caused him to veer toward what he thought was the slow lane. *'This is the fast lane you great steaming idiot.'* He said to himself. *'Better get a move on.'*

On board the BA 747 to JFK, Henry determined, he would drop a hint to Jim Baxter who would no doubt tell the Brits and the Brits would no doubt ensure that the Prince is not bumped off on their patch. Only at that point could he finally turn his mind off and go to sleep.

CHAPTER 9

ALL IN THE GAME

The telephone on Sir Peter's desk rang once and was picked up instantly.

'Yes.'

'Terry here guv, we have another call to Vostok's office.'

'Same as before Tee?'

'Almost guv, this time the call was made from a phone booth in a Service area on the M1. Must have a special gizmo that works on a public phone, only got the "Hello it's me" bit.'

'Our man again?'

'I would say so guv.'

17th November Kensington Palace

Early morning, three days after the events on Tuesday, Lady Katharine Forsythe, lady in waiting to Alice Princess of Wight, tapped lightly on the Princess's bedroom door.

'Your highness, are you awake?'

'Ah h, y-e-s Kathy,' she yawned, 'do come in.'

'Kathy opened the door and excitedly ran to the Princess's room plonking herself on the bed next the still drowsy Princess. 'Alice, Alice the guard has gone.' She said excitedly.

'Gone where?'

'I don't know, he must have been called away during the night, we're free.'

'Are you sure Kathy, he hasn't just sloped off for a cuppa?'

'One hundred percent. I heard him talking on his radio thing, last night, so I took a peek.'

'And?'

'He was gone and he's not there now.'

'Wow!' Before Alice had even thought about it; she had picked up her mobile and punched in Mohammed's number.

'Hello.' Mohammed casually answered.

'Ahem, err it's Alice, err Princess of Wight.' She said nervously.

Never in a million years would she have thought of being so forward as to actually pursue the man, but for some unknown reason in this instance her usual reserve had diminished. Perhaps it was because she was quite taken with this young Arabian Prince and her thoughts had been of little else. Although she tried to conceal it, the excitement in her voice was apparent, as she blurted out the well practiced line. 'I just thought I would let you know I have a gap in my diary.'

After about five minutes of small talk and a couple of childish giggles, she ended the conversation with a demure, 'goodbye.'

Alice switched off her mobile and turned to Kathy who was

still sitting on the edge of her bed; slowly a smile formed and broke into a scream of delight accompanied by the excited slapping of the duvet. 'We're going to meet,' she squealed, 'Hyde Park, at eleven.'

Kathy determined to retain control of her emotions, responded cautiously. 'Oh Alice, are you sure, this all seems so contrived Edward could have set the whole thing up to trick you into divorce.

'No, I don't think so, he may have had something to do with the removal of the guard, but I'm sure Edward has no connection with Mohammed.'

'With or without Edward's knowledge, you will have a hard job trying to get out of this place without being recognised.'

'I know, that's why I going in disguise and you are going to help me with the make up.'

'O-k-a-y,' Kathy replied thoughtfully, 'on one condition, that you help me with mine, because I'm coming with you.'

About one and half hours later, two cleaning ladies left Kensington Palace by the servants' entrance, unchallenged. John as a matter of course made his way to Mohammed's suite. He expected to go through the usual body search scenario with the Egyptian maulers and then have to assist Mohammed to dress. As the door opened the two bodyguards looked up briefly, saw who it was and continued to check their weapons and put on their overcoats. *What's going on?* John thought as he made his way unchallenged, to the Prince's room.

Mohammed was in the process of pushing one arm into the overcoat being held open by the Indian manservant.

'Ah John, just in time, we're going out, go and get your coat, it's a cold today.' John could see this was not the time to ask questions, so he returned to his room and collected his coat.

Mohammed had been right about it being a cold day, especially in Hyde Park, but why and what, they were in the park for, John didn't have a clue. The penny didn't drop, even when, the group were approached by two dark haired ladies wearing dark glasses. A broad grin spread across Mohammed's face, as soon as he realized who they were. John on the other hand was confused and it wasn't until he heard Mohammed that it clicked.

'Oh Alice, it is so good to see you.'

'I didn't think you would recognise me in these clothes and wearing this dark hair piece.'

'I would have known you anywhere, with or without your disguise.'

Oh no – give me strength. John pursed his lips and feigned embarrassment.

'We dressed like this to avoid being recognised.'

Blatantly obvious, John thought, reacting to the grins now spread across their faces, *like a couple of daft kids.*

'Your beauty cannot be disguised. Highness,' Mohammed said as his gloved hands encased hers. He looked longingly for a moment into her eyes. 'Shall we walk?'

She nodded politely and automatically linked an arm through his. Mohammed and Alice, wig, dark glasses and all, set off arm in arm. *Prince bloody charming indeed.*

'Lady Katharine Forsythe, Lady in Waiting to Her Royal Highness the Princess of Wight.' The other dark haired lady took steps towards John, hand outstretched. 'Saw you at the horse trial in Windsor Park,' she said.

'Pleased to meet you,' he said taking her hand, 'John Godfrey, diplomatic service and companion to the Saudi Arabian Crown Prince, Mohammed Bin Aziz Al Saud.' John gently shook her hand, before gesturing that they should follow the couple in front. They walked together, about five paces behind the Royal couple and the bodyguards stayed at a discreet distance behind them.

'I'm sorry Lady Katharine, but I can't recall seeing you at that horsey thing.'

'Ah that may be down to the disguise, I'm actually blond under this dark wig, as is Princes Alice.' Katharine looked down at her shoes as they ambled through the Park and nothing was said for a while, before lifting her head to speak. 'You do realize don't you, that these disguise's are not just for the benefit of the public?'

'Well, Lady Katharine, I—.'

'Call me Kathy, please.'

'Well Kathy, I could imagine, Princess Alice would have problems getting out of the palace without her escorts.'

'Yes, it was too dammed easy, but that's another worry.'

'Worry?' John put in, somewhat perplexed.

She nodded solemnly. 'If I told you John, there was another more serious reason, would that surprise you?'

'I haven't really thought about it.'

Kathy paused, head down again, watching the progress of her feet. Her head came up and she stared at John, *Shall I trust this man.* She thought, and instantly concluded that she would.

'Okay, - I believe Prince Edward arranged this meeting and has probably got someone watching us now.' John was taken slightly aback, but decided to let Kathy offer an explanation, before giving his opinion.

'Hum – interesting, but why?'

'Edward desperately wants a divorce.'

'Does he, but I thought—.'

'Oh yes, desperately, he's having an affair with a married woman and wants Alice off the scene. As soon as he's free Edward will run to his lover and publicly cry on her shoulder, or pretend to. He is very good at pretending you know, even pretends he and Alice live together. In fact we only see him on official engagements.'

'I'm missing something here Kathy, if the situation is a bad as you say, why don't they just divorce and have done with it.'

'In short John, the King won't let them.' She paused a moment to consider her phrasing. 'You see the monarchy is going through a bad time. Public opinion is against them and there have been calls for a republic. The one thing keeping the Royalist cause alive at this time is the popularity of Princess Alice. The King knows it, as do the rest of the Royal family and they despise her for it. I don't know if the King is aware of Edward's bit on the side, or indeed his marital arrangements, but nevertheless he has cautioned Edward not to do anything that would upset public opinion. As sure as God made little apples, if Edward divorced Alice it would prove to be the final straw for the monarchy.'

'I'm beginning to see where you're coming from.' John put in, giving Kathy a chance to catch her breath. 'If Edward can make Princess Alice look deceitful, having an affair with an Arab, he may just turn the tables in the popularity stakes.'

'Exactly!'

'And you think he could be having us watched.'

'Yes, after the horse race in Windsor, the Princess and I have been imprisoned in Kensington Palace.'

'So I gathered when I noticed her, and it must have been you, being whisked away in the Jag, that day.'

'We had a guard on the door twenty-four hours, this morning he was gone. Not even our ever present detectives are anywhere to be found.'

'I see - umm.' John seemed to be thinking the situation through before responding, but Kathy continued.

'Alice could if she wanted, blow the whole thing, file for a divorce naming names, desertion the whole ball of wax, but she must consider the future for her son. If the monarchy were to fall, where would that leave the young Prince?'

'Well Kathy, from what you have told me it certainly sounds as if Prince Edward could be up to something, but I can't see how he could have legislated for Prince Mohammed to be involved. From what I have been led to believe, the Royal family made it clear the Saudi Prince is not welcome here and have kept him at a distance. Apparently it took a lot of gesturing, and a bit of arm twisting to get an invite to Tuesday's fiasco. But most importantly, when that soldier fell off the ramp and rather painfully broke an arm, which I'm sure wasn't deliberate. I prompted the Major Salmon, to let the Prince stand in. I had told him that Prince Mohammed was an excellent horseman, which indeed he is.'

'The Prince rode a splendid race, didn't he?'

'Yes he did and because he did, he got to meet the Princess. No way could Edward have contrived a meeting from those circumstances.'

'Perhaps you're right John, maybe I worry too much.'

Alice and Mohammed had stopped and were facing each other, when Kathy and John joined them.

'An old friend of mine has a houseboat on the Thames; it's empty at the moment. Mohammed and I were thinking we could spend some time there, by ourselves.'

'I don't think we should allow that.' John said. 'You're both getting into something here that could have catastrophic consequences.'

Before either could object, Kathy put in. 'If you go, we should go with you.'

John looked at Kathy. 'I don't think we should be encouraging th--,' but before John could finish, Prince Mohammed responded to Kathy.

'Good that's settled, lets head to the houseboat.' He turned and walked back to the bodyguards and speaking in Arabic told them to taxi back to the hotel. There seemed to be some mild protest, but after what appeared to be a roll of banknotes being handed over, the two bodyguards sloped off.

John Godfrey was not a field operative, but he was a dab hand at surveillance, equipment and techniques and as he turned to watch Mohammed talk to the bodyguards, the hairs on the back of his neck stood up. *Am I paranoid, are Kathy's comments getting to me?* Then he stiffened, as he caught sight of a man wearing jeans and a blue blouson jacket, carrying a rolled up newspaper, and loitering about fifty yards behind the bodyguards. The way he was holding the newspaper could have contained a zoom type microphone. This guy was now aimlessly wandering on the grass. John knew instinctively he had been watching the group, what's more this guy knew he'd been pinged.

'What's the matter John?' Kathy asked, seeing the concern on his face.

'Oh it's nothing Kathy.'

John began to scan the park. *He must be part of a team, where's the relay.* John scanned the background. *Got yah!* A glint of sunlight reflected, seemingly caught something like a lens, Way off in the tree line. *Hope that's not the telescopic site of a rifle.* John thought. *Just in case, I think it's time to get the hell out of here.*

As Mohammed wandered back, John spread his arms around the group herding them together.

'Let's go folks, need to move.' John ushered the group along. Mohammed and Alice complied without hesitation, still lost in each other's charms. Kathy on the other hand wasn't easily fooled.

'What's the problem John? And don't tell me there isn't one.' John took her arm and pulled her in close, talking quietly out of the corner of his mouth, as they hurried along the path in the direction of Marble Arch.

'We are being followed, Mohammed's certainly being watched and probably listened to by an amplified microphone, wired to that guy about eighty yards back.'

Kathy could not resist a quick glance behind. 'He's still following us.'

'Yes, I know.'

Mohammed turned to John. 'Hey John, shouldn't we be going in the other direction for the car?'

'Thought we'd make a day of it and give you a new experience.' *Besides,* John thought, *the car is probably bugged.*

As if reading his mind, Kathy whispered. 'Who do you think it is John?'

'I'm not sure, there's a Russian who no doubt would want Prince Mohammed dead, but why did he not shoot, why listen. It doesn't make sense.'

'Do you think this could be Edwards doing?'

'Could be I suppose, but I can't figure how they'd have recognised you and I'm fairly confident these guys weren't around when you showed. What's more, they are coming from the direction of the Park Lane car park, where we parked our limo, not from the direction of Kensington Gardens.'

John turned his attention back to leading the small group 'Okay gang this way.'

'Marble Arch Underground?'

'Wow I've never been on the underground before John.' Mohammed said excitedly.

They jumped on the first train and at John's insistence, got off at Oxford Circus. Then they jumped on another train getting off at Euston and heading to the Northern line platform. Princess Alice stopped in the middle of the crossover tunnel, forcing the crowds of passengers to mill around her.

'Mr Godfrey, would you please tell me what it is you are doing?'

'We do seem to be spending a long time down here John.' Mohammed chirped in.

John looked at the two of them. 'Please bear with me, I promise you a full explanation, but right now is not the time or place.'

'He's right we must hurry.' Kathy said.

Thank goodness for Kathy's intervention.

Nothing more was said, they changed trains again at Charing Cross to Putney Bridge, where they finally emerged into the sunlight.

'Right, let's get a coffee somewhere and I'll explain all.'

'Good, the houseboat is just there.' Princess Alice said pointing at a group of houseboats moored at the riverside.

'No, not just yet, it would be prudent to be a little more patient, please bear with me.'

'I'm sorry John, but I think you are being dammed unreasonable.' Alice nodded in agreement with Mohammed, Kathy again intervened.

'Perhaps we should listen to Mr Godfrey.'

'Thanks Kathy, its just that I've got this uneasy niggle and I've learnt never to ignore niggles.' John said, saying the first thing to come into his head. The others looked at him quizzically, but nevertheless trooped off behind him in search of an establishment where they could acquire some refreshment.

The small café was on the corner of a side road a block away from the main road and the houseboat.

John, coffee in hand, was about to explain to the others seated around a table, the reason for his erratic and somewhat over cautious behaviour. That's when he caught a glance through the corner window, of a white van, just coming to a stop in the side street opposite, about fifty yards away. Again the neck hairs bristled.

'My God!'

'What!' Came the collective response.

John thought for a moment. 'Excuse me your highness.' John started to run his hands and eyes over the Prince's clothing, who was somewhat taken aback by John's familiarity.

'You go too far, take your hands off me this instance!' Mohammed snapped, keeping his voice low, so as to avoid being overheard in such a small place.

John paid little heed, remaining focussed, looking intensely for something. He failed to discover anything, and sat back feeling perplexed, that was until he saw the overcoat on the stand by the door. Moving over to it John ran his hands all over it and finding inside the lining at the hem, something the size of a coat button. John pulled at the stitching releasing the object.

'What on earth are you doing now?' Princess Alice asked, her curiosity could no longer be contained. 'Are you some kind of a lunatic?'

John just ignored her. 'Ah,' he said holding his find between his thumb and forefinger, 'what we have here boy and girls, is a miniature transmitter.' Again he was about to explain the situation, and the presence of the white van, when he noticed blue jacket and another were heading in the direction of café. 'Time to go folks!' He declared and made to leave.

'But we haven't finished,' came the protests, as the three of them picked up on Johns apprehension and scrambled to follow John to the door. As he stepped out into the street, John noticed the two surveillance guys immediately turned their attention away, looking into the window of a Hairdressing salon.

They walked a little way in the direction of the main road, passing a small wooded urban garden with a high privet perimeter hedge. The gate of the wrought iron, matching railings surrounding the garden, was ajar. John realising that they were not being followed, turned to Kathy. 'Take these two in there please Kathy and keep them out of sight.' Then he turned to the other two. 'Excuse me for a minute, I'll be back soon.' At that John set off toward the busy road. On the near side of the road, there was a line of vehicles waiting at the intersection for the traffic lights to change to green. John noted that one of the vehicles was a builder's pickup, so he quickened his pace to get to it before it moved off. As he walked by he threw the transmitter into the back. The pickup then pulled away when the lights changed and headed in the direction of Westminster. John stepped back into a shop doorway and waited.

Sure enough a minute or so later the white van passed, heading in the same direction. *'Okay,'* he said to himself, *'time for some answers,'* and he headed for a telephone kiosk.

'Sir Peter? John Godfrey.'

'Yes John, what can I do for you?'

'I'm not really sure sir, could be our security has been compromised.'

'Compromised you say, - where are you?'

'In a public box on the outskirts.'

'Can you be more specific?'

'I'd prefer not to at this time'

'Why, are you in some sort of danger?'

'Not really sure, however I do have a small problem.'

'Oh - what sort of a problem?'

'We are under surveillance, a team of three possibly four, professionals and possibly ours.'

'Are you sure?'

'Oh yes, the car's probably bugged, as well as Mohammed overcoat.'

'Overcoat, you say?'

'Yes but what bothers me most about that is that the bastards must have access to Mohammed hotel room.' There was a little pause. John could sense Sir Peter was thinking it through before responding.

'You spotted them eh? - Should have guessed you would.'

Somehow John was not surprised, Sir Peter could be very devious and always several steps ahead.

'I see, so you arranged it, would you mind telling me why sir?'

'Not at all John, Special Branch dirty tricks department, not the brightest sparks on the block, it would appear. A little insurance, you understand, just in case Mohammed turns anti-Western again when he gets back home. You never know, but if he does, we can show him and perhaps his father just how much he loves our culture and our women.'

'That's diabolical sir.'

'Y-e-s....All in the game John, - all in the game.' Sir Peter's voice now had a stern edge to it. 'No need to remind you who you work for, is there John?'

'No sir.'

'And I can rely upon you to keep this information to yourself?'

'Yes sir.'

'Good, in that case, I'll have your car debugged and returned to the hotel, you will not be followed again, at least not for that reason. Oh, by the way John, thought you may be interested to know, Vostok's assassins in town.... Good bye John.'

'The – the bastard, he's winding me up,' as the line clicked dead. John slowly replaced the receiver. *The old buggers up to something, I just know he is.*

 On the houseboat, both ladies removed their disguises and were very relaxed and seemingly happy. John had not found it necessary to explain his odd behaviour, suffice to say there had been an incident, which he ensured, would not happen again. Over the next few days, visits to the Boathouse became a regular occurrence and romance blossomed. The restraint, level headedness that John intended to portray, was lost in his own infatuation with Kathy.

Inevitably Mohammed and Alice disappeared into the bedroom. It wasn't long before excited groans and sounds of bouncing springs emitted through the timber partition wall. At first they tried to ignore it, staring at each other trying not to show any embarrassment. It was Kathy who nonchantly throw a pillow onto the wooden floor, took hold of John's arm and pulled him to the deck with her. *This is one episode that will not be going in my report, Sir Peter.*

Purely from the point of view, of the scandal and the obvious advantage the Prince of Wight would gain from Princess

Alice's infidelity, John tried his level best to put a stop to the relationship, trying in vain to discourage Mohammed from further contact. They met on more royal engagements some official, but most unofficial. John found himself giving priority to finding ways of avoiding the press and paparazzi, ditching bodyguards and other hangers on, just to find some time for the four of them to spend time in each others company, usually on their secret hideaway boathouse.

'What are we to do John; we've got to somehow put a stop to this affair before it gets out of hand.'

'I agree Kathy, but I think it's gone too far, perhaps the answer will be to separate them, he is due to go home soon that should do it. Although he keeps hinting that he would like to stay longer, this isn't a surprise.' They both laughed and then Kathy's eyes lifted toward John.

'I'm going to miss you, John Godfrey.'

'And I you, Lady Katharine Forsythe. Let's do it again, for old time sake.'

'Let's.' She threw down the pillows dragging John to the floor with her.

That was to be the last encounter John would have with Kathy. However Prince Mohammed could not conceal his desire for the Princess, and insisted on going to events were she would be in attendance. John had little option but to go over and over the consequences, but it wasn't until John explained the danger to Alice, that Mohammed capitulated and allowed John to reschedule the diary to avoid contact.

This in no way stopped the telephone conversations.

John began to think that whole scenario had been dreamt up by Sir Peter for some obscure reason.

John was seated in Sir Peter's office reporting the complicated situation that he now faced. 'I'm fast running out of ideas, there is no way I can keep a cover on this affair any longer. As much as I will miss the guy, I think we should consider sending him home.'

Sir Peter rubbed his chin. 'Do that John and we loose control.'

'I can't see the need sir, Mohammed is not going to publicly retract, but I now know that when he becomes King, his attitude will mellow and the threat of him being assassinated just hasn't materialised.'

'Oh Vostok's assassin is here alright and we know he has been watching you and the Prince, but for some reason that's all he's doing.'

'Why?'

Sir peter pursed his lips and shook his head. 'I've a feeling that all will be revealed fairly soon, so for the time being I want to keep him under our wing.' He paused thoughtfully. 'Didn't you tell me that the Saudi King has a yacht moored in the South of France?'

'Err yes sir, St Tropez I believe.'

'Well that's the answer, get him out of Vostok's reach, away from Princess Alice and out from under our feet. Y-e-s, that's the answer, get him on that boat John, soon as.' John sat there gobsmacked and before he was able to offer any objection, Sir Peter continued. 'Oh and John, you make sure you're with him.'

'Well err … Yes sir, as you wish.'

'Another thing John, you'll be quite close to Monte-Carlo, will you not.' Sir Peter winked exaggeratedly. 'Good gambling there, I here.'

'Yes sir.' John nodded, fully understanding the devious thoughts behind Sir Peter's smile.

As John left the office, Sir Peter pressed the intercom. 'Get that Marj?'

'Every word.'

'Better pop in.'

Marjorie walked in with her note book in hand and flopped onto the Chesterfield. 'What about this Abramovich guy, Vostok's gunman?'

'I'm not sure; I'm convinced Vostok has taken the bait and is now sold on the idea that the British secret service will execute the demise of Prince. So what need does he have for a gunman?' Sir Peter thought for a moment. 'I suspect Vostok will ship him out and keep him on ice until the deed has been done. Then he will probably have him bumped off with something incriminating planted on him.'

'Incriminating?'

'Yes, something to say he was hired by the Brits or the Yanks.' Marjorie nodded thoughtfully. 'Interesting, but what if Vostok isn't convinced and he instructs Abramovich to put down the camera and use the gun?'

'Humm, possible I suppose, but somehow I can't see Vostok passing up such an opportunity. He's got to think we're as mad as hell at this jumped up Arab Prince and will only see our anger. Look at it from his side, this young Prince fellow, who, after we appear to have forgiven him for saying such damaging things about the West, throws our hospitality back in our face by having an affair with the future Queen of England.' Sir Peter shook his head. 'No Marj, Vostok's probably rubbing his hands at the thought of us Brits doing his dirty work for him.'

'Okay so John gets the Prince on the yacht, what's the next step?'

Sir Peter sat back in his chair and clasped his hands behind his head. 'I now have control of the game and I'm going to play it my way.'

'What do you have in mind?'

'Contact with Spider.'

CHAPTER 10
REASON TO LEAVE

John Godfrey made his way back to the Ritz following the meeting with Sir Peter. He took the elevator and went directly to the Prince's stateroom, nodding to the bodyguard stationed in the hall outside the room, as he rapped on the door. The bodyguard stationed on the inside opened it, BG1 and 2 John called them. Both of them stocky built Egyptians. These BG's never spoke, just gestured, hands making as if they were wafting away a bad smell meant that John had to raise his arms and spread his legs. Then the BG would run his hands all over, fond of a grope these guys.

BG1 motioned with his hand that the examination of John's body was complete; he could now proceed into the Prince's lounge. The Indian manservant Rahjad Singh insisted on making the unnecessary introduction.

'Mr Godfrey to see you, your Highness.'

'Hello John.'

'You're Highness. Err- I have some news. We need to talk, in private.'

John waited until the manservant had disappeared, before taking the seat opposite the Prince without waiting for an invite.

'That sounds very serious my friend.'

'Yes Mohammed it is.'

John leaned back and sighed. 'Time to level with you. We, by whom I mean British and American Governments, have for some time now been in pursuit of a very powerful Russian businessman by the name of Vladimir Vostok..'

'I've heard of him.' Mohammed interrupted.

John ignored the comment and continued. 'It seems our Mr Vostok has one big ambition, which is to control the worlds, or at least the Western worlds, oil reserves. His efforts to achieve this goal include inciting fundamentalist's hatred of all things Western, supplying arms to anti-western terrorist groups and writing exaggerated anti-western speeches for young naïve Prince's to recite at religious gatherings.'

Mohammed sprung up in defence. 'My very good friend Sheikh Ahmed Al Bosfar told me that every thing I was to say was true and had been instigated by the Americans.'

John waved his hand gesturing the Prince to sit down. 'I can tell you because I was there, the Sheikh ran in fear of his life when he discovered it was the Russians and not the Americans who had supplied that garbage for you to announce.'

'Allah be merciful.' Mohammed sighed. 'I cannot now take back what has been spoken in the midst of our holiest shrine.' Mohammed shook his head covering his eyes with his hands. John went on. 'One other thing, Vostok is trying to kill you.' Mohammed's eyes flared through splayed fingers, but he said nothing.

'Your father and I discussed the matter at some length. We concluded that it would be wise to take you away, somewhere where we could give you some protection, and somewhere away from the anti-western influences. Let the situation cool, there just might be a chance the whole speech episode would be forgotten. So that's why you came to England, we thought we could offer you some protection from the Russians assassins.'

'Only thought, you could protect me.' Mohammed chirped in. John was not going to be drawn into discussing the rudiments of MI5 or Special Branch; BISS of course did not exist, so again he ignored the Princes comment.

'That's why I am with you, while you are here in England. I did personally assure your father, the King that I would take care of you.' *Only a little lie.* John thought.

'I know my father is concerned for my safety.' The Prince said. 'He always makes some comment on the subject each time we talk. It was on his insistence that those two baboons should accompany me to England supposedly for my protection.' The Prince shook his head from side to side, feigning mild protest of the arrangement.

'Well they just might prove to be of some use now that Vostok's executioner has arrived in town.'

'When?'

'Last week, the twenty-second to be precise.'

'That's eight days ago, why haven't you arrested him?'

'What for, he hasn't done anything, yet! All we know is that he's checking you out, follows you everywhere, no doubt waiting for the right opportunity.' John was trying to sound relaxed about the whole situation, pausing for effect, letting the gravity of the matter sink in. Mohammed was just about to offer a response when John started up again.

'That isn't all, this affair you are having with the Princess of Wight is ruffling some very high placed feathers. There is reluctance in certain quarters to stop this Russian fellow completing his task. If the newspapers were to get wind of the affair, I dare say there will be those who will offer him some assistance.' The seriousness of the situation had immediate effect, Mohammed tight lipped and head bowed, slowly lifted his eyes to meet Johns.

'We love each other John, if I must die then it is Allah's will for I cannot live without her.'

'No need to bring Allah into it, I have an idea which will give us some breathing space and a chance to work it all out.'

'I put myself in your hands.'

'Good, this is what we'll do. First, send all of your entourage packing with the exception of your manservant and I suppose you'd better hang onto the bee-gees. Then order your Lear jet to be fuelled and ready to leave Friday morning. We will file the flight plan just before take off.'

'Tomorrow'! John nodded. 'To where?'

'Nice, we're going to spend a few weeks on your fathers yacht, cruising the Med, they say the casino at Monte Carlo is a must see.'

Mohammed's eyes brightened at the thought. 'But what about Alice?'

'Look Mohammed, while you're here Princess Alice is being confined in Kensington Palace, a virtual prisoner. Maybe a couple of days after we leave, she will be allowed some freedom. Then you can send for her, if that's what you want. For now it is imperative that no one knows your whereabouts that includes Princess Alice and your farther, also you will avoid the calls from those Muslim extremists.'

Late afternoon the next day, the Princes small party arrived in St Tropez by helicopter from Nice airport. A limousine conveyed the party from the heli-pad to the quay.

The yacht was quite impressive, although John was expecting something much grander; being a 'Royal Yacht' and all, but still she was 125ft long, coloured dark blue on the shell to the main deck, the upper structure comprising of two decks, boat deck and bridge were white with a gold embossed crown above the nameplate at mid-ships, her name, the Golden Crown.

She was secured forward with lines to anchored buoys, and spring lines to bollards, mooring her stern on to the quay. The gangway was in position, flanked shore side by the crew of eight, all wearing blue polo shirts with a golden crown embroidered on the breast pocket. The Captain was a Syrian, the engineer Greek and the six deck hands were all Indian.

'Welcome aboard your Highness,' the Captain said, not sure if he should bow or shake hands, he settled for a rather half-hearted sloppy salute. 'If I might lead the way your Highness I will give you a tour of the ship and show you to your quarters.'

For his arrival Prince Mohammed had changed back into his Arab clothes, white throbe, white silk kertifi with a braided black headband, and black cloak trimmed with gold thread, at his waist he wore a jewelled dagger. He had rightly thought his appearance would project an air of authority. Not only that, but he stood out from the crowd. It would not be long before the whole of St Tropez would know that there was an Arab Prince in town. No doubt the reporter for the local rag was already sharpening his pencil.

When John met the Prince in the saloon, he had changed into typical British attire, brown cords with an Arran sweater. 'I think we had better make plans to move Mohammed before the world and his dog find out where you are.'

'Agreed John, where shall we go?'

'Tell the Captain to set a course for Nice.' Rahjad appeared from the galley carrying a large silver tray, and began to set out the first course of dinner on the table.

Mohammed lifted the intercom, gave the order to sail within the hour, he turned back to John. 'Let's eat, shall we.'

John and the Prince took their place around the table and began a leisurely dinner, while the crew scampered around the decks pulling at various ropes and things.

'Pity, I would have liked to have seen more of St Tropez.' Mohammed said, not looking up from dissecting his steak, with the throb of the diesel engines and the noticeable sway of the craft, it was apparent that the ship was underway. By the time they had finished dinner the ship was well out to sea the faint lights along the French 'Cote d' Azur' disappeared then re-appeared through the port side windows in the heavy swell of the winter Mediterranean.

'Sure we should be doing this John?'

'Its necessary Mohammed and I think it would be prudent when we get to Nice, to send all of the Indian crew home, possibly with an air ticket, a wage cheque and perhaps a bonus by way of a thank you.'

'Will we be able to sail without a full crew?'

'No problem the ship can virtually run itself, the crew are only required for docking, maintenance and that kind of thing. We'll retain the Engineer to keep the engines turning and the Captain to steer the ship. And besides, I'm ex-navy; if a spare hand is needed I'll be there.'

'Well if that's what you think, then that's what we will do,' with that Mohammed picked up the ship to shore telephone and relayed the message to the Saudi Palace staff. 'Every thing will be in place by noon tomorrow,' he assured John.

The ship docked in Nice during the night; John awoke to the sounds of a city coming to life and the bustle of the crew on the outside decks, trying to look busy. Mohammed and the BG's were heading down the gangway to a waiting limousine, no doubt arranged by his father's staff.

Mohammed returned about two hours later and immediately gathered the crew to make the announcement. About an hour later six smiling Indians boarded a mini-bus for the airport. Golden Crown cast off her lines and headed out to sea again.

CHAPTER 11
THE CRUISE

It had been just short of four weeks since the operation, twenty-five days to be precise. The hand was healing quickly, a fact Steven put down to the frequent dips in the sea and he was now able to get some coordinated movement to the false finger, although he had no feeling there. When not working out, Steven would spend a lot of time on the base shooting range, practising firing with both hands and was becoming proficient with either hand. Another notable attribute, the false knuckle and digit gave him a fist as hard as a ball hammer enabling him to deliver a forcible blow, should the need ever arise.

Steven exercised the false digit almost constantly, wherever he was, which could be a little off putting to anyone not knowing the circumstances. Fortunately Jennifer, a very attractive nurse at the clinic, saw the come on look in his eyes and ignored the provocative finger movements. That was the start of their relationship, a relationship that was becoming more intense as the days went by. This instinctive attraction between them was based purely on lust. Although Steven tried to deny deeper feelings existed, she was filling his every thought. *Is this love?*

Jennifer knew she had fallen head over heels for the guy, but played it cool hiding her feelings, because Steven had made it clear from the start, that he could never commit.

They had decided to take a week out together, sailing Morning Star, Steven's motor yacht, to the Channel Islands. The forecast wasn't good and the sea was lumpy as Morning Star pulled out of the harbour entrance.

'What do yah reckon Jen, shall we risk it?' Steven said from his seat at the helm.

'It's up to you, I'm just happy being here.' She said from the seat next to him.

'Is a bit pointless I suppose, would you be disappointed if we just anchored off Studland?'

Jenifer shrugged her shoulders and flashed a smile. 'Anywhere with you Hun.'

'That's settled then.'

So they abandoned their Guernsey plans in favour of calmer waters in the lee of Old Harry Rock, just off Studland.

Apart from Steven's early morning workout and the necessary trips to the galley for food, they had spent most of the first three days in bed together making love Not wanting to be disturb they had switched off their mobiles and didn't give the outside world another thought.

Steven rolled over on his king size bed; bringing his arm to rest gently on Jenifer's shoulder. She was on her side with her back towards him and knees drawn up, almost in the foetal position. Steven eased his naked body next to hers, snuggling into her slim body feeling the warmth of her soft skin his mind began to fill with sexual thoughts, his pulse quickened and he could feel his heart pounding like a beating drum within his chest.

The body he was nestled into, murmured with a deep sigh, which told Steven the lady was still very much asleep, it was after all only five in the morning. *Control yourself Steven.* He eased himself back, gently moving her long blond hair and settled for giving her a kiss on her exposed neck. Then he slipped out of the bed, leaving the sleeping beauty to her slumber. *Time for a swim, I need to cool my ardour.*

Morning Star was at anchor off Studland in the lee of the Old Harry Rock. The sea state was now good with only a slight swell. Steven wearing a wet suit with short legs and a pair of rubber-wet shoes wandered out onto the aft deck and took in a mouthful of fresh morning air. A few limbering motions to chase away any overnight stiffness before venturing onto the stern bathing platform before and diving into the cold water. He swam out into Poole bay swinging left along the side of a man made reef known as the training bank towards Poole harbour, the swim was about three miles to the harbour entrance. Fortunately the tide was running in, otherwise it would have been almost impossible to swim against the out flowing current, even for a strong swimmer like Steven. On reaching the ferry landing on the Studland side, he set off to jog the four and a half mile back along the road, mostly uphill. As he came down to the beach nearest to Studland Village, he could see Morning Star gently swaying on her anchor lines. He plunge into the water again for the short swim back to the boat.

Once onboard he headed for the master bedroom en-suite bathroom, noting as he went that Jennifer was still fast asleep. Nothing unusual in that, it was only a little after eight, his fitness routine these past four mornings had taken about three hours and as usual Steven decided that he would let her sleep a little longer.

After a quick shower he towelled off in the galley before making a cup of tea for Jen and a cup of coffee for himself. With the towel now wrapped around his waste, he carried them into the master bedroom.

'Come on sleepy head, are you going to stay there all day?' Steven put down her cup of tea on the bedside table.

'Humm, what's the time?'

'Just after nine, I've been up ages.'

'Didn't feel a thing,' she laughed. 'Get back in this bed and do it again.'

Steven needed no further persuasion; sending the towel flying in the general direction of the ensuite, he pulled back the duvet and nestled into Jennifer's warm body. They tried to make the art of love making, spin out as long as possible. But as in all good things they finished, laying side by side quite still and breathing deeply, savouring the moment. Jennifer was the first to move, she rolled over to look at the clock.

'My goodness, just look at the time, it's nearly ten. We almost made that last an hour.' She giggled as she slipped out of bed and headed to the shower. A few minutes later she emerged and put on her dressing gown. Steven was still lying in bed staring at the ceiling.

'I'm starving; I'll go and prepare breakfast. What do you fancy?' Steven smiled a lecherous look in his eye. 'I'm looking at her.' He declared, for which he received a direct hit from a damp towel.

It was decided, following Jenifer's inspection of the galley that certain stocks of fresh food were in need of replenishment. So that afternoon Steven and Jennifer took the inflatable and headed ashore. The intention was to replenish the stocks from Studland village stores, calling at the 'Bankes Arms' for the odd pint on their way. Thirst quenched they walked hand in hand up the hill into the village. It was plain to see that they were enjoying each other's company, laughing and joking as they entered the shop. Jennifer set about selecting foodstuffs. Steven browsed the small selection of newspapers, picked up the 'Bournemouth Evening Echo' initially to check the local weather forecast and the predicted sea state on page two, but instinctively turned his attention to the 'Articles Wanted' section.

That's when he saw the coded message requiring him to make contact.

They walked back down to the beach without speaking passing the 'Bankes Arms' without pausing. Something was wrong, but seeing the determined look on Steven's face, Jennifer considered it prudent not to ask any questions.

He will tell me when he is good and ready.

As soon as Steven boarded Morning Star he made for the cockpit and retrieved his mobile. Switching it on as he settled into the leather chair at the helm and began to send a text. Jennifer sensing his need for privacy had gone down a deck to the galley and started to put away the groceries, at the same time, making a pot of tea.

She returned to the saloon with two mugs, Steven was still sat at the helm and she could see the troubled look on his face.

'Our cruise is over then?' she said, trying to save him the embarrassment of having to concoct a fairy story.

'Perceptive as ever Jen....I'm afraid.... I'm really...really sorry, but duty calls, and all that.'

She didn't question him; she knew there would be no point. They both sat quietly, sipping their tea, periodically looking up from their cup to catch each other's eyes and immediately returning their gaze to the cup, both wanting to avoid further discussion on the matter.

'I'll get you to the village at lunch time tomorrow and arrange for a taxi to take you back home.'

'No need for a taxi, I'll catch the bus.' She said with a nonchalant lift of her shoulders.

CHAPTER 12

MY WAY

The Jaguar took a left turn at Studland, then a right, passing the 'Manor House Hotel' and down the hill towards the 'Bankes Arms.'

'Have you been here before Peter?'

'Yes, some time ago, as I remember the 'Bankes Arms' used to have a good selection of real ale. Could all of changed by now of course.'

'We shall no doubt find out, soon enough.'

Sir Peter smiled as he steered the Jag into a 'National Trust' car park next to the pub. 'This is the only car park, but fortunately it is unmanned this time of year, so I wouldn't envisage any queries as far as overnight parking goes.'

'Sure we are staying here overnight?'

'That's what Steven's text suggests, be at Bankes Arms three pm, with overnight bag, follow when I leave.'

'Well I guess we are.'

It was three- thirty when they arrived at the 'Bankes Arms.

'What would you like to drink Marj?'

'A red wine would be good.'

'A rcd wine and a pint of your real ale, please.' Sir Peter said to the barman, as he surveyed his wallet for a suitable note.

Taking their drinks they headed for a table near to the huge log fire at one end of the room. They noted the without acknowledgment, the handsome dark haired man sitting in the adjacent corner.

Fifteen minutes later the dark haired man got up and left via the front door. Sir Peter and Marjorie, pretending not to notice, drained their glasses, a minute or so later, they also got up and headed for the door.

Steven was waiting where the beach path meets the road. As soon as they had spotted him he set off down the beach track. Marjorie and Sir Peter, cases in hand, followed at a discreet distance.

The daylight was fading fast, just a little after four. The low winter sun was already lost behind the trees and the heavily wooded path was getting dark and quite eerie. By the time they had gone about fifty yards, Marjorie was feeling trepidations. Little wonder that she gave out an audible gasp when Steven appeared from out of the shadows.

'Sorry Marjorie, didn't mean to frighten you...It is getting dark.'

'Yeah we're late, the ferry isn't running, had to come the long way round.' Sir Peter said.

'The beach is deserted this time of the year,' Steven said, as he preceded them onto the beach and began to push the inflatable into the water, 'best take off your shoes and socks the water isn't cold.'

An understatement, but nevertheless Marjorie and Sir Peter did as they were bid without one word of remonstration.

Morning Star was gently swaying on her anchor line about two hundred yards offshore, nothing else was said until they were onboard.

'Welcome aboard.' Steven said as he helped each in turn to alight from the inflatable.

'Hi Steven, how's the hand doing?'

'Healing very well sir, I've almost recovered full use, a few more days should see me right as rain.'

'Good to hear it, but that wound looks to have been much worse than you led me to believe.... Isn't that a false finger?'

'Yes.' Steven said, holding up the digit for inspection.

'Titanium....Hell of a weapon.'

'I don't doubt.' Sir Peter said pursing his lips, slowly shook his head and tut tuttered, as if he was about to scold a naughty child.

'A very expensive finger at that sir must have cost Colonel Bradley a packet.' Steven said in jocular fashion, a broad grin exposing his brilliant white teeth. Then he immediately changed the subject.

'I've put you and Marjorie in the forward VIP cabin, this way.' Their bags in his hands, he led the way down the staircase.

'Wow!' Marjorie said as she stepped inside.

'Make yourselves at home, freshen up if you wish, there are towels in your bathroom. I'm about to put the kettle on, anyone fancy a brew?'

There was a spontaneous. 'Yes please.'

They were sitting around the dining table in the deck saloon, having eaten a very nice meal and were having a general conversation over a glass of red Zinfandel. Steven knew the reason they were here would surface when Sir Peter was good and ready, so he didn't push it. The moment came when, without comment Sir Peter reached down into his brief case and withdrew an unmarked file which he dropped onto the table. 'Your next assignment Steven.....This is everything we have on record, a fair bit of reading I'm afraid, but it would probably be as well for you to get through it now, give us a chance to discuss the situation tonight.'

'Humm.' Steven hesitated momentarily and was met by Sir Peter's glare, so he picked up the file and headed forward. 'Help yourself to wine, this will take me a little time.' He said over his shoulder.

Forty minutes later Steven returned to the deck saloon and dropped the file back onto the table in front of Sir Peter.
'A volatile situation, how would you like me to help?'
'Before I go any further I must warn you what I'm about to propose is a delicate matter and one that will not have any involvement by BISS or any hint whatsoever of British involvement. Do I make myself clear?'
'As crystal sir.'
'Good, let's get down to it.'
Sir Peter opened the file. 'We will start with the latest on Abramovich, the likely assassin. He took off the other day to Zurich.'
'Why there? Surely he doesn't think the Prince is there.'
'I doubt it Steven, at this juncture I don't think he gives a toss where Prince Mohammed is, or why, but we'll get to that later.'
Marjorie pulled a photograph from out of her bag. 'Time to mention this character,' lightly tapping the print as she placed in on the table. 'His name is Hiendric Kunze, said at one time

to be one of the richest men in Europe. Strangely, later records don't seem to exist; however, we do know that he is still a Swiss Banker. He runs a huge financial empire from his office in the very first bank started by his great grandfather, in all places, Zurich.'

'And you think there is a connection between Abramovich and Kunze?'

'Not quite', Sir Peter put in. 'From the file you will note, a group of ten rich men gathered in the UK and we believe, elected to have Mohammed eliminated. The sum of twenty million pounds was mentioned. Although these men are not named in the file, other than Forbes and Fairchild that is, we are fairly certain who they are.

They names are of no real significance to us, at this juncture, except for Hiendric Kunze, who we believe has been given of the task of collecting twenty-million.'

'Abramovich is after money.'

'Well, yes in my opinion, but at this stage, I've no idea how; perhaps you ought to keep that in mind.'

Sir Peter got to his feet and adopted his usual thinking stance, head bowed, hands clasped behind and began to pace out the saloon floor. 'The way I see it, Giles Fairchild is without doubt one of the member's and I'm convinced he is also Vostok's man. He probably instigated the hit knowing he had an assassin waiting in the wings. It would have worked well. Vostok gets the Prince assassinated in England whilst under British protection, points the finger at British security and bang goes our credibility, along with the Saudi oil. Then Fairchild collects the eighteen million, which incidentally he needs, its not public knowledge yet, but his financial empire is about to go bottoms up.' Sir Peter spun around and looked directly at Steven. 'What bothered me about the whole scenario is that Abramovich has not made any attempt at the hit. Why wait?' Sir Peter was asking himself, rather than opening the question for debate. 'I think Abramovich was told to hang fire, until Fairchild could get a hold of the cash and we know Fairchild doesn't have it yet.' Sir Peter turned to Marjorie. 'How long do you reckon it would take to pull that amount of cash together, Marj?'

'All depends; I assume we are talking black money. Someone of Hiendric Kunze's genius with things financial would be able to access many accounts, routing monies around the world in and out of bogus accounts, before landing it in one nest, I would say a week maybe two.'

'Thank you Marj....We are aware that Fairchild handed Abramovich an envelope before he left, we think that contained some sort of reference or code necessary to recover the money from the bank in Zurich.'

'Makes sense, Kunze would know Faichild, so he sends Abramovich.'

'Got it in one Steven, at least that's the way I see it.'

'What if Abramovich decides to hang onto the cash, after all he is a gangster.'

'Your guess is as good as mine, but I would imagine the same thought would have crossed Vostok's as well Fairchild's mind.'

The atmosphere became very relaxed; the conversation had gone away from discussing the mission to lighter general topics.

 Steven thought it would be best, if he did not mention Jennifer. He also had a gut feeling that Sir Peter was not telling him everything. *He can be a devious old bugger; what's he holding back and why?*

'I've noticed Steven that you haven't got the full use of that finger, have you?'

'No sir, not quite, but it's coming along nicely, gets better every day.'

'Umm the hand is still very swollen.' Sir Peter was now looking intently at Steven's damaged limb.

'That's partly down to the oversized titanium ball and socket which replaces the knuckle joint.'

'You sure you're fit enough for active service?'

'Yes sir.'

Then Sir Peter casually steered the conversation back to the mission.

'Tell me Steven, how feasible would it be for you to spend Christmas in the Mediterranean, with Morning Star of course?'

Steven looked a little surprised, using his own boat, registered in his real name that would never have been considered on any previous covert operation.

'In connection with the operation?' Steven exclaimed. 'Yes Steven.'

'A little unusual for an undercover operation, isn't it, the boat is registered in my real name?'

'If this operation is a success, it may prove to be an advantage, just an Englishman abroad enjoying a holiday, rather than somebody abroad with a false identity.'

'Fair enough sir, if that's the way you see it.'

'I do Steven, I do.'

Steven rubbed his chin. 'Let me get this straight, you want me to sail Morning Star to the Med?'

Sir Peter nodded. 'That's the general idea.'

'I suppose I could cross the channel into France, using the canal and river network, make my way down to the Mediterranean....But I'm not sure if the bridges will be high enough and some waters freeze up at.....'

'I was thinking of something a little less high profile.'

Steven was taken aback. 'You mean the sea route?'

'More discrete wouldn't you say.'

'Could take an age, the Bay of Biscay can be pretty rough at the best of times, then there's the fuel....'

'I'm sure you'll manage....Don't worry about the cost, we can help you with that. Assuming it was feasible, how long would it take you, to get to Monaco, say ...approximately?'

Steven looked at the chart again, tracing his finger along the French, Portuguese and Spanish coast lines, figuring likely refuelling stops. 'Quick turnaround, good weather, and very little sleep, I would say about ten days.'

Marjorie delved once more into her trusty bag.

'We have pre-empted you a little Steven and have deposited five hundred-thousand Euros in Mr Kunze's bank, Zurich branch of course. Thought you might need a reason when you look the place over. It's a numbered account, internet access; your password is spider001, of course.' She handed Steven a note with fourteen random numbers. 'Best if you memorise them dear and destroy the note, no connection with us, you understand. Here is your visa card, should you require credit or money from a cash point, the bank have instructions to keep the current account topped up at ten thousand Euros, while your funds last, that is. That's about it Steven, except for this.' Marjorie handed Steven another note. 'It's the telephone number of the Zurich branch, should you need it, again memorise and burn, try not to get then mixed up dear.'

A broad grin spread across Steven's face.

Sir Peter, who had been quiet for a while, now adopted his thinking position again and began to speak. 'Getting back to taking Morning Star down to the Med. If you are going to take ten days, you will need to leave here no later than the day after tomorrow, if you are going to make Monaco by the seventeenth, wouldn't you say?'

'I guess.' Steven said sounding a little perplexed.

'Perfect I'll inform John Godfrey, get him to set things up.'

Steven didn't know what John Godfrey was setting up or why, but he knew he couldn't bump into the guy who thinks he's Charles Evans.

'What has me taking Morning Star to Monaco, got to do with John Godfrey?'

'Oh yes, haven't mentioned that, have I. Well that's where the Arab is now, spending a little time with John onboard the Saudi Royal yacht, it's all set out in the other file.'

'What file?'

Sir Peter looked at Marjorie; she was already in the process of taking an envelope from her bag, which she slid across the table. Sir Peter opened it and took out two photographs.

'Golden Crown,' he said, tapping the pictures, the Saudi Royal Yacht, taken in St Tropez, but by the time you meet up with her she'll be in Monaco.'

'And John?'

'On his way home, I would think.'

Steven read the situation, the Arab Prince was being used as bait to attract Vostok's assassin, where no doubt he would take him out. *All very elaborate.*

Noting how Golden Crown was berthed at St Tropez, Steven added. 'If I'm to keep the Prince alive, I would suggest she anchors a good half mile offshore.' He didn't perceive the sideways look at Marjorie before Sir Peter replied. 'I'll be done Steven, just as you want it.'

Still thinking along the lines of protection Seven continued.

'And perhaps it would be better to leave Morning Star further down the coast....Take a hotel room, from where I can keep an eye on things.'

'Hmm, well yes I suppose, but that would be up to you, your prerogative.'

'Do you know her complement?'

Marjorie answered. 'At the moment she carries an all year round crew of eight, plus the two bodyguards, the Prince's manservant, Prince Mohammed and John himself, making a full complement of thirteen.'

'Lucky for some.' Steven said.

'However,' Marjorie continued. 'John has persuaded the Prince to let six of the crew go.'

'Well I suppose he has good reason.'

The next morning was relaxed, the pending mission was not mentioned, that was until Sir Peter and Marjorie were about to leave.

'I'm going to leave you this.' Sir Peter said as he withdrew a sealed envelope from his brief case. 'It contains your specific instructions.' Steven looked puzzled. 'I thought we'd covered that.'

Sir Peter shook his head as he pressed the envelope into Steven's hand. 'I want you to read and digest the information after Marj and I have left.' Sir Peter looked at Steven with a sombre expression. 'You are completely on your own on this one; how you play it is down to you, your prerogative.' Then he added in a serious voice. 'When read I expect you to destroy it, no trace, you understand Steven?'

'Understood.'

Steven flopped onto the saloon couch paper knife in hand which he inserted into the envelope flap. Extracting two sheets of paper, he read the first which set out a number of anticipated circumstances and the possible scenarios. 'Didn't make much sense,' he thought, so he turned his attention to the second sheet headed 'Operation Objectives,' they were short and specific and as he read, a feeling of despair filled his mind. The paper sheets slipped from his hand dropping lightly onto his chest, and the shock of what he'd been asked to do, registered like a kick in the crutch.

'Bloody hell! No way! You, you conniving old bastard,' Steven shouted as the sound of his voice echoed around the emptiness of the boat. And for the first time in his service career he did not want to undertake the mission.

Jumping up off the settee, he balled up the sheets of paper and threw them, with all the anger and frustration he could muster. 'No! No! No! Dam you, you bastard; find someone else to do your dirty work.' He paced quickly up and down the saloon trying to stamp out the anger. Finally he flopped into the leather helm chair and stared blankly through the screen. After some time his anger subsided, he didn't how long he'd been sitting there, but it was dark and he was transfixed at his own sombre image reflecting back from the blackness of the windscreen. *I've got to analyse the situation, there must be another way.* He sat there just staring his mind blank again, sub consciously refusing to get involved. Then it suddenly seemed apparent, he did have an option.

'Okay Sir 'bloody' Peter Thompson-Smythe.

My prerogative, MY WAY!'

Steven pulled the inflatable up the beach at Allum Chine trusting it would still be there when he returned. He then set off to jog along the road to Westbourne, eventually stopping outside the Clinic.

He put his hands on his knees and stood in that prone position until his heavy breathing eased.

Good I'm in time.

'What on earth....'

'Hi Jen,' Steven said, flashing the white teeth and the irresistible smile, 'thought you'd be here.'

Before she could respond another member of the Clinics staff approached. 'Hello Mr Pinder, I'm afraid the Clinic is closed. If you are having problems, you'll have to go to the Hospital.'

'Oh I....'

'It's alright Miss Jones, I'll sort it....If you want to take off, I'll lock up.'

'You're sure?' Jennifer nodded back. 'Okay then. Goodnight Nurse Walsh, Mr Pinder.'

Steven held his breath until he heard the Miss Jones exit and the door close.

'Just who do you think you are and what right do you have to come here....and... and what's more how did you know I was here.' She spun around so that her back was toward him, and folded her arms, feigning anger, but in truth, the smile she was trying so hard to suppress began to surface and she stared at the wall opposite not wanting Steven to notice.

Steven leaned in, lightly kissed the nape of her neck and whispered. 'Love you Jen.'

That did it, she spun back round. 'I know you, what is it you want?'

'Only you Jen.'

She was now smiling. 'Pull the other one, you're up to something.'

'In truth Jen, I need your help.' The pleading look was enough.

'Knew it.'

Seriously Jen...I love you, but I have this mission....I can't do alone.'

'Such as?'

Steven didn't tell her everything, but what he did divulge was a flowered version of an attempt to kidnap a Saudi Prince.

'You do realise if I come with you now, I'll loose my job.'

Steven nodded. 'It may be sometime before we come back, you may not want to.....'

'What about you, the Marines....'

'You know, I'm not really a Marine.'

'Sure I do, did you think I hadn't guessed. Your secret meetings, bullet wounds, on and off duty as you please. The operation on your hand, that's something else. You my dear have got to be one very special person indeed to have received such treatment.' She paused more for effect. 'I was merely wondering if you'd be missed.'

'All taken care of, anyway I intend to make this my final mission, get married settle down...If you'll have me that is.'

'Is that a proposal?'

'I guess it is.'

She nodded a nonchalant expression on her face. 'Okay then, I accept.' They laughed and kissed.

'One more thing before we leave, I need you to borrow some of that gas the anaesthetist uses to knock out the patient. I'll have Sir Peter replace it before it's missed.'

'Sorry no can do.'

'But a telephone call in the morning and it will be replaced,'

'It's not that, the gas is kept in a secure place and I don't have the access code.'

'Damn! Sorry Jen, I was kind of counting on that.'

They looked at each other in silence for a long moment.   Steven shook his head from side to side. 'There's no plan B Jen, got to knock him out somehow.'

'We do have bottles of Chloroform, purely as a stand by, would that be of any use?'

A smile widened across his face and broke into a broad grin that flashed his white teeth again. 'You little beauty you bet it would.'

'We keep it in the dispensary, for which I do have a key.'

Jennifer ensured that the clinic was all locked and the security alarm was on.

'How long before this is missed?' Steven said as she handed him a 250ml bottle of Chloroform.

'Not for some time, it's from a new batch of replaced stock; it's only there for emergency use.'

'I'll get my boss to organize its replacement as soon as.'

Jennifer had placed a letter on the clinic manager's desk, saying she had been called away on urgent business and would use up her holiday entitlement for the time she would be away. She never gave a thought to how long that would be or even if she would ever return.

At 5am on the morning of the 7th December, Morning Star shipped her anchor. With her two Volvo D12 diesel engines springing to life, she nosed out from the lee of Old Harry into Poole Bay channel, passing Swanage, off the starboard side and out into the English Channel. Steven set a course for the Channel Islands, being the first leg of their journey to the Mediterranean Sea.

CHAPTER 13
MONTE-CARLO

The Prince had deliberately put off giving the Captain a destination until the ship had cleared the harbour. Not long after leaving Nice the Golden Crown was tying up along side a pier in Monaco.

'John I'm desperate to call Alice, do you any objection?'

'Who am I to stand in your way, you are fully aware of my views on the matter and you know the consequence of continuing your relationship with the Princess.' John hunched up his shoulders suggesting complacency, 'I can only advise you against such a liaison, whatever you do is your choice.'

John had hardly got the last word out before Mohammed had picked up the telephone.

'No doubt you'll need a little privacy, I'll be in my room should you want me.' John headed up the stairway and along the upper deck companion way to his stateroom, as he went he took out of his pocket a small receiver and placed it into his ear. The wire ran down the inside of his coat to a piece of equipment the size of a 20 pack of cigarettes. He had placed a bug in the on board telephone and was intent on listening to Mohammed's conversation. Unbeknown to John, BG1 appeared behind him.

Since being on this damned boat the Englishman had an upper deck stateroom next to the Prince's stateroom, while he and his partner were in the cramped lower deck cabin next door to the engines and that incessant generator.

BG1resented John and the position of trust he held, often overplaying his authority with unnecessary body searches in an attempt to humiliate him.

Time for me to grope you English.

The big Egyptian Bodyguard quickened his pace, but John, still oblivious to the fact that he was being pursued, entered his room closed and automatically locked the door.

The Bodyguard was just a fraction too late, and experienced the indignity of the door being slammed in his face.

John sat on the edge of his bed listening intently to Mohammed's conversation with Princess Alice. *'Hardly surprising,'* John thought as he heard them express their love for each other. Her movements were still being restricted, although there were signs that that was easing. She was allowed to spend more time with her son, but she was accompanied all the time. From out of the corner of his eye, John saw the handle on the cabin door slowly moving. Someone was trying get in, definitely not the Prince he was still on the telephone and he didn't trust anyone else on board. Click then a discernable push, another click as the handle was slowly released and returned to its original position, this was followed with a knock, from a heavy hand.

'Yes,' John shouted, no reply, another knocking this time heavier and louder.

'Who's there?' Still no reply, the knocking became continuous and louder. John turned the key and shouted angrily through the open door.

'What the h---!'

He was cut short as the shape of BG1 filled the doorframe; he was holding a gun in his left hand, which was now aimed in John's direction. John froze, mind blank, staring fearfully at the weapon. In that instance and before John could recover his senses, the palm of the BG's right hand caught John squarely on the chest sending him crashing back into the wardrobe door. John was a deskman not a super fit field agent, but when you work for Sir Peter Thompson-Smythe, you have to achieve a certain level of skill in the martial arts. Memories of these skills, unused for so many years, flashed through John's mind, probably brought on by anger and the surge of adrenalin coursing through his veins.

The wind was knocked out of him; John was hurt, but not as badly as his agonising cry made out. BG1, a smile on his face, lowered his weapon and swaggered toward the slumping body of the Englishman. In one movement, with perfect timing, John threw his head forward, his forehead impacting on the bridge of the BGs hooked nose. BG 1 staggered back in surprise, but before he could react, John swung his right leg with force, the tanned leather of his Oxford brogues making full and hard contact with the Egyptian's testicles. The kick was instantly followed by another, this one just below BG's left knee. In the same movement John's protruded knuckles of his left hand stabbed out landing a blow on the windpipe, his right arm automatically shot out to block the gun, which BG was instinctively bringing up. The big Egyptian reeled, but didn't appear to be too affected by John's onslaught. He was tough, no doubt about that, but he was slow and cumbersome. His reaction was to pull the trigger of the gun which John was now pushing away, firing it twice; the bullets were embedded into the cabin wall. He sent a swinging right aimed at John's head.

John caught the blow behind the ear, landed with the inside of the Egyptians arm. That only served to give more impetus as John spun his body under blow grabbing a handful of BGs collar with his left hand and the wrist of the gun hand with his right.

He ed twisted his body under the Egyptians, sticking his bottom into the top of the legs. Continuing the flowing movement, he dropped to his knees and pulled down as hard as he could. It was a classic judo throw, executed perfectly; the Egyptian's weight added to the momentum as he flew through the air and landed heavily against the bulkhead smashing the wall mounted flat screen television with his flaying size twelve's. The gun was thrown off across the room, disappearing somewhere on the other side of the bed.

This was one tough cookie, John thought, *can't allow him to get up.*

As BG 1 turned onto all fours in an effort to get to his feet, John took a running kick at his head, the leather brogue connected with force in the region of BG1's mouth and jaw.

'What's going on?' In the doorway stood Prince Mohammed, at his side BG 2 with gun drawn, who immediately stepped forward and pressed the barrel into John's temple. John limply raised his hands to just above his shoulders turning his head, as much as he could and his eyes to look at Mohammed. As the Prince came into focus, he saw that the Captain and the Engineer were now stood in the doorway, both bobbing up and down like demented puppets trying to get a better view of the proceedings. The Prince still waiting for an answer, raised his right arm pushing BG2's outstretched arm and gun into the air, much to John's relief.

John, panting replied. 'You'd huh, better huh, ask this huh, son of a bitch, you're huh, highness.'

The Prince then looked at the still prostrate BG 1, who was moaning and groaning and bleeding profusely from several facial areas. Mumbling something in Arabic and shaking his head from side to side. BG 2 headed into John's en-suite, returning a moment later with a wet towel and began to attend his colleague's wounds. The Prince moved closer to the BG's and began to speak in Arabic. It was then that John realised that the BG's did not speak English and he of course did not let them know he could converse in Arabic.

The Captain and Engineer had concluded that the excitement was over and had disappeared.

After a few minutes deliberation, the Prince turned to John, 'Abdul says that you are a British spy who has been sent to kill me. That's why we are here, away from England and why you have persuaded me to get rid of the crew.'

'Oh yeah, well he's the one with the gun.'

'He tells me, that you listen to my telephone conversations.'

John having regained his composure replied. 'Load of nonsense, why on earth should I want to listen to your telephone calls.'

A sideways look from the Prince and BG 2 reached into John's pocket and removed what looked like an ordinary cassette recorder. He pressed rewind and then play. A broad smile cut across Prince Mohammed's face as the sound of the Bee Gee's singing 'Staying Alive' echoed from the machine. John held out his hands, palms up and made an innocent face to Mohammed. 'Happy now.'

The Prince was so convinced that the Bodyguard had screwed up, apologised most sincerely to John and threatened both Bodyguards with instant dismissal if such a thing were to happen again to any of his guests.

In an effort to forget this incident and as some form of appeasement, the Prince suggested a visit to Monte Carlos casino would be in order. He hoped this would repair the damage and restore his friendship with John. No one, thank goodness, had bothered to check the telephone for the bug. *Must remember to remove it before I leave.*

Sometime later Mohammed telephoned his father and relayed the terrible event, but declined the offer of a replacement bodyguard. That would have meant giving away his location, and he had no intention of returning home just yet. He was still fearful of being pestered by anti American extremist, of which there are many in Saudi Arabia. At least that was that was what he was telling his father, but he had an ulterior motive involving a continuing relationship with Princess Alice.

John removed the receiver from his ear, locking it and the recorder in the desk drawer. And then continued to get changed into his tuxedo, ready for a night on the town.

While John was in the casino he took the advantage of there being only one bodyguard to look after the Prince. Knowing that BG 2 would not leave Mohammed's side, he made the excuse of going to spend a penny, but instead headed to the telephones.

So far, so good, all was proceeding according to plan.

The next morning, John did some exercises on deck, mainly to pacify the ache in his muscles, a result of yesterday's fracas, muscles that had been unused for such a long time.

He noted BG 2 was still on duty. *Poor sod's pulled BG 1's shift, as well as his own, he must be shattered.*

Prince Mohammed was in the saloon when John walked in.

'Good morning John.'

'Morning Mohammed.'

'How are you today?' The Prince asked in a quizzing manner.

'After the incident yesterday, do you mean?' Mohammed nodded. 'Well I'm feeling a little stiff here and there, but I'm in no doubt better shape than your bodyguard.' Mohammed again nodded his head in agreement.

'And last night, did you enjoy yourself?'

'Yes I had a great time; I didn't loose a lot.'

'Err, John.'

'Yes Mohammed.'

'I've been thinking.'

'And.' John knew exactly what was coming.

'I want to bring Alice here now; I am not prepared to wait any longer.'

'Your prerogative Mohammed, but as we discussed she is very high profile. The moment she arrives here you run a very big risk of your affair being exposed and all the repercussions that would entail. Once the press gets a whiff of a scandal, they would descend on The Golden Crown like wasps around a jam pot. Then the extremist will know where you are and not least so will Vostok's hit man.'

'I've considered all of the issue's and I am prepared to run the risk just to have her here.'

'Yes, but is Princess Alice prepared to take the risk, knowing the consequences of divorce from the future King of England.'

'Perhaps I am being selfish, but life without her is becoming unbearable. I'm sure she feels exactly the same way.'

'Okay if that's what you want....You do realise that I can't be here when she arrives. It mustn't be construed that the British diplomatic service condones this association.'

'Sure John, I understand.'

John hesitated making it look as if he was giving the matter a great deal of thought. 'If the Princess is coming, I think we had better ensure that she, and you for that matter, have maximum protection.' He rubbed his chin as if further pondering the matter. 'Only one fit bodyguard, my fault I fear.'

'Yes, the Captain took Abdul to the hospital last night while we were at the casino, he'll be out of action for a few days, five stitches in a cut above the eye, broken nose, split lip, bruising around the larynx and big purple coloured bollocks. He's having trouble walking and talking.' Mohammed couldn't help smiling as he relayed the bodyguard's incapacitation.

'Tough, if that bastard had had his way, I would probably be on a slab in some morgue, or at least sampling hospital food, I was lucky, I got in first.'

'Abdul over stepped the mark, but as things are I could do with him around.'

'I know that's what I'm trying to discuss. In your situation you need security right now, not in a few days time when your bodyguard is feeling better. That's why I am offering my services as a security advisor and protector until BG1 is back on duty.'

'Most gracious of you.'

'Firstly, and most importantly, we should get this boat moved away from the quay and the harbour, out of reach of the paparazzi and any lurking Russian assassin.'

'Makes sense, I suppose.'

'If we put 'The Golden Crown' at anchor in the outer harbour it will make it more difficult for the perpetrators telescopic lenses, or the telescopic site of a snipers rifle.' At that Mohammed looked visibly shaken.

They sat for a few moments deep in thought, Mohammed, as John thought, was thinking though the security situation, but how wrong he was.

'Was Abdul right, are you going to kill me John?'

John was somewhat taken aback by Mohammed question which seemingly came from out of the blue and there was a stunned silence before he looked Mohammed squarely in the eyes.

'No Mohammed, I don't kill people, I've never killed anybody, I don't even carry a weapon.'

'But the way you handled Abdul.'

'I've told you Mohammed, he thought he was going to push his way into my cabin and knock the shit out of me. The last thing he expected was for me to retaliate. I learnt some martial arts, years ago in the Navy.....Funny how you don't forget things,' John mused, 'like riding a bike.'

'Say no more, we shall do as you say and move the ship.' Mohammed reached for the intercom and relayed the instructions to the Captain on the bridge.

As the engines kicked into life, John was on the quay casting off fore and aft, and onto the main deck to winch in the gangway. When the Golden Crown was underway, John headed back to the saloon in time for Rahjad to serve breakfast.

'Very useful to have around,' Mohammed said.

'I try Mohammed, I try.'

Later that day Mohammed telephoned Princess Alice. John sat on the edge of his bed, with the earpiece in place.

'Hi, how are you?'

'Hello darling, a lot better thanks. Apparently as long as I keep up the appearance of the loving wife and mother, the firm is happy and I'm even allowed some freedom, particularly since you disappeared. Enough about me, tell me what you've been up to?'

'Not much of interest Al, we went to the casino yesterday, I had a little win but I didn't particularly enjoy the evening.'

'Why, what was wrong?'

'Oh nothing really, it's just me I don't seem to be able relax, I have this one singular thought and that's to get you here with me.'

John could guess what she would say, so he disconnected and locked the equipment away in the draw. *Think I'll surprise him, if only to show I'm not listening.*

John wandered into the lounge, Mohammed, as he knew he would be, was on the sofa with the telephone stuck to his ear.

'Oh sorry, didn't realise you were on the phone.' John said timidly turning as he spoke as if about to go back out. Mohammed waved frantically indicating that he should stay.

'Alice, you've got to get away, come to me, please think of what I have said. My 'Lear jet' is on stand by waiting for you at London Airport.'

'Love you.'

Mohammed replaced the receiver. 'She will come John, at the first opportunity.'

'That's good; I'm pleased for the both of you.....Unofficially of course.'

John had appointed himself daytime security and personal protector, as well as a companion escorting the Prince on his frequent visits to the casino. This gave the only bodyguard the opportunity to catch up on some well-needed shuteye. The other bodyguard, BG1, was still recovering from the beating John had given him, but he was getting better, it wouldn't be long before he could resume his duties.

John concentrated, as far as Prince Mohammed was aware, on not allowing any exposure to an assassin's bullet. Pretty hard really, but John with his analytical mind had carefully noted all the logical points along the shore line and of course other boats, from where a sniper could operate. So he tended to shuffle the Prince about the ship, out of any possible line of sight and when they went ashore, John positioned himself always to shield. A point that didn't go unnoticed by the Prince.

The Golden Crown lay at anchor outside Monaco harbour, about half a mile offshore, due east of the Monte Carlo casino. The Captain was constantly surveying weather reports for any change, which would send the ship back to the sanctuary of the harbour, but the sea state was relatively good for this time of year.

It was now the 10th December six days after their arrival in Monaco.

Sir Peter had specifically requested that the Prince should be encouraged to stay in Monaco until the 17th, why, John had no idea, but he had the feeling, that that could prove as hard as stopping a snipers bullet. Unless... *She was to join him.*

'It's been four days since I had the fight with your bodyguard Mohammed, and I really think it's about time he started to pull his weight.... He must be fit enough by now.'

'Couldn't agree more John, why don't you go and tell him to get back to work.'

'Me!'

'Yes, why not, it'll give you the chance to patch things up with him.'

Reluctantly John agreed. *Wonder if I can get BG2 to have a word.*

With this in mind headed below decks to talk to BG2. He partly wished now that he'd used the intercom like he normally did, but instead he had to go 'sticky beaking' where the hired help hang out. He could hear them talking in Arabic as he came through the engine room. They were talking quite loudly over the constant hum of the generators and their cabin door was partly ajar. BG1 in his usual obnoxious manner was making his feelings felt, and John, of course was the subject.

'I tell you my friend the English pig is up to something, I'm sure he intends to kill the Prince and us no doubt.'

'I don't agree Abdul, he's been working hard to protect the Prince and without his help these past days I could not have managed.'

'Listen to me my friend, what are we doing here, eh? I tell you, the Englishman wants us here.' There was a pause and a sound of movement, John held his breath and pushed his back against the bulkhead. The cabin door flew open and BG1 stuck out his purple-patched bruised face.

'You spooked or something Abdul,' BG2's voice came from inside of the cabin.

'For a moment, I thought I could smell him.'

BG1 stepped back inside and closed the door. John without hesitation tiptoed up to door and placed his ear against it.

'I don't trust him Tariq the cat plays with the mouse before he bites off the head. The Englishman now plays with us....I feel it. He is keeping us here for a reason, perhaps to kill us one by one.'

'I tell you Abdul you are becoming paranoid, the Englishman has no weapons and just how do you think he will kill us?'

'I don't know how, but I do know he's up to something and I don't intend waiting to find out. When I get the chance, that son of a pig is going to get stuck and fed to the fishes.'

John had heard enough and he made his way back to his Stateroom on the upper deck level. 'Damn! That's all I need, what the hell do I do now?'

That evening one of the lifeboats was lowered, and brought around to the lowered gangway. The small party going ashore consisted of the Prince accompanied by John and protected by BG2. The boat was piloted by the Greek Engineer.

A limousine was waiting on the quay. The chauffeur jumped out as the party approached and held open the rear door for the Prince and John. BG2 after furtively checking around, right hand tucked inside the breast of his coat, holding his wallet no doubt, got into the front. As the car wound its way up from the quay and onto the 'Avenue d'Ostende' John could see the lights of the Golden Crown in the bay and could just make out the navigation lights of the life-boat, come tender making its way back to the ship.

I wonder what that tow rag BG1 is up to now. I wouldn't mind betting he's searching my cabin, or maybe putting cyanide in my toothpaste.' He snapped out of his trance on hearing Mohammed. 'Here we are again, at the casino.'

Mohammed's voice was a flat drawl, the excitement of a few days ago, had given way to one of monotonous routine. John realised that he would have to do something about the situation; otherwise he would have little chance of convincing Mohammed that they needed to stay here a little longer.

As the party entered the casino main hall, Mohammed's mood instantly changed; his eyes became fixed on the spin of the roulette wheel. *He's obviously got the bug.* John took the opportunity of Mohammed's fixation to slope off to the telephone.

Sir Peter's voice was reassuring.

'Okay John I'll see what I can do, in the meantime might I suggest that you book into the hotel for a couple of nights, get your land legs back. Spend some time seeing the sights, visiting the likes of Nice and Cannes. I'm sure the Prince would like that. May help to take his mind off the Princess and it will get you away from that nasty bodyguard.'

'Thank you sir.'

John's suggestion of hotel accommodation was accepted without question, he could almost see the sparkle return to Mohammed's eyes.

They had spent two days touring the area, but now on John's insistence, were back in the Monte Carlo hotel preparing to return to the ship.

'Why do we have to go back to the ship?' as question that John was finding difficult to answer. He could hardly say that that was his instruction, so he tried to stall. 'Because.' He said.

'Because what John?'

'I assure you this ......'

Saved by the bell you might say when Mohammed's mobile buzzed. The Prince put the appliance to his ear and turned his head away.

The look of glee on Mohammed's face was evident as he turned back. 'She's coming John, she is on her way.' He said excitedly.

'Now we must go back to the ship, I need to collect my things and head home.'

.

As John made his way to his stateroom, he sensed he was not alone; he turned sharply to find the bulk of BG1 close behind. The best course of action John felt was to face off the guy. 'You want to play again? Eh!' He spat out and then he switched to Arabic and said. 'I smell you, you fat son of an Arab pig!'

The confused look on the bodyguards face was unmistakable; he stood staring at John. After a moment of indecision BG's hand instinctively went to the inside his jacket. *Woops! I don't think he's going to scratch his shoulder.*

The bodyguard momentarily let his hand stay there, probably considering the consequence of shooting his gun again.

Rather than show fear, John decided to exploit the bodyguard's hesitation and said, again in Arabic. 'Use that gun pig face and the Prince would have you executed.'

The guard froze, paralysed by indecision and John looked hard into his eyes and moved menacingly towards him, secretly hoping the guard would have second thoughts and back down.

'Abdul now is not the time.' The shout in Arabic came from the end of the passage. 'You are to come at once the Prince has need of us.' It was BG2, BG1 glared at John, slowly removed his hand from inside his coat, at the same time taking backward steps before turning and disappearing down the passage.

Phew, that was close. John hurried back to his stateroom and locked the door. He could now feel his heart pounding and was visibly shaking. He dropped onto the bed and lay there until the hype from the adrenalin calmed and his pulse settled.

Five minutes later John was sufficiently recovered to start packing and began to throw his clothes into a soft leather carryall. It was then that he noticed the indicator flicker on the transistor. At first he thought it was Mohammed making further arrangements, but then realised the call was incoming. *How come, only Alice has this number and she must be in transit, or is she?*

He could no longer resist the temptation and putting in the earpiece, he listened in.

The caller was King Faud.

'Mohammed my son, (ahh) it is time (ahh) for you to come home.'

'My father, I'm still very concerned about the pressure I will get from the anti Western extremist in our country.'

The King spoke slowly gasping mid sentence, clearly suffering shortness of breath. 'That problem is, (ahh) sorted, I have (ahh) talked to the Americans, (ahh) and they are willing to (ahh) increase the price they pay for our oil.'

'I shall give your words much consideration my father.'

There was a pregnant pause and John could almost hear the tension building, then the King snapped.

'Enough! Enough of this nonsense, (ahh) you take me (ahh) for a fool. Do you (ahh) think I don't I know about (ahh) your affair with the (ahh) English Princess. You shall come (ahh) home at once, no more lies. The affair is to (ahh) end now, do you hear!' The King again paused probably to catch his breath and calm himself, for when he spoke again, it was almost whispered. 'Such an alliance (ahh) would be against the Islamic faith and would threaten the (ahh) Saudi dynasty.'

'My father, I love her.'

The King raised his voice again. 'You (ahh) will end it! Now! Or you will never (ahh) become King.'

There was another long silence then Mohammed spoke.

'Imshallah, if Allah wills it, then so be it, my father.'

John switched of the recorder and flopped onto the bed. 'Well I'll be blowed,' he mumbled. 'how the hell did he find out where we where?'

But he sort of knew that the leak was probably instigated by Sir Peter Thompson-Smythe.

CHAPTER 14

SAIL OR STAY

'John's here, Sir Peter.'

'Send him in Marj and you had better come in as well.'

A single rap on the door and John Godfrey walked into Sir Peter's office, closely followed by Marjorie, who held out a note pad in front of her, leafing through the pages as she entered. She was only going through the motions, for she knew only too well that notes were seldom taken at Sir Peter's meetings.

'Morning sir.'

'Morning John, do have a seat. How was the trip?'

'Not too bad sir, a bit of a wait at Orly, I eventually got home just after ten.'

'Anything to report, you haven't already told us?'

'You'd better listen to yesterday's tape; I think you'll find them interesting.' John handed over the micro tape, Sir Peter put the miniature cassette into the machine on his desk and played the tape over the speakers, the three of them listened in silence. When the tape had finished, Sir Peter slowly got up out of his chair and adopted his usual thinking posture, with his head down and his hands clasped firmly behind him, began to pace the office floor.

'Hum, I knew about Princess Alice rushing to Prince Mohammed's side, of course, I arranged it. However convincing King Faud wasn't as straight forward, particularly since the American climb down had got the Prince off the hook.'

'You told the King the Prince was having an affair with Princess Alice?' John's outburst had more than a hint of anger to it.

'Well, not personally, the Ambassador actually did the telling.'

'Why on earth?'

'My dear fellow I find your fondness for this Arab very touching, but I'm afraid there is no room for that kind of sentiment in this job. Do I make myself clear?'

John slowly crossed his arms and put on a determined expression. 'As crystal...Sir.'

Which Sir Peter ignored. 'Now then, where was I. Ah yes, I knew what the reaction of our Royal Family was to the affair. They are livid. It occurred to me that we hadn't considered how the Saudi Royal family would take the news. Thanks to the tape John, we now know that there are just as angry.' Sir Peter stopped pacing for a moment, tapped a fore finger against his lips and then he walked over to the desk, picked up the telephone and dialled an outside line. Both Marjorie and John looked puzzled.

'Hello, Sun Newspapers, could I speak to the Editor please. It's private. Yes I'll wait a moment.'

During the wait Sir Peter turned to look at the others, a smug smile on his face.

'Editor...

I have some information which you may find interesting....

I have it on good authority...Princess Alice is having an affair....

Yes, a love affair....

With the Crown Prince Mohammed of Saudi Arabia. She's with him right now on his yacht Golden Crown, moored off Monte Carlo.'

No. I'm not looking for a reward.

Yes, I prefer to remain anonymous.....

Yes, the Prince who made that speech.

Sir Peter replaced the hand piece. 'It should be a world exclusive by this time tomorrow.'

John couldn't contain himself any longer. 'All this time I've tried to keep it secret and you've exposed them, just like that, even to the point of telling the world where they are.'

'Are you going to allow me the courtesy to explain?' Sir Peter said glaring at John.

John didn't respond, just glared back.

'Consider the situation now, if you will. If sometime in the near future Prince Mohammed dies, under, shall we say, suspicious circumstances. Imagine the conjecture; was it an accident or assassination, if so, by whom? The Americans, or was it the Brits, perhaps it was his own people, or more likely one of the many Islamic fundamental factions. And just possibly, with one or two carefully chosen words leaked to the media, even a certain Russian billionaire could be put in the frame.' Sir Peter turned to face John.

'So you see John, by exposing the affair I have also offered him some protection. It would not now be easy for Vostok to accuse us or America of the crime, when there are so many others in the frame...Including himself.'

'I doubt Mohammed or Alice would see it that way. Sir.'

Sir Peter ignored John's comment and turned to Marjorie. 'Any idea where our man is, Marj?'

A man, John thought, *what is he up to now?* But he knew better than to ask.

'There was a money transaction on the thirteenth at a bank in Frejus, in the south of France.'

'Good, he's ahead of schedule.'

'Morning Star,' cruised slowly into the marina at Frejus, tied up to a designated berth and shut down her engines. Steven and Jenifer headed towards the BISS computer station, which was hidden behind a secret panel in the fore section on the saloon deck. Steven located the secret button and activated the panel opening mechanism. 'Let's get down to it shall we,' and he switched on the computer. 'The first thing we need to do is to transfer some funds and then we'll go for a walk into the town, visit the bank and the post office.'

'Why the post office, are you expecting a letter?'

'I need an authentic identity; with you as look out I'll open a box, get a name, and maybe the address, if not, we could find it listed in the telephone book.'

Four hours later they returned by taxi to Morning Star, Steven with arms full of Auchan carrier bags meant they had also taken the opportunity to re stock on provisions. He put them on the galley worktop for Jennifer to sort.

'Okay Jen?'

'Sure I'll put this lot away and prepare our lunch. You go and do what you need to, on the computer.'

Steven sat at his state of the art system and logged into the BISS network. 'Now then let's reproduce a French identity card,' he said to himself as a blank of the document appeared on the screen. He took his personal details and photograph, off his passport and inserted them onto the card under the name of, Monsieur Jacque Mateau, using an authentic NI number lifted off the French National register. After reproducing the identification card, he went on to produce a driving licence and other documentation adding Monsieur Mateau's address 32 Avenue de la Grande Corniche, L'Armitelle, Saint Raphael. Jennifer appeared from the galley carrying a tray set with two meals, bread and two glasses of wine.

Putting the tray down on the table, she walked over to Steven who was still sitting at the computer and draped her arms over his shoulders she moved so close that her face gently brushed against his.

'Oh there are good, Monsieur Mateau, very good. You know I've never made love to a Frenchman before.'

'Ah oui oui Mademoiselle.' Steven jumped up and flung his arms around her, she screamed and lightly beat both hands on his chest. 'No no, you mad Frenchman you,' laughing loudly, they rolled together on the carpeted saloon floor and instinctively started to remove each other's clothing.

They lay together naked, joined only at the lips in a long kissing embrace, slowly they moved their hands to explore each others body, fondling lovingly. She pulled him to her and they made love.

'That was fantastic.'

'Hum not bad,' she said, and they laid there in silence a little longer.

'Well I suppose the lunch ruined it must have gone cold by now.'

That's for sure, big boy,' she said, 'it's a salad.' And they both laughed again.

'Okay, must be serious now, we have work to do.'

They got dressed ate lunch and set off back into town to buy Monsieur Mateau a nearly new estate car, nothing flash but roomy and reliable.'

They settled for a silver 'Peugeot 406'hdi estate, only forty thousand kilometres on the clock. Not bad for a diesel and it looked to be in good condition. Although it was to be a cash sale via a bank transfer, time was needed for registration and insurance, together with a check of the purchaser's credentials. Fortunately Monsieur Jacque Mateau's were in order. But the red tape involved with registration, meant the car could not be taken until the fifteenth. Again that wasn't a problem there were still lots of details for Steven and Jennifer to go over, to lessen the risk of failure. Steven needed to reproduce more false identification documents and Jennifer wanted another practice run.

So much now depended on Jennifer, was he being fair to her, or just selfish. *Please God don't let anything happen to her.*

They had decided to take the coast road to Monaco. Jennifer was driving the Peugeot in order to familiarise her self with the route. Dropping down into Monaco she followed the Boulevard Albert onto the Boulevard Larvotto and into Monte Carlo, where she pulled the Peugeot into a parking space in the Jardin Japonais.

To cover up the real reason they were Monte Carlo, they played at being holidaymakers albeit being out of season, taking in the sites, especially the one of Golden Crown moored out at sea. The wind from the sea had a chill to it and Jennifer pulled up the collar on her trench coat and snuggled into Steven's side, linking her arm in his.

'About half a mile, wouldn't you say Jen?'

'You know better that I, but it certainly looks a long way.'

Steven had a pair of binoculars which he brought up periodically, there were so few people about he didn't need to worry too much about discretion. 'I've only managed to pick out four individuals so far, the Prince and John Godfrey are not among them.' 'Pointless exercise without the Prince, what do you think we should do?'

'I'm not quite sure; if the operation had been called off I'd have been notified and after all, we are ahead of schedule. We aren't supposed to be here until the seventeenth, so I guess we should wait until then before considering our next move.'

'I agree. I think we should spend at least another day here, keeping an eye on the Golden Crown.'

'Makes sense I suppose.'

Jennifer looked over her shoulder as she spoke. 'And we can stay in the hotel near the casino. I do believe they have an excellent boutique.' Steven, binoculars still raised and pointing out to sea, turned his head and gave Jennifer a knowing look.'

'What!' She exclaimed trying to sound innocent. 'We'll need a change of clothes and some overnight things...Won't we?'

'Ever had that feeling you're being taken for a ride.'

'Come on you know you like it, play your cards right and you'll get your wish.' She giggled as he made to chase her back to the car.

Steven signed the register, Jacque and Nickolette Mateau.

'Room 1042 sir,' the clerk said, handing Steven the key.

'Merci.'

Steven with Jennifer on his arm, headed towards the elevators at the far end of the lobby. The room, as he had requested was on the top floor with sea views. As they approached, the elevators there was a *'ping'* sound and one of the lift doors opened. A man stepped out and furtively looked around, in an instant Steven recognised a bodyguard when he saw one and at that same time he heard the distinctive English tones of John Godfrey's voice coming from within. He smartly wheeled to the left as if heading into the lounge area. Jennifer shot him a bemused look, but quickly understood as he brought his forefinger to his lips. John Godfrey was so wrapped up in his conversation with the Prince that he failed to notice as he walked by, a man not three feet away, whom he knew as Charles Evans.

The three of them headed out toward the 'Place du Casino. Steven and Jennifer did a quick about turn and jumped into the empty elevator before the doors closed.

'Phew that was close, but at least that's one problem solved, it would seem our friends are having themselves a spot of shore leave.'

A quick check of the room and balcony confirmed that they had a good view of Golden Crown and almost all of the Port de Monaco.

Ironically that particular balcony would be at the top of John Godfrey's security watch.

'Good choice Jen, suits our purpose, now let's go and get you something to wear; you will go to the ball tonight, Cinders.'

'And so will you Prince Charming.'

'Well well, we've got some activity out at sea.' Steven was standing just inside the open patio door looking through the binoculars.

'What's happening?'

'They are lowering one of the rib type lifeboats, probably going to use as a tender. I wonder if the Prince has had enough of the casino life.' They took turns with the binoculars to follow the lifeboat's navigation lights into Port de Monaco. Sometime later they watched as the tender returned, when it became visible in the Golden Crowns lights, it disappeared onto the seaward starboard side.

'Very wise, they've lowered the gantry on the starboard side, unfortunately for us we can't see who, or if anybody, has come onboard.'

'We'll have to wait and see what happens tomorrow. All that time to kill, I wonder what we should do,' Jennifer gave out a sexy humm and rolled her eyes. 'Oh I wonder.'

They had had an early breakfast in the room to limit the risk of bumping into John, just in case they hadn't returned to the ship and were taking turns on watch.

'Steven, we have some activity. Here take a look, see what you make of it.' Jenifer passed him the binoculars as he emerged from the bathroom.

He studied the scene for a moment. 'They are lowering both of the lifeboats.' Thinking out loud he muttered. 'Why?'

'Perhaps they are testing them or something.'

Steven still with the binoculars focussed on the activity, replied. 'No I don't think so, the port boat with a crew of one, has just set off for the port, the other seems to be holding station on the starboard side.'

Then it became clear as Steven tracked the first boat into the harbour and watched it tying up to the fuelling jetty. 'He's filling her tank, with petrol. Interesting.'

'What's so interesting about it?'

'Well, just something I hadn't thought about. I was expecting to see two small craft with diesel inboards. What we've got are two eighteen foot ribs with four stroke outboards. Not the most practical lifeboats.'

'Will it affect our plans?'

'Nope, in fact things have just got a little better.'

Steven lowered the binoculars and handed them to Jennifer. After a few moments of her scanning the lifeboat fuelling, she turned her attention back to the ship. 'There seems to be more activity onboard.' She passed the binoculars back to him. He lifted them to eyes and scanned the decks of the ship.

'Can't see very much, but something's definitely happening.'

A few minutes later the starboard boat appeared.

'Bingo, we have lift off, now let's see who's going for a little boat trip. Well that solves that, our friends must have returned to the ship last night and now appear to be leaving again. I can see the Prince, John Godfrey with a carryall bag, two, I would guess, bodyguards...Umm, one looks to have been in a fight, he has two black eyes and a plastered nose. And there is another man at the helm.'

He passed her the binoculars. 'What do you reckon Jen?'

'I'd say our Mr Godfrey is heading home and the Prince is seeing him off.'

'I agree.....Why didn't the Prince say goodbye on the ship, I wonder?'

'Perhaps he just wanted a trip out, probably will go with him to the airport, if that's where they're heading.'

'Hum perhaps. Whatever the reason, you know what that means.'

Jennifer nodded her head. 'Sure we've got to wait until he returns before we can determine our next move.'

'Got it in one.' Steven watched as the tender disappeared behind one of the many luxury yachts in the harbour. Several minutes later a limousine left the quay. *That could be the Prince's party leaving now.*

'Anything happening?' Jennifer said as she craned her neck in an attempt to follow the proceedings.

'Not sure, the tender hasn't showed as yet, could be it's been told to wait and if that's the case, I wouldn't mind having a chat with crewman, how's your Greek?'

'Lousy, why?'

'The crewman isn't the Captain, so he must be the Greek Engineer and my Greek's lousy too.'

After several more minutes the tender still hadn't appeared, 'Okay I'm going to head down there, do some digging, are you coming, or are you holding the fort?'

'I'll hold the fort, could do with a nap.'

The crewman was slouched on a bench seat on the quay just above where the tender was moored, his legs were crossed and straight, his arms folded and his chin rested on his chest.

'Salaam Aleikum.'

'Oh no, not another kisser of thee ground. Go away, I no understand, I am Greek.'

There must be a common language on board. 'Do you speak English?'

The Greek undid an arm and oscillated the fingers. 'A little, maybe.'

'So sorry, I thought you might be able to help me, I'm looking for a crew member from the Saudi Royal yacht Golden Crown.'

'Who is it you are?'

'Oh, I'm Edgar Peterson, reporter for the Times Newspapers.'

Steven delved into the inside pocket of his coat and produced a fake, (naturally), press card. Judging by the absent look on the Greeks face, a monopoly get out of jail card would have sufficed equally as well. Steven sat down on the bench next to the Greek. 'I'm doing this article, you see, (which of course he didn't) on the Saudi Royal family. And I was rather hoping to get some information I could use.'

'What information?' the Greek snapped, rather briskly.

'Anything really, I'd be willing pay of course.'

'How much?'

'Err one hundred and fifty Euros.' The Greek puckered his lips and stared out to sea.

'I take it you don't know any of the Golden Crown crew?'

'Five hundred.'

'Three hundred, if the information is good.'

'Show me.' Steven withdrew his wallet and took out six fifty-Euro notes, which were immediately plucked from his grasp and disappeared into the Greeks trouser pocket.

'What is it you want to know?'

'How many of the Saudi Royals are onboard and who are they?'

'The Prince is all, but he no here now.'

'You mean not on the ship?' Steven nodded as he spoke, emphasizing each word.

'Si, he no here.'

'Which Prince?'

The Greek shrugged his shoulders. 'I not know.'

'Where is the Prince now?'

'He go airport, I think, maybe he say goodbye to the English.'

'Englishman?'

'Si, good man. I like English, no good he leaves. St Tropez we have much crew, many hands, now only the Captain and me, I am Engineer,' prodding himself in the chest with his thumb.

'I pull no the fuckin rope, no fix the fuckin line, no clean deck. English, he very good, many times he help me. I laugh, ha ha, when he do good the job to face of thee Egyptian pig.'

'You mean?' Steven made a fist and made a short jab.

'Si, how you say, err fight. He makes much blood from the pig.'

Well I never, didn't think John had it in him.

The bruised face on one of the bodyguards flashed through his mind.

'What can you tell me about the Prince?'

'No much, he come the ship two weeks, laughing no.' The Greek waved a finger, pulling down his chin at the same time. The gesture was not lost on Steven.

'But today he laughs much.'

'Why?'

The Greek shrugged his shoulders again, 'I not know.'

'How long will the Golden Crown be at anchor out there?'

Again the Greek shrugged his shoulders. 'Maybe we go soon, but today no possible, the engines need the gasoil. 'Maybe the barge, it comes tomorrow sometime, maybe.'

Steven returned to the hotel room, a broad smile on his face.

'Hi Jen.'

'Hi, how did it go?'

'Somewhat confusing, but I've managed to establish that the Prince is laughing, probably in the airport, and the ship can't sail until tomorrow, maybe.'

'Sounds like you've been enjoying yourself.'

'For sure, I reckon we should shoot back to Morning Star and get the gear we need, so that I'm prepared if Mohammed decides to jump the gun.'

'Okay, sounds good, I could use another dummy run. Check the route and timing. Are we keeping this room on, as a base?'

'Yes I think so, makes sense for one more night. It may not be available tomorrow. As soon as the Prince gets back we'll take off.'

Steven picked up the binoculars and walked out on to balcony. He had been there for about half an hour, when he spotted the tender. 'Here we go the tender's on its way back.' Steven focussed the binoculars. 'Bloody hell!'

'What?' Jennifer was now stood at his side. Steven slowly lowered the binoculars and passed them to Jennifer.

'The old bugger was right, even to the day. I was really hoping he'd got it all screwed up.'

Jennifer had no idea who Steven was referring to as she adjusted the binoculars to her eyes. 'Wow! That's Princess Alice, isn't it?' Steven just nodded.

'You were expecting her, weren't you?'

'Y-e-a-h, that's the bit I didn't tell you, I was kind of wishing it wasn't going to happen.'

'This changes everything.'

'No, not at all Jen, what we practiced for one can easily be adapted for two.'

'I'm not sure I can do this, I don't feel its right; -- she's a loving wife and mother of a future King.'

'Believe me Jen you don't know the half of it and if we don't do this there may not be a future King.'

Jennifer shook her head not really grasping what Steven was getting at. 'I don't understand Steven, I trusted you.'

'I know it's hard for you to accept, but the real purpose of the op was to take her out, not him.' Steven cupped her face and looked into her eyes. 'We've got to do this Jen, as we've planned, we're committed.'

Jenifer stared back at him, and saw the sincerity. 'Well, I agreed to come along, don't suppose I should quit now.'

'You're still with me then?'

'I'm still with you.'

'Thanks.' He kissed her letting his hands slip gently away from her face.

At that Jennifer turned back, lifting the binoculars to her eyes and re-focussed, tracking the progress of the tender and its occupants across Monaco bay. 'Oh no, there are two men with her.'

Steven took the binoculars from her and focussed onto the tender. 'She's brought her own bodyguards.'

'Bodyguards'!

Steven lowered the binoculars, slightly shook his head in disbelief. 'Now that I didn't expect.'

'Oh Steven, I don't like those odds. At least four armed men to one. I think we should abort the operation.'

'Can't do that Jen, there's too much at stake. Don't worry, I'll have surprise on my side, I hope.'

'You sure?'

'I'm sure.'

'Okay, if you think, let's do it.'

'We'll head back to Frejus and pick up the things I'm going to need.'

The low winter sun shone in through a chink in the heavy curtains of the hotel bedroom window and bounced off the dressing table mirror, rousing Steven from a sound sleep.

'What's the time?' Jennifer murmured, she was not yet in the wide-awake club. Steven propped himself up on one elbow and squinted at his watch.

'Bloody hell, it's nearly ten; I never ever slept this late before.' Steven scolded himself.

'For heavens sake Steven it was after four when we got back, Jennifer still murmuring snuggled her face into the pillow.

'Didn't your mother ever tell you not to talk with your eyes shut?' Steven's attempt at humour fell on deaf ears, so he eased himself out of the bed stretched and scratched and pulled on his underpants.

'Better take a look at the Golden Crown, see if she's still there,' he said, more or less to himself; as he nonchalantly picked up the binoculars and slid open the patio door. The cold wind from the sea instantly blew back the heavy curtain. Even before his eyes had adjusted to the sun's glare and the glasses focussed, he sensed the commotion. He could see the Prince and the Princess scurrying from the forward deck, back along the starboard gangway heading towards the saloon area. They were followed by a hysterical looking Indian. *Must be the manservant.* They are being frantically waved at by one of the new bodyguards. Catching this fleeting moment, in the movement of the binoculars he glimpsed something else, readjusting the sight line he found another bodyguard on the boat deck, with binoculars! Trained on him! Steven's heart seemed to skip a beat, as he automatically flung himself back into the room. 'How?'.... He automatically fell to the floor, lying on his stomach and began to inch forward. Snaking his way back onto the balcony, it suddenly dawned on him when he heard above the wind whistle, zzzclick zzzzclick, coming from the balcony below. Training his binoculars back to the ship and the bodyguard, Steven concluded. 'He's not looking at me, thank god.' He pushed back into the room. 'Jen Jen where's your mirror.' Still with eyes firmly shut, an arm flopped out and waved in a vague direction and she muttered in a hardly discernable voice. 'My bag.'

'It's alright Jen don't get up.' He found the mirror and headed back to the balcony, again he was on his stomach just in case the bodyguard was scanning the rest of the building. He put the hand holding the mirror through the wrought iron balustrade, angling it so that he could see the balconies below. Sure enough, the sight of a large telescope with camera confirmed it, 'Paparazzi.' 'The cats well and truly out of the bag now, this could really screw up our schedule.'

They sat on the edge of the bed gazing out through the patio door. 'What do you think?'

'Well if I was the Prince, or the Princess for that matter, I would want to get my arse out of here, PDQ.'

'Umm, I'm not so sure, I think they could to try and bluff it out, pretend she's here holidaying with a friend. On that premise, maybe they'll stick around for another day or so...But I can't take that chance. I've got to find a way to keep them here until we are all set.' Steven fingered his chin in a thoughtful manner. 'But how?'

'We only need them to be here tonight; surely we can do something.'

'They can't sail now because they are in need of fuel, if there was some way to delay the fuel barge, it may just be enough to keep them here until first light tomorrow.'

'Sounds good.'

'My Engineer friend has given me an idea. With a bit of luck and a lot of confusion, it may work.' Steven smiled at the thought of the mayhem he would cause.

'What do you think Jen, a Greek, speaking pigeon English to a French receptionist in the wrong office, with enough confusion so that the fact, the call isn't being made from the ship may not be noticed, especially if I can get transferred to the right office through her switchboard.'

'Well I'm sure as hell confused.'

'Bare with me all will become clear.' Steven picked up the telephone and dialled reception.

'Oui Monsieur.'

'Could you connect to the Port Authority, s'il vous plait?'

'Ah oui.'

'Merci.' Steven waited a moment until the connection was made. 'Bonjour, Port Monaco control.'

'Oui, heberger autorite, doue vous ri-couaire la pilot?'

'Eh! No no, you no comprende. No want pilot! Want the gasoil. I number one best of Engineer on Golden Crown, engines need the gasoil.'

'Une moment Monsieur, I will transfer you to the fuel depot.' There was a delay accompanied by various ring tones emanating from the hand set. Steven looked at Jennifer and rolled his eyes. 'Si, si, yes, oui; I need the gasoil, diesel, you comprehend! I talk me the fuel tanker.' Steven put his hand over the mouthpiece. 'Good they are transferring my call to the fuel depot office.'

'Ah oui Monsieur.'

'Oui I need the diesel.'

'You are Golden Crown?'

'No I Engineer, Golden Crown my ship.'

'La barge is on its way.'

'No no, small problemo, la gasoil no possible now, require chez trois.'

'Monsieur, you now want the fuel barge at three, is that correct?'

'Ah oui, trois tou-de' pour la barge – er, merci.'

'You require we reschedule your delivery?'

'Yes, oui, you bring the diesel at three today. Good the bye.'

'As you wish Monsieur.'

At that the receivers were replaced at both ends.

'Phew, I think I've done it, the fuel barge has been rescheduled for three this afternoon. The light will be fading, by the time refuelling is complete it'll be dark, so there would be no point in making a hasty retreat from the cameras. I'm gambling that the Captain won't bother to raise the anchor and set a new course until first light.'

'It could work the other way, he may consider it a good option to slip away under the cover of darkness.'

'Yes I know, let's keep our fingers crossed that he doesn't. In fact the Prince may even want to hang back to catch the first editions, just to see what they are saying.'

'And what if the Captain telephones the depot wanting to know where his fuel is?'

'He probably will, I'm just hoping, when he does, his allocation has been allotted elsewhere and he has to get back in line.'

They sat there for a while seemingly deep in thought, then Jennifer said. 'When are we leaving the hotel?'

'I reckon now's a good a time as any.'

ALL AT SEA

'What was that all about Robert?'

'Paparazzi, your highness, on a hotel balcony with a camera,' the bodyguard replied, as he ushered the Prince and Princess into the saloon.

'Oh dear, now we'll be hounded.'

'We shall sail at once,' Mohammed said, pressing the intercom to the bridge.

'We are awaiting fuel delivery sir.'

Mohammed looked anxious, not really sure what to say. 'Can we not get the fuel elsewhere?'

'Our tanks are so low sir, I doubt we would make but a few kilometres. I shall contact the fuel barge and try for an earlier delivery.'

'Yes...Please do so.'

Mohammed released to button and turned to Alice, 'We'll have to sit it out for while.'

'Why run,' she said, 'they've no doubt followed me here, hoping to find a story, if we leave now; we would only provoke their suspicion. It may be better for us to announce that I am recuperating from illness as a guest on your yacht.'

'Y-e-s you could be right; perhaps it would be prudent to leave in a day or two. Although I am concerned that somebody is spying on me.'

'Whoever it is, is no doubt spying on both of us.'

'Perhaps, but it seems so coincidental that my father now knows about us and then the paparazzi appear from nowhere.'

'At least we're together.'

A smile spread across Mohammed face and in that instance all other problems paled into insignificance.

They had waited for nightfall in a dark corner of a car park, where Steven had changed and made his preparations. When the time was right, Jennifer drove down to the foreshore and stopped near to the waters edge, the dark shape of the Golden Crown could just be discerned in the starlight.

'Well, we're in luck, she's still sitting there.' Steven looked at his watch. 'One-o-clock Jen, you ready?' He said as he eased himself out of the car.

'Ready and raring to go,' then with a serious look on her face she called after him, 'Steven.'

'Yes.'

'Be careful... I love you.'

'Love you too.' He reached back and gently squeezed her arm. Steven wearing a black wet suit, black rubber shoes and with his face cam cream blackened, moved away from the car a few steps and vanished into the darkness. Just for the slightest moment she caught a glimpse of his shadow set against the lights from the town reflecting in the water. She waited a few minutes before starting the engine and her journey back to Morning Star.

At the waters edge Steven had checked the waterproof bag was secure on his back. Around his waist he had tied a length of black-knotted cord holding a small folding rubber clad grappling hook, which was tucked into a pouch on his belt. Happy that he had all he needed, he spat into his mask rubbing the spittle around the inside of the glass to prevent fogging. Then he placed the mask over his eyes and nose, giving it a little jiggle to ensure the neoprene was sealed to his face, the last thing Steven wanted was to have stinging salt water spoiling his vision. He waded into the sea and began the long swim towards the dark shape of the Golden Crown.

He swam most of the way in an over arm crawl style, until he was about fifty yards from the vessel. Then he switched to breaststroke to limit the disturbance to the waters surface, taking five strokes underwater. On the sixth stroke, he allowed his head to break the surface for air and to get his bearings. The Golden Crown had switched to low level lighting to counter intrusions from long-range camera night lenses. Apart from a couple of dim glows along the gangways the ship was a big black mass that loomed above Steven as he approached the anchor chain. There wasn't much movement on the water just a slow and regular swell.

Steven trod water, one arm crooked around the chain to steady himself as he unwound the grappling hook. With one end of the cord secured to his waist, he estimated about 20 feet. *Should be enough.* He slipped off the holding ring, allowing the rubber-coated prongs to snap open. Wrapping arms and legs around the anchor chain he began to shin up. He was hanging upside down, with the grappling hook dangling from his waist and disappearing into the water. Getting as high as possible he retrieved the grappling hook swinging it gently over the stem and snagging it on the gunwale in the first attempt. He pulled down sharply to ensure it had snagged, before transferring his weight onto the cord. Hand over hand he completed the climb, sliding silently onto the forward deck. The cloud cover shut out any light from the moon and stars and apart from the dim lighting on the main deck port and starboard gangways, it was almost total darkness. Steven removed the mask, opened his waterproof bag taking out the 9mm automatic with silencer, gave it a quick reassuring check and tucked the weapon into his belt. He pulled out a PNG and placed it on his head; he could now see that the chloroform bottle wrapped in bubble-wrap was still intact. He untied the cord from around his waist; wound it into ball before folding the grappling hook and replacing the retaining ring.

All set, Steven figured there would be at least two guards on duty, probably at the stern, so he stealthily made his way along the port side gangway, keeping lower than the windows in case one guard was securing the saloon area.

He heard him before he saw him, one man moving around at the stern rail. Steven moved silently into a position from where he could take in the whole aft area and check for another body. Scanning with PNG vision he ascertained that the target was on his own, in that location at least. Moving silently Steven came up behind the man, getting in real close and then he simultaneously clapped his left hand over the targets mouth whilst bringing the full force of the grappling hook, now doubling as a cosh, down onto the mans head. The blow caught the guard just above the right ear, there was a muffled cry as the target went down like a bag of bricks.

'Hey! What the fuck are you doing down there? You dumb Egyptian shit.' One of the English bodyguards shouted as he started to descend the stairway from the boat deck above. The torch in his hand, cast a beam of light over the stern deck, and Steven could see he had a gun in his other hand. Steven shrunk back into a shadowy recess beneath the stairway.

The English guard jumped the last two treads onto the main deck then froze for a split second as the light beam picked out the body of the Egyptian. He spun around quickly. Steven sprang forward bringing the grappling hook crashing down on the bodyguard's gun hand. Gun and hook went flying across the deck. The bodyguard's reaction was immediate and instinctive, smashing the torch across Steven's face. Fortunately for Steven the PNG took most of the force, as it was knocked off his head, relieving Steven of his night vision advantage. But the bodyguard didn't stop there; he continued the onslaught, swinging the torch like a club at the faint shadow, which was Steven's head. Steven caught some of the blows on his arms but a couple connected and he fell back, partly from the pain and partly as a reaction to avoid the further flailing. Somehow he managed to catch hold of the torch as it came down, twisting with and under the path of the blow, wrestling the torch from the bodyguards grip. The torch came away easy, far too easy for Stevens liking, he now found himself in a crouched position with his back to his opponent and holding a torch. This was not to his advantage, as the continuous barrage of blows to his head and shoulders would attest. With all the power he could muster, he swung around aiming the torch, now in his hand, at his assailants head. The swing was blocked with such a jolt that the torch left Stevens hand and it too went skimming along the deck. The bodyguard still had the upper hand and continued his attack with a fusillade of karate punches, chops and kicks. In the dark Steven could not see them coming and reacted instinctively to block the blows, using all of his energy to defend himself. Eventually a kick landed just beneath his rib cage sending him backwards, crashing into the superstructure. That knocked the wind out of him and he doubled in pain. However the few yards the kick sent him, had given him some distance away from his assailant and the time to recoup, albeit brief, before the next onslaught. It also brought the pursuing bodyguard, into glow from one of the overhead dim lights, just enough for Steven to perceive a drop to the shoulder, the swung back arm and the bunched fist. Knowing what was coming Steven feigned to his right as the bodyguards fist whistled past his ear, at that instant he brought up his right hand with all the strength he could muster, the titanium knuckled fist connected with the guards jaw sending the head back which such force that it almost left his shoulders. An adrenalin surge and Steven was on the offensive. He caught the bodyguard with a swinging left to the head and one more blow from that vicious right hand to the chin, sent the guard staggering backward trying desperately to stay upright but failing. It was all over bar the shouting. Steven had no choice; the guard could place him on the ship this night. 'Sorry pal you were a hell of an adversary.' He put an arm around the guard's neck, put his knee in his back and pulled sharply up.

Steven took a long time to gather himself, lying on top of the dead bodyguard, an arm still wrapped around the neck. He stayed like that until he could feel his pulse settle and the pain ease. Shit! My backpack, he suddenly remembered being slammed the ships structure. Slipping the bag off his shoulder he opened it, found his pen torch to inspect the contents. 'Oh no the chloroform! Damn! Damn! Damn!' He cursed under his breath. The bottle had broken in the fight, but on closer inspection, all was not lost. The chloroform, broken glass bottle and soggy bubble-wrap were sloshing about in a sealed plastic bag which miraculously hadn't punctured.

'Thank goodness I've still got it, better get cracking.' Slipping on a pair of latex gloves, he was about to set off when the

Egyptian bodyguard started to moan as he came round. Steven thrust his hand into the plastic bag, feeling the cold of the liquid permeate through the latex. He then grabbed the guard around the nose and mouth, feeling the body go limp again as the vapours from the residue of chloroform on his glove took effect. 'Must get on with it now,' he said to himself as he made his way to the master bedroom, using the pen torch for guidance. Slowly and quietly he tried the door, only to discover it was locked. *Typical.* He felt in the bag for his wire levers. It was relatively easy to pick the lock, after pushing the key inside.

Slipping silently into the dark chamber crawling on all fours, he could hear the deep breathing of two sleeping people. Keeping below the bed line he shone the pen torch into the bag. Taking a piece of cloth, he soaked it in the plastic bag, making sure it was resealed to preserve the precious liquid. 'Not the most economical way to administer chloroform, but any port in a storm as they say,' Steven mumbled to himself. 'This will be the trial, Jen talked about, hopefully without the error.' As he approached the king size bed, Jens words ran through his mind. 'Chloroform slows down the rate of the vital organs, administer too much and you could stop them altogether. Administer the drops very slowly and keep checking the pulse rate. I would try to judge half the normal rhythm as the enough point, but it's all trial and error really.' *Thanks for that Jen, pity you didn't tell me what to do when you don't have a means to drop the stuff.* With the pen torch in one hand, soaked cloth in the other, he moved the torch until the small beam of light picked out Mohammed face. *Damn and blast, he's lying on his side, face almost buried in the pillow and he is snuggled into Alice's back. No way can I check his pulse rate without disturbing them.* Rather cautiously Steven gently laid the cloth over what he could see of Mohammed's nose and mouth, allowing the chloroform vapours to work. After only a few seconds there was a discernable slowing of the Prince's breathing. Steven waited for the breathing pattern to be half the speed it was when he entered the room, before taking away the cloth. Soaking the cloth again, he repeated the same procedure with Alice. 'There that ought to keep them quiet for a while. Just in case it doesn't, I'll lock them in.'

Steven quickly located the Captains cabin on the same deck; the door was unlocked. The Captain was lying on his back, snoring quite loudly, arms across his chest conveniently exposed outside the blankets. 'How very obliging sir,' Steven draped the cloth over the face, picked up a wrist locating the pulse with his fingers and started to count the Captains pulse rate to himself. He was in and out quickly; making sure the door was locked after him, just in case the chloroform wasn't having the desired effect. 'That's a thought, what to do if these guys wake up before I'm through. Sod-it, I'll cross that particular bridge when and if I come to it.'

The manservant was next; he was also on the same deck, with an unlocked door. Not quite as obliging as the Captain position wise, but nevertheless surprisingly easy. 'Thank goodness for small mercies, I'm behind schedule.'

Steven made his way to the lower deck. By now the chloroform was getting low and he was getting quite heady and drowsy from his exposure to the vapours.

Irrespective of the schedule he needed to take time out, refresh himself, or he would end up his own victim. He went into the bathroom flicked on the light and locked the door behind him. He spent a good five minutes, splashing cold water on his face, until he could feel the chloroform effect diminish.

Bang! – Bang! – Bang! On the door and a gruff Arabic voice, which Steven had no trouble understanding. 'Hurry up in there, I need to piss.'

That can only be the Egyptian bodyguard, the one who John thumped. He gave out a grunt of acknowledgement. How do I deal with the situation, I don't have the time or the energy to get involved in another fight.'

Bang! Bang! 'Hey you in there, hurry your pig arse up, I'm about to piss myself.' In Arabic of course, believing he could not be understood by the others on that deck.

Steven gave another grunt. *Desperate for a pee, would give me an advantage.* 'What the hell, I didn't want to chance anyone being found with a bullet in him, but I guess in this guy's case I can make an exception, I'll just have to hope he's never found.' Pulling the automatic from his belt, he threw open the bathroom door. 'Spit.' One shot to the head. Steven caught the slumping body before it hit the deck, dragged him into the bathroom and sat him on the pan.

'Okay you want a pee, feel free.' The wet patch on his pyjama bottoms indicated that he already had. Steven put the light off and closed the door.

Two to go, locating the cabin where the last bodyguard was, proved fairly easy and Steven had no trouble dealing with him in the same way as the others, remembering to remove the guys gun from the end of the bunk bed, before locking the door.

'That's it, only my Greek friend left. He'll be bunking in the engine room that will also give me the chance to check the engines over while I'm down here. He made his way into the engine room checking the level gauges on the tanks as he passed by, noting that they were full, reassuring himself that the fuel barge did make it. He crept towards the bunk where the Engineer was lying asleep, the sound of his snoring was so loud, it was in competition with the generator for the highest decibel count, and was probably winning. He administered nearly all the chloroform he had left to the Engineer, saving only the droplets that were nestled in the folds of the plastic bag and bubble-wrap. Better save these remnants for the guy I hit with the hook, he's probably about to recover and may need another dose.

Steven ran to bridge, and started the engines, easing her bow forward, as he engaged the winch motor, raising the anchor. 'Nearly two thirty, I'm running late.'

As the anchor clanged up the stem and into the housing, Steven gently pushed forward on the two throttle levers. The twin diesels kicked into action and Golden Crown pulled away from Monaco heading due south.

'Moderate sea conditions should average 26 knots,' he said to himself as he set the course and speed. Steven switched on the radar, mainly to check the position of any other traffic in the area. There was none, so he shut the system down to avoid chance detection. He then set up the autopilot to the GPS, logging the waypoint where he was to rendezvous with Jenifer and Morning Star. He would wait until the ship was out of sight of land before switching on any internal lights.

Confident that the ship was holding course without too much of his input, he commenced the clean up operation, periodically returning to the bridge to make any necessary course adjustment. Both ships were due at the waypoint at three-thirty. He was just about shattered and there was still a lot more to do. Having checked that his live victims were still in an unconscious state, he had carried each and placed them in the starboard side lifeboat, wisely he collected the English bodyguard from below decks first, the heavy Egyptian second, the Greek Engineer, then the Captain. Finally he carried the Indian manservant to the lifeboat and carefully placed a pre-prepared sealed envelope inside the Indian's pyjamas.

A bottle of whiskey found in the saloon came in useful giving each of the lifeboat occupants a whiskey wash, just to disguise the effect and detection of the chloroform, the empty bottle went into the Med.'

Steven removed the compass, a hand held sat-nav, transmitter and the flares from the craft, and these followed the whiskey bottle. He then removed the fuel lines from the twin outboard engines and lifted the now full petrol tank out of both lifeboats, dropping them on the deck. He would use the petrol later to douse the furniture in the staterooms and saloon.

For additional containment of the sleeping lifeboats passengers, he re-secured the tarpaulin cover, tying it down tightly. Just in case any of the passengers decided to awake before they should.

The two dead bodies were placed in cabins on the lower deck, doors left open for access of crabs, fish, and any sea life in need of a meal.

Steven checked his watch, 'Ten past three, better check on the course.' He said as he ran to the bridge. Wow! I'm a good mile to the east of the projected course. 'Autopilot's not worth shit.' He said under his breath, while making the necessary adjustment to the course and realigning the projected direction to the GPS waypoint. 'I'll have to nurse this baby for a while, can't afford to waste any more time on another deviation, may as well check out the radar while I'm here.' As he switched on the unit, the screen lit up showing specks and shaded patches in an all round direction as the antenna revolved. 'Okay,' he determined, 'no shipping anywhere near.' Switching off the radar, he turned his attention back to the GPS. 'Good the new course is being maintained, gotta get cracking, there isn't much time left to complete phase two.'

Just as a precaution, he took the automatic from his belt, turning the key with his left hand, he unlocked the door to the master bedroom. Switching on the light he could see Princess Alice and Prince Mohammed were still very much asleep, replacing the gun back in his belt he walked over to the side of the king sized bed, as he did so he caught sight of himself in the mirrored wall. 'Bloody Nora! What a sight, gave myself quite a shock, a black shape with white eyes and streaks of caked blood.' Steven made a quick inspection of the wound on the side of his head, which was no doubt made by the flailing torch, and determined it was only minor. Turning his attention back to the bed he pulled down the duvet and exposed the naked couple who were laying there. As he did so, he noticed the soiling on the sheets. 'Well, they seem to have had a little fun before leaving their Royal life.' He said to himself as he began to remove the items of jewellery from each of them. 'These things won't be of any use to them where they are going. 'Ah, the famous engagement ring.' He mused as he eased it off Alice's finger.

Using the sheets he wrapped each of them like a mummy, got to maintain their modesty to some degree.

Sometime later Steven was back the bridge the ship was running completely dark, to lessen any chance of detection he had switched off all of the internal and navigation lighting.

As Golden Crown neared the rendezvous area, Steven turned on the radar and did a check; there was contact, a vessel sitting at the designated waypoint. 'Must be Morning Star,' he concluded and taking a torch he flashed out a signal and received almost instantly, the correct response.

Using only the GPS he manoeuvred Golden Crown until she lay about 25yards off, and parallel to, the starboard side of Morning Star. He throttled back and slipped her into neutral, letting the diesels tick over, the two boats bobbed along together nicely, keeping their distance. At this time neither boat was showing any lights, so he expected that Jennifer had registered from Morning Stars GPS that he was now in position.

Before leaving the bridge Steven switched on the deck lighting, *Can't work in the dark.* He thought, as he lowered the port side gangway he could hear the purr of the outboard engine on the inflatable, he shone the torch to guide Jennifer in.

'Ahoy there! Permission to come aboard?' She called.

'Come ahead.' He called back, and within minutes she was climbing up the gangway.

'Come here gorgeous.'

As she came near Jenifer notice the congealed blood on Steven's face and gave him a concerned look. 'Your face.'

'Oh that,' he said, dabbing the caked blood and cam cream, 'it's only superficial.'

'How did it go?'

'Oh, you know, one or two little snags, but all in all, pretty much as we planned, your end okay?'

'No problems, the items you wanted are in the inflatable. And as suggested I've tied on an umbilical line, so hopefully Morning Star is at the end of that rope.' Jennifer pointed in the general direction with her head, although nothing was visible in the darkness.

'Great, we'd better get on with it, give me a hand, to lower the lifeboats.' The davits and winches were operated by electric motors, so that task, apart from untying the securing straps turned out to be a relatively easy. They lowered the starboard lifeboat first just to the lower deck level. While Jenifer lowered the port craft, Steven collected a fifty-foot length of rope from the inflatable and tied one end to the stem of the starboard craft and secured the other end with a loop loosely to an aft bollard. He then lowered it into the sea and pulled on the ties to release the davit grab type lifting blocks. The boat drifted back until the rope tether restrained it.

By the time Steven had done that, Jennifer had the port side boat tethered to the side of the inflatable and Steven's pre-packed bag on deck at the head of the gangway. Steven then made his way down the gangway and handed Jenifer his waterproof bag, ensuring the contents, including the automatic pistol, were not left on board the Golden Crown.

'You ready Jen?'

'As ever.' She shouted back at the same time starting the dinghy's small outboard. Steven pulled the ties to release the davits.

'See you later Jen.' He cast her off, and lifted the gangway. The dark shadow of the crafts moved slowly away from 'Golden Crown', a combination of the small outboard and hauling of the umbilical rope, would, hopefully see them safely back to 'Morning Star.'

Steven collected the bag, had a quick check of the contents to reassure himself that he had all that he needed. He then collected the former lifeboat petrol tanks and spread the contents of one liberally around the ship, leaving a small quantity of the liquid in the tank so that its destruction would be ensured.

In the bag, Steven had packed plastic explosive, detonators, a roll of wire, a large battery and a wind up alarm clock. He placed most of the plastic explosive around the sea cocks on the water intake and inserted a detonator in each; with these blown the ship will flood pretty fast. But to help this happen a little quicker he placed some plastic against the fuel tank at the supply line. He wasn't sure if the fuel would explode but it would definitely ignite, 'same result at the end of the day.' He mused. Then he ran a wire into the master bedroom and using the petrol from the other tank he dowsed everything, including his canvas bag, which he placed in the wardrobe. Leaving some petrol in the container and placing it against the bed, he put plastic in the neck and inserted the wired detonator. Lastly he placed some of the plastic explosive with a wired detonator, on the aft bollard holding the tethered lifeboat.

Checking that all the detonators were wired, he linked up to the battery via the alarm clock and set it to make contact in one hour.

Back on the bridge he shutdown all the lights and re-set the course on the autopilot to due South. He pushed both throttles to their limit, the bow lifted and the water foamed and churned at the stern as Golden Crown took off on her last voyage. Steven ran from the bridge and dived over the side into the dark water.

By the time he had surfaced Golden Crown could not be seen and the noise from her engines was fast fading into the distance. Steven started his swim back towards the light from Jennifer's torch.

She too had been busy, the inflatable was stored away in the stern housing, the small outboard lifted off the transom and stored. The lifeboat was tied fore and aft across the stern diving platform, riding against a pair of fend-offs. She had also found the time to drill a couple of holes in the canvas inflated sides, so that they flopped deflated over the sides of the GRP hull.

'Hi big boy, welcome aboard, just the heavy work to do.'

'Woo just a sec.' Steven held up a hand. 'I need to catch my breath, I'm shattered.' Steven was standing on the platform, back bent, with his hands on his knees, water dripping off him. Jennifer pretended that she wasn't one bit concerned announced as she threw him a towel. 'You'd better dry off a bit before you set foot in the saloon and get your face cleaned up, you're not a pretty sight.'

'Thanks Jen, nice to see you too.'

Fifteen minutes later the heavy work done, Steven ran the cordless drill through the hull, and the lifeboat began to fill rapidly; he jumped out and quickly untied the craft allowing it to sink. It would probably take a while to disappear completely, if indeed it ever would. Steven and Jennifer weren't going to wait around to find out.

It was 6.10am when Morning Star entered Frejus marina, fortunately it was still dark and very quiet as she tied up at her berth. Nobody, as far as they could tell, had noticed she'd been away.

CHAPTER 16

WELCOME ABOARD

'Shall we do it Jen?'

'Can't wait, I'll get the tea.' They made their way down to the forward VIP guest bedroom. Steven unlocked and pushed the door open, Jennifer tray in hand squeezed past him.

'Thank you, kind sir.'

'Ah, good morning folks, trust you slept well?' Not waiting for any response. 'Bet you'd love a cuppa, sort that dry throat out.' She said as she placed the tray on a bedside table.

Steven was still standing at the door, a fixed grin on his face, trying hard to radiate a friendly persona, as some kind of reassuring gesture.

The two figures on the bed made a futile effort to sit upright but the sheets were bound around them too tightly to allow the freedom of any limbs. Their glazed eyes seemed to be stood out as if on stalks, which only emphasized the bemused look on their faces. It was obvious they had only just come round and did not comprehend anything that was happening. Steven noticed their predicament with the sheets he had wrapped them in several hours previous. So he stepped forward, cradled his arm under Mohammed and propped him into a sitting position ensuring the sheet was loosened, before stepping back to his position by the door, the broad grin still fixed on his face. Jenifer must have noted their situation at the same time, for she did the same for Alice. During the process, there was no sound or protest from either of the shrouded bodies.

'Right.' Jennifer said, looking busy. 'Milk and sugar?' Turning to look at the guests to catch their affirmative nod, and continued to talk as she poured. 'There are clean towels and all the toiletries you will need in the bathroom. There is a selection of clothes and shoes for each of you in the wardrobe, in your sizes.'

Putting down the teapot she then started to gesture to the various areas, looking like an air stewardess pointing to the exits. 'In this drawer, there is a selection of underwear for him, and in this drawer for her.'

Still no sound escaped from either of the couples mouths, as Jennifer continued her one sided conversation. 'Oh yes, I've put a small amount of jewellery in the top draw. Not much, his and her watches, male signet ring and an engagement ring. Nice, but not flash and a white gold wedding band for you dear. Oh and there are one or two other trinkets, hope you like them.'

She made her way to the door, turning back as she got next to Steven. 'Oh before I forget there are two 'Paracetamol' on the tray. When you feel up to it, please feel free to pop up to the saloon for a chat.' At that Jennifer left the bedroom. Steven still smiling like a Cheshire cat and nodding like a donkey turned and followed, closing the door behind him.

'Did well there Jen, I think you put them at ease. Pop up for a chat, I like it. Oh, by the way the weather is really good today.' Steven said in a mocking feminine manner, and received a playful dig in the ribs.

'Don't be flippant, big boy.'

About an hour later Mohammed, now dressed, appeared at the top of the stairs, Alice close behind.

'Ah come in take a seat.' Steven said pointing to the settee.

'We'd like to know, what's going on? Who are you? And what right do you have to abduct us?'

'Our names are of no consequence really, but as long as we are sharing this space and being sociable, I'm Steven and this is Jennifer. As for the whys and wherefores of our action I will explain.'

'This is blackmail, isn't it?' Alice interrupted. 'How much do you want?'

'Blackmail. Far from it my dear, in fact quite the opposite.' Steven didn't feel the need to expand any further on that subject.

He was sat facing the bewildered couple on the settee opposite, stroking his chin he pondered what he considered to be the best way to phrase the story, so that their situation would be made clear.

'If I may I'd like to tell you a story.'

'I'll make us some more tea.' Jennifer put in, as she got up and headed to the galley.

'Once upon a time there was a handsome young Prince.' Steven looked directly at Mohammed as he spoke. 'Heir to the throne of the Kingdom of Saudi Arabia. Very rich, had the world at his feet, you might say. Anyway one day, this Prince said something, which perhaps in hindsight he shouldn't have, caused a bit of an international incident and upset a few people. Okay so the young Prince was naïve. It would be best for him to go away for a while, just until things settle down. Then everything will be all right, and so it was.' Steven paused momentarily to judge the reaction in Mohammed's eyes. 'However being in a different environment brought its own problems, for it was then that the Prince realized he didn't have everything. What he found, hit him square in the heart the moment he laid eyes on a very beautiful Princess. Ironically this Princess felt exactly the same, love at first sight.' Steven glanced at Alice for a confirmatory nod. 'The passion and

desire, so strong, every thing else paled into insignificance.'
Steven noted that both of them were nodding in agreement with his analysis. He had hit the nail squarely on its head.

'Unfortunately, as was the way with this Prince, he did have a tendency to tread on toes, piss in another's pond, so to speak.' In a slightly raised voice, he continued. 'The beautiful Princess was only to be the future Queen of England, the wife, of the soon to be King and mother of the future King.' This time Steven looked directly at Alice, his voice back to its normal pitch. 'The British Royal family were very angry. To have an affair is disgraceful enough, but with a Muslim. Such an affront to the British Monarchy and the Church of England is intolerable. Some would even suggest that the affair is an act of treason and should be punished accordingly.'

'The Royal family didn't give a dam about me,' Alice protested. 'Their biggest problem was that I am more popular than Edward or any of the other so called blue bloods.'

'Granted, no doubt that was the situation, but what would the publics opinion be once the details of this affair gets out, eh?' Both Mohammed and Alice opened their mouths about to offer some protest, but Steven held out a hand signifying that he was not finished. 'By the same token the Saudi Royal family aren't best pleased, their concerns would be similar to that of the

British Royal family. The difference being, it would be an insult to Allah. A future King and custodian of the holiest places in all of Islam cannot be allowed any association with a female infidel. There are many extremists groups in the Arab world who would feel that the Prince and Princess should be publicly executed for their sins.' Steven paused for a drink of tea just brought in by Jennifer. 'There is also the Law of the Protection of Values from Shame.' Mohammed instantly understood the Islamic view of the matter, dropping his head and sighing.

'So you see, if you add in this Russian who also wants this Prince dead for his own reasons, you have every man and his dog now wanting to dispose of these lovebirds.' Steven waved a finger in the air. 'But would all those threats persuade this couple to end their relationship, if not for themselves, then for the safety of their partner, eh?' Steven raised his eyebrows, as a gesture to invite comment, but he knew no comment would be forthcoming. 'Not on your Nellie. These two wanted each other so badly that they were prepared to risk everything, even life itself, to be together. How very nice and very romantic, if only they could have walked off into the sunset and lived happily ever after.'

Steven sat quiet for a long moment, allowing the nervous couple in front of him to consider the implications of their situation.

Mohammed looked at Alice and took hold of her hand and they both sighed realising that there was little they could say to defend their actions.

As a distraction, Steven picked up the remote and put the TV on, the Prince and Princess swivelled their heads in unison to watch. BBC News 24 was discussing the affair with pictures of the couple embracing on the fore deck of Golden Crown. He flicked over to CNN and then to Al Jezeerah, all were carrying the same story. 'See what I mean.'

'It is all true, what you say,' Mohammed said. 'I shall contact my father he will find a way to help, Allah wills it.'

'You haven't quite got it yet, have you? You no longer have a father, or anybody else for that matter.' Steven looked at each in turn. 'Princess Alice, Princess of Wight and her lover, Prince Mohammed Bin Aziz Al Saud, died in a boating accident aboard the Saudi Royal yacht Golden Crown, sailing in the Mediterranean. Last night to be precise, - so you see, they are no longer, they do not now exist, they have ceased to be.' Steven paused for the couple to digest the facts, before continuing. 'And I might add for the sake of our Islamic friend,' purposefully not using his name. 'Should, in any mysterious way Allah's will is involved, it would be to give you and your wife a second chance at a life together.'

'Wife,' Alice declared, 'but I'm already mar---.' Then it slowly dawned.

'I know it's a hell of lot to take in. Take five.' Steven sat back, crossed his legs and took another mouthful of tea.

'Probably in a day or so, a lifeboat will be found drifting in the Med', on one of the occupants will be found a letter written in Arabic describing a suicide pact, signed by the Prince and the Princess. A good forgery if I say so myself, it's even sealed with the Saudi Royal seal.'

'You give us no option, other than to go along with you,' Alice said and who appeared now to be more abreast of the situation than Mohammed.

'Good! This is the way it is to be.' Steven said as he got up, went to his desk and took out a large envelope full of various documents.

'Firstly read and digest this.' He passed them two sheets of paper each. 'It's your respective lives and family up to today. When you've memorised it, we'll shred them.'

Just so they understood, Steven read from his copy. 'Your names are, William Morris Chambers and Jordan Danielle

Chambers, nee Hornby-Turner. Birth certificates suitably aged, together with your National Insurance numbers and your Marriage certificate, passports and driving licences. Altogether, these are all the necessary documentation which would constitute your lives. The passports and driving licences do require your photographs, but we can do this, after Jens had a chance to alter your appearance.'

'I am no longer Muslim?'

'No, you are both non practicing Christians, but if you feel a need to follow the Islamic way, do it in private. However, in my opinion I strongly recommend that you forget about religion altogether, concentrate on being the average English couple who don't go to church every Sunday.'

Mohammed's head dropped, he clearly didn't like the thought of giving up his religion to any extent.

Steven noting the dismay on his face, decided to cajole him. 'I understand, this whole scenario, will take some coming to terms with. But come to terms with it, you must.'

Mohammed now Morris, showed no reaction other than to continue sulking. Steven only just, managed to restrain himself from giving the spoilt brat a slap.

'You do realise don't you? The extent of risk we have taken, just to give you this second chance at life. Don't blow it, Morris.'

Still no reaction, he just sat there staring at the saloon floor. 'If you have a problem with this, then you had better let me know now, while there is still time to drop the both of you, somewhere in the Med.'

A look of horror shot across both their faces.

Steven continued his voice sombre. 'However should you wish to take on these new identities, I must stress, and in all honesty, if ever your former identities are discovered, all, and I mean all, of our lives won't be worth shit. There is no going back. Do you understand!!!'

Jennifer could see Steven was becoming very exasperated. So she decided to continue the instruction, in a softer calmer voice. 'We want you to spend some time with us, here on Morning Star; we can even go for walks into town, which by the way is Frejus.' Noting the blank look, she added, 'That's on the South coast of France next to San Raphael. There should not be a problem with you being recognised, as the weather is very suitable for the wearing of hats, scarves and for having one's coat collar pulled up.' Jennifer turned first to Mohammed, gently lifting his still lowered head with her fingers under his chin. 'I think without your beard and your hair bleached, you would look completely different.' She studied his face a little longer, but more importantly, giving Mohammed the opportunity to note that she cared. As Jennifer took her hand away, the head stayed.

Turning her attention to the former Princess, she continued. 'And for you Jordan, dark hair and some gold rimmed spectacles, clear glass of course.' Taking a step back, she looked again at the couple. 'Yes, that would do it, I think.' Steven eased himself up. 'I guess you'll thank us one day.' Not being able to suppress the comment any longer.

'Oh, but I would like to thank you now, I only have one regret and that is I'll never see my son again, as a mother that is.' Mohammed – Morris looked at the former Princess and nodded in agreement. 'You're right, how could I not see that you are my life and my life is with you.' He looked at Steven, then at Jennifer. 'You have given me a life and for that I thank you.' Steven smiled. 'I'm glad you now see it our way. The first thing we must do is to alter to your appearances, so that we can complete the documentation.' At that, Jennifer produced a box full of utensil needed for the transformations.

'You first Morris,' she said, as she draped a towel around his neck and delved into the box for the shears. Jordan peered into the box and selected a hair colorant.

'If I could take this to the bathroom, I'll take care of my own hair.'

'Fine, if you can change the style as well, even better.'

'Before you run off Jordan, I have something else to say.' Steven said.

'Please make sure, for the time being at least, when you go on deck, or leave the boat, that you cover up, we can't take any chances that you may be recognised. I'm afraid this routine will have to be maintained until we are happy that whole situation has been forgotten. Oh and one more thing, I am going to leave you in Jens capable hands, for a day or so. I have some business to take care of. I sure hope you both will be comfortable here.'

CHAPTER 17
DISCOVERIES
Zurich

Steven arrived at Zurich International Airport, parked the Peugeot and headed to Customs and Immigration. Flashed a very authentic looking warrant card, at the desk sergeant and demanded to see whoever was in charge. 'That would be the Chief,' he said, 'if you care to follow me, sir.' The sergeant wrapped on an office door, awaited a response, before opening it and ushering Steven in.

'Detective Inspector Jacque Mateau, Interpol,' he said in flawless French.

'How can I help you Detective Inspector?'

'I'm trying to trace this man.' Steven said taking a photograph from out of his pocket. 'His name is Demmitri Abramovich, a known Russian gangster, said to be big in the Mafia.'

'So this is not a nice man, what's it got to do with me?' The Chief said flippantly.

Steven flicked through a note pad, 'On Saturday 3rd December Demmitri Abramovich boarded the ten am Swissair flight from Heathrow to Zurich.'

'We don't keep passenger manifests after a flight Monsieur.'

'Oh I know, but this guy's Russian, travelling under his own name and passport, he must have completed an immigration card. You do keep them don't you?' The officer thought for a moment.

'Y-e-s...We must, in order to keep track of aliens. We take the information from the card and put it on the computer.'

'So have you got him on your computer?' *Like drawing teeth.*

'It may be possible.'

'Please...If you wouldn't mind....Could you take a look?' Steven said, trying to remain patient.

'The third, you say, we may have something.' The Chief tapped the keyboard. 'Ah...'

'Problem?'

'Yes, we have an asterisk against his name.'

'Meaning?'

'We considered him undesirable and would have passed his details to the Police....Sorry.' The Chief said, making an apologetic gesture with his shoulders.

'So if you don't have his details on your computer. What's the chance that you still have the original immigration card?'

Again the Chief responded with a lift of his shoulders. 'Hum, possible, but why not contact the police, you have the authority don't you?'

'Believe me this is a very delicate matter, corruption may be involved, need I say more.'

The customs officer nodded, touched the side of his nose with his forefinger, and lifted the telephone receiver. 'Fabienne, please come in.'

A moment later, a very attractive blonde entered the office. 'Ah Fabienne, would you be so kind as to show the Detective Inspector to our archives. He will be looking for a particular immigration card early December.'

'Yes sir.' Then turning to Steven. 'Would you care to follow me, sir?'

'Most certainly.'

As soon as Steven had left the room, the customs officer, tapped Detective Inspector Jacque Mateau into the computer and attempted to access Interpol files. He didn't have clearance to do an in-depth search, but he did manage to come up with Steven's picture and a brief description. *It's enough.* He thought. *D I Mateau appears to be genuine.*

Fabienne pointed to the most likely box file and left Steven to it. 'Please Monsieur, turn off the light when you leave and return all the cards to the right place.'

'Thank you.' He said, as he delved into the masses of cards.

Thirty minutes later, Steven held up a card written in Russian, with a French translation scribbled at the bottom. Abramovich had listed his address as an apartment on Badenerstrasse. 'Hum this is interesting.' He tucked the card into his pocket and made his way back, remembering to turn out the light.

He entered the Chiefs office without knocking. 'Ah Inspector, did you find what you were looking for?'

'Sort of, Abramovich lists his occupation as a Salesman for Schneider Klaus. Who are they?'

The Chief customs officer hit a few keys and a page of information on Schneider Klaus appeared. 'I'll run a copy off for you, Detective Inspector, you can see for yourself.'

Steven lifted the telephone in an airport pay booth.

'Hi Jen, how's it going?'

'Everything's fine, the Chambers actually seem to be enjoying themselves. Are you all right?'

'Yes I'm fine, but I would like you to do something for me.'

'Sure, what?'

'Access my computer and send an e-mail to guy named Terry, his address is in my contact list.'

'I know your code name, but I can't remember your access code.'

'Not a problem, I'll text it, just remember to delete it from your inbox once you're in.'

'Okay, so what am I asking this Terry?'

'I want him to dig into a company here in Zurich, Schneider Klaus, anything he can find.'

'Will do.'

'I'll give you a ring tomorrow evening hopefully you'll have the answers.'

'Is that all?'

'That's it Jen, love you, see you later.'

'Love you too, bye.'

Steven replaced the receiver, looked around the milling crowds in the arrivals hall and ascertained that he was not the subject of any unwanted interest. *Right, next step, find a hotel on Badenerstrasse.*

Steven had found himself a hotel, which had proved difficult so close to Christmas, but a combination of warrant card flashing for a surveillance operation and a very large donation to the hotels charity box, secured him a room, although not directly opposite, did look onto the apartment building on Badenerstrasser. He had already checked the apartments list of the occupant's on the door and had ascertained with a few direct question to some of the residents, that Abramovich was a resident in the apartment with no name tag.

The next day Abramovich appeared. He left the apartment building, walked to the end of the block and disappeared from Steven's view. 'Probably going to pick up his car,' Steven thought. *Doesn't appear to take his job seriously either, almost noon, if he's going to work, I reckon he'll be late.*

Steven waited a while to make sure Demmitri wasn't going to reappear, before putting on his grey three quarter wool overcoat with a red scarf and kid leather gloves and going out into the cold and damp street.

Light flakes of snow dusted the crowds of shoppers milling along the pavements and in and out of the shops, no doubt preparing for the forthcoming holiday.

With his collar pulled up Steven crossed the busy street and entered into the doorway of the apartment building. He randomly selected one of the residents listed, he pressed the call button.

'Ja.'

'Package for Heinz.' As the buzzer sounded, Steven pushed the door open and took the stairs to Abramovich's apartment, number ten on the second floor. He had a quick check to see if the door was clean, it was. *Obviously doesn't feel the need for caution.* Putting an ear to the door, he heard a faint female voice humming an undeterminable tune.

It was a Yale type lock, awkward, but should be easy enough. With a visual check of the landing he ensured the coast was clear and took the lock levers from out of the large inside coat pocket and twiddled them in the key slot. After a few moments he rotated the lever in the slot and rolled back the latch. He quietly opened the door, stepped inside, gently closing it behind him and tip toed into the hall heading towards the sound. The bedroom door was open, bedding in disarray and articles of woman's clothing were strewn across the floor. The humming now louder was accompanied with the occasional splashing. *Some one's having a bath.* The bathroom door was partly open and wisps of steam escaped into the passage. Without further hesitation he pushed the door open and lent a shoulder against the frame, taking in the sight of a blond woman in the bath. Her hair tied up with a pink ribbon, eyes closed, lying in a bath of foaming bubbles. Sensing that someone was standing in the doorway, she said in Swiss French.

'You tell me you would be gone sometime time, Monsieur.'

'Did he?' Steven said in the same language.

The shock caused her to sit up, eyes now open she stared wildly at Steven. 'Who the hell are you?'

Steven didn't answer, he just smiled.

Without any sign of modesty, she stood up and attempted to reach for the towel on the chair near to where Steven was standing. She made no attempt to cover her more private bits and the foaming bubbles that had initially clung to the skin above her breasts, began to run down her body like a low cut dress that was fast disintegrating. The soapy foam dripped from her very prominent pink nipples and ran down her stomach collecting for a moment to hang like a bunch of grapes on her pubic hair before continuing their journey down her legs.

'What the fuck do you want? (Or the French equivalent) How did you get in?'

Steven took in the sight before him, couldn't help it really.

'Had a good look, have you?'

Steven smiled and nodded as he picked up a towel off the chair and with an outstretched arm, handed it to her.

'Oh me, I'm just a humble policeman doing a hard and poorly paid job, and how I got in and what I want is of no concern to you.'

'You bastards flatfoot pigs, you can't leave me alone. I've every right to be here, he called me. It wasn't a pick up.'

'Just get dressed and get out.'

'I haven't been paid.'

'If you're not out of here in five minutes, you can tell that to the magistrate.'

The prostitute got the message and was out of there post haste.

Steven had made himself comfortable in the lounge armchair, his coat and scarf lay neatly on the settee, the contents of his pockets, including the 9mm automatic with silencer and his flick knife, arranged on an occasional table at his side.

Steven had searched the place and had discovered a black note book taped to the back of a painting which was hanging on the bedroom wall. He sat back studied each page, while sampling a glass of Demmitri's Vodka.

Most of the information in the book related to what Steven thought was mafia business, except that is, for an entry on the back inside cover, which seemed to be, somewhat out of place. It was a set of twenty numbers arranged in pairs with a different letter set over each paring.

The click of the latch and the groan of a door opening, and Steven became alert. He slowly picked up the 9mm automatic, thumbing off the safety and let it rest lightly on the top of his crossed legs.

'I'm back.' Was shouted, in passable Swiss French.

'Glad to hear it, old boy.' Demmitri spun around in the direction of the voice at the same time his hand went inside his coat.

'Ah ah, we don't want to do that, do we?' Steven was now aiming the automatic at Demmitri's head. He got out of the chair and took a couple of steps towards the Russian. Plunging his left hand into Demmitri's coat, he retrieved the weapon that was tucked under the Russians arm, at the same time bringing the butt of the 9mm automatic crashing down onto his temple. Demmitri dropped like a bag of bricks.

It was almost half an hour later when Demmitri came round, there was a banging inside his head and bright flashing lights danced in front of his eyes. At first he was puzzled and confused as to why he was so cold and unable to move his limbs and then he slowly realised that he was spread-eagled on the bed. His hands and feet were tightly tied, there was tape over his mouth and he was completely naked, but somehow he had the impression, this was not going to be a kinky sex session. As his vision slowly returned, he saw Steven's smiling face towering over him.

'Sorry about that old boy, can't have you playing with guns, can we?' Then Steven placed a towel filled with ice over Demmitri's forehead. 'There that should help to dull the pain a little. Now, all I want to do is to ask you few simple questions, get a few answers, and then I'm on my way. I am about to remove the tape, no shouting please.'

Steven removed the gag. 'Who the fuck, are you?'

'You're the second one to ask that question today.'

'What do you fucking want, are you some kind of fucked up pervert?'

'Demmitri, Demmitri, this is not the way to play the game. I ask the questions, and you give the answers, right.'

'Fuck you.'

Steven pressed the button that allowed the six inch blade of his flick knife to spring open in front of Demmitri's eyes. He then ran the blade down the side of Abramovich's face without breaking the skin, but with the desired effect.

'Wrong answer, now shall we start again?' Demmitri gave a very delicate nod. 'About three weeks ago you were in London. Why?'

'I was sightseeing.'

'I'm so sorry Mr Abramovich; I forgot to explain the rules. If I get a wrong answer, I run my knife down your body, starting, I think, at your neck. Every wrong answer, I'll go a little further until I reach your manhood. Although, I haven't yet decided what to cut off first, your balls or your dick.'

Demmitri could see in Steven's eyes, that he meant every word. *Who is this bastard who knows my name, where I'm living and where I've been.* But Demmitri could not, rather foolishly, resist the challenge to be defiant.

'Okay, I shall ask you again, why were you in London?'

'To see the fucking King!'

Steven's knifepoint touched the skin and he applied a little pressure. It was so sharp that a rivulet of blood appeared like the turned over soil that follows the plough. The knife travelled to the sternum, the skin peeling open, but it was not a deep cut. Steven had wisely replaced the gag to subdue the scream he knew Abramovich would let out, especially when he liberally dusted the wound with a layer of salt.

Steven lifted tape. 'Well?'

'Okay, okay, I'll tell you everything you want to know.' Demmitri said as Steven lifted the knife.

'That's the spirit.' He said, at the same time using a sheet to clean the wound.

'Are you going to kill me?'

'Not unless you force me, your death would be of little benefit.'

At that the relief on Demmitri's face was evident, there was no reason to believe Steven, but it would less painful if he did.

'Let's start again, why were you in London?'

Demmitri hesitated, wondering just how much this man knew. His inhibitions soon disappeared as he felt the point of Steven's knife on his stomach.

'I, I was paid a large sum to kill an Arab Prince.'

'Ah, good now we're getting somewhere, and did you?'

'No, it was all a cock up. I was told to kill the Arab make sure the Americans took the blame.'

'How was it a cock up?'

'I get to London with a plan to make a bomb; it was to be of American sourced materials. I was going to plant it under the Arab's car.'

'And?'

'This guy, who was supposed to get me the stuff, gave me a fucking camera and told me to shoot pictures. Hey, what the fuck. I'm not going to argue, so long as I get paid.'

'Who was paying you?'

'He'll kill me.'

'So shall I if you don't tell me about Comrade Vostok.'

He knows, oh shit, who is this fucking guy. Demmitri's mind was in a spin and the throbbing pain shooting from his temple and across his brow did not help.

'Well Demmitri are you going to tell me?'

'Yes, yes, you know already.'

Steven nodded. 'I'm still waiting.'

'A very powerful man, from the motherland, name of Vladimir Vostok.'

'Thank you, now no more time wasting, Demmitri, eh.'

Demmitri now shaking with fear, made a barely discernable nod. 'What do you know of Giles Fairchild?'

'He was the contact in London, the one who was to get me the explosive. - Any chance of a drink, whoever you are?'

Steven got a glass of water, propping an arm behind his head gave him a drink.

'Ah, thanks.' Demmitri let his head go down and his eyes roll up to stare at a spot on the ceiling.

'I had it all figured, I gave that Fairchild man a list of items I would need. But instead he gave me a camera, you know the ones with the big lens, there's been a change of plan, he said you just take the pictures, I'll tell you what, where and when.'

Demmitri rolled his eyes to look at Steven.' So that's what I did, I took pictures.'

'Pictures of whom?'

'The Arab and some blond tart.'

'How much was Vostok paying you?'

'Six million roubles, plus expenses, half at the start and half when the Prince is dead, I'm still waiting for Vostok to pay up.'

'Why, is the Prince dead?'

'How the fuck do I know.'

'There's something else isn't there Demmitri, something that you aren't telling me?'

'No, nothing, there is no more to tell.'

'Oh dear, just when I thought we were friends.'

Steven pulled back the sheet and held up the knife letting the glint of the blade flash in Demmitri's eyes again, as he repositioned the tape over Demmitri's mouth. The sharp point of the blade pierced the skin on the end of his manhood. The penis shrunk all of its own accord, trying to bury itself within the foreskin.

'Mmmm-mmmm.' Demmitri shook his head violently from side to side. As Steven removed the tape gag, Demmitri blurted out. 'No! No! I tell you anything you want to know.'

'Too late old man, I've started so I'll finish, perhaps the next time I ask a question, I'll get the right answer.'

Steven replaced the gag and positioned the blade back to the stomach. Slowly he let the blade travel another six inches towards his umbilical, again dusting the wound with salt. 'Good healing power, salt, may sting a little.'

Demmitri's eyes bulged and the cheeks expanded as the tape muffled the scream, but the pain was genuine.

'Now then Demmitri, no more pissing me about, eh?' Demmitri nodded opening and closing his eyes at the same time.

'What do you know about twenty-million pounds Sterling?' Steven removed the gag and lowered an ear towards Demmitri's face to hear the gagging voice.

'Twenty-million, what! – I know nothing, please believe me, I don't know.' Demmitri was almost crying as he pleaded with Steven.

And I'm inclined to believe you. Steven thought.

'I only took the pictures. I gave the film and the camera back to Fairchild. He gave me a Swissair ticket to Zurich and the address of this apartment which had been pre booked in my name. Believe me, that's all I know, someone else would make the hit on the Arab. I was to wait here until he was dead. Then Vostok would pay me what he owes.'

'Your still not telling everything, are you?'

'What do you mean?'

'The envelope!'

Demmitri knew that it was pointless trying to withhold information. This stranger seems to know more than he knew himself.

'Oh the envelope, Fairchild gave it to me. I was to hand to Vladimir Vostok, no one else.'

'Is Vostok here in Zurich?'

'Of course, he arrived just before I got here.'

'Where is he?'

'I don't know where he is living, but he spends a lot of time in his office.'

'His office, where?'

'The Schneider Klaus factory on Bellerivestrasse.' Steven didn't let his surprise show.

'You opened the envelope of course?'

'Err yes, when I got here, because Vostok did not come when I arrived. I didn't know what to make of it, there were ten small envelopes inside and each of them had a square piece of paper inside.' Abramovich hesitated, as if he was again considering how much more he should divulge.

'Go on, Demmitri.' Steven prompted, as he waved the blade over the Russian's face.

'On each piece of paper was a capitol letter with a two digit number under. All were hand written, by different hands.'

'And?'

'I didn't know what it all meant, so I went out and bought similar envelopes put them back as there were and gave them to one of Vostok's heavies when he showed up here.'

'These numbers?' Steven opened the black book, sticking his thumb in the back cover to hold it open at the entry. Demmitri gasped then let his jaw drop, ever so slightly nodding his head.

London

'I've just received the communiqué Terry intercepted from the French coast guard Peter.' Marjorie said on the intercom.

'Sounds interesting, you'd better bring it in, dear.'

Marjorie entered Sir Peter's office, her eyes scanning a piece of paper as she walked in and sat down.

'It's in French of course, roughly translated it says,

'Early this morning a fishing vessel out of Sardinia picked up five survivors from a lifeboat, believed to be from the MV Golden Crown. One of the survivors was carrying a letter written in Arabic referring to a suicide pact and it was signed by Prince Mohammed Bin Aziz Al Saud and Princess Alice, Princess of Wight.'

'Well blow me, I think he's done it, he's just bloody well gone and done it.' Sir Peter's face then turned sombre. 'Hum, unfortunately now's the time to sort this little matter.' Taking a file from the draw, he stapled a white form with a large black 'D' to the file front. 'Have MI5 action that, please Marj,' handing Marjorie the file.

'But that's Spiders file, isn't that a bit drastic Peter?'

'I don't have any choice; this is the one time when all bridges have to be burnt. The fewer people who know about our connection with this the better and useful though he is, he is one of the too many people.'

Marjorie, file in hand stood looking at Sir Peter trying to comprehend.

'And I would like them to expedite this as well, PDQ.'

Zurich

'Hi Jen, how's it going?'

'Yeah good.'

'And our guests?'

'No worries there Steven, they are so wrapped up in each other, nothing else matters.'

'Good, have you heard anything from Terry?'

'Got the info about an hour ago.'

'Anything interesting?'

'Uh uh, pin your ears back lover boy.' Jenifer gave out little cough just to emphasize that she was about to read.

'Two Germans Gunter Schneider and Helmut Klaus founded a Swiss precision engineering workshop in 1888 making watches. Schneider died forty years later no heir. Klaus, only had a daughter, she copped the lot when old man Klaus kicked the bucket. This is where it starts to get interesting; Olga Klaus's married name was Kunze, with me so far?'

'I'm way ahead.'

'The Kunze banking empire grew from the profits of the engineering roots. Our banker friend Hiendric Kunze, the last of the Kunze family, lost the engineering side of the business three years ago in a hostile takeover by-.'

'Let me guess.' Steven put in. 'Vladimir Vostok.'

'Got it in one lover, how did you-.

'Oh I've just had a meeting with one of his employee's.'

Well, apparently the engineering business switched from watches to weapons when Vostok got involved.'

'Thanks for that Jen.'

'There's something else I thought you would like to know, on this mornings TV, the lifeboat has been found, five survivors.'

'Good, I'm pleased they survived, sort of worked out as we planned.'

'Sure did.'

'Bye gorgeous, catch you later.'

'Bye lover. - Oh Steven.'

'Yes'

'Be careful.'

CHAPTER 18

PAY BACK TIME

Steven parked the Peugeot in a side street two blocks away from the bank and set off to walk the short distance. The Kunze International Bank stood on the other side of Stockerstrasse. It was a large imposing building constructed of stone block, rather plain and not aesthetically pleasing. Steven crossed the street and entered the building via a large double leaf steel clad timber door, on the inside of which stood an x-ray type security screen, and three guards. He was not stopped, perhaps because the guard, who was scrutinising the screen, was looking for obvious weapons. He was now in the grand hall, a large open floor area with stone supporting pillars in grid form carrying the high ceilings.

The grand hall, was bustling with investors, borrowers, tellers and advisors. Steven noted the security cameras covering every area of the floor. *Thank goodness I left the gun behind.* He mused as he headed towards the main reception desk, which was positioned in the middle of the floor, but set back toward the rear wall of the hall.

Of the two receptionists, one he noted was old and no doubt prudish. *A proper jobsworth by the looks, won't get far with that one.* The other was a lot younger and seemed to be much less proficient and from time to time, she appeared to be seeking the older ones advice.

She'll do for me, I'll just hang back until the older women is involved with a customer, then I'll catch the young ones eye.

'I'd like to see the Director please.'

'Do you have an appointment, Monsieur?'

'No.'

'Ah well I don't think that would be possible.'

Steven passed her an envelope, written on it was "PRIVATE and URGENT".

"For the attention of Heindric Kunze Director."

'Oh I think he will want to see me, would you make sure he gets this immediately.'

The young receptionist made to take the envelope, then pulled her hand back and looked for some assurance from the older woman, there was none was forthcoming, so she gingerly took the envelope from Steven.

'I'll be waiting over there.' Steven said, pointing to a bench seat in the middle of the hall.

'Who shall I say it's from sir?'

'It's not relevant.'

'Do you have an account with us Monsieur?'

'Yes, it's a numbered account.' Steven turned his back on the receptionist and headed to the seat.

'Please Monsieur I need to fill in your details.' Steven ignored her and as he sat down, he made a point of staring at the young girl.

She's getting flustered now, biting her bottom lip, not knowing whether she should pester her colleague again or leave her post to run the errand.

Eventually she did the right thing and made a telephone call. Steven guessed she was relaying his message by the way she would occasionally nod and look in his direction.

Ten minutes later a rather tall stiff looking man with thinning hair and wearing a black suit with a white shirt that had a starched straight up collar with wing tips, came out of one of the lifts. At first glance, Steven thought he was a preacher and then noticed that the man stopped briefly at the desk and talked to the young receptionist, who in turn, pointed at Steven. The man collected the envelope and headed in Steven's direction. He approached clicking his heels together as he halted, so close that he towered over Steven. Looking down his hooked nose, he said. 'Would you care to follow me sir.' And without saying another word, he smartly turned, as if on a parade square and headed back to the lifts. Steven jumped up almost broke into a trot in an attempt to catch up.

The man and Steven took the lift to the seventh and top floor. Neither spoke.

Directly in front of the lift, across a passage was a door. As a matter of fact, it was the only door Steven could see on that landing, apart from a fire door at the far end of the passage with the word 'SORTIE' stencilled on it. What's more, only the one lift, yet there was a bank of four on the ground floor. Steven followed the man through the door into what was an outer office. In the centre of the opposite wall, there was another large very ornate double leaf rosewood door and at each side of it were red cushioned chairs. A little way back and to one side there was a very clerical looking desk, no doubt the stiff's place.

The man indicated that Steven should be seated on one of the red cushioned chairs. 'Wait here, please.' Giving the large door a cursory knock, he opened it and disappeared inside.

A few moments later the stiff emerged and ushered Steven in. Steven was wearing a navy blue suit white shirt and red silk tie, his three quarter overcoat and scarf lay neatly over his left arm. Lightly adhered to the forefinger of the left hand and concealed by the coat, was a miniature transmitter. The black disc was about 8mm diameter by 2mm thick, with a strong adhesive coated the outer face.

Kunze's office was huge, rosewood panelling, or full height rosewood bookcases around the walls. There were two other smaller doors at one side, possibly led to a conference room and perhaps a washroom. Large portrait oil paintings with gilt frames adorned the walls, some no doubt, paintings of the founders, as some of these portraits bore a strong resemblance to the present Director, who was sat at the far end of the room behind a grand 'Rosewood' desk. Steven noted the hard hostile stare he was getting from the diminutive and rather wizened figure of Hiendric Kunze.

Likes his 'Rosewood, He took in the surroundings as he approached the distant desk, as got nearer he noted with some satisfaction that the telephone was black. He also noted the paper, his note, shaking slightly even though Kunze held it with both hands.

As Steven got within ten feet of the desk, he quickened his stride, extending his right hand out to the Director and making sure his was at the telephone side of the desk. His approach was so forceful and overpowering, that Kunze was obliged to remain seated, as Steven reached over and trust his hand forward.

'Ah Director Kunze how pleased I am to meet you.' Steven said. As he leaned across the corner of the desk to shake hands with Kunze, the index finger on his left hand uncurled itself from the cover of his overcoat and deposited the little black sticky disc on the back of the telephone. Kunze, now trying to stand was neither up nor down, being forced by etiquette to accept Steven's hand. Which he did half-heartedly, offering a brief limp response. 'Monsieur.' He gestured for Steven to take a seat, with a nod of the head in the direction of a solitary chair facing the desk.

'I don't know anything about twenty-million pounds, your note cannot be correct.'

Really. Steven thought. *Then why did you bother to see me. This is a worried man, he isn't even attempting to ask my name.*

'Perhaps Herr Kunze, this may help you throw some light on the matter.' Steven took another envelope from his pocket, the envelope and its contents were exactly as Demmitri Abramovich had described.

The colour drained from Kunze's face even before Steven had taken out all of the smaller envelopes. Steven made no attempt to remove the slips of paper, he perceived the mere sight of the envelopes was enough. Beads of perspiration formed on

Kunze's brow and trickled on to the lenses of his gold-rimmed spectacles.

'Impossible!' He shouted, jumping to his feet and sending his chair flying backwards. No doubt very rattled now, he brought his fist down on the desktop. 'Who sent you? There is no such account! What do you want?'

Account eh, that's interesting, I do believe I've hit pay dirt. Let's wing it, see if I can really stir some shit.

'Who sent me? Why you and your friends did. The task is complete, now I want what was promised.'

'Err I don't know what you are talking about. - I want you to leave, right now.'

Steven wondered why Kunze kept furtively glancing at the local newspaper folded neatly on the corner of the desk.

'Do I have to call security?'

Yeah go ahead, why don't you, I've really put the shits up you, haven't I, better than I could have hoped for. 'No, no need, I'm leaving.' Steven said holding up the palm of his right hand.

'Maybe Herr Kunze you want time to reconsider, but I'll be back and that's a promise.'

Steven got up and walked quickly out. As he passed through the outer office, the stiff jumped to his feet and stared hard and menacingly. But Steven paid him no heed as he sped through the door making sure it was closed behind him. He hit the lift call button, the doors opened instantly. Entering he pressed the button for level one, jumping out before the doors closed and headed instead for the door marked 'SORTIE' leading, he was sure to a stairwell.

There was a camera high on the side wall of the stairwell, but fortunately it was pointing down the staircase, Steven figured that the landing directly under the camera would not be in shot, a black spot and he pressed into the void and hoped. There was also a camera on the wall covering the flight of staircase going up, which more than likely led to the roof and lift shaft motor rooms.

As soon he was confident that he was not being watched, he withdrew a wire from his inside pocket which was connected to a receiver and just a moment after the earpiece was in place.

Purr, purr, purr, 'Vostok.'

'Vladimir, it's Hiendric, we've got big problems. You told me everything was taken care of and I wasn't to be involved. No need to set up the account, you said.'

'Hiendric! Get a grip of yourself, you wimp. What's the big problem?'

'I've just had a man here, in the bank, wanting the twenty-million pounds for getting rid of the Prince.'

'Quiet you fool! Watch what you're saying, idiot.'

'How, how, did he know?'

'Hiendric, this is not a matter we can discuss on the phone.'

There was a moment's pause. 'Where is this man now?'

'I think he is on his way out, but he did say he was coming back.'

Stop the bastard now! I'm on my way.'

Click –the receiver went down, only to be picked up again.

'Gunter.'

'Yes Herr Director.'

'That man who has just left my office, stop him, do not let him leave the building.' Click. The phone went dead.

Steven took the earpiece from his ear, tucking it and the wire back into his pocket. Well I think the shits well and truly hit the fan, now what do I do, can't go up and as sure as hell can't go down.

The outer office door opened and the lift motor was activated. Steven peered through the wired glass panel set into the door, just in time to see the blur of a figure he assumed to be Gunter, disappear into the lift.

'Come on Steven what would you do in their situation?' He pondered. 'I'd immediately block the exits, give the guards my description, until I could lift a photo off the tapes, then I would check the camera footage. When they realise I may not have left they will probably carry out a search room by room. If they don't find me, will they assume I've somehow escaped? No I don't think so; they will check every body in and out of the building.'

He heard a door bang somewhere below and the sound of a number of pairs of boots running up the stairs. One thing's for sure, I'm not staying here. Steven checked the passage. 'Good all clear.'

He made his way to the lift and was about to press the call button when the motor began to whirl. *Time for a re-think.* He had no other option but to make a dash into the outer office. Desperately he looked around for somewhere to hide. Behind Gunter's desk were two doors, one left and one right, he chose the right one, it was a washroom.

Where can you hide in a washroom? Well at least the pan is enclosed.'

There were sounds of many footsteps, and a few voices, one of which was Gunter's, issuing orders.

A crash as the washroom door was flung open and then another as the security guard pushed open the toilet cubicle door and had a quick look in. On seeing it empty, he left the washroom closing the door behind him. 'All clear in there, Herr Gunter.' *That was close,* Steven thought, *thank goodness for high ceilings.* He stayed suspended above the pan, legs and arms pressing into the sidewalls, back against the ceiling. The tie was tucked into his shirt and he was now wearing the buttoned up overcoat.

It's getting to be most uncomfortable up here, can't stay here any longer and he slowly lowered himself down to the floor and sat down for a breather on the pan. Hope Gunter isn't taken short. The earpiece was put back in place, when he heard Gunter entering Kunze's office.

'Pardon the intrusion Herr Director, but the man did not leave the building. We are not sure at what floor he left the elevator, so we are searching all floors. May we check the conference room?'

'Yes, of course.'

At that moment the telephone rang. 'Herr Vostok and two other Gentlemen to see you Herr Director.'

'Yes I am expecting them, send them up.'

Click.

'Gunter, continue your search, Herr Vostok is on his way up. I will require some privacy.'

'As you wish Herr Director. You there, check the stairwell.'
Gunter barked out his orders as he left Kunze's office.

Steven heard both the inner and outer doors close and the noise that accompanied the search abated. Seconds later the noise of the large rosewood doors being thrown open rang in Steven's ear.

'Err Comrade Vostok, good of you to come.'

'No it isn't you slimy bastard, I had to leave a very important meeting because of your whimpering. – Now what's this all about?'

'Err this is a private matter, Comrade.'

'Very well.' He slowly turned, nodding at two heavily built gentlemen. –'You two outside.'

Steven heard Kunze's office door close again, with as much noise that had accompanied its opening and presumed that the two thugs were now standing outside the washroom door, in the outer office. 'Hope they aren't in need of a piss either.'

'This man entered my office with an envelope demanding payment of the Twenty million for completing the task.'

'Probably a set up by your Brotherhood friends to ensure you keep your end of the deal.'

'But he had the account numbers.'

'Impossible there are only two sets, one in your safe, the others in mine.....Then again, my copy came from the Englishman. Surely he would never have the balls to cross me.....Or would he?'

'You mean London copied the numbers before giving them to you.'

'Y-e-s, it all fits, the bastards must be trying to double cross me.'

'What about this man, he seemed genuine. Could he have done, you-know?'

'You are so gullible Kunze, you worry me sometimes. Believe me from what I've read about the probable loss of the Golden Crown it would have taken more than one man to undertake an operation of such magnitude; no I smell a rat, an English one at that.'

There was a long pause; Steven listened intently trying to envisage what was happening.

'I'm going to have him for this. – How dare he even think about crossing me? And that goes for you too Herr Kunze, cross me at your peril.'

'Oh no Comrade I would never dare.'

'Where is this man now?'

'We are still searching the building. We think he is still inside.'

'Find him... I want answers.'

'Y-e-s comrade.'

'When you have him, hold him, I want to know for sure who sent him. My companions specialise in extracting information, with some relish, but of course, you know this....Do you not. When we have what we need, we will fit him out with a pair of concrete boots, ha ha ha.' Vostok let out a false sounding laugh 'And watch him swim in the lake.'

There was another pause in the conversation accompanied by the sounds of somebody pacing back and forth.

'Enough of this waiting, I don't have time for this. I must return to my meeting. You will telephone me when you have him. Goodbye Herr Kunze....Oh, and if you don't find this man, I'm sure we can find some boots that will fit you.' Steven heard doors opening and closing and the sound moving away.

He may have left the gun in the car glove compartment, but he was not without a weapon, he had managed to smuggle in the flick knife which he placed in his top pocket of his jacket, along with a couple of pens.

Easing himself out of the washroom, ensuring the coast was clear; he headed to Kunze's office. Pushing open the double doors, he jumped inside; back straight and left arm extended holding the hilt of the knife. With luck from a distance, the knife handle would resemble the barrel of a handgun.

'I'm back! Ah, ah, hands where I can see them please, Herr Kunze.' Even from the other side of the room Steven could see the fear in the Directors eyes.

Without averting his attention he closed the door behind him, turning the large iron key until it clicked locked and pushing home the shoot bolts in one of the leaves, before quickly striding towards the shaking figure of Herr Kunze.

Once in knife range, Steven threw the knife up so that it spun in the air, rather like tossing a pancake. As he caught the handle he pressed the button and the blade flicked out. In the same movement his arm extended, so that the tip of the blade lightly touched Kunze's nose, instantly turning the face ashen. 'That proved a point.'

'Let's cut the crap Herr Kunze, I was sent here by some very powerful business men to make sure this account was opened with the money they entrusted to you.'

'I, I, can't.'

Steven didn't give him a chance to continue. 'Oh yes you can, I was instructed to advise you in the event of this scenario happening. These very powerful men will take your business plunging you and your family into financial ruin and you will of course.' Steven paused long enough to push the blade ever so slightly, but enough to cause a droplet of blood to disperse on the desk blotter. 'Be executed. Eventually!'

Herr Kunze appeared to get the message. He knew how powerful these men could be in their own right, combined, awesome. Steven watched as Kunze visibly shaking, opened the newspaper at the ads' section. Kunze then reached over for the envelopes Steven had laid on the desk. He found himself struggling with the shakes, unable to extract the slips of paper easily. The telephone rang and Kunze physically jumped, scattering the paper pieces and envelopes, across the desk. Steven leaned over and grabbed Kunze's right hand, holding it solidly in a vice like grip, positioning the blade tip lightly under his chin. 'Answer it, very, very carefully Herr Kunze.' Kunze picked up the receiver, gave a little cough to activate his voice box. 'Y-e-s.'

'Gunter, Herr Director.' Steven mouthed the prompts for Kunze. 'Did you find him Gunter?'

'No Herr Director, we have checked the all screens and searched the building there is no sign of him. We've replayed the videos from when he entered the bank, but can't find any of him leaving the building.'

'All right Gunter, did you check out the vaults?'

'No Herr Director.'

'Then do so. Report back to me only when you have found him. And Gunter.'

'Yes Herr Director.'

'I'm in the middle of some very important paperwork of a discrete nature, my door is locked, please see to it that I'm not disturbed.'

'Yes Herr Director.'

Steven gestured to replace the receiver, and he did. It was best that Kunze did not call off the search for him. It may have led to Gunter suspecting Kunze was being forced.

'I do hope for your sake Herr Kunze, that Gunter believes you have locked yourself in for the sake of paperwork.'

'It is a common occurrence, Gunter will not suspect anything.'

'Shall we proceed?' Kunze nodded, his shakes had settled and some colour was starting to return to his face.

'Tell me; did you kill the Arab Prince?'

Steven pondered the question. 'Yes, I did, with a little help; you can take it that the Prince is dead.'

'And how, may I ask did you come by these numbers?' *Got to wing it again.* Steven thought. 'I was employed to watch a certain Englishman and report on the progress of this package. When it became clear that nothing was going to happen, I stepped in, did the job, then had a little chat with the then carrier to retrieve the envelope, not to dissimilar from the one we're having now. I can be very persuasive. He'd already passed on the envelope, but was wise enough to make a copy.'

'Y-e-s that would explain it.....I remember, I used a blue ballpoint, not black.'

Kunze stared blankly at Steven for a moment. 'Then you should be paid as the Brotherhood agreed.'

Steven got the impression that Hiendric Kunze had changed; perhaps the threats from his Brotherhood friends had had the desired affect. Kunze now seemed calmer and more assured as he switched on the computer. He collected the slips of paper and set them out, in order of the corresponding letters in the newspaper ad. 'CDHZPLMYBW' the two numbers under each initial formed the twenty-digit number, which Kunze entered into the computer.

'That is your account number; you will need to give me your personal details for a recognition code so that only you can access the account.'

'I would prefer to put in my own code.'

'Feel free.' Kunze turned the monitor to face Steven.

'Hands where I can see them please Herr Kunze.' Steven put down the knife, and turned his attention to the computer screen.

'If you insist, but let me tell you, whoever you are.'

The second time I been called that.

'I have no intention of causing you any problems.' Steven nodded and started to enter a six-digit name as a personal recognition code.

'Oh yeah, why the sudden change of heart?'

Kunze looked at Steven for a long moment, before replying. 'From the very start, I was afraid someone like you would turn up. When you did, I was shocked and I panicked. In these past moments I've had the chance to consider my situation. All I have left now is my pride and hopefully if I can retrieve it, my allegiance to the Brotherhood.....To start with, I intend to honour my commitment to them.'

Kunze sat up straight and swung back the computer screen with some vigour. 'So I've decided, to make things right.' Kunze was punching numbers into the computer as he spoke. 'The twenty-million pounds, was only sixteen-million, two of us didn't contribute. I exchanged this to Euros, and was forced to transfer the money into this account.'

Steven muttered, even before he saw the screen, 'Vostok'

'Ah you know him?'

'Oh yes I know him, although we've never met, he's the bastard who started the whole thing. His greed for Arab oil sparked terrorist action all over the Middle East, eventually leading to the assassination of a Prince and Princess.'

Steven looked into Kunze's eyes. 'I figured he was pulling your strings.'

Kunze stopped tapping the computer keys and sat motionless for a few moments, staring somewhere in the distance.

'I am so sorry for the loss of those young lives; I never wanted to be involved.'

So now he admits involvement.

Kunze continued. 'Some four years ago, Vostok, although I didn't know it at the time, contrived to take over my engineering empire. It started slowly, someone, over time, buying all the available stock in each of my sixty-nine world wide engineering companies. I was so tied up with my bank. I didn't even notice. Then it started to happen, loss of orders, wildcat strikes, contracts going pear shaped through shop floor errors. It was a nightmare, works after works closing down. The redundancy payments alone were crippling me. I found out much later that these workshops were being bought up for next to nothing by the same body that had bought the shares.'

'Vostok.'

'Indirectly, yes, at first I thought they were crazy, until I realised one man was behind them. By then of course I needed money to cover the mounting debt. There were the liquidated damages claims and the legal costs. – One contract in particular, cost me dearly. We had supplied the glazing support structure for a tower block curtain wall system. This proved to be faulty and the engineering integrity of the whole glazed wall was in jeopardy. I approached a well known establishment for a substantial loan.' Kunze's eyes began to water; the tears seemed to hang on his cheek for sometime before disappearing down his shirtfront. 'Perhaps rather naively, now I think about it, I was persuaded to put up my banking empire as surety. Imagine if you can my feelings, as Comrade Vostok along with his two henchmen, stood in this very office with a foreclosure notice. He just happened to own the loan company as well.' Kunze deflated and sank back into his chair.

'I've lost everything. Yes, Mr' whoever you are, everything, including this bank.' Kunze paused, sadness on his face, the tears still welling in his eyes.

'So you see, your threats of financial ruin are of no consequence. And your threat of execution could even be a comfort to me.' Steven quite genuinely reached out and rested his hand on Kunze's shoulder. 'I'm so sorry.'

Kunze smiled weakly, nodding his head in acknowledgement. He took out a handkerchief and dabbed his eyes. 'Of course nobody but Vostok, and you now, know that, to the staff I am still Herr Director.' Kunze looked very solemn. 'This bank, among other things, Vostok took with force.'

Steven's turn to look surprised. 'How?'

'As you may imagine I was not going to give in that easily to Comrade Vostok, like you, locked my office door and let his two goons go to work on the parts of my body, which are usually covered. I have a very low pain threshold. It didn't take them that long before I was signing over my banking empire, together with the deeds to the Russian.

As you so eloquently put it, I had no choice but to let Comrade Vostok, pull my strings. He made it quite clear, I was to do as I was told, and in return I could keep my position at the bank.'

The twinkle seemed to return to Kunze's eyes he sat up straight again and a faint smile cut across his face. 'As you have no doubt worked out, it was Vostok who instructed me to divert the funds from the Brotherhood into his account.'

Kunze looked solemnly at Steven. 'One little matter to deal with first.'

Kunze picked up the telephone. Steven's hand shot out and grabbed Kunze's wrist. 'Please trust me; I don't want Gunter listening at the door.' Steven released his grip.

'Reception, do you know where I can find Herr Gunter?'

'Yes Herr Director, I can see him by the main door. He is coming now sir.'

'Yes Herr Director.'

'Have you found that man yet?'

'Not yet sir, but we are still looking.'

'It is no longer a priority matter, leave that to security. I want you to go to investments, check, and list out for me all contribution into the Certina account over the past five years.'

'As you wish, Herr Director.'

Kunze replaced the receiver. 'That should keep him busy for sometime.'

Steven couldn't help but feel he was now talking to a completely different man, from the pale faced shaking person he had first encountered, only a few minutes ago.

'Just by talking to you, I've been able to face this situation and what I'm just beginning to realise is that I still hold some cards.' The faint smile broadened across Kunze's face, as he began to tap away on the computer again. 'What has just occurred to me, to carry out his instructions, I had to have all the details of his account.' At that Kunze hit a key and figures filled the screen. He turned the monitor towards Steven. 'The current balance of Vostok's Swiss account, no doubt he has others, is eight hundred and seventy-million Euros. I'll transfer thirty-million into your account, it is rightfully yours.'

'What about the rest?'

'That's Vostok's; it would be unethical for me to tamper with personal accounts.'

'Well by my calculation I would say Vostok owes me at least another ten million and the balance I would say is about the sum Vostok stole from you. Transfer forty million into my account and the balance into your account, use it to re-establish your family business and close Vostok's account clearing all reference to it from the memory.'

Kunze looked shocked, that scenario had clearly not occurred to him.

'Lets face it, Herr Kunze; you may as well get hung for a sheep as a lamb.'

'Yes, perhaps you're right, but I don't want his money.'

'Your money!'

'Under normal circumstances it would be unethical of me to even consider such a move....'

'Hardly what I would call normal.' Steven interrupted.

'....But I think in this instance I may make an exception, just to get one over on Vostok.' Kunze tapped at the keyboard, the screen cleared and came up with, 'Account Closed.''

'Ah doesn't that feel good, now transfer the funds to your own personal account.

Kunze tapped the keyboard skilfully and then sat back. 'All done,' he declared.

'There you go, isn't it nice to have your family fortune back.'

'There's no point really, I have no family. - My wife died last year. She had a heart attack, brought on I'm sure by the stress of us losing everything.'

'I'm sorry, that bastard has a lot to account for.'

'I miss her so much, it would not be a hard for me to join her, but I shall deny Vostok that pleasure.'

Steven's initial intention was to come to Zurich in search of Abramovich and to establish the existence of the twenty million, but things had moved on a pace, much to his satisfaction. He had never expected to find Vostok here, but now that he has --. Steven's mind began to whirl.

'I think Herr Kunze we should be more positive. If, for example, Comrade Vladimir Vostok was to have an accident, probably fatal, would that not throw a different light on the matter?' Herr Kunze looked surprised, but not shocked. 'As you said yourself only you and Vostok are aware of the full extent of his hostility towards you.'

'He is very well protected you know, bodyguards, bullet proof limousines and a small army guard the armaments factory.'

'Surely he doesn't spend all his time at the factory, where does he stay when he's in town?'

The smile returned again to his face, just as if the sun had appeared from behind a dark cloud.

'Ah, now that's a different matter.' Kunze pulled open and began to rummage in the desk draw; Steven tensed, half wanting to appear trusting and half wondering if Kunze was about to produce a weapon.

'Here we are.' Kunze produced a bunch of keys, and dangled them in front of Steven. 'My business empire was not the only thing that Vostok stole from me. Our lovely lakeside home was among his acquisitions. When we lost that, it was the final straw for my Hilda.' Kunze swallowed, tears again welled in his eyes, but he quickly composed himself, as he put the memories from his mind.

'The house stands empty most of the time, apart from the gardener and the house keeper who were retained. They are married and live in the gatehouse cottage, about a kilometre from the house. Sometimes, when Vostok is not there, I visit the place and reflect on happier times, the servants are still loyal, understanding and very discreet. Vostok, so confident that my fear of him would keep me forever subservient, never bothered to change the locks on house and the furniture is as we left it. He never planned to use it that much, to him; my home was just another thing to take from me.' He paused for a moment reflecting on better times, before continuing. 'It felt so good to be home, the house the gardens; you know I could still smell Hilda's perfume and feel her presence in the house.' Kunze seemed to instantly snap out of his trance like state, coming back to the reality of the situation.

'But not everything was as I left it, Vostok has installed a security system, cameras and flood lights as far as I could tell, but I've no idea where the cameras are fitted.'

Kunze paused again for a long moment, to let the nostalgic memories filter through his mind. Steven waited, letting him enjoy the thoughts.

'Two things Herr Kunze, I want to know every inch of your former home. And I want to know how to get out of here without having to pass any of the security staff.'

'No problem with the house.' Kunze took out the pocket watch from his waistcoat. 'As for getting out of here, through that door is a meeting room.' He said, pointing to the door at the rear of his office. 'Beyond that, there are the lifts and a staircase. Two floors down on level five is an open plan office. There are fifty employees on that floor dealing with the currency markets' Kunze looked at the watch. 'Er-, in one hour precisely, half of the staff on that floor will be going to lunch, if you time it right, you could mingle and maybe avoid the security cameras and the guards. Your capture is no longer a priority, so there's a chance that you won't be noticed in the crowd.'

'Are the stairs and lifts on camera?'

'Err. – Y-e-s, but there are no cameras inside the lifts, didn't think there would be necessary.'

'Perhaps it would be easier if you could tell me where else isn't on camera.'

Steven left Kunze's office by the main door. As he went through the outer office he picked up chair and headed to Kunze's private lift. The passage and lift area, to that level, he knew were not on camera. He pressed the call button, which immediately started the lift on its ascent. As the lift doors opened, Steven pushed in the chair and laid a pen in the door track to prevent the doors from closing and further lift use. Standing on the chair, he pushed open the access hatch and pulled himself up into the upper lift shaft. He was just about to replace the hatch cover, when he noticed Herr Kunze take the chair away. If all goes to plan, Kunze will pick up the pen in five minutes time, that should be time enough to pull him up onto the beams supporting the winding gear.

He had already put on his overcoat, and though uncomfortably warm, figured it would protect his blue suit from the grease and grime associated with lift shafts and he had already pinned the security tab that Kunze had given him, to his suit lapel.

The red tie's got to go. He sat astride the motor support beam, removed it and dispensed with it down the lift shaft. The other lifts only went up to the sixth floor, but shared the same motor room. Their winding gears were in constant use going up and down to the various levels.

Steven moved and was now on the support beam over another lift shaft. He looked at his watch. 'Only one minute to go.' Right on queue the lift below came up and stopped at the sixth floor. Without hesitation he lowered himself down on the lifts cables. *Don't rate my chances if this thing moves.*

He dropped on to the lift car roof, removed the hatch and dropped in. Herr Kunze took his hand out of the door allowing them to close, at the same time handing Steven several tissues to remove the grease from his hands. Steven removed the now grease stained overcoat, folding it inside out and placing it neatly over Herr Kunze's outstretched arm.

'Level two Monsieur.'

'Merci, danke schon.' Steven jovially responded with a thank you in both French and German, languages he knew Herr Kunze to be fluent in. When they arrived at level two, Kunze stepped out. 'Good luck.' He said under his breath to the stranger who had just turned his life around.

As if on cue the lift shot up to level five where a dozen or more souls crowded in accompanied with much chattering. *Perfect.* Steven shrunk into the corner; nobody had paid him any attention.

The doors opened and the group poured out into the main hall, Steven had manoeuvred himself into the centre and struck up a conversation with a pretty young lady. Steven's good looks had not gone unnoticed and there was a look of delight on the girl's face. 'Pardon Mademoiselle, this my first day at the office, would show me a good place to buy lunch?'

'Most certainly Monsieur.'

'David, please.'

'Hello David, I'm Angellic, why don't you come with us.' She nodded at a group of girls who had now surrounded him.

'Love to.'

A chorus of 'great' followed by giggles was the reply.

The group made their way towards the exit accompanied by a lot of chatter from the girls each bombarding Steven with a fusillade of questions, to which Steven nodded and grunted, all of the time he had one eye on the numerous bank guards milling around the floor. He had passed several guards without incident, however as the group neared the large doorway, he caught the look of doubt on a guards face.

The guard moved after the group, jostling for a better position. If only he had not hesitated he would have been in a better position to make a positive identification of the man they were looking for. As it was, he could not be sure, no overcoat, no red tie that's what had thrown him, but everything else fits. So he made a desperate effort to push through the ever-increasing number of bodies, moving in and out of the bank and through its main hall, much to the protests from the bodies he rudely pushed, in his haste to catch up with the tall man in a blue suit. Steven noticed the disturbance behind and knew he had to put some distance between him and his pursuer. 'Excuse me ladies, but I must retrieve a package from my car. – I will catch you up.' Steven quickened his step.

'But you don't know where we're going David.' Angellic called after him.

'Strange behaviour.' Said one girl.

'Must have been you.' Said another.

By which time Steven was well out of earshot and had made it to the door. The guards there were clearly harassed by the volume of people moving into the bank through the security screens, that little notice was taken of the crowds rushing out for lunch. *Must always be the same at this time of the day.* Steven thought, as he stepped out onto the pavement.

CHAPTER 19

TERMINATION TIME

Damn, more trouble. He spotted two guys in a black Mercedes parked roadside about ten metres to the left of the bank's entrance. *Vostok's thugs, no doubt looking for me. And they've found me.*

Steven knew instinctively by the guys' reactions that he'd been twigged, so he automatically headed to the right and increased his pace. *Okay,* he reasoned, *Vostok wants to talk to me, which means these bastards aren't out to kill me....Not just yet, anyway.*

Hopefully the two gorillas hadn't realised that he'd spotted them. So Steven paid them no heed as he walked quickly, angling his path across the now getting busier Stockerstrasse, weaving his way between the slow moving traffic in both lanes. He didn't look back, but knew instinctively that they would be pursuing him and that's just what he wanted.

Almost at his car, Steven did, casually glance back to just to check, there was only one of the thugs following and he wasn't too far behind. This thug, a big solid looking bloke with a shinny bald head and wearing a black wool overcoat, periodically lifted, what Steven thought was a mobile telephone to his mouth, no doubt reporting progress to his mate back in the car.

Hard to miss. Steven mused as he got into his car and pulled out into the slow moving traffic. He noted baldy had stopped but still talking into the device he was holding.

As the line of cars crawled along, Steven spotted the Mercedes coming fast swerving in and out of the oncoming traffic, screeching to a stop and baldy jumping in.

Okay...Showtime.

Steven swung the Peugeot out, throwing a yewie. The car cut through the line of oncoming vehicles, to a loud chorus of car horns and no doubt the sound of crunching metal as several shunts occurred. It mounted the pavement, amid the screams and jumping bodies of the pedestrians and weaved precariously at speed around various obstacles, bouncing the car back onto the road and back again, maintaining his speed.

Judging by the cacophony behind, the Mercedes had carried out the same manoeuvre and was closing the gap. After about fifty meters of pavement, Steven threw a right onto a relatively traffic free street and he pushed the pedal down hard. The car responded and some distance was gained on the pursuers. He had to judge this right; he wanted to elude the thugs but not entirely. So he ever so slightly eased his foot off the accelerator, just enough to catch sight of the Mercedes in the rear view. If his plan was going to work, he needed to head back to his hotel, but not directly, he needed to put on a show which would involve a chase through the back streets of Zurich. Again his judgement needed to be right; he did not want to evoke a police response, although that was no doubt happening back on Stockerstrasse, he did not want to damage his vehicle, and he not want to lose his pursuers.

Adjacent to the hotel, was a large multi storey car park, access to which was by way of a 'take a ticket', which initiated the lifting of a barrier. Two levels of the car park where underground with some of the spaces on the lowest level reserved strictly for hotel guests. *I've got to time this just right..* He waited at the ticket machine until he caught sight of the Mercedes, then pulling the ticket, headed down to the lower level. If the thugs in the Mercedes had seen him, and he felt sure that they had, they would, with a bit of luck, head upward. Steven parked the Peugeot in one of the hotels spaces that was near to the lift and stairwell access to the hotel lobby. After a short time he caught a glimpse of the Mercedes winding its way slowly down the ramp towards him. Quickly he ducked low and out of sight behind the parked vehicles opposite to where he had parked the Peugeot. Gun in hand he waited. The Mercedes slowly eased to a stop opposite Steven's Peugeot. It stayed there, engine ticking over for a couple of minutes. Steven figured that they were probably telling Vostok of the situation and awaiting his instruction. He edged himself forward so that he could see what was happening in the Mercedes.

The car door opened and baldy got out and headed to the lift. Thankfully the lunch time rush had subsided and this must have had an effect on the car park as there was little movement and plenty of empty parking spaces. Steven considered this to be the optimum time to strike and so he stealthily made his way to the passenger side of the Mercedes. In one movement he swung the door open and pressed the guns silencer against the driver's temple. 'Drive,' he said quietly in Russian.

'To where?' The driver said rather shakily.

'Just move,' Steven jabbed the end of the weapon into the drivers head.

The car started to circulate the car park. 'Over there.' Steven instructed. 'Here will do, turn off the engine, please.' The Mercedes was now parked in an isolated space at the far end of the lowest level, but not too far from the hotel lift access. 'I'll take them.' He said as he reached across and took the keys out of the ignition, at the same time he pressed the gun to the driver's chest angling the barrel downwards. Spit! The shocked look on the man's face was still apparent as the body slumped forward against the restraint of the seat belt. *'Hope there isn't a lot of blood,'* Steven thought as he straightened the man in the seat. *Can't see any exit wound.*

Steven got out of the car and headed back to the lift area, getting there just as the baldy thug came bounding out of the double leaf access door. He stopped short and looking perplexed as he frantically looked from side to side, no doubt wondering where his partner had gone. Steven again keeping low edged his way along the wall allowing him to come up behind the thug. He was just about to make a move when the lift doors behind baldy swung open. Baldy spun around and shot a hand into his coat. That would have been enough to scare the hell out of the young couple as they came through the door, but they were so busy chatting to each other, that seemed to pay little heed to the big Russian. Steven shrank back, letting baldy panic a little.

Won't be long before he figures out what's happened.

At that moment another couple entered the car park from the hotel lift and at same time another car came down the ramp and parked close to the hotel lift access, its occupants passed both sets of couples and baldy in the walkway. Fortunately both couples vehicles had been parked close to the doorway and in a matter of seconds each couple had gotten into their respective vehicles, started the engines and were gone. Quiet again... Steven made his move.

He stepped forward prodding the silencer end of the gun into the thug's lower back. He then reached under the thugs coat and removed the gun that was secured under the thug's armpit. While pocketing the gun, and again speaking in Russian he invited the man to walk with him.

'Ah no need to lift up your arms Ivor, we don't want to draw attention to ourselves now, do we?'

'What have you done with Boris?'

'Boris eh, your partner, he's just having a little lay down, let's not worry about him, shall we.' Steven motioned him towards the Peugeot and lifted the tailgate indicating that the thug should sit down on the back of the car. The Russian thug complied without protest. 'Now then Ivor, is that my photograph I see in your hand?'

'The Russian nodded and held up a print that had been lifted off the bank's security cameras. 'Umm not bad, I suppose you have informed Mr Vostok of my whereabouts?' Again the Russian just nodded. 'Well what were his instructions?' The

Russian just stared at Steven. 'Oh dear I don't have time for games.' He transferred the gun to his left hand and swung his right titanium knuckle so that it connected with the Russian's jaw. As the Russian fell back with the force of the blow, Steven pointed the gun at his forehead. 'Forget it,' he said, 'I'll ask Boris.'

'No no I will tell you.' Rather dazed and clearly in some pain, the Russian managed to pull himself upright and without any further prompting began to explain Vostok's instructions.

'We are to confirm that you stay here, make sure you are here and then wait for you.'

'Wait, for how long?'

'As long as it takes, one night, two,' the Russian shrugged his shoulders as he spoke. Steven seemed to relax a little, carefully considering his next move. The Russian now feeling better, realised that the gun was still in Steven's left hand and was no longer pointing at his head. That together with the distraction of another car on the down ramp gave baldy the opportunity to reach out and try wrestle the weapon from Steven's grasp. Steven in such situations was never that much turned off.

'Spit.' The bullet entered just below the larynx, passed through the heart and embedded itself in the lung. The Russian's hand was still clasped around the barrel of the pistol, when with eyes wide open looked unbelievingly at Steven, before releasing his grip and falling back, dead. In a deft move Steven picked up the Russian's legs, swung them around and pushed the whole body into the back of the Estate car and in the same movement, he lowered the tailgate. The occupants of the car coming into the parking didn't seem to notice anything.

Steven got into the Peugeot and drove it down to the back of the level, parking in one of the many empty bays adjacent to the Mercedes.

Finding a roll of heavy-duty large black bin liners, he snapped one off and furtively checked around, ensuring the coast was clear, before opening the Mercedes door. Easing the Boris's body forward, at the same time releasing the seat belt, he placed the bag over the upper torso. Letting the body fall over his shoulder, he lifted it out of the Mercedes and transferred it into the Peugeot dumping the body next to the former partner. Then he systematically removed all forms of identification, weapons and jewellery including watches and placed them in a plastic bag. The Russians clothing had absorbed most of the blood, but for further containment, Steven fitted further bin liners over the upper torsos of both victims, tying the plastic the bags tight around his victims' waists.

He was in the process of concealing the bodies, when the Russian's mobile started to ring. He quickly covered the bodies with a blanket, shut the tailgate and sat in the front seat of the Peugeot, before answering it. Guessing it would be Vostok wanting a progress report, he decided to answer in a deep voice, similar to that of the baldy thug and without waiting to be asked, spoke into the phone. 'The subject is in his room, I am near to his door, must be quiet.' At that Steven turned off the telephone and removed the sim card.

Before leaving he got back into the Mercedes and taking out his handkerchief wiped around all points of contact, locked it and put the keys into the plastic bag. Again double checking that he had not been seen, before driving the Peugeot back to park adjacent to the hotel lift access door.

Locking the car, he casually walked into the hotel lobby, and requested his key at the desk. 'Ah Monsieur there has been a man looking for you.'

'Big guy, shaved head?'

'Oui.'

'We've met, a business problem, all sorted now.'

Steven took the key and headed upstairs to his room to freshen up and pack. Later that evening he would check out.

Steven pulled the Peugeot off the main road and proceeded cautiously down an ice packed track that led to the lakeside on the south side of Lake Lucerne. Selecting a sheltered spot relatively close to the waters edge, he parked the car, cutting the engine and the lights. It was one am, the sky was clear and the moon reflected on the water silhouetting pieces of floating ice.

Steven changed into an all in one rubber dry suit, pulling it over a thick cotton top, wool socks and joggers. He blacked out the areas of exposed skin on his face with cam cream and then pulled on rubber waterproof gloves.

The first task was to carry his two victims to the waters edge. Wading into the water he collected large rocks and pebbles from the lake bed, filling plastic bin liner bags and the victims clothing with them. He tied the weighted bags to each body and then dragged one of them out as far into the water as he could. Fortunately the bottom of the lake fell away sharply just a few feet from the shore line. Tethered with a rope he let the body sink judging the depth at about twenty feet. Diving down he ensured the body was securely tied to large boulders on the bottom. That done he dragged the other body to a different spot and repeated the operation.

The other identification items, telephone and car keys would be disposed of later, perhaps in the Mediterranean on his way back. Task complete, Steven thoroughly checked over the Peugeot to ensure there was nothing incriminating. All looked okay, so he put his head back reclined his seat and took five.

'Once More into the breach.' He said to himself, putting on his pre-packed waterproof backpack and his mask, as he waded into the cold water.

Steven was winging this one, the plan he had in his mind was based purely on information provided by Hiendric Kunze. He had no idea apart from a bank of eight screens linked to cameras somewhere, what other security measures Vostok had in place while he was in residence.....Aside from the fact that there would be no dogs, Vostok apparently moved around too much, there was no permanent security staff at the house. According to Kunze, that is.

His judgment and the map confirmed it would be almost a mile swimming in the freezing water to the Kunze former residence on the other side of the lake.

Part way across he could discern the glow of the floodlights now surrounding what he presumed to be the house. As he got within fifty yards of the shore, he noted that there were no lights at the waters edge. 'Good.'

Just as Kunze had described, there was a large boathouse jutting out into the lake. From this boathouse there were steps leading up the plateau where the house stands. The garden, from the house down to the edge of the plateau was about seventy metres set in a series of terraced lawns; a gravel path meandered down from the house to the edge of the plateau by the lakeside.

Steven swam into the relative darkness of the boathouse and lifted himself onto the timber decking. Through the wooden slats of a Louvre panel he could see the steps rising about fifteen feet. If there are any security devices down here, they are more likely to be on the stairway, but it was too dark to see anything. To be on the safe side Steven decided to swim out and around the boathouse and scale the rock face up to the garden. This he did with consummate ease, pulling himself up and over a small perimeter wall on the lower garden terrace; from there he could clearly see the house. It looked quite large, the lower perimeter was bathed in the light from a number of floodlights; the upper section and roof formed a dark shadow against the night sky. The gardens had a layer of ice with large patches of snow that lay in clumps where it hadn't quite melted before freezing over again.

The house had a French influence, a chateau type, formed in a rectangle with a round tower at each end. From what Kunze had told him, the rear, being the aspect Steven was looking at now, were the only rooms likely to be occupied.

Between the round towers, the roof was ridged and pitched steeply with five pyramid shaped dormer windows set at mid slope and spaced evenly along the roof. Below the dormers and set into the side wall were three first floor windows each a small balcony with stone spindled balustrade. And directly below these windows were three French doors opening onto the ground floor patio terrace. The terrace was at a raised level of about two metres above the garden and was surrounded by a stone balustrade similar to those around the first floor balconies. Steps in the centre of the patio terrace, ran down to the start of the gravel path.

The property boundary at either side was difficult to define as the lawns merged into the shadows of conifers trees.

Steven had already worked out a plan of action from information Her Kunze had provided. He would merge into the shadow of the tree line, work his way up to the side of the house and simply let himself in through a service entrance, after all, he had the spare set of keys.

Steven waited in the shadows about twenty yards from the house, just watching, checking for any movement. Had his presence been detected? Are the guards, if there are any, doing a check on the grounds, if so at what intervals?

It seemed an age in coming, but eventually it did. The distant sound of a door being opened and then closed, followed by a cough and the rustle of an overcoat being pulled together. Then a man, assumedly a guard, appeared at the edge of the patio terrace and shone a powerful spotlight into the gloom of the garden and the trees. Steven dropped flat to the ground as the beam passed over. The guard let the beam move slowly across the garden in waves until in his judgment he had covered the garden. Once or twice during this ritual he would let the beam linger in some spot for a moment. Steven concluded it wasn't a thorough security check; the lingering amounted to nothing more than malingering. The guard disappeared around the front of the house, no doubt to perform the same ritual there.

Five minutes later, a door opened and closed security check complete.

Opening the waterproof bag Steven took out his automatic and pushed it into his belt. Then he took out a small glass bottle, held it between thumb and forefinger and examined it against the light coming from the floodlighting. It was still intact. He headed for the side door keeping in the shadow between the floodlights when a light in the house came on. He froze as the light cut into the shadow and exposed him; again he instinctively dropped flat to the ground.

A man could be seen through the window. That must be the kitchen window. Steven ran Kunze's diagram through his mind. And that man must be another guard, judging by the gun holstered at his shoulder. Moments later the man was pouring hot water from a kettle into three cups. Ah must be a coffee break and it looks like three on duty. The guard put the cups on a tray and disappeared, turning off the kitchen light as he left. 'No lights at this side or at the rear and unless they are drinking their coffee or whatever in the dark, they are probably stationed in a room at the front of the house, which confirms what Herr Kunze had said.

Steven checked the time, three-thirty; need to get a move on. He unlocked a small door at the side of the house let himself in and with a torch in hand, made his way to the stone spiral staircase in one of the round towers. According to Kunze both round towers have stairs used only by servants for discreet access to the main rooms, it would be unlikely that there were in use.

This one, Steven would guess certainly hasn't been used for some time, its dark, dank and bloody freezing.' He made his to the former servants' access on the first floor landing and carefully and slowly opened the door. He was immediately hit with the waft of the warm air on his face and the brightness of the light momentarily stung his eyes. Gathering himself, he inched the door open and checked out the landing.

'Damn!' – And eased the door closed again, he stood in the darkness contemplating the situation.

Not at all, what he was expecting. A guard was stationed midway along the gallery, at the head of an ornate staircase and outside a bedroom door.

'That's obviously Vostok's bedroom.'

As Kunze had guessed, Vostok was using the master bedroom, middle door of three on that landing.

Again fortune to some degree smiled on Steven, as he considered alternative options, there was a loud snore. He cracked open the door again and noted the guard was now lying almost horizontal in the chair, apparently fast asleep. 'That's better.'

In a ground floor room under the central staircase, two guards sat in front of bank of TV screens, not paying any particular attention to the flickering images, but were laid back conversing in Russian. 'Its now four, time for you to check the grounds comrade.'

'Do you think its necessary Gregor?'

'Orders are orders my friend.'

'Why can't Ivor do it?'

'Because he did it last night, so get your arse into gear.'

With some reluctance the guard stood and collected his overcoat. 'Bloody cold out there.' He said, muttering his objections.

Hoping the guard was a heavy sleeper Steven tiptoed across the landing. He wouldn't have time to fiddle around, so he had to take his best guess as to the implements he would need.

Vostok he knew had a lock fitted to the bedroom door, he was guessing that the door would be locked and that the standard lever lock key would be in the lock. Not entirely all guesswork thanks to Kunze again.

The guard was in essence doing him a favour; the noise of his snoring covered any indiscreet squeak Steven's rubber shoes may have made on the polished floorboards. A slow turn of the doorknob and a gentle nudge with the shoulder, confirmed the door was indeed locked. Checking the keyhole, he affirmed that the key was still in the lock.

A loud snore accompanied with lip smacking and head shaking came from the guard, as he almost woke himself up. Steven held his breath and pushed himself flush against the door, to lessen the risk of being spotted. The guard settled down to his dreams again and Steven relaxed his breathing. He set about opening the door using a very special precision-engineered tool. It looked very much like a very slim clutch pencil, which he gently inserted into the keyhole until it contacted and gripped the end of the key. In a fluid movement, he turned the door knob and the tool; there was a faint click as the lever came back. He then released the tool, opened the door, stepped inside and locked it again to prevent any unwelcome intrusion.

The bedroom was quite large, it was three rooms made into one and the Kunze's had used it as a sitting room and a study as well as a bedroom. Beautiful views over the lake from that room. Kunze had mused.

Steven located Vostok with the pen torch, following the sound of deep breathing, with the occasional snore. The bed was at the far end of the room where Herr and Frau Kunze had placed it many years ago. Putting the torch in his mouth he rummaged in his bag and removed a case containing a hypodermic needle, which he quickly assembled. He then took the bottle out of its plastic container; again giving it a good shake, ensuring the particles had fully dissolved before pushing the needle into the little glass bottle, and withdrawing the contents into the barrel of the syringe.

It had occurred to Steven, that he had for years been carrying a cyanide tablet, standard issue, never ever fancied taking it. So crushing and mixing it with water, would do the job.

He jumped on top of Vostok putting his bent knees on either side of Vostok's body, pressing the duvet tight around him to restrict his movement. At the same time he clasped his hand firmly over Vostok's mouth and plunged the hypodermic needle into the nasal cavity. Vostok's eyes seemed to bulge out of his head and he tried desperately to struggle. Steven kept his full weight on top of Vostok in a vice like embrace until the body was motionless.

'Goodbye comrade Vostok, you'll have no need for money now.'

Steven switched on the light, and tidied the bed, making Vostok's position look as natural as possible.

A Monet print on the far wall covered the safe. It was a key and combination type. Steven had a spare key and providing Vostok hadn't changed it, the combination....He hadn't. Collecting what he came for, he locked the safe, transferring the items into his backpack.

Everything tidied away, waterproof bag on his back, he turned off the light and put an ear to the door, thankfully the guard was still snoring. Placing the clutch tool on the key he passed it through the key hole. Quietly unlocking and opening the door, he checked all was clear before stepping out and closing the door behind him. Using the tool, he re-locked the door, unclamped the tool, leaving the key on the inside of the locked door, as he had found it.

The two guards in the security room were having an in-depth conversation about the lack of job prospects in the motherland. Seemingly oblivious to Stevens exploits.

Steven left the same way he arrived

As he neared the lay-by where he had parked the Peugeot, he slowed his stroke and began to tread water while he scanned the area for any movement. Now away from the floodlit garden, his night vision had returned and there was sufficient light from the moon and stars to discern the shape of the parked car. After a few minutes he decided that nobody had taken an interest in the vehicle, so he continued his swim.

Once at the car, he recovered the keys from under a previously selected stone and unlocked it, but before opening the door, he peeled off his dry suit, for no other reason than it would have been difficult to do in the confines of the car. Opening the tailgate Steven picked up the dry suit and backpack throwing them and himself into the rear of the car, reaching up pulled the door shut. Finding a dry towel, he rubbed himself vigorously all over to get some warmth back into his body. It was at that point he realised just how cold and tired he was.

Dressing quickly, he pulled on an Arran sweater over the cotton top and replaced the joggers with brown cords. Slipping on a pair of mid brown leather shoes with thick rubber soles over his woollen socks.

Steven relaxed for a moment to appreciate the new found warmth and the tingling sensation that occurs, almost as good as an orgasm and he immediately thought of Jennifer.

Feeling in his canvas bag he found the baby wipes and eventually after using half the packet, managed to remove the entire cam cream from his face.

'Time to pack,' he said to himself, rolling up his spare clothes, wet gear and equipment fitting them neatly into the bag. He rolled over the back seat and got out of the car by the rear door, taking with him a dark brown leather jacket that he wasted no time putting on. 'Had enough cold for one night, thanks.' Walking back to the waters edge, he stripped the keys off Kunze's key ring. Throwing each one as far as he could into the water and in different directions, including the key ring itself. From the back of the car he collected the used tissues and wrapped them around the little glass bottle. He then proceeded to smash it with a large pebble, into grain of sand size pieces. Which he again scattered into the water. The bottle top the hypodermic and its plastic case were given a similar bashing. This time he left the pieces in the tissues, making a hole in the pebbly shore, he placed all the tissues and pieces into the hole poured on petrol and set fire to it. There was a bright flash as the fire flared then almost instantly died leaving nothing but ash. Steven kicked back the pebbles. 'Right, I'm out of here.'

It was still dark when Steven posted the brown envelope into the bank night safe, again marked PRIVATE for the attention of Hiendric Kunze Director, but this time, Steven thought

Kunze would be rather pleased with his post. The streets were beginning to get busy with traffic, the time was six-thirty and people were heading to work for the last day before the Christmas break. Steven turned the Peugeot into a garage forecourt, making sure for the benefit of anybody reviewing CCTV footage that Jacques Mateau's Peugeot was heading out of town and could not be construed as coming from the direction of Lucerne. He filled the car up with diesel before buying a few things from the food store section.

'Have you been open all night?' Steven asked the assistant, knowing they had.

'Yes, I'm off at seven, not before time, I've done enough for one night.'

'I'm just starting; thankfully it's my last day before the holiday.' The assistant methodically scanned the items as Steven talked. 'That will be forty-three Euros, sir' Steven handed over a fifty note and the assistant proffered the seven Euros change.

'Keep it friend, have a Merry Christmas.'

'Thank you sir and the same to you.'

Just in case he needs to remember me.

Steven headed back into town, to the apartment block on Badenerstrasser. Parking the Peugeot in the car park; he crossed the street with a carrier bag in each hand. Transferring them to one hand, he fished around in his jacket pocket for the keys he had purloined from Abramovich.

He cautiously let himself into apartment number ten, just in case Abramovich had somehow escaped, and was waiting for him. But he relaxed when he saw the feet still tied to the bed. He called out in Russian. 'Hello dear, I'm home! Phew what a mess, you don't smell so good Demmitri old man.' Demmitri Abramovich was semi conscious; the blood stained sheet partly covering his body was now heavily stained with urine. Although the sheet covered the lower regions, the smell left Steven in no doubt that he had also shit himself.

'Better get you something to eat you must be starving and then we'll get you cleaned up.' Taking out his flick knife, Steven moved towards the bed. As the blade sprang the fear showed in Abramovich's eyes at the same time trying to call out.

'Mmmmm!'

'Steady on old man, just cutting your bonds off, not your balls.' Steven removed the cord and duck tape gag putting the pieces in one of the plastic carrier bags. He sat Abramovich up and gently massaged most of the areas of his body that had been pressed against the bed. 'We'll give your arse a miss for the time being Demmitri old sport, if that's okay.' Steven said, still gagging at the stench. Abramovich flopped, shoulders down, chin on chest and making a low moaning sound. 'Just sit there and don't move while I fix us something to eat.' Knowing full well that Abramovich was going nowhere; Steven picked up the carriers and went into the kitchen, finding a large bowl he made porridge in the microwave. While that was cooking he went into the bathroom, checking Abramovich hadn't moved, as he passed the bedroom.

The sweet smell of the prostitutes perfume hit him as he opened the bathroom door. Images of the bubbles collecting on her pubic hair, came flooding back. *Get a grip.* Pulling the plug he let the now bubble-less cold water run out, at the same time turning on the hot water tap to check there was hot water in the system. The ping of the microwave coincided with the emptying of the bath, replacing the plug he left the hot water to run, adding a good drizzle of bath oil before heading back into the kitchen.

'Here we are old man.' Steven held a spoon full of creamy porridge laced with honey to Abramovich's lips. He took the first spoonful slowly. That seemed to stimulate his appetite and his resolve. He took the bowl and spoon off Steven and rather shakily got stuck in.

'Good on you Demmitri, coffee and toast to follow, don't go away.' Steven checked the bath, before heading to the kitchen, adding some cold water to get the temperature right. As he left the bathroom he caught sight of a naked body on hands and knees, heading for the door. 'Whoa there Trigger, you'll need some clothes on its freezing out there. Steven pulled the out the gun from under his jacket and waved the barrel in front of Demmitri as he turned to face Steven. 'Come on Demmitri, we'll forget about the toast and I'll let you have your coffee in the bath.' Steven was finding it difficult to keep sounding cheerful, the sight of such a pathetic figure was making him feel sick, not least because he knew he shouldn't lose sight of the fact that this was Vostok's assassin. Abramovich seemed to realise further resistance would be futile, he had neither the strength nor the inclination to resist. Steven helped him to his feet and walked him to the bathroom.

Abramovich smiled for the first time as the pleasure of the warm water caressed his aching sore body.

Steven left him in the bath, while he had some breakfast, making sure that any dishes he used were cleaned and put away. Now for the serious bit, Steven picked up a package and went into the bathroom. Abramovich was looking relaxed his eyes closed, the weal's on his arms and legs made by the rope, were still prominent but not angry, the cut on his chest, now clean was hardly discernable.

Steven stood over looking down on him. 'Well Demmitri, when I told you your death would not be of benefit to me, that wasn't quite true, unfortunately, for you that is. As you are aware, you are indirectly involved in a conspiracy to assassinate the Crown Prince of Arabia. And knowing what you know, I cannot allow you to live, sorry old chap. I really am.' Abramovich looked gob smacked, a pleading look in his eyes, and he started struggling against the slippery surface trying to get up and out of the bath. Steven gave him a firm push sending him sliding back down. Abramovich kicked and splashed for a brief moment, before Steven dropped an electric fire, already plugged in and switched on, into the water. Abramovich stiffened letting out an agonising cry before entering into unconsciousness. The power surge tripped the main supply switch. Steven had thought it might, so he pushed Abramovich's head under the water holding it there until he was sure the termination was complete.

Death wasn't pretty it never is. Termination sounds like the ending of a bus ride, such a non-personal name for such a personal act.

Steven, for all his training hated being the one who did the deed. Four Terminations today, all of them justified in his own mind.

He unplugged the little electric fire, letting it drain into the bath for a while before drying with it a towel. He made his way to the switch box to restore the power back to the apartment. And then he tackled the bedding, sluicing the shit down the loo and putting the sheets in the washing machine and scrubbing the mattress with disinfectant. By the time he had finished the apartment smelt a lot better. He finished tidying the place putting the food he'd bought into the cupboard and the milk into the refrigerator. 'Everything clean and tidy, only one person lived here, R.I.P. Demmitri Abramovich.'

Steven push down the button on the Yale ensuring that latch was locked from the inside, leaving Abramovich's keys on his bedside cupboard. He then climbed through the kitchen window and out onto the fire escape. With a piece of fine filament fishing line wrapped around the window handle and both ends in his hand, he managed to close the window from the outside pulling down the latch, then letting one end of the line go, he was able to pull it out through the minute gap.

It took some time to descend the escape stair. The snow had not lain on the steel stairs, so no footprints were visible, but he had to be very careful he was not seen from the back street and from any apartment window.

He hit the back street, letting the short access ladder spring back up, confident that he had not been noticed; he merged in with the crowds of shoppers on Badenerstrasser.

CHAPTER 20
THE WINERY

By the time Steven reached Saint Raphael it was dark and the streets were quiet. He parked the car, dropping the keys into a pre-prepared envelope along with the vehicle registration documents. It was marked, Jacque Mateau, 32 Avenue de la Grande Corniche.

The front of the house was in darkness. He placed the envelope on the doorstep, rang the bell, turned and quickly and quietly walked away. *Merry Christmas Jacque Mateau thanks for the use of your name.*

Steven with a Bergen on his back and a newly acquired canvas bag in one hand broke into a steady jog. It would take him about twenty minutes to reach the marina in Frejus and Morning Star.

'Hi gorgeous, miss me?' Steven said, letting the bags fall to the deck, and holding his arms outstretched to receive Jennifer's onrushing body in an embrace.

'You bet!' She wrapped her arms around him and held on tight, as if never wanting to ever let go. They embraced for a long moment, before Steven peering over Jennifer's shoulder noticed the other occupants.

'Hi there, you two.'

'Hello.' Jordan said, 'good to have you back.'

'Salaam A-.' Steven raised his eyebrows. 'Err, I mean, hello Steven.'

Steven and Jennifer sat down opposite their guests. 'My, my, our Jens performed a miracle on you both, you look so different.'

Morris decided to speak for both of them. 'We've had four days to take in what you said, we've talked,' turning his head to get a confirmatory nod from Jordan. 'Jordan and I, that is, both agree that our former lives weren't really lives at all.'

'We love the feeling of being free,' Jordan put in.

'Freedom to be ourselves,' Morris concluded.

'That's good; I was kind of hoping you would feel that way.' Steven looked directly at Morris, 'because I now have another test which you in particular may find difficult.'

Morris frowned, turning again to Jordan for reassurance. 'What more must I do?'

'Celebrate Christmas with us, as a Christian.'

'It's not a problem, a new experience maybe,' Morris shrugged his shoulders, 'but for me, so is this life.'

'Right then, that's settled.' Steven rubbed his hands together and turned back to Jennifer. 'What's the sea state Jen?'

'Fair overnight, becoming moderate tomorrow.'

'Okay we'll go for it, if we leave now we may just be there for Christmas Day.'

'Where?'

Steven tapped the side of his nose with his forefinger and began to rummage in his new canvas holdall. 'But for now a little reading.' Passing each of them a book.

'Practical Spanish?' Jordan said in a quizzical manner.

Steven just smiled. 'Let's get the show on the road, Jen.'

Benicarlo, Spain

The first leg of the journey to Barcelona had taken most of the night, Jennifer and Steven had planned to take alternate watches, or so it was decided. In truth Steven didn't have the heart to wake her, and it was five am before she wandered up, of her own volition, to the main helm console. She was yawning, and rubbing her eyes, at the same time.

'Ah-h-ha, what time is it Steven?'

'Almost five'!

'Steven, you should have woken me. Take yourself off to bed, right now.'

'Oh Jen, I do like it when you get bossy.'

'Go on, get below.' She said trying to be firm, but the smile was letting her down.'

'I'll just take five on the settee; we should be nearing Barcelona soon, you'll need to wake me when we are within harbour control.

A short nap later, Steven was up supervising the refuelling in Barcelona. After which he took 'Morning Star' back out to sea steering south-south-west and hugging the Spanish coast. Morning Star entered the marina at Benicarlo five pm on the 24th December.

Steven finished securing Morning Star in the designated berth and had gone to the marina office to discuss the terms and duration of their stay. While on shore he rang around a few old friends he had not seen for sometime, he also rang a local car hire company arranging for the vehicle to be delivered to the marina quayside.

Later that evening the hire car, a Nissan Primera was delivered, all formalities were taken care of, Steven shut down and locked up 'Morning Star.'

The four of them then made their way along the pontoons to the quay.

'Feels very strange being on dry land again,' Morris said, 'I feel as if I'm still in motion.'

'A common feeling,' Steven said as the ladies nodded their heads and made affirmative sounds.

They climbed into the car, Morris and Jordan in the back seat, Jennifer up front with Steven.

'The suspense is killing me; won't you at least tell us where we are going?'

'Okay Jen I'm taking you to my home, for Christmas.'

'Your home?'

'Yep my home, I haven't spent a great deal of time there, been far too busy, but I will one day.'

'I don't know why I'm surprised; you're such a dark horse.'

He turned his head, looked right at her and gave her a huge grin. 'It's really a family home on my mother's side. She was the only child and I am her only child, so you see I copped the lot, warts an all.'

'I never thought to ask about your parents; sorry to hear your mother has died.'

'Oh but she hasn't, mother and father are both fine, they retired years ago and are enjoying life in Australia, everything was signed over to me before they left.'

Morris leaned forward. 'How far are we going Steven?'

'About twenty miles inland, a little village called Canet Lo Roig.'

Steven drove through the village, to a very large detached house on the outskirts. The wrought iron gates stood open, lights were burning from the ground floor rooms and flood lights bathed the façade in a yellow glow. Steven swung the car into the drive and up to the large wooden door.

'My great Grandfather used to have a vineyard; he had this place built to house the presses and vats. It's still called the 'Winery', but it was Grandfather who modernised the place when olive trees replaced the grapes, to the mansion it is today.'

'It's fantastic.' Jennifer gasped as she got out of the car and surveyed the building from the drive.

Friends had been in to make the house hospitable; a log fire was burning in the grate in the lounge. The kitchen larder and refrigerator had been well stocked with fresh food, including a turkey, specially supplied for the Christmas dinner.

Christmas day morning, the four gathered in the lounge, each with a cup of coffee, exchanging presents as a start to the day's festivities. Steven had bought Jennifer a few small presents and an expensive Swiss wristwatch and there were presents for each, from each.

'Now's the time,' Steven declared as he looked at Morris and Jordan. 'You've no doubt guessed that Spain is to be your new home and of course you are more than welcome to live here in the Winery, for the time being, until you find where you want to be.' Steven picked up his canvas bag and rummaged inside, taking out two blue cards. 'Here is a start for your new life, I've made application on your behalf for Spanish residence that will take about three years, and in the mean time here are your NIF non resident numbers. You will need them for any special purchases and for bank accounts in Spain.... Speaking of which this is a bank account in both your names, if you want you can have the balance transferred to any bank of your choosing. Invested wisely it should keep you in clover for the rest of your life.' He handed them an envelope containing the account details, debit cards and a cheque book.

They both turned to look at each other, then back to Steven, emotion welling up in them as they noted the amount of twenty million Euros.

'We can't take this Steven, how do we repay'----.

Steven cut him short. 'You don't have to, it's a gift.'

'I err, don't know what to say, I had no idea-.'

Steven held up a hand. 'The pair of you are so used to the comfort of money, it would never have occurred to you as to how you would survive without it.'

'Thank you very much Steven.' Jordon put in. 'We will use it wisely.'

'Good for you,' said Jennifer.

That night, when Steven and Jennifer were in bed, she lay on her side with her head resting on his chest. 'It's been a smashing day Steven, lovely house, great food, nice area and good company.'

'I agree it's been very enjoyable, you do realise don't you, it would be difficult to sail Morning Star back to England in such bad weather. We may have to stay here until spring, you don't mind do you?'

'Mind, why should I, I think I'm going to love it here. No doubt I'll lose my job, but what the heck I'll soon get another.'

'Come to think of it, I'm in no hurry to get back I've just about had about enough of the violence and deception.' Steven said as he stared blankly at the high ceiling. 'Time for a little "us time", don't you think?'

'Will whoever it is that employs you allow it?'

Steven shrugged. 'Maybe, maybe not.'

'What will we do for money?'

'No worries, I'm not short of a bob or two.' He gave her a little squeeze. 'If we get stuck you can always get a job, there's plenty of work round here, for a strong girl like you.' Pinching the muscle on her arm, 'mucking out the pigs for one.'

'You, you cheeky swine.' She gave him a playful punch on his chest; he tried to feign injury but couldn't stop himself from laughing.

'Shush they'll hear you.' And she rolled over until she lay on top of him. 'Now get out of that, lover boy.'

'Easy.' He cradled his hands behind her head pulling her gently down until their lips met.

CHAPTER 21

REDRESS THE BALANCE

Guildford

Sir Peter was busy raking the wet sodden leaves into piles at the bottom of the very large garden of his home on the outskirts of Guildford. Muttering to himself, 'dammed obvious that gardener chap hasn't been for a while, I shall have to have a word with him after the holidays.'

The detached house built in the Georgian style had five bedrooms, two bathrooms and stood in an acre and a half of land.

Resting on the rake he gazed lovingly back at the house, with its beautiful gardens. *Too bloody big really,* he thought, *but I love it, only wish we could spend more time here.*

'Peter!' Marjorie was on the patio waving, Sir Peter waved back. 'Coming.' He stood the rake against a tree and headed back to the house, kicking off his Wellington boots at the patio door where Marjorie was standing.

'Problems?' He said cocking an eyebrow.

'No, quite the contrary, there's a message down loading on the secure line, thought you might be interested.... It's Spiders ID.'

'You've decoded it?'

'Running through the decoder as we speak.'

They headed into the study, Marjorie retrieved the four-page report and put it through the copier, making a spare set for her to peruse.

They sat in silence studying the report. Sir Peter, at his desk, Marjorie in an armchair, opposite.

'Intriguing,' Marjorie said, 'our man has been busy, hasn't he?'

Sir Peter looked up. 'They must have discovered Vostok's body by now. Anything on the Swiss police network?'

Marjorie got up and went to the computer, punching in a set of codes. 'I'll check with Cheltenham.'

It took a few minutes to complete the connection and subsequent communication, and a few minutes more to get a response.

Marjorie sat at the keyboard, as the screen began to fill with text, when it finished, she acknowledged and closed the connection.

'Not a thing; no mention in any police telephone or radio traffic, concerning Vostok, or the house by the lake.'

'Over twenty-four hours ago. Surely the bodyguards have discovered the body by now, so why aren't they reporting the incident to the authorities.'

'Spider's positive that Vostok was dead.'

'Y-e-s,' Sir Peter mused. 'If you were responsible for guarding Vostok, what would you do in this situation?'

She pondered. 'If I were in their shoes, I would think Vostok, my meal ticket, died in his sleep of natural causes. The sooner his death is reported, the sooner I'd be out of a job.'

'Exactly what I'm thinking; so supposing they talked it over and decided to act as if nothing had happened.'

'The question is Peter, how long can they keep it quiet?'

'Hum, that could be indefinitely, if they left him who would know? It could be weeks before the body was discovered.' Sir Peter rubbed his chin deep in thought. 'Consider this scenario Marj; we know they haven't so far, but let's assume they decide to report the death, say within the next hour as the earliest time from now. The police would have to be involved, along with a doctor. And if the circumstances on the face of it are not suspicious, why make it an urgent matter. Such a lot of red tape you know and all the important people are on holiday. The chief of police is probably on the ski slopes right now.' Sir Peter concluded. 'Y-e-s, with a bit of luck and red tape, Vostok's demise may not be reported until after the holidays.'

'I think the guards will just take off, grabbing what they can, no point in hanging around.....I doubt they'll even tell their two buddies.'

'Whatever Marj, I think we will have sometime before the demise of Vladimir Vostok is made public, hopefully after the markets reopen......I wonder if we can use this time, to our advantage.'

Marjorie knew Sir Peter had a germ of an idea because he was now pacing across the study floor in his thinking position, head down and hands clasped behind his back. She knew she shouldn't say anything, but couldn't stop herself. 'We don't know, there will be a delay, it's only a supposition.'

Sir Peter released a hand and brought it up in a 'stop the traffic' gesture. 'Won't really matter, better kept quiet for while, but if not, it's not a big deal.' He returned to the desk. 'This secret society, "the Brotherhood," refer to each other by the place name they are from.' She nodded. 'So that would make Henry Forbes, 'Washington,' would it not?' Marjorie nodded again in agreement. 'Would it be possible to get his private e-mail and telephone number?'

'Might take a few minutes.'

'Okay, I'd like you to send him an e-mail.' Marjorie found a pen and turned Steven's report over poised ready for action.

WASHINGTON, CONTRACT IS COMPLETE AND PAYMENT MADE. RE YOUR MAJOR SUPPLY PROBLEM THIS COULD BE RESOLVED WITH THE PURCHASE OF STOCK OF A SOON TO BE AVAILABLE LARGE INDUSTRIAL EMPIRE. OUR FRIENDS MAY BE OF HELP. IMPERATIVE YOU ACT IMEDIATELY. ZURICH.

Ten minutes latter, Marjorie returned from the computer. 'All done.'

'Good.' He responded, more to himself than an acknowledgement to Marjorie. 'Now for the wake up call.'

Sir Peter went to the desk and picked up the cordless telephone. 'Is this the number Marj?' She nodded. 'It must be nearly six in the morning in the States, let's see if our Mr Forbes is awake. If I speak with a foreign accent, and if Forbes is still half a sleep, I just might convince him, I'm Zurich....But I'm hoping he'll be listening to what I say rather than the way I say it.'

Sir Peter punched in the numbers and let it ring for a good five minutes until he heard the clicks of the receiver being fumbled. Then a tired voice answered, 'Forbes.'

'Washington.'

'Yeah, who. Who is this?' Henry Forbes immediately came awake on hearing his Brotherhood name.

'It's Zurich, check your e-mail, the stocks are "Vos Oil," it is imperative that there is no delay in your acquisition, goodbye.'

Sir Peter pressed the red button on the handset cutting the call.

'Not bad, could have fooled me,' Marjorie said.

'If it comes off Marj, what a coup, America could end up owning a third of Russia's oil reserve.'

Marjorie took the hard copies of Steven's report and put them through the shredder, then she deleted all the files in connection with this operation, from the system.

Christmas day, Sir Peter and Marjorie watched the Kings speech on TV, even though they had a good idea what the main subject would be. Sure enough the King had gone through the usual rhetoric and aspirations, before he touched on the loss of his niece.

'My niece Princess Alice, Princess of Wight has been missing for seven days now.' He paused for affect. 'It is with a heavy heart, I feel we must fear the worst. My wife and I are saddened and we send our deepest sympathy to our nephew the Prince of Wight and their son. Our thoughts go out to the families and friends of all those lost in this tragic incident. It is now that I shall take steps to request my ministers make the necessary arrangements for a memorial service, early in the New Year.'

Sir Peter looked at Marjorie, the remote control in his hand.

'Heard enough Marj?'

'Y-e-s,' she nodded thoughtfully, 'he never said what the tragic incident was, or mentioned the Saudi Royal family who have lost their son and heir.'

Sir Peter switched channels to catch the news. 'No it all seemed very matter of fact.'

'This is Darren Turner for BBC News 24, with news every hour, on the hour. Here is our main story.

It is believed that Her Royal Highness Princess Alice the Princess of Wight, has perished in what appears to have been a tragic accident in the Mediterranean involving the Saudi Arabian Royal yacht. As far as we know, the yacht left Monaco sometime in the late evening of the 17th or early morning of the 18th December. Nothing has been heard from her since.'

Darren paused to read the second part of the report from the auto-queue.

'Hopes are now fading fast, of finding any more survivors from the lost ship MV Golden Crown. The search, involving ships from the Royal Navy as well as vessels from the French and Italian Coast Guard, is to be scaled down.

Bad weather is said be hampering the search efforts. A spokesman has told News 24, that HMS Devonshire will remain on stand by in the Mediterranean until the New Year.

We can say with some certainty that HRH Princess Alice, along with the Saudi Arabian Crown Prince, Mohammed Bin Aziz Al Saud, were on board the yacht when it was lost. They and two other passengers, said to be bodyguards, are still missing somewhere off the coast of Sardinia.

It is said that the health of King Faud has seriously declined following the loss of his son and heir. Prince Abdullah bin Aziz Al Saud, is being prepared to take his brothers place as the next King of Saudi Arabia.

Here in Buckingham Palace the King, moments ago, made his Christmas Day broadcast, in which he sends condolences to all involved. This will start an official week of mourning for a much-loved Princess. Crowds of thousands have been gathering at the palace gates, awaiting any news. There are tearful scenes, and hundreds of floral tributes lining the Mall. We will show a full coverage of these scenes in a special programme following the news. Right now we are going over to Nicholas Davidson our reporter in Cagliari for details on the search and rescue operation. Nicholas.'

'Yes, thank you Darren, as you know five days ago, a fishing vessel out of this port rescued five people from a drifting lifeboat about 20 miles to the west of here. One of the survivors, believed to be Prince Mohammed's bodyguard is still in intensive care in this hospital behind me. The others are resting in a hotel. They are the Captain, the Engineer, another bodyguard and the Prince's manservant. We have just learnt, officially, that the manservant was carrying a suicide letter, tucked inside his pyjama jacket. Analysts confirm that it was written by the Prince and signed by both the Prince and Princess.

The statement from the Captain says that no one knows what really happened. He only remembers being carried by a bodyguard and thrown into the lifeboat. I must have hit my head, he said, because I lost consciousness, my head was spinning and banging inside. I heard a very loud explosion; the flash came through the slits. It was impossible to tell what had happened; the bodyguard had tied the canvas cover down. But I remember the boat nearly capsized with the shock wave, and then I must have passed out again. Two days, I think, later, we were picked up.

The rest of the survivors say pretty much the same thing, but the Indian manservant Rahjad Singh had something to add. He was with the Prince when he took a telephone call from his father. The Prince was very upset by something his father had said about his relationship with the Princess Alice. I think the bodyguard of the Prince was ordered to do it, so no shame would be brought to Islam. He was to die a Marta for Allah and virgins would await him in heaven.'

Nicholas tucked the draft statements back into his pocket and looked back into the camera. 'That bit about the bodyguard being the instigator, is speculation at this juncture.'

'What news of the search Nicholas?'

'Darren, I have it on good authority that there are several spy type satellites passing over the Med at regular intervals. In all known cases the cameras shut down over this low risk area. So if, as we believe there was an explosion, it was not picked up on the spy in the sky network.'

'If it was an explosion Nicholas, wouldn't there be any debris floating about and probably an oil slick?'

'The problem as I understand it Darren, the lifeboat was picked up about twenty miles west of here. It is not known which direction it drifted from, or really for how long. So it is proving difficult to pinpoint a search area. Finally bad weather and rough seas are not only hampering the air search but are making the spotting of any oil slick or debris almost impossible.'

'Any thing else to tell us on the search Nicholas?'

'We are still awaiting further news from the Devonshire on the search for survivors operation. It is still hoped the other lifeboat, Golden Crown carried two, will show up. I'll let you know when I get it.

That's all for now, I'll hand you back to London. Nicholas Davidson, Cagliari, Sardinia.'

'Thank you Nick. We are now going over to the BBC's search and rescue expert, Robert Cartridge in our Cyprus studio.'

At that, the screen filled with the image of a young man standing in front of a large wall map of the Mediterranean.

'Hi Bobby, what can you tell us about the efforts to find Golden Crown and her other life boat?'

'Well Darren, not much I'm afraid, all naval and air efforts are centred around this area.' He turned and circled, with an electronic marker a large area of sea to the west of Sardinia.

'This is our best estimate as to where the ship went down, and where the other life boat, hopefully with survivors, will be found....So far we have not sighted anything, and our search is being hampered by the weather conditions.

'Can we be sure the yacht sank?'

'We are fairly sure, having of course checked out coast lines and ports within the maximum sailing time and range.... Nothing. We have no idea what time the yacht left Monaco or the direction it took.' Pointing at the map again Bobby continued.

'This is where the survivors were picked up. And this is the starting place to compute the probable location, but finding the wreck may take years.'

'Thank you Bobby.'

The screen returned to Darren Turner at the news desk.

'Now for the rest of the day's news.

Early this morning the body of financier Giles Fairchild was pulled out of the Thames at Tower Bridge. The police have not released any details, but foul play is not suspected. Giles Fairchild believed to be at one time, one of Britain's richest men, recently lost the bulk of his fortune, following a number of bad investments and was said to have been depressed. He was a regular visitor to the palace and a personal friend of the Prince of Wight. The Prince is now facing two tragedies, the tragic circumstances surrounding the disappearance of his wife. And now the loss of a friend. It is however believed the incidents are not connected.'

Sir Peter hit the button. 'Well that's that sorted.' He said sombrely. 'We may have to find Steven another code name.'

Marseilles

Sitting in the corner of a water front bar in Marseille, a Greek sailor nursed a glass of ouzo and stared blankly at the TV screen on the opposite wall. The commentary was in French so he understood not one word, but he did wonder if all the sea searching activity had any connection to what he saw last week.

He was night watch on a small cargo boat out of Iraklion, Crete. Early on the morning of the third day, he had seen a bright flash on the Northern horizon and was about to wake the captain to report what he had seen. And he would have, had he not realised that he'd consumed two thirds of a bottle of ouzo trying to keep warm that night, so the incident wasn't logged.

The sailor shrugged his shoulders, grunted and drained his glass. 'No matter.' He muttered to himself as he got up and left the bar.

Washington

Dring, dring, dring. 'What the,' Henry Forbes, more asleep than awake, couldn't fathom what or where the noise was, suddenly he realised it was the telephone. He lazily threw an arm out of the duvet in a fumbling search for the bedside light switch. The phone continued to ring, dring, dring, dring. 'For crying out loud, just a goddamn minute!' Eventually bringing himself to a state of awareness, just, as he answered the phone.

'Forbes. – Yeah, who. Who is this?

Err, okay.'

Henry Forbes now sat on the edge of the bed and replaced the receiver back onto its cradle.

'Hum, who was that honey?'

'Father Christmas,' then said to himself, 'at least I hope so.'

'That's alright then.' His wife said, still very much in a dream like state.

Intrigued, Henry put on his dressing gown, slipped his feet into his slippers and headed for the study.

He was still sitting at the computer when she walked into the study. 'Merry Christmas darling.' Putting her arms around his neck from behind she bent forward and kissed him on the cheek.

'And a Merry Christmas to you dear.'

'Oh Henry, What are you doing?'

'Just checking some facts, shan't be long.'

'Work, work, work, that's all you ever do, can't you take just one day off, you know the children will be here soon. You should be in the sitting room when they arrive so we can all open our presents together.'

'Sorry dear, this is very important, just have to make a couple of calls, I'll be along shortly.'

She shook her head and pursed her lips as she headed to the door, she knew fine well, when Henry gets his teeth into something he's like a dog with a bone. He wont let anything distract him, but she loved him anyway. 'I'll bring your coffee and toast in here, mind you're not too long.'

'Thank you, dear.'

Henry shut down the computer and just sat there, staring into the now blank screen, deep in thought. He had gleaned all the information on Vos Oil he could find, which wasn't very much. I know someone who'll have the answers, he said to himself. He swivelled around in his chair and picked up the telephone, at the same time thumbing through the pages of a notebook for a very special number, which he tapped into the keypad on the handset. 'Hello this is President Baxter,' sounding very formal and official. 'Hi Jim, Henry Forbes, Merry Christmas.'

'Godamit Henry, you know this number's for emergency use only.' The President paused momentarily. 'It isn't an emergency, is it?'

'Not really.'

'Thank goodness Henry and a Merry Christmas to you. I take it this is more than just a social call, so what can I do for you?'

'Yeah, sorry about using this number Jim, but I need some information, could be of National interest.'

'Fire away.'

'I'd like to know all there is to know about a Russian company, 'Vos Oil' part of Vostok Industries?'

There was a silence on the other end of the line, not the reaction Henry expected. 'You still there, Jim?'

'So you finally got there Henry, I'll send what I have, unclassified, to your e-mail. The Brit's know more of course, they've been handling it.'

'Thanks Jim.' Henry replaced the receiver, a blank faraway look in his eyes, only snapping out of his trance when Jean put the tray down in front of him.

'You should have stayed in bed honey,' she said, 'you look all in.'

'Oh I'll be fine, just a couple of calls to make then I'll sort myself out.'

'Make sure you do it before the children arrive.'

'Y-e-s d-e-a-r.' He muttered as she disappeared through the study door closing it behind her. Deep in thought again, as he took a mouthful of coffee and a bite of toast. I need to call Houston. He put down the coffee, holding a piece of toast between his teeth, thumbed through his book again until he found the number. Still with toast in his mouth, he tapped it into the handset keypad. As it rang, Henry chewed on the bread, swallowing as the answer phone kicked in.

'Hi yah all, Cliff T Hartford junior speakin, can't get to yah right now, leave yah name an number, an I'll give yah all a call...

'Houston its Washington, if you are there, pick up. There was a few seconds delay before Henry heard the click of the receiver being lifted. 'Washington, hi, what can I do for yah?' Cliff knew when Brotherhood names were being used there was no place for small talk

'Houston contact Portland and Denver, we need a meeting, tomorrow evening, the Maryland house.'

'Okee dokee, bit kind of short on notice ain't it?'

'Time is of the essence.'

'Understood, can I ask yah what it's about?'

'Yeah..... I received a message this morning from someone pretending to be Zurich.'

Henry replaced the handset, took another bite of toast and a slurp of coffee.

He heard the car pull up on the drive outside, better get my finger out, one more call. Going through the same routine. Damn! I only have the bank number; I'll have to try it. Purr, purr, purr, 'Bonjour.'

'Zurich, Washington, I didn't expect to get you at the bank today.'

'Why shouldn't you, I spend most of my time here, these days. What is it that you want?' Blunt and to the point, that's Kunze,

'Meeting tomorrow evening, seven-thirty pm US time, Maryland, can you make it?'

'I will be there.'

Maryland

The Forbes's country retreat was in secluded woodland setting, perched on a hill. It was possible to see the sweep of Chesapeake Bay, above the trees, less than a mile away. The house wasn't particularly large, more or less a log cabin, but it made an excellent bolt hole for Henry and Jean, when the pressures of Washington got too much. The children haven't been there for some years now; they are both married with children of their own, so as no others knew of the retreat, interruption would be unlikely.

Portland was the first to arrive, Henry made him welcome gave him a drink and they sat in the lounge on opposite settees, a large coffee table between them, in front of a log fire. About fifteen minutes later Houston showed up and ten minutes after that Denver arrived. 'Well gentleman, its six-thirty, I think we can get started.'

'What about our European cousins?'

'Ah, I didn't invite them, except for Zurich that is, he'll be here at seven-thirty.'

'Are yah gona tell us why?'

'Sure Houston, one thing I need to know first. Am I right in saying, just us four Brotherhood members, know about the US oil situation?'

'For sure.'

'Sure only us four.'

'Yep only us guys.'

Each answered. 'And nothing was mentioned to another member outside us four?'

'Nope.'

'No way.'

'No.'

Henry stood up and collected his briefcase from the dining table and opened it, taking out some notes, a copy of which he passed to the three members. 'Read it and burn it, please.'

Denver felt it was his duty to state the obvious. 'How the hell does Zurich know our situation?'

'That's just it, he doesn't; the e-mail was from a no reply false source, followed by a phone call, allegedly from Zurich, but sounded nothing like him.'

'Then who, - why?' Denver stammered.

'I believe someone is trying, in a subtle way, to get us involved in the purchase of Russian Vos oil and by us so doing, we would save the good ole US from the pending oil crisis.'

'Well that's a great theory you got there Washington ole buddy, but who in the hell, -sides us, knows about the oil situation?' 'Well I guess the producers in the cartel have a clue, but I'm as sure as hell, not one of them knows dick shit about the Brotherhood.' Huston piped in.

'Ahem.' Washington suppressed a little embarrassed cough. 'I have a confession to make to you guys.' There all went silent and stared blankly at Washington.

'Before our last meeting I met Jim Baxter to find out what the government were going to do about the consequences of the Arabs speech. The President was so unconcerned about the issue, that out of sheer frustration I told him about the state of our oil reserves, it seemed to get his attention for a while, but he was still prepared to continue with the no win, food for oil deal. In my attempt to convince him, I may have let slip that I was a member of a secret society.'

The others all looked surprised by Washington's indiscretion, but nothing was said for a long moment, each one trying to think of a way to make a protest without upsetting their host. It was Denver who finally broke the silence.

'Okay what's done is done, so the President knows there is a pending US oil crisis and that there is a group of people who don't like this particular foreign policy of his, so what! It does not make Jim Baxter the sender of the e-mail.'

'Yeah I'd go along with that, an how tha hell would he know bout Zurich?'

'Whoa.' Washington held his hands up. 'It's just that Jim Baxter knows something we don't, about Vostok Industries and I know he is most concerned about our oil situation and he knows about the brotherhood. I can't think of anyone else outside of this room that has all of this information.' Henry paused and looked at the blank faces on the opposite settee, and at Houston's, sitting next to him. 'That sounds pretty conclusive and I must confess a little hard to believe.' Portland said.

'Still don't explain how he knew about Zurich' Denver chirped in.

'Could of had tha CIA to check us out,' Huston said nonchalantly.

The four sat back in their respective settees and fell silent again, after a moment, Washington spoke again. 'Whatever, someone out there knows what we're about and I've got a feeling that Zurich knows something too. That's why I've invited him, when he arrives, please leave the talking to me and don't mention our oil crisis.

Zurich arrived as expected, at seven-thirty, on the dot; the others welcomed him, stuck a drink in his hand and sat him at the end of the settee nearest the fire.

'Are we not waiting for the others?'

'They couldn't make it, Christmas and all that.'

'I see,' Zurich said, but didn't seem at all perturbed. 'Just as well really it will be of no use for them to know the truth.'

The four Americans looked at each other, it was Washington who spoke.

'And what is the truth, Zurich?'

'You know as well as I, Washington. Thanks to the man you sent, I now have my bank and my fortune back.'

Washington decided to play along; the others were wise enough to say nothing. 'Yes he did well, but what I don't understand is where Vladimir Vostok fits in this affair?'

'You don't know.....Do you?'

'No Zurich, we don't know, we have heard of the Russian oil magnet of course.'

Hiendric Kunze sat back in the settee, and looked in turn at the four Americans. 'You understand, a lot of what I'm about to tell you is speculation on my part. Based on comments which until recently only became clear to me, from that and information your man gave me, I have managed to piece things together.' Kunze hesitated, as if running the whole scenario through his mind.

'Vostok has spent a considerable amount of time and money trying to get his hands on the Saudi oil reserve, at your, Americans, that is, expense. I do believe he supplied arms to Middle East terrorists and he contrived to get rid of the Saudi Prince making it look like the Americans or the English had done it. The aim was clear; create bad Saudi - West relations, culminating in the Saudis kicking the West out of Arabia.'

'Why the conniving son of a bitch.' Washington held up a hand to stop any more comments.

'Please go on, Zurich.'

'When the Prince went to England it was an ideal opportunity for Vostok to have him assassinated. Giles Fairchild formerly known as London, an unworthy member of our Brotherhood was to provide the means and opportunity for the assassination. He had been in league with Vostok for sometime.'

'I always suspected he was up to something,' Washington put in.

'Yes, Fairchild was a devious man; apparently he owed Vostok a lot of money, so he concocted this deal to get himself out of the red.'

'Did I hear yah say was?' Washington put his hand on Houston's shoulder.

'Lets tackle that one later, please continue Zurich.'

'As you know, he persuaded the Brotherhood to finance the hit. Vostok's assassin, who was all primed and ready to go, would do the deed as ordered, and the eighteen million was to be split with Vostok. After the assassination, Fairchild's plan was to finger the hit man, he was a Russian mafia villain named Demmitri Abramovich. Vostok was to have Abramovich eliminated on his return to Russia and then leak the information to the press that the assassin was hired by four Americans, and he names them.' Kunze fixed his eyes on each of his companions in turn.

'Son of a bitch!' Both Portland and Denver gave out.

'Tha double dealin bastard!' said Houston.

Washington shook his head from side to side. 'I guess the constraints I put on the payment, had an effect.'

'I'm quite sure it did from Fairchild's point of view, but I'm not sure what.' Kunze paused. 'All I know is that Vostok somehow believed the job would be done. Shortly after our meeting in Yorkshire, he walked into the bank with his two heavies and demanded the twenty million be deposited in his account. For my part, I won't bore you with the details, suffice to say, Vostok took my home and my empire.' Kunze took a deep breath and tried to contain himself.

'What?' Washington said the others had the courtesy to remain silent.

'That's another story; you had better ask the man you sent. However the result is that he ordered your money to be paid into his account.'

'All of it?'

'Don't worry your man was heaven sent. After he'd carried out the contract on the Prince, he eliminated Vostok and with my help he took the agreed payment. At the same time, he got me my bank back, plus the money Vostok cheated me out of.'

'Our man seems to have done a pretty good job, are you telling us, that Vostok is dead?'

'Oh yes, he's dead alright.'

'I've done a thorough check on Vostok Industries, checked news sources; there is no mention anywhere of Vostok being dead.'

'It's like this Washington; Vostok was staying in what used to be my house, with six bodyguards I believe. The housekeeper and the gardener were retained to look after the place when Vostok is not in residence. They live in the gatehouse away from the main house and have been with my family for years. So they called me when they found the front door to the house wide open and the bodyguards gone. The bedroom door had been broken open and Vostok was dead in bed. I advised Marcel and Martha to touch and say nothing. Return to the gatehouse and admit to no one what you have seen. I think the bodyguards will also keep a low profile, probably still drawing their wages, as long as it's believed Vostok's alive.'

'That's very interesting Zurich, the bodyguard theory offers an intriguing proposition.' Washington paused as if the idea was just occurring to him, 'What do you think the chances are that we can buy a sizeable share of Vos Oil before the shit hits the fan?'

Kunze smiled. 'Ahum, a very enterprising thought Washington, could that be the reason you wanted me here?' Washington just smiled, Kunze continued. 'Let me just say that I'm confident that I can determine through contacts in the World Bank where one can get hold of Vostok assets....With some discretion, of course.'

Washington poured more drinks and the mood was jovial, not one of them pursued Kunze for further explanations or more detail. 'Well then Zurich you were going to tell us what happened to London?'

'Please my friends, I cannot consider this man a member of our society, therefore I'm not prepared to give him the honour of using his Brotherhood name.' Kunze took a drink before continuing. 'I knew Fairchild was very involved, but I got the impression it was Vostok calling the tune, having confirmed Vostok was dead. I wanted to make sure Fairchild didn't know about Vostok's acquisitions.' Kunze paused again to look at the four very attentive Americans. 'Acquisitions at my expense, so I telephoned his private number, nothing. Then I telephoned his home, his wife answered.'

'Hell I didn't even know he was married.'

'Neither did I.'

'The point is that Giles Fairchild was fished out of the river Thames on Christmas Eve.'

CHAPTER 22

LOOSE ENDS

Queen Anne's Gate, London

Sir Peter was waiting in his office for a pre-arranged meeting with Sir Robert Palmer head of MI5, the intercom buzzed.

'Yes Marj?'

'Sir Robert's here.' 'Wheel him please Marj and you come in as well.' There was a tap, and then the door opened.

'Ah Bob my good fellow, Happy New Year.' Sir Peter stood hand extended, which Sir Robert grasped.

'Morning Peter.'

'Please have a seat.' Sir Peter gestured towards the Chesterfield. 'Sorry to have dragged you in during the holidays, but I need to put this situation to bed, you understand.'

'Of course Peter, it's no problem.'

'Did you get it?'

'I hope so.' Sir Robert delved inside his briefcase and brought out a manila envelope. He handed the envelope to Sir Peter; he took a quick look at the contents then passed the package to Marjorie. 'Would you take a look at that lot Marjorie; I'd like your opinion on whether or not we have them all.'

Turning back to Sir Robert, 'and the camera, Bob?'

'That was left,' he nodded toward the envelope, 'but we retrieved the sim card, its in the envelope.'

'Good.'

Sir Robert paused for a moment. 'As requested the D notice was served.'

'Thanks Bob, good job, I'll let you know if there's anything else.' Sir Robert took the hint, stood up, shook Sir Peters hand and nodded toward Marjorie.

'Glad to be of service. Happy New Year to you both, bye.' At that he left the office.

Sir Peter waited for security to announce that Sir Robert had left the building before turning to Marjorie.

'What do you think Marj?'

'We've got them all, thirty-six hard copies and the sim, that's what Fairchild said he had.'

'Destroy them now and let's head back to Guildford for what's left of the holiday.'

Sir Peter was going through the motions of setting the alarm to his office when the telephone on Marjorie's desk rang. Marjorie stopped what she was doing and picked up the receiver.

'Hello.'

–'Hello Miss Fawcett....Front door security. I've got John Godfrey here at the desk, wanting to see Sir Peter.' Marjorie turned to look at Sir Peter, who gave a little nod as he began to cancel the alarm and unlock the office.

'Okay, send him up,' Marjorie said and replaced the receiver.

'Hello John, he's waiting for you.'

'Hi Marjorie,' John followed Marjorie, she tapped and opened Sir Peters office door, stepping back allowing John to walk in.

'Ah John, season's greetings.' Sir Peter said at the same time gesturing for John to sit in the chesterfield armchair.

'Same to you sir. I thought you probably would be at the office today, so I took a chance you'd see me.'

'Well we're here, what can we do for you?'

John hesitated and gave out a nervous cough before he could spit out what he'd come to confront Sir Peter with. 'Ahum...Are we responsible?'

'For what?'

'For the sinking of Golden Crown and the deaths of the Prince and Princess?'

'Come on John you know better than to ask such questions.'

John pursed his lips and just nodded. 'Are we?....Sir.' He demanded.

'Of course not, we were looking after them.....Weren't we?'

'Guess so...Sorry sir.'

'Quite alright, John.' Sir Peter responded in a condescending manner.'

'And what about Giles Fairchild?'

'I do believe he committed suicide, John. Prince Edward is devastated, having just lost his wife and now a close friend.' Sir Peter paused. 'It would probably do him good to get away for the weekend.'

'Weekend sir?'

'Well as you can imagine John, in view of the circumstances, the Prince cancelled all official engagements for this month. But I gather, not the private ones.'

'A private weekend?' John suddenly realised he'd been hooked. *Changed the bloody subject...Why is he telling me this crap.*

'Yes, some weeks ago Charlie Mc Bride invited the Prince to a shoot in Dorset, the 28th of January.'

'The Prince, without the Princess?'

'Apparently....I do believe a certain Mrs Grey is also invited.' Sir Peter gave John another knowing wink. 'You have a friend in the press, don't you, John?'

John nodded. 'An acquaintance.'

'Hum interesting. But I'm sure you didn't come here to talk about the Prince of Wight.'

The crafty buggers fed me a line. 'No sir. When can I get back to Baghdad?' John's turn, to change the subject.

'Not so fast John, I'd like you to stay around a little while longer, until the situation has cooled, just a precaution you understand, let's say Baghdad February.'

'Fine sir.'

John got up and headed to the door, Sir Peter reached into his desk draw.

'As you are here John, I wonder, would it be possible to deliver this package by hand for me? It is most important.'

'Of course sir, where would you like me to take it?'

'You're living in Croydon at the moment, aren't you?'

'A little way past there sir, in a small village called Kenley.'

'Not too far from the M25 is it?'

'Not too far at all sir'

'Mmm – even better, that could prove to be very convenient for my purpose. These documents need to be in the hands of a certain person, at four am tomorrow morning precisely. The address is in Brentwood, I shall write it down, please memorize it for I am about to destroy it, standard procedure, you know.'

Sir Peter wrote out the address and held it up for John to read.

'Got that?'

'Yes sir.'

'Good, don't forget it must be there at four precisely.'

'No problem sir.' Sir Peter then tore up the paper into tiny pieces and disposed of them.

What's the old bugger up to now?

John placed the telephone back in the holder, hesitated and picked it up again, tapping in digits, etched in his memory.

'Kathy it's...'

'I'm afraid Mrs Forsyth is no longer in residence.'

'Oh....Can you tell me where I can get hold of her?'

'Sorry sir can't help you.' Click...Purr...The line went dead. He decided to try her mobile, on the off chance of one of those rare occasions when she had the machine switched on...She hadn't. The automated answering service gave out the usual rhetoric about leaving a message. *Pointless.*

John looked at phone, deciding his best bet to trace Kathy would be the company computer, so he placed the instrument back in its holder and went to bed.

It was just after three a m when John left his lodgings and headed for the M25, in a Vauxhall Astra hire car. The motorway was surprisingly quiet at that time of the morning not much traffic. John found himself thinking of Kathy; he wondered how and what she is doing, now that she doesn't have a lady to wait on. If she is not in the Palace, perhaps she's at home with her husband. Then as images of their sex romps flashed through his mind a broad smile cut across his face.

It was about then that he noticed the single headlight, which he took to be a motorbike about one hundred metres behind, keeping pace with him. 'That's odd I'm not going fast, why isn't he overtaking?' John speeded up, but still the light maintained the same distance. Somewhat perturbed, John accelerated until he lost sight of the light behind. As the car entered the lit up area of the Dartford tunnel pay booths, there was no sign of any motorbike. He had just entered the tunnel when a motorbike came into view not far behind him. 'The crafty sod had turned off his head light, what the hell is happening here?'

John decided to speed up through the tunnel; he had bad vibes about this. *Got to get away.*

The motorbike seemed to have anticipated John's reaction and drew level with his car. John saw the man on the pillion pointing a torch like object at him. There was a flash so intense that John was momentarily blinded and instantly lost control of the vehicle; it veered across the carriageway smashing into the tunnel wall.

There was the noise of screeching tyres and crunching metal that seemed to last for an eternity, then silence.

John couldn't move, but he could feel a tingling sensation all over his body, he realized this numbness was desperately trying to mask the pain he was about to feel. He also felt the warm liquid running down his face. The air bag hadn't prevented something from hitting his head, but he had no idea of what, or of anything else for that matter. Through his now hazy vision he saw the dark visor of the motor biker's helmet peering at him. 'You alright mate?' John tried to speak, but no sound came out. He saw and he could smell the whiskey as it was poured over him and he saw, but did not feel the hypodermic needle as it sunk into his neck. He felt no more.

Canet Lo Roig

The thing about living in a place like Canet, you knew everybody and everybody knew you. Felipe has a stall on the markets, so he is up early every morning taking the dogs for their walk before heading off to the various towns with his wares.

As part of his fitness programme Steven would do a ten mile mountain run, often timing the end so he could wind down, walking back with Felipe and the dogs.

'Buenos dias Felipe. How are you this morning?'

'Ah Steven, I have some news for you.'

'What news?'

'Yesterday, Benicarlo market day.' Steven nodded, he knew very well the market day of each town in the area. 'Jaime, my amigo, he came to see me, you know him, no?' Steven nodded. 'He sells the boats, next to the marina.'

'Yes, Felipe, I know him.'

'Well he is telling me, a man is watching your boat. Jaime he see him, there are no strangers about at this time.'

'Sure it was my boat he was watching?' Felipe just shrugged his shoulders and they continued to walk quietly for a while. Felipe could detect Steven's concern.

'Steven, you take the Dobby and the Lila, my dogs, they like you, no stranger would get near you with these two around.'

'Thanks but no thanks Felipe, no offence Dobby, Lila,' he said. The two large Boxer dogs, on hearing Steven say their names, responded with excessive wagging of their stubby tails.

'Probably nothing in it.' He said nonchantly. 'I'll give Jaime a ring, check it out.

Steven dived into pool and swam as fast as he could for as long as he could, that was the best way he knew to get rid of his frustration, nay anger! He was fairly peeved to put it mildly; it had not crossed his mind that Sir Peter would want him terminated. He heaved himself out of the pool without effort and just stood there in a trance like state weighing up all the connotations.

He towelled off, put on his robe and walked into the house through the patio door almost bumping into Jennifer as she was heading out.

'You alright?'

'Sorry Jen, yeah, - fine.'

'You look as if you're miles away.....Penny for them,'

Steven took her by the hand and led her to the settee and they both sat down.

'You know I told you we wouldn't go back to the UK until the spring.'

'Y-e-s.'

'Well how would you feel if we could never go back?'

Jennifer let the thought run her head. 'Whatever... I'm with you boo-boo.'

'I'm serious Jen.'

'So am I lover, so why not get to the point and tell me what's bothering you?'

Steven sat back and took a deep breath. 'I think someone is watching the boat waiting for me to show....Intending to terminate me.'

'What!'

'Believe me Jen, I understand the scenario all too well, you see, I know too much.'

'I don't understand....I..'

Steven interrupted. They have no idea where I am, that's why they're watching my boat. Thankfully I doubt that they are aware of you or involvement, otherwise we would have been traced through your mobile.'

'You're serious aren't you?'

Steven nodded. 'Deadly.'

'Surely Steven whoever you work for.' She held up her hand. 'And I don't want to know who, must have need of you.'

'Well I admit that's what I thought, but upon reflection what I have up here.' Steven tapped a finger on the side of his forehead. 'Probably out weighs any feelings of loyalty they may have for me.'

'What are we going to do?'

'You my dear are staying put; I on the other hand intend to do some checking.'

Steven picked up the telephone, chose a number from a list by the table and pressed the digits.

'Olla Jaime.'

'Ah Steven, I been waiting your call, you call about this man, no?'

'Si.'

'I see him now. He take coffee, always he look your boat.'

'What makes you so sure it's my boat he is watching?'

'Morning Star the only boat on pier 4. The marina manager he say, this man asked him if Mr Pinder has rented the berth.'

'Gracia Jaime....That would do it for me.'

'Steven he know you only rent to the end of the month, he wait for you.'

'Tell me is he there all night?'

'I don't know, maybe he sleeps somewhere.'

'Okay thanks Jaime, adios.'

Steven replaced the receiver. *He knows my name and possibly has my photograph.* 'Jen, I need your skills, I want to age forty years.'

An old man sat in one of the bars at the side of the marina, nursing his coffee and cognac. He took in the younger looking man who seemed to fully occupied watching 'Morning Star' oblivious to all else around him. The old man weighed the young man up.

Bomber jacket, jeans, desert boots and close cropped hair. Definitely ex-army, probably Para. Big guy but flabby, wonder how fit he is.

Steven moved around the various bars and restaurants in the marina area, not spending too long at any one spot. He watched the younger man without making it obvious, the guy so intent on watching the boat, hadn't a clue he was being observed. Steven concluded that the guy was alone and amateur. He felt a little peeved that Sir Peter should think he warranted such an unworthy opponent. Perhaps he was wrong, the guy hadn't been sent to wipe him out....Or perhaps that crafty old bugger Sir Peter is just going through the motions....In which case that guys expendable.

The next morning, Steven as usual met up with Felipe.

'Are you at Jana this morning?'

'Si.'

'Will you do me a favour?'

'For sure, what is it, you want?'

'When you pack up at two, take the Primera to Benicarlo, make sure you wear one of your blue track suits, same as this one you sold me last week.' Felipe nodded. 'And one of them bobble hats you wear at the football.'

'For what?'

'I want you to take some things onto Morning Star pretending to be me.'

'It will be dangerous. No?'

'I don't think so, but just in case make sure the pier gate is closed after you.'

As Felipe entered the pier, the man sat up. *Very amateur.* Steven thought, as he watched from the roof terrace restaurant. No sooner had Felipe boarded Morning Star than the man walked over to the Primera and planted a magnetic tracker. *So bloody obvious.* Steven shook his head in disgust, as he punched the numbers into Jen's mobile, he had deliberately given his own a water test somewhere in the Med. 'Felipe you can come out now, I'll meet you in Lidl's car park.'

Steven, makeup removed and clothes changed, was waiting in Lidl's parking area as the Primera came to a stop. They exchanged cars and Felipe, without hesitation took off in the Land Rover.

Steven was now wearing his blue track suit and a bobble hat, and driving the Primera, headed towards Peniscola. He glanced from time to time, in the rear view mirror to ensure he still had the contractor in tow. He took the south coast road from Peniscola for two kilometres and parked in a lane at the foot of a mountain track to the Ermita San Antonia.

Dressed in a tracksuit with a small backpack and still wearing Felipe's bobble hat, he set off on the uphill five kilometre rough track run.

As the track climbed and wound, it was quite easy to keep an eye on the man way below, who was busting a gut trying to keep up. At the top, the track turns sharply to the left ramping a further fifty metres to the Ermita terrace. The triangular piece of land formed by the turn was originally a garden, which still had the remains of a stone store. That's where Steven decided to wait, unseen from the track below.

The man seemed to have gained a second wind and was now moving easier albeit more cautiously, running from cover to cover, making him a hard target. *Ah, so the old training is coming back.*

When the man reached the track directly below the garden, he was out of view. Steven would have to judge the right moment when he believed the man had passed his hiding place. He waited for what he perceived to be the right time to quietly slide down a crumbling stonewall and onto the track.

Keeping concealed by the foliage growing out of the bottom of the wall and at the track side, he was banking on the man, now ahead of him and half way up the slope, being more interested in the Ermita and the terrace above, than watching his back. The man was about ten yards ahead with his back against the opposite wall which supported the terrace above and now had a gun in his hand which he was pointing up at the terrace. He was making his way slowly up the slope, looking in an upward direction and trying to keep pressed, or as near to the wall as he could. Unfortunately, for him that is, he reached a point where the undergrowth at the bottom of the wall was so thick that he had to move out into the track to get around it. That was the moment Steven quietly emerged from his cover and quickly came up behind the gunman, taking him by surprise.

'The gun isn't necessary.' He said softly. The man spun around in shock, but before he could react, in a flash Steven's left hand grabbed the gun by the barrel and with a twist, turn and jerk movement, plucked the gun from the man's hand. In the same turning motion, Steven brought up his right elbow catching the man in the throat, sending him backwards to an ideal distance for Steven to launch a high kick with his right leg which caught the man on his chest. With a further series of spinning kicks he forced the man backwards up the slope. The man made a brave attempt to fight back and tried desperately to fend off the kicks, but the exertion of the uphill pursuit had taken its toll, his arms and legs ached and his movement was slow and leaden. Steven had no trouble hitting the target and blocking a rather telegraphed swinging right arm, countering with another spinning high kick.

By this time Steven had in fact, pushed the man to the top of the slope, so that he was standing, just about, on the edge of the Ermita terrace. With a finally movement Steven landed his right titanium fist on the side of the man's jaw.

When the man came round, he was on the Ermita terrace slumped against the wall, the blood had caked around his mouth and the side of his face had doubled in size. Steven was sat on a stone bench a few feet away drinking water from a plastic bottle, the gun was on the bench by his side.

'Ah you're awake, fancy a drink?' The man made an attempt to nod, grimacing with pain as he did so and Steven passed him the bottle.

'Well now, what shall we do with you?' Steven said as if pondering a chess move.

'Let me run this by you. Oh, and feel free to stop me if I've got it wrong.' The man again attempted an acknowledging nod.

'I would say you're an ex squady, probably Para, no family ties, never done anything like this since your army days, I would say more used to throwing trouble makers out of night clubs than being a contract killer.'

The look on the man's face said it all, Steven was bang on.

'How much did they offer you?' The man mumbled. 'What was that, I didn't hear you?' Struggling to talk he eventually spat out the words.

'Hundred grand......Half upfront, half when it's done.'

'Well I'm blowed, what a pittance, I feel somewhat insulted. What's your name?' The man looked unsure.

'It's not going to matter a jot whether I know your name or not.'

'Gary, my name's Gary, Gary Holdsworth.' He mumbled.

'Mine's Steven but you know that of course. Speaking as one who has done this, killing the bad guys' kind of thing, many times before, this is how it goes, for you that is.' Steven paused for affect. 'You are given a name, a photo and a location. They tell you that they are HM special services and will pay you to terminate Steven Pinder, me, right so far?' Gary nodded. 'One important bit try to make it look like an accident, but take this gun just in case. Perhaps it didn't occur to you earlier, but you and I are about the same size, looks wouldn't matter.

So why do you think they would send, - no disrespect intended Gary, an amateur like you to terminate a professional like me?' With some effort and a lot of determination Gary responded in a hardly discernable voice.

'I didn't know about you, just some bloke that had to be rubbed out. I think you've broken my jaw, I'm in some pain here.' Steven rummaged in his backpack and handed Gary a strip of paracetamol. 'Take two of them and have another drink. The point is Mr Holdsworth; it's you who is meant to end up at the bottom of some cliff. In my hire car, with my papers and personal items. Just for identification purposes, you understand. Obviously I would take the trouble to ensure your face would be unrecognisable, before the fatal trip. That's why your looks wouldn't matter.' Gary's eyes went to the gun on the bench next to Steven. 'Don't even think about it, I'd drop you before you could get up, besides it's unloaded.'

'What if I had killed you?' He mumbled.

'Highly unlikely don't you think. You see, my employer just wants me to disappear for a while, Steven Pinder, which would be you, - dead, that would do the trick. I suppose the intention is, I would re-emerge sometime later, in the future with a new name, probably yours.'

At this point, despite the pain in his jaw, Gary was not prepared to accept that Steven was superior in any way.

'Supposing, I had shot and killed you.'

'Highly unlikely, but if you had managed to terminate me it would be somewhat inconvenient for my employers, losing an asset, they have invested millions in. Nevertheless my loss at the end of the day would be inconsequential in the grand scheme of things. In your case however the matter's already decided and your fate is sealed. As soon as you tried to collect the other fifty grand, you would be dead. And if you don't collect, you will be tracked down and terminated anyway.'

Gary thought for a moment and then he looked at Steven and mumbled.

'Then I'm in deep shit aren't I?' Steven pursed his lips and nodded.

'Don't worry Gary there just might be a way out. It really would be a pain for me to change my name at this time for various reasons that I wont bore you with. Do you think you can walk?' Gary nodded and started to get to his feet, although he was very unsteady. 'Good I'll explain on our way down, but first we have to get you to the hospital at Vinaros and get your jaw sorted.' Automatically Steven came up under Gary's arm to give him support.

'Hi Jen, you alright?'

'Fine, where are you?'

'Better not say, these mobile phones you know.'

'Understood.'

'Listen Jen, I have one or two things to do I may be away a couple of days. Would you do me a favour?'

'Sure.'

'Take Felipe with you to Edison, there's a Mercedes 4x4 with English plates, parked in the lane, the keys are tucked inside the rear bumper and the documents are in the glove compartment, including a bill of sale in Felipe's name, if he doesn't object to a right hand drive he can have it. Get the car re-registered with Spanish plates as soon as.'

'That it?'

'That's it.'

'No problem, you take care now, bye lover.'

'Bye gorgeous.'

Steven left Gary in the hospital heading for the print works where the local newspaper is produced. A bribe of one thousand Euros was enough to have his obituary, with details of the car accident, printed in the last run of tomorrow's paper, about three hundred copies, which hopefully would not be noticed in the overall circulation. Before leaving he lingered by the end of the printing line and picked up as many copies as he could, throwing them all, apart from one copy, into the waste skip.

The next morning Steven placed the folded Spanish newspaper, with the obituary highlighted, into a large brown envelope and headed to Benicarlo post office. Sending the package marked private for the attention of Sir Peter Thompson- Smythe, Queen Anne's Gate London.

Steven started 'Morning Stars' engines and slowly inched forward, the figure on the jetty casting off the lines had a white bandage wrapped around his head a wire frame over his face and looked like a ninja with a bad case of mumps.

'Cast off the forward spring,' Steven shouted and then eased the levers into reverse so that the craft inched back to relieve the tension on the stern spring line.

'Cast off aft and come aboard.'

Morning Star eased her way out of Benicarlo marina through the inner and outer harbour into the open sea. Once clear of other shipping, Steven set a course for Marseille and set the autopilot. Gary was sat in the saloon with a pencil and paper so that he could respond to Steven without speaking.

'Oh I do love this captive audience situation,' Steven said laughingly, but Gary was not in a jovial mood.

'First things first Gary old chum, that fifty grand they've given you....Still got it?' Gary scribbled away.

Spent most of it on the Mercedes.

'Good, you can forget about the other fifty.'

Gary just shrugged his shoulders, after all Steven must have told him a dozen times already.

'Okay I repeat myself, but what I haven't told you yet is that I've opened an account for you in a Swiss bank, only eight hundred thousand Euros, I'm afraid, but it should be enough to last you a while, so don't go wasting it. Gary's eyes lit up and for one brief moment he forgot the pain as he wrote.

Thank you, thank you very much—

And turned the paper around, for Steven to read.

'You're welcome mate.' Steven went to his desk draw taking out a lot of documents. 'This is your new passport and all the documents you will require for your new identity. Your name is now Keith Forward.' Gary now Keith scribbled again. *–Wow!! –* And underscored the thank you.

'When we get to Marseille I will book you into a private clinic, all paid, for a three week stay and when you've sufficiently recovered, I want you to head east. I'm sure that HM special services are satisfied that you were involved in a road accident, using my name and hire car and you are deceased, so there should be no attempt to trace you.'

Keith picked up the pencil and started to write again.

Still don't understand why someone had to die, for your sake. Steven took his time reading the note, searching his mind for an explanation he himself was unsure of.

'Well Keith in one way my death, charade or otherwise, will provide my employer some insurance, but I wouldn't expect you to understand that scenario. However, I think it would be more understandable, if I were to tell you that the arrangements made by my employer for your demise, was they way of reminding me that they still had control my life and whether I live or die.'

Keith would have shook his head in disgust had it not been painful. Steven and Keith looked at each other in silence for a long moment, before Steven picked up the thread of what he was saying earlier. 'Yes, I suggest you head east and make a new life for yourself, but I must stress. - Never! Never return to the UK, and most importantly, forget everything you know about me.'

Keith nodded and scribbled. *I promise.*

CHAPTER 23

FAREWELL

TV News London

Sunday 1st January. Today, thousands of people, thronged around St Paul's Cathedral for a memorial service to mourn the loss of the much-loved Alice, Princess of Wight. The choice of St Paul's over Westminster, says a communiqué from the Palace is due to no mortal remains having been found of her Highness and her companion Prince Mohammed of Saudi Arabia. The service is to be simple and straightforward with no honour guard. This service is for the benefit of the Royal family to come to terms with the situation and their way of accepting her loss as final. Edward Prince of Wight is to read the eulogy.

There are many rumours circulating among the crowd, the general feeling is that the Royal family are only going through the motions and don't really care about the Princess. Particularly, as she may have been having an affair with the Arab Prince. The Palace have been at pains to point out that Prince Mohammed was a friend of the family, the Princess was taking a well earned holiday onboard the Saudi Royal Yacht to recuperate after illness. The Saudi Royal family reiterate the statement from the Palace.

The Saudi Royal Yacht, Golden Crown was last seen on the 17th December at anchor off Monaco Sometime between the 17th and 18th she left Monaco and it thought to have sunk somewhere off Sardinia. Princess Alice, Prince Mohammed and two bodyguards are believed to have gone down with her. All attempts to locate further survivors and the wreck have now been called off. HMS Devonshire is on her way home.

Swiss Television Report

Zurich 4th January, Police today attended the Lakeside estate formerly of the Kunze banking family, now the home, when in Switzerland, of Vladimir Vostok, head of the giant Russian concern 'Vostok Industries.'

The Police were called to the house by the housekeeper. Vladimir Vostok was found dead in a first floor bedroom. From the level of decomposition death is believed to have occurred approximately two weeks previously. They suspect Vostok died of natural courses, because of the circumstance surrounding the body. The police are not offering an explanation as to what these particular circumstances are, but they are very keen to interview Vostok's six bodyguards.

In a statement given by the housekeeper, Frau Rhinehart, the bodyguards left the estate in somewhat of a hurry on the 23rd December.

Frau Rhinehart lives in the gatehouse cottage a kilometre from the main house. Her duties strictly forbid her attending the main house, while Vostok is in residence, but she became concerned when the guards did not return and Vostok's car was still in the drive. She put off checking the place, until today. A post-mortem will be undertaken tomorrow.

Zurich News

Zurich 9th January, Post-mortem result on Vladimir Vostok, indicates that traces of poison were found in the body. The coroner's verdict is death by misadventure. The Police are anxious to interview the former bodyguards, but so far, have been unable to trace any of them.

Zurich 24th January, Police where called to an apartment on Badenerstrasser, today, following reports from the neighbours of a bad smell. A body of a man believed to be that of Demmitri Abramovich was removed, foul play is not suspected. A Police spokesman at the scene says there are faint marks around the wrist and ankles of the corpse are indicative of bondage at some time before death. Our enquiries so far with other residents, lead us to believe prostitutes visited the deceased frequently. This gives rise to the theory that the bondage was inflicted during a sexual act. At this juncture we are not looking for anyone else in connection with the death.

Abramovich was a salesman for Schneider Klaus, an Engineering company owned by the recently deceased Vladimir Vostok. The Police feel there is no connection between the two deaths. It has been revealed by the team investigating the scenes, that in both instances, the deaths occurred in a locked room, or in Abramovich's case, a locked apartment, locked, from the inside.

CHAPTER 24

PAPARAZZI

London Paparazzi Office

William Thompson had returned from the south of France to bathe in the relative glory of the pictures he had taken. As it turned out, the last pictures taken of the Saudi yacht Golden Crown. But what was more important, they were last pictures of the Princess Alice and Prince Mohammed. Bill was certain the two were having an affair, but the photographs had been inconclusive.

Too late for them now.. He'd looked into Princess Alice's eyes through his giant telescopic lens and had seen a happiness that he'd never seen on the hundreds of other photographs he had taken of her. So sad for her loss, Bill like thousands of others, Royalists or not, had a deep affection for the Princess. *In away,* he thought, *I'm glad that I didn't cause her the pain and the problems that exposure would have.*

He was sitting, almost lying down, in his swivel chair, legs crossed and supported on the desk in front of him, hands clasped behind his head. He was staring at the proofs on the wall in front of him.

'Hey you, bollock brain, got a job for you, get your arse in here.' That was paparazzi boss, Joe Wyman in his usual friendly manner. Bill pushed himself up and sauntered over to the glass screen door of Wyman's office. 'Come in Bill and shut the fucking door.'

'What's the job boss?'

'I've just had a call from a good contact of mine, never been wrong this guy. He tells me that HRH Prince of Wight is giving one to a married chick name of Cecelia Grey and has been for some years. If Princess Alice was having an affair, it wasn't before time. Anyway according to my source HRH delighted in taunting the Princess with all of the details of his infidelity.'

Bill let his feelings show. 'The bastard drove her to it.'

'You've got it, which begs the question, for what purpose?'

Bill thought for a moment. 'All these rumours, surrounding their deaths, maybe, it wasn't suicide, or maybe it wasn't Muslim extremists, perhaps it was a conspiracy by our own Royal family.'

'I can see your point Bill, she always was a cut above that prick of a husband, but fuckin' proving there's been a conspiracy.....Well that's a whole new ball game.'

'Yeah but it won't hurt to do a little digging.'

'Better not to go there Bill, you're pushing a bucket of shit with a short handled stick, leave the suppositions to others. Just get me the fucking pic's and I'll nail the bastard'

'Do my best, what do want me to do?'

'I want pictures of him with this woman. My source tells me that these two plan to meet this weekend, at a shoot in Dorset. Apparently she was invited to shoot quite independently of him, so that their meeting didn't look at all contrived.'

'If there's a picture to be had, I'll get it. Where in Dorset is this shoot?'

'As far as I know, on the Encombe estate, which I believe is on the south coast near a place called Corfe. If you take off now it'll give a couple of days to suss' the place. Go on then, fuck off.'

'Okay, okay, I'm out of here.'

'Such a polite man, our Joe.' Bill muttered as he threw a few odds and ends into a canvas bag along with a camera a selection of lenses and spare rolls of film, he preferred the old type of film rather than the digital because it gave him the freedom to send the rolls on, computers are not always available.

Bill arrived Friday morning in a little village called Kingston just outside the larger village of Corfe on the Dorset coast. Eager to get involved in the local scene, he booked accommodation for two nights in the local pub, the Scott Arms. Leaving the canvas bag on the bed he headed down to the bar, to pick up a little gossip from the regulars. As far as the locals are concerned he would tell them that he was there to do an article for Dorset Life magazine, on country estates.

Bill thought he would get all the local knowledge he wanted by chatting up the bar maid. Only this barmaid turned out to be a barman. Not to worry, the guy proved to be a fount of local knowledge and very helpful.

'It just so happens, this here village used to belong to the Encombe estate, that be just down a ways.' The barman pointed off to his right. 'That there estate be avin a shoot this comin weekend.'

'Oh really, that's a spot of luck, I should get plenty of material on that, for my article.'

'Now ar doesn't bother too much with the shoot these days, but young Ian he goes reg-lar. Should be in t-night.'

'Thanks for that, I'll make a point of talking to him.'

Bill walked over, pint in hand and sat in front of the log fire and immediately struck up a conversation with four gentlemen sitting at a corner table, who as it turned out, were just as full of the local information as the barman and just as eager to relate it. Apparently at one time the Scott Family owned all the land around, the large Encombe house was the family home, that all changed when the house and the immediate surrounding land was sold off. A bit of useless information Bill thought, nevertheless he had learnt that Encombe house, sits in a horseshoe shaped valley, the open end being the sea, and the hills around the perimeter are steep and wooded. There are also public footpaths along the hilltop on each side of the estate. 'Good I'll go for a walk.' He said, putting the empty glass on the bar as he passed.

About half a mile up the road, he found the path, which would take him along the hilltop to the coast. The scenery was breathtaking in more ways than one. By the time he had walked up down and around the estate, he was absolutely knackered. When he eventually got back to the Scott Arms he was so cold and tired, that he headed straight for the chair by the fire and flopped. At least he now knew how the land lay.

Feeling somewhat refreshed after a rest and a shower. He made his way to the bar again. This time to meet Ian, one of the beaters on tomorrows shoot, he was very informative.

Apparently all of the drives are set up on the hillsides in various locations around the estate and the pegs for the guns are set in the valley bowl. For the final drive, the obelisk, the guns are lined up on their pegs in the valley as usual, but this time, not far from the house. On this shoot each gun would have a loader to pop the cartridges into the barrels, behind them, stood well back, were men with dogs to pickup the downed birds.

Bill was wearing a camouflage hat and jacket and he had a piece of camouflage netting, propped with twigs covering him and the cameras telescopic lens. He had selected a spot in the woods on the hillside, which would be behind the guns and picking up teams, in an ideal position to observe the last drive of the shoot. After a long wait, he saw the beaters wagon stop on the road below him, drop off a couple of guys with flags, who set off to climb the hill up to the obelisk, presumably to act as stops. The wagon with the rest of the beaters disappeared from view. Bill knew these beaters were going to come in from behind driving the birds over the hill crest and over the waiting guns. A few minutes later vehicles some caring the guns and some with the picker-up teams, began to arrive on the road below and the personnel started to assemble at their chosen place.

Prince Edward was easy to spot, he was the only gun to have two loaders, no doubt bodyguards and a rather out of place looking man stood behind them. *Probably the manservant.* Cecelia stood at her peg pretending that she hadn't really noticed HRH, but Bill looking through the telescopic lens, had caught them several times glancing at each other.

The birds appeared in waves over the crest of the hill opposite, dropping down into the valley and over the waiting guns. It was then that things got little perturbing, a lot of birds flew directly over Bill's position and some of the shot birds dropped from the sky hitting the ground only metres in front of his position. Fortunately the picking up dogs seemed to be more interested in grabbing the downed birds and carrying them back to their masters, rather than sniffing around him.

The whistle blew to signify the end of the drive and guns were being unloaded, rested and made safe. Then it happened.

Instead of joining the other guests on the short walk back to Encombe house, the Prince made for the Range Rover. The two bodyguards turned to follow the Prince, at that moment the manservant stepped forward to block their path, spreading his arms to herd them into a huddle. Bill noticed the head movement as the manservant talked and it seemed obvious to him that the bodyguards had been told to ignore the situation.

The guards turned away and began to collect up the equipment and spent cartridges. Bill turned his attention and camera back to the Prince. 'What the fuck is he up to?' HRH climbed into the vehicle and started it. Bill so wrapped up in watching the Prince through the telescopic lens, failed notice Cecelia who seemed to have appeared from nowhere climbing into the other side of the vehicle. It then sped away in the opposite direction from the house. 'Shit!' Bill desperately gathered up his gear and scrambled up the hill, slipping and sliding back, getting snagged in the brambles and undergrowth. He was nowhere near the top of the hill when he heard the Range Rover go past on the road above.

Breathless and panting he eventually got to the road. He dropped the canvas bag on the grass, put his hands on his knees and his head down, and cursed. 'Shit! Shit! Shit!' A minute or so later, his breathing almost normal again, he straightened. 'What now, Bill failed again Thompson, what the fuck do you do now.' Then it twigged. 'Hang on old son,' he said to himself. 'I was on this road yesterday and I know it isn't the most direct route out of here. I wonder, are they still on the estate? Yeah – why not, they've had weeks to plan. It would make sense to have a private type place lined up for a dirty weekend preferably on the estate, less public and if memory serves, there's an estate cottage nestled in the woods along this road, noticed it yesterday, let's check it out old son.'

Picking up the canvas bag he set off in the direction the Range Rover had taken.

A couple of minutes later he caught sight of the cottage roof above the thick bushes planted along the perimeter fence, the double leaf gate was constructed in timber and clad with vertical lapping planks six foot high. Bill put down the bag, took hold with both hands on top of the gate and eased himself up so that he could see over the top.

'Thompson, you lucky bastard.' There at the end of the gravelled drive stood the Range Rover.

Dropping back down to the ground, he considered the options. He needed to get in discretely, the gate is too exposed, he had to pick a place from where he could approach the cottage without been seen.'

A short while later, Bill had climbed the fence and had dropped down into a natural gap between two bushes, he was adjacent to the sidewall of the cottage, no windows. Opening his bag he took out the camera fitting a standard lens, and flash. With this baby on he'd have to get in real close, probably only going to get one shot, let's hope it's a good n.

He moved swiftly around to the front of the house keeping to the wall and stooping low under the windows. Turning the old-fashioned type knob on the front door, he gently pushed it open and it groaned as it swung on the multi coats of old paint on the steel hinges. Bill froze, at the same time cursing his luck. Nothing happened, so he stepped into the hall. As he reached the foot of the stairs, he heard faint groans and the squeak of bedsprings coming from one of the upstairs rooms. 'Not really on, this old sport,' he said to himself. 'This is without doubt, breaking and entering, well entering and definitely invasion of privacy.' But he felt compelled to continue the slow step-by-step torturous journey up the stairs. 'This one is for you Alice, I'm going to nail that bastard,' he whispered under his breath. Finally he stood poised outside the door, from where the bouncing, panting and groaning sounds were emanating. Shoulder lightly against the door, camera at the ready, right hand on the doorknob. Bill was ready, he took a deep breath. 'One two three, in we go. Smile!' Zzz click. Both of them were starker's, HRH was on the bed, and Cecelia was astride him, riding him like a horse. Their clothes were strewn all over the floor. They had been so keen to unite their bodies that they had not taken the time to get into the bed. Zzz click 'That's nice.' Cecelia was screaming and tugging at the duvet trying to get something to cover her modesty, HRH was more aggressive.

'What the! Who the bloody hell are you!'

'That's good, hold it.' Zzz click.

'Get out of here!' The Prince retrieved a small black box and pressed the button, which was probably an alarm call to his bodyguards.

'I'm out of here.' Bill took off down the stairs, out of the door up to and over the fence picking up the canvas bag on the way, without breaking step. And he kept running as fast as he could, heading towards the village. He felt elated; perhaps it was the adrenaline, no, more than that, he'd just got the bloody scoop of the century, worth thousands.

He heard the car coming down the stone chip estate road, and without hesitation, he dived full length into the undergrowth of the woods. The ground was damp and cold and was covered with small tongue shaped ferns and bramble runners, which clawed their way across his face and tore into his clothing. Not without some discomfort, the bramble runner across his face arrested the momentum of his dive. Tucking the bag into his body, he lay quite still, hoping the camouflaged fatigues would blend with the limited cover. His arm crooked across his forehead initially to push off the bramble. But staying in that position he was able to peer out from under, just in time to see the car with the two bodyguards, speed past in the direction of the village. 'What the fuck do I do now,' he asked himself, as he sat up the adrenalin banging in his veins, masking the soreness of the bramble scratches across his face. Any bodyguard worth their salt, and he was sure these guys were, would be checking him out at the local pub. Right now they'll probably know the make and size of his underpants and have his car picked out in the pub car park. 'Okay,' he said to himself, 'just relax old son, think it through what would you do in their shoes. I'd leave one man to watch the car while the other drove back checking out the possible route I may have taken. Y-e-s that's what they'll do.'

He concluded that a return to the Scott Arms was out of the question. So Billy boy, what are you going to do, can't stay here, that's a fact.'

He decided to continue straight on through these woods and down the hill, instead of taking a right into the village, it must come out somewhere near Corfe Castle.'

Without further to do Bill got to his feet and set off at a brisk pace, he was just about to scramble over a dry stone wall at the bottom edge of the wood when he heard the car driving slowly on the road some two hundred metres behind. Turning to look in that direction he noticed the trail of flattened ferns where he'd planted his size nines. 'Bugger if they spot that I'm done for.' But the Range Rover cruised slowly by and hadn't seemed to noticed the tell tale path of flattened vegetation.

'Phew....Lucky, or what.' And so he pressed on.

Corfe Castle stood on a hillock in front of him, it looked so close he felt he could almost touch it, but that was half an hour ago, and he didn't seem to be getting any closer. Finally after almost an hour since leaving the wood, he was standing in Corfe village square, with torn clothing, feeling exhausted and very sore from the bloody scratches across his face.

The young lady in the Post Office looked at him quizzically. 'Fell into a bramble bush,' he loudly proclaimed to anyone showing an interest in his dishevelled state. Bill picked up a large brown envelope from the shelf, took it to the side counter where a pen dangled on a piece of string. He addressed the envelope to Joe at the office, marking it private and confidential. He then took the roll of film out of the camera and dropped it into the envelope. 'How do I get Joe's attention?' Picking up the pen, he wrote across the top, as big and bold as he could.

NAILED HIM!

'Could you send this for me please, first class recorded delivery?' 'Yes sir. Is there anything of value?'

'I should cocoa.'

The lady had her pen poised over the value box on the form.

Better not get too cocky Billy boy.

'If you put £10 in that should cover it.'

'With the envelope, that will be £1.98p sir.'

Bill peeled off a teener and passed it under the glass screen.

'Thank you, please sign here.'

With that done Bill took himself into a corner behind a rack of postcards. Just in case those goons catch up with him, they'll want the film. So he put a new roll into the camera and fired off six shots, mainly of the postcard collection on a rotating stand.

Having been given a number for a taxi, the nearest happened to be in Wareham, Bill headed to the local telephone kiosk, and tapped out the number.

'Hello, taxi, yes could you send one straight aw-.'

Something hard, which he suspected was a gun, stuck him in his lower back. A hand came over his shoulder and clicked off the phone.

'You can hang up the receiver now sir, your taxi is here.'

Bill was bundled unceremoniously into the back of the car and pushed onto the floor. A boot with some force stamped on the back of his head pushing his face hard into the floor, the pain was excruciating. Nothing was said, but he knew one of the men was examining the contents of his canvas bag, while the other was driving, to where, he hadn't a clue. Then he felt a hand checking out his pockets, his car keys and wallet were removed.

Sometime later he was dragged out of the car by his hair and thrown to the ground. He was in woods again, but not the same woods, the vegetation was different. *Get up Billy boy, all is not lost.*

There was a thud! The pain filled the back of his head, then blackness.

That was the last thing William Thompson felt.

Tabloid Press Reports

Tuesday 31st January. Lawyers acting on behalf of his majesty the King worked quickly to prevent the compromising photographs appearing in the tabloids, inciting liable action for breach of privacy laws. However all the daily papers carried a watered down column indicting the Prince of Wight was believed to be romantically involved with a married woman.

Except that is, for the Spanish issue of the Daily Mail which was in print before it could be amended. The front page showed a photograph of HRH the Prince of Wight in a compromising position with Mrs Cecelia Grey. For the sake of modesty, the paper had blanked out the naughty bits.

However the internet was not slow to take advantage of the uncensored photographs floating around cyber space. And the National papers across most of the rest of Europe were quick to follow were the internet had led and printed the unconcerned versions with complete disregard to the British legal system. In all instances the cover story accompanying the picture was the same, in the relevant language.

These photographs were allegedly taken last weekend at a cottage in Dorset, on the south coast of England.

A Buckingham Palace spokesman, in London, refused to make any comment, but sources close to the Prince say he has being having an affair with Mrs Grey for years. Sceptics are wondering what effect the affair would have had on Princess Alice, some are even remarking, given the present circumstances, on the convenience of her death.

Paparazzi Office

Two men walked into the Paparazzi headquarters and knocked on the glass door of Joe Wymans office.

'Come in!' Joe shouted without looking up from a set of prints spread on his desk top.

'Mr Wyman?'

'And who the fuck wants to know?

'I'm DI Jackson and this is my colleague Sergeant Foster, from the Met.' Joe sat back in his chair and looked up at the two plain clothed police officers.

'About bloody time you guys showed up.'

'You reported one of your operatives as missing, a person by the name of William Thompson.'

'Sure did, you guys found him then?'

'Not quite sir. We have found a blue Mondeo X667 ODT registered in your name.'

'Sure that's the company car Bill was driving.'

'Not good news, I'm afraid sir. Dorset police were called to investigate tyre tracks running across a field and disappearing over the cliff edge near a place called Chapman's Pool on the south coast.' Joe, probably for the first time in his life, was gobsmacked, DI Jackson continued. 'Apparently the water around that area is quite deep and I'm led to believe, is quite treacherous. However, Dorset police inform us that they are unable to affect recovery at this time, but have had a police dive team in place.'

'So where the fuck is Bill?'

'I'm coming to that sir. The driver's door and all windows were open, the body could be anywhere. No doubt it will turn up in a day or, somewhere along the coast.' DI Jackson took a note book from his pocket, flicked over a few pages and began to read.

'The divers have recovered Mr Thompson's wallet, a canvas bag containing cameras and lenses, several empty paracetamol foil strips and an empty bottle of whisky, empty of whisky that is.'

'Bill couldn't stand whisky.' Joe protested.

DI Jackson seemingly ignored Joe's outburst and continued. 'In view of the evidence recovered so far, we are prepared accept that Mr Thompson has taken his own life and we will not be pursuing the matter further.'

'You pack of bastards.' Joe snarled. 'You've done him in.' The two men left the office under a storm of abuse.

Joe Wyman never saw their warrant cards, but he suspected these guys whoever they were, were not Metropolitan police officers. A call later, to a friend in the force, confirmed that to be the case.

CHAPTER 25
CONSPIRACY
Windsor Castle

The Jaguar XJ passed through the main gate, up the road and into the castle courtyard. As the car came to a stop the chauffeur got out and opened the rear door. Sir Peter Thompson-Smythe eased himself out.

'Thank you Dennis.'

As he straightened, a smart young man stepped forward. 'You are expected Sir Peter, please excuse me, procedure you understand.' The young man ran his hands over Sir Peter's body, looking for weapons or other such nasty devices.

'Thank you sir, now if you'd care to follow me.' Leading the way the young man took Sir Peter to the Kings private study. He knocked on the door and awaited a response before opening it and announcing. 'Sir Peter, your Majesty.' He then stood aside to allow Sir Peter to pass, leaving and closing the door behind him.

'Peter, so good of you to come.' Which really meant Sir Peter didn't have choice.

'Your Majesty.' Sir Peter said bowing politely.

The King ushered Sir Peter to sit opposite in a high-backed winged armchair.

'Cognac, Peter?' The King took two glasses already poured, from an adjacent table and handed one to Sir Peter.

'Thank you sir.'

'I've just been reading the papers, fortunately managed to silence our guys, but those bloody foreign Jonnies.' The King paused for moment. 'Well there isn't much room left for doubt.'

'Err no sir, I don't suppose there is. Frankly I don't know who tipped off the paparazzi in the first place, but who would have expected them to get such candid pictures.'

'Who indeed,' the King said as he shot Sir Peter a knowing look, but decided to let the question of who may have tipped off the press, drop.

'I only hope sir that this escapade has not put the future of the monarchy in jeopardy.'

'Oh, don't worry about that Peter. The young fool was going to get caught sooner or later. It's about time that affair was brought out into the open. It's just a pity Alice had to be sacrificed because of it.' The King swirled his cognac and took a sip before continuing. 'I suppose the silver lining is that the press are now so busy hounding Edward and Mrs Grey they are leaving the rest of us alone.'

'Very revealing photographs, if I may say so your Majesty, for a future Queen, that is.'

The King reacted with a raised voice and glaring eyes. 'She will never become Queen if I have anything to say about it. And I intend to make damn sure there will be no Royal titles forthcoming for that madam. As for Edward, it will be a long time before he gets to wear my crown. Plenty of life left in this body of mine, see out a couple of decades at least, I should think.' He gave Sir Peter a wry smile. 'By the time Edward becomes King, this incident will be a faded memory.' The King took another sip of cognac. 'Besides the monarchy has survived many such dark days in the past, I do not doubt we shall continue to do so.'

They paused for a moment to study the golden liquid in their glass, each taking a sip before Sir Peter felt compelled to continue the conversation.

'Well your Majesty, on the whole everything has gone to plan.'

'Yes indeed, the Arab turning up was very convenient.'

'Ah yes, that situation, developed better than I dared hope.'

'Another bonus, I suppose, was getting rid of that sycophant Giles Fairchild.'

Sir Peter swirled his cognac and stared down into the glass, transfixed by the moving liquid he uttered in a sombre voice.

'Hardly a bonus sir, - in fact a great pity, a great pity indeed.'

The King looked a little puzzled, hesitating before he offered a response. 'Are you saying this Fairchild chap was one of ours?'

'Oh yes your Majesty, very much so. Giles Fairchild, codename "Gadfly" had served us for some time and played his part very well, very well indeed.....I recruited him when he was at Gordonstown with Prince Edward. There were pals, seemed a logical move at the time. With the help of the Treasury we created for him a healthy bank balance, which in affect allowed him the privilege to operate within, begging your pardon sir, Royal circles, my eyes and ears, for Prince Edward's benefit, you understand.'

'Well I'll be blowed, you crafty old bugger.'

Sir Peter nodded, taking the King's comment as a complement. 'When you first asked me to look at the situation, my instructions to Giles Fairchild was to encourage Edward in keeping Alice away from attending public duties, just to see if her popularity diminished. But when she met the Arab, it presented me with an opportunity too good to miss. I therefore did all in my power to steer them in the right direction.'

'How on earth did you know that she would fall for the Arab?'

'In truth your Majesty, I didn't, just a stroke of luck, but it was their love affair that inspired me to combine the two situations.'

'Kill two birds with one stone.' The King said knowingly.

'That was the idea.'

'What about those photographs, did Fairchild plant them?'

'Of course and Edward knew he had, all part of the plan you see. Giles used Vostok's assassin to take pictures instead of pulling a trigger with the intention of fooling Vostok into thinking an outraged Edward would get the SAS to the business on the Arab. It also bought me a little time; I didn't want the Arab Prince eliminated, before I could make my own preparations.

I engineered Giles association with Vladimir Vostok when it came to light that he was supplying the arms to the Islamic terrorists.'

Sir Peter paused for a moment to reflect and then took a sip of Cognac before continuing.

'The real bonus was Fairchild's membership of the Brotherhood, an organisation that has afforded me a lot of useful information over the years. Through Giles, Vostok was persuaded to wait three weeks to get the Brotherhood involved. With them in the play, there would no doubt be an opportunity for financial gain and a cartel of rich Westerners at which to point the accusing finger for the demise of the Saudi Prince.'

'You must have contrived the whole thing.' Sir Peter again nodded modestly. 'I can now understand your thinking.' The

King said. 'The Russian, the Americans, the Brotherhood, the Islamic fundamentalists and us, it would appear, all wanted shot of Mohammed. So who would get the blame when he was bumped off and who could have guessed Alice would be caught up in it?'

'Who indeed, your Majesty.'

Sir Peter took another sip of Cognac and the King drained his glass, and looked at Sir Peter over the rim. 'Can I take it Peter that all those involved in the incident are now taken care of? We don't want any recriminations, do we?'

'Rest assured your majesty every one involved with the death of Princess Alice and aware of BISS hand in this affair, have been dealt with.'

'Excellent, then I think Peter; we can now put the whole situation behind us.'

The End

Printed in Great Britain
by Amazon